The Insiders

The Insiders

TIJAN

ST. MARTIN'S GRIFFIN
NEW YORK

First published in the United States by St. Martin's Griffin, an imprint of St. Martin's Publishing Group

www.stmartins.com

Library of Congress Cataloging-in-Publication Data

Names: Tijan, author.
Title: The insiders / Tijan.
Description: First edition. | New York : St. Martin's Griffin, 2021. |
Identifiers: LCCN 2020056325 | ISBN 9781250210777 (trade paperback) |
    ISBN 9781250210784 (ebook)
Subjects: GSAFD: Romantic suspense fiction.
Classification: LCC PS3620.I49 I57 2021 | DDC 813/.6—dc23
LC record available at https://lccn.loc.gov/2020056325

First Edition: 2021

10 9 8 7 6 5 4 3 2 1

To all the "outliers" that were/are never an outlier

The Insiders

ONE

There was someone in my room.

I sensed them just as I turned the lights off. This was the nightmare every girl had at some point in her life. It was here. It was happening to me, not to someone else. Me. Coming back from the bathroom, going to my bedroom, their shadow caught the corner of my eye.

Hairs on the back of my neck stood up. A chill went down my spine.

A split second. Not even. That's how long I had to compute what was about to happen before a hand grabbed my arm. Another slammed over my mouth.

"Shh!"

He moved fast, backing me into the wall. He was tall, a couple inches on me, and *strong*. That chill just doubled, and he bent his head low, whispering into my ear, "In two minutes, men will break into your home and take you hostage."

My lungs stopped working.

This didn't happen to people like me. I was no one special. Okay, that wasn't altogether true. The only special thing about me was a lame nickname I got in elementary school, but that was years ago. I was Bailey Hayes, twenty-two and going to start graduate school in three months. My mother raised me on her own, working doubles at the local hospital. We had a thousand-square-foot house, three bedrooms, a basement, and a sad backyard with a half-built tree house. Midwest born and raised. My mom and I were barely keeping our heads above water. She was a nurse. I was a brainiac. That was it, for real. That was the only "special" thing about me. Brainiac Bailey. A lame nickname and nothing else.

A whimper came out.

He only pressed harder. "Shh!"

I was going to die. Not him. Me!

"Stop!" He pushed me against the wall even harder. My eyes shifted to my free hand. I could ram my finger in his eyeballs, but as if reading my thoughts, he grabbed the hand. Pulling back, he had both my hands in one of his and he pinned my arms above my head. I was paralyzed, unable to fight back.

"Listen to me!" He was growling, yelling, and whispering all at the same time. He readjusted for a tighter grip. "If you want to get out of this alive, stop fighting and pay attention. I will not let them hurt you. Got it? But if you squeal on me, we're both dead. Nod your head. Let me know you're following."

I nodded, just briefly.

His voice went quiet again. "I was sent to detain you. Arcane is waiting for me to bring you out. When I don't, they will break in here. They'll ask what took me so long—" His hand moved like lightning again, and he ripped the front of my shirt open.

His eyes never left mine. "Got it? They're going to think I raped you, and you'll cry."

I nodded again.

"You'll whimper."

Not a problem. I let another one loose, but it was muffled by his hand.

"And you will go limp when they try to drag you out of here. Limp. Your body is going to become your weapon. You have no chance of surviving if you go with them. You'll be on their territory then. Keep them here. Force them to make their stand here. Got it? Your house. Your territory. Your only shot of living."

My only shot.

Words that shouldn't be in my head, but were.

I nodded again. "Go limp. Body is my weapon." It was stamped there forever.

Then—he was gone.

I stepped back from the wall. The room was empty.

I glanced to my window. The thought of crawling out and running flared in my head, but just as I thought it—

Crash!

Thud.

They kicked the door in, and it seemed like the entire house shook.

I should run for the window, but that guy's voice was in my head. He was supposed to have detained me, raped me.

Feet stampeded up the stairs, and below me.

I had one second.

They were checking the house—where had that guy gone?

The window. It beckoned me. And screw it, I went for it.

I got one step before he was back. He grabbed my arm roughly, and called out, "I got her, boss."

After that, everything blurred.

Time skipped for me.

Go limp. Drag me out. Body is my weapon.

"This is her?" A boot kicked me in the side.

Boots.

I tasted blood.

"Thought she was rich. Her daddy hasn't been supporting her or something? The whole thing depends on the dad."

My dad? I didn't have a dad . . .

———

"You cleared the upstairs, right, Chase?"

Chase. Chase was the guy who showed up first. Chase was my maybe ally.

"He better have, or was the two pumps not long enough?"

A full belly laugh came from the boots guy.

"Shut up, Rafe. Clemin. Both of you." Chase's voice was strained.

I was being hoisted up in the air.

My one shot. My one chance. My neighbor.

A bloodcurdling scream ripped from my throat.

"*Aahhh!*" Breathe. "He-e-elp me!"

Please, Mrs. Jones. Please hear me.

Chase dropped me back to the ground, and instead of a hand, I saw a boot lift up—

Then—

Sirens.

The cops were coming.

TWO

I wasn't being taken to a police station.

I was told that I was fine at the hospital. But after being told I was also in shock, after being told all the big words that I knew the definitions for, like *dissociation, minimization,* and *deflection*—I could only focus on one thing now. After leaving the hospital, I was not going to the police station. I knew the maps, the geography, and that's where I should've gone.

Right? But no. The hospital was behind us where the station was too.

We were heading out of Chicago, and maybe another half hour or so from the small town where my mom and I lived.

Wait. Second thought—where we *used* to live?

What would my mom do now? Could Chrissy Hayes remain in that house after I was just attacked, almost taken hostage? I called my mother by all kinds of names—Chrissy Hayes, Chrissy, or Mom. Or, well, a whole other kind of names too, because to say she's a character is putting it mildly. And we have an interesting relationship to say the least.

I might be deflecting here.

Numb. I was numb. I should be pissing my pants, but instead I'm ruminating over how I refer to my mother.

Could *I* stay in that house after what just happened?

I'd been planning to spend time with Chrissy, helping with the house and working at the local computer store to make some extra money before I left for school. But now . . . fuck if I knew.

Myriad curses went through my mind as I realized Chrissy would have to move.

Shivers pierced me as I went over what had happened tonight, but then we were pulling into a driveway, next to a booth. A large gate barricaded us from moving forward.

Official police business, my tech ass.

Then again, nothing seemed official. I was told that I was being taken to my mother, but I left with two detectives. Bright and Wilson. They introduced themselves, then said she couldn't see me in the hospital. They didn't explain why, but I was to go with them to see her.

I went.

I was in the backseat of their unmarked car a few minutes later.

Bright's window rolled down. She flashed her badge. "We're expected."

The attendant nodded, hitting a button. The gate opened, showing a campus of buildings behind it. Some made of dark red brick. Some seemingly made of reflective windows, top to bottom. Some painted totally black. A large parking lot sat in the middle of the buildings. "Phoenix Tech" was on a sign in front of the first building, but we went past, heading around it and toward a smaller building on the opposite end of the lot.

My tongue was glued to the back of my throat. We were at Phoenix Tech headquarters.

I had yearned to get an internship there every year since fifth grade, and then through college. I kept applying, but they kept denying. Some might say I was being desperate. I prefer determined. It's a quality that I feel is honorable. Plus, I wasn't above hoping they'd take pity on me one day. It worked, because while I might not have been good enough to walk their hallways, I *was* good enough for them to give me charity. They awarded me the majority of my grants for undergrad, so I'd been able to go to college debt free. I'd been expecting that to change for graduate school, but it hadn't. Or, well, it kind of had.

I was hired as a graduate assistant, starting in the fall, which gave me a stipend, but the rest was covered by another scholarship from Phoenix Tech.

Phoenix Tech was one of the world's leading companies on cyber security. I was going into information systems, which was close enough. A job here would be a dream.

"My mom is here?" I asked, when Bright parked, and both her and Wilson got out of the vehicle.

Neither answered.

Bright opened my back door and motioned for me, slipping her sunglasses over her eyes. "It's time for you to find out some answers."

"What?"

They took off for the door.

I trudged after. "I thought you were going to interrogate me."

Her mouth went back to that disapproving and very firm line. "Not likely. We're just the go-between."

We were moving fast. We went down an empty hallway. When she got to the very last room, the door opened for us from the inside. Wilson was walking behind us, but remained in the hallway.

Bright took me in.

It was an interrogation room, or looked like one. Details were still fuzzy on what I was supposed to be expecting here. The only light was hanging directly over a table, pushed against the far wall. The corners of the room were dark, and as we walked inside, a security guard was standing behind the door. He ducked out; the door swung shut.

"Sweetheart?"

"Mom?"

Chrissy Hayes was sitting in a back corner, and she stepped

out from the shadows. Her hair was a mess. Ends were sticking up everywhere. Her eyes were glazed, the pupils dilated. Rings of worry fell underneath them, matching the wrinkles around her mouth.

My mother was a good-looking woman. I knew this. I'd suffered the consequences growing up, as teachers or mailmen or even restaurant owners tried to butter me up to get to her. She was a petite woman, with a usually gorgeous blond mane of hair, and they always fell for her blue eyes. It wasn't just her looks, though.

She had a personality where she was tough as nails at times but flighty and ditzy at others. She was fun, too. Chrissy Hayes enjoyed a good bargain, a good time, and a good adventure. She was clear on that motto in life, but this version of my mom wasn't one I'd met many times.

She was wrecked. Totally and completely. Destroyed.

My heart twisted. Pain sliced through that numb wall.

I was almost the total opposite, with honey-brown eyes and jet-black hair. My hair was so dark that it had a slight tint of blue to it at times. Sometimes it was there, sometimes not. I got asked by stylists what color I used for it, but it was all natural. I used to hate it, but like the weirdness of my brain, it had grown on me.

We had the same build.

We were both petite, though the couple extra inches I had made me feel like I towered over her.

"Oh, honey." She rushed to me, her flannel shirt enveloping me as she pressed my head to her neck. Her hand smoothed my hair down and back and then swept up to repeat. She shuddered, holding me. "I was so worried." Her head buried into my shoulder, and she pressed a kiss to my forehead. Pulling back, she tucked my hair strands behind my ears, framing my face. Her eyes raked over me and she shook her head, biting her lip. "I am so sorry this happened to you."

My hands came up to rest on her arms.

I noticed her jeans, tight, with sparkles intermixed so there was a light glitter dusting over them. They were her date jeans, and that flannel shirt. It was unbuttoned, with a white shirt underneath. I said flatly, "I thought you worked last night." No. It was the same night. I corrected, "I mean tonight. Earlier." Christ. What time was it? "You were on a date."

She grimaced, still biting down on her bottom lip. "Yes, but is that really important now? You were almost kidnapped, sweetie."

Detective Bright cleared her throat, stepping closer to the table. "You two can have a talk later. There's quite a bit we need to discuss first."

I took one of the seats closest to the wall. "You don't usually lie about dates." But there was one guy she *would* lie about. "Was it Chad Haskell?" I did not like Chad Haskell. No one should like Chad Haskell. "He beat up Simone Ainsley's mom. Remember?"

Chrissy flicked her eyes to the ceiling and waved at me. "Oh, come on. You were friends with that girl for four months your sophomore year in high school. She was a liar. You got mad because she was only using you to get a date with that Bobby guy from your debate team."

"Mom. Seriously." My blood was boiling. "And it wasn't debate team. It was the computer club, and . . ." I saw the look on Detective Bright's face. "And she didn't use me to get a date with Bobby Riggs—she used me to get an in with his brother, who I was tutoring because, unlike Bobby, *Brian* Riggs wasn't the smartest guy on the football team."

Chrissy was fighting back a smile. "And you had a crush on Brian Riggs, didn't you?"

I jerked back in my chair. "I'm just telling you that while I was friends with Simone, she told me her mom got beat up by Chad Haskell. Don't date him, Mom. Trust me." I gestured to my head. "Out of our two minds, mine doesn't forget things." Ever.

She softened. "I know, honey."

I heard the *but* coming . . .

"But," she said, "he owns the bowling alley. You could bowl there for free every weekend." She was off. We were embarking in Chrissy Hayes's fantasyland. Sometimes I was allowed to visit. "You could bring all your friends every Friday night—or hey! You could help rewrite his computer system. I bet he'd take you on as his personal IT department."

This was what we were talking about? Here?

My mom was dating Chad Haskell so I could have free bowling Friday nights?

I rubbed at my forehead. A headache was coming. Chad Haskell's influence had invaded Chrissy Hayes. Chrady. That's the name for both of them.

She should just go by Chrady now.

Chrady turned toward Detective Bright. "Do you know about my daughter? She was awarded all of these prestigious scholarships, and she got into Hawking. She's going there for graduate school."

"Actually . . ." Detective Bright waved for Chrissy to take the last empty seat by me, as we all sat. Her tone turned businesslike. "That's why you're here."

Consider the mic dropped.

The guys who tried to kidnap me, the cops being so insistent and pushy, the fact that my mom was already in an interview room and not at the police station—everything started piecing together.

My mom was wrecked, but was sighing about a delusion that would never happen.

She was worried, but she *wasn't* confused.

I frowned, mulling it over. "Those guys wanted me for a reason." I didn't know if I dared look to the side, but . . . "I don't remember the whole thing, but they mentioned my father."

Chrissy sucked in some air.

And I was tense. I was so tense. What did that mean?

I looked now. "They *mentioned* my dad."

She wasn't looking at me. That told me a whole lot, maybe too much.

My voice dropped low. "You said he was in the military, that he died overseas."

She mashed her lips together. That was it.

My stomach flipped over, knotting. I kept on. "You had Barney tell me about him. Pike. Masteron." There were others too, all friends of my mom at the VFW. And I was replaying some of those times when they told stories about him, all the shifting in the seats. All the looks they gave each other, not knowing I saw it too. The small tugs at their mouths, like they were uncomfortable, or how they watched my mom when she was in the room with all of us.

How she told me his name wouldn't be in any computer database because he would be in classified files.

How he was estranged from his family.

How there were no pictures of him because she said she destroyed them in a fit of rage one time while she was grieving him.

She had a flag folded up in a display case.

Detective Bright sat back on her chair, drawing our attention. She folded her arms over her chest. She was eyeing my mom, her head turned almost sideways, then let her arms drop. "You're very smart, Bailey."

Before I had a second to digest that statement, she pushed forward. "You were brought here because those men didn't want you to work on some software code. They tried to kidnap you." She paused.

I was doing the math.

Bright was silent. One second.

A kidnapping attempt.

Bright's eyes shifted, staying on my mother.

They *mentioned* my *father*.

Chrissy's head lowered, her gaze falling to her lap. Bright pursed her lips together once again, in disapproval.

We were at Phoenix Tech.

"Why are we here again?" My voice was hoarse. "Why not the police station? Why not somewhere else?"

Bright was waiting. She knew I was putting it together.

All those scholarships.

The way my brain worked.

Only 2 to 15 percent of all children have a photographic memory, and an even lower percentage retain it into adulthood, but I had it. And I knew one other person who had it. His face and name were plastered everywhere—websites, magazine covers, documentaries.

He had dark hair that, in a small group of photographs, looked like it had a bluish tint to it. The details might have been missed. But I was savvy with the computer, and he was my childhood idol growing up. I was obsessed with learning as many facts about him as I could—another computer genius who worked with the government and ran a Fortune 500 empire that specialized in computer security.

There was a lock unlocking.

Click.

Click.

It connected, one last, final, and resounding click into place.

Detective Bright broke the silence. "You were taken because your birth father is—"

I spoke at the same time as her, and together we said his name. "Peter Francis."

Peter Francis was the CEO of Phoenix Tech.

THREE

Bright's voice was emotionless, cold almost. "My partner and I are here as a personal favor to your father. We've done work with him before and are familiar with your case."

Father. I had a father. Not the one I thought I had, but someone else. Someone new. Someone powerful. Of *course* he'd want to be cautious.

There was a camera pointing at us from the corner of the room.

Bright cleared her throat. "You're here as a precaution."

"For what?"

She didn't answer, watching me a moment before her eyes slid toward my mother.

I couldn't follow. I couldn't look at her. If I did, if I spoke to her, I'd lose it.

She had lied. All this time.

Chrissy Hayes raised me right. Violence was bad, unless defending yourself. And even though it felt like someone was attacking me at the moment, I was too shocked to do much except sit here, pretend I was a fully functioning human at the moment.

But.

Holy *effin* shit.

Peter Francis.

"Honey." Chrissy knew it was her turn to step up to the plate. I had to give credit to her survival instincts. Her voice was starting quiet, all demure like.

I couldn't look at her, but my voice dropped low. Hoarse. "You

gave me my first *Computer Weekly* in fourth grade. I found it
early. It was supposed to be a Christmas gift, but you gave it to
me anyway. You special ordered it from the UK." I remembered
the feel of it, how much it weighed, how it felt like the clouds
parted and choir music started singing. "They did an article on
him. November twelfth." I saw his picture, how black his hair
was, how he had honey-brown eyes too, but they were covered by
glasses. "I can tell you the journalist's name, the byline under it.
'Computer Genius, Peter Francis.'"

"Honey."

I was not done. Not now, when I was just starting.

My voice matched Bright's, emotionless and monotone. "I
have two uncles, one in California. The other in New York. Both
work in Phoenix Tech branches. Four cousins to the California
one. Another cousin in New York. Two half brothers. One half
sister. He has an estate on the outskirts of Chicago, in Ashwick."

Which was an hour from where I lived.

I looked. I had to.

My mom was looking down at her lap, her hands twisting
around the sleeve ends, and after her chest rose and fell once,
she lifted her head.

Still no words. Fine. I could keep going.

"You said you worked for him one time." Fifth grade. She told
me over the phone, when I asked if I could join the computer
club. They had an extracurricular program. "I nearly crapped my
pants when you told me."

"I took care of his mother when I was in nursing school. In
Saint Louis."

"I asked if you *met* him." My voice rose, same as my blood had.
"I asked you. You said no!"

"I didn't say that . . ." But she looked away, because she had,
and she knew she had.

"Okay. Let's pause for a moment." Bright held up a hand. She
was wincing. "You're shouting."

I hadn't realized.

I didn't care.

I wrote my application essay on my father, the father that was a goddamn lie. I thought he served in the military, and I wanted to show my respect in my own way. But it was a lie.

Calm. I needed to be calm. Calm was mature. I was twenty-two. I could be calm.

Screw it. I couldn't be calm.

I threw my arms up, shoving the chair back and standing at the same time. "What else have you lied about?!"

"Nothing!" Chrissy shot to her feet, her hands up. "I swear. Nothing else. It was—"

I stopped. Everything stopped. I felt my heart thump hard. "What? It was what?" My head inclined forward. I rolled to my toes, lifting off the balls of my heels. "You *what?*"

"Nothing." The temporary fight left her. Her shoulders folded in on themselves, and she sank to her seat. Her elbows rested on the table. She buried her head in her hands. "I'm so sorry, Bailey. I really am. I—" She choked off her next word, looking up with haunted eyes.

I looked away. I didn't want to see her torment. *Her* torment.

I grimaced, but I was angry. I had a right to be. There was an entire family I didn't know about, and she made that decision. Not me. Did he—no, no, no. The spinner was on in my head, going round and round, but I was feeling overwhelmed.

I whipped around, heading for the door. "I have to get out of here. I can't think—"

The door opened, and Detective Wilson stepped inside.

I moved aside, reaching to catch the handle after he let go.

He didn't. He shut the door and moved in front of it. Then he folded his hands in front of him. "You're not leaving this room."

My mom spoke up, sighing. "Let her go. She just needs to walk for a bit. She'll come back with eighty percent of the answers already figured out."

Wilson's response was to fold his arms over his chest. He locked eyes with me. "Sit down. You have to make a decision before we can pass you off."

A decision? I needed out of there. I needed air, and space, but I also needed answers.

I looked right at my mom. "I'll stay." A beat passed. "If she goes."

Chrissy's mouth dropped. "Bailey . . ."

I wasn't normally a cold person, or an angry person. I joked. They were lame jokes, but it was my thing. It was early morning by now. The attack at my house was last night. It felt so long ago. It was 4:18 a.m. when I was being taken to the hospital. Another two hours waiting, being looked over. One more hour to get released, and the last hour it took to be brought here.

It hit me then, why we're here.

All of this—everything that had happened after they tried to take me—was all for him.

I looked up at the camera then.

He was watching me.

I gutted out, "You gotta go, Mom."

She went.

FOUR

Everything happened simultaneously after that.

Bright's phone buzzed. She gave the nod to her partner, and the door opened again.

I don't know who I was expecting to come through that door. It could've been Chrissy coming back, or my father deciding to meet me in person, but I was not expecting the man who stepped inside our room. If I could call him a man, because he looked like a young man, like he was only a few years older than me. But no. Thinking on it, I was right the first time. He was all man.

He was *hot*.

Cognac-brown eyes, hair almost as dark as mine, a strong jawline. There were indentations around his mouth, making his lip so pronounced, and so tempting. His cheekbones were high and chiseled. Broad and defined shoulders. Lean, athletic build.

There wasn't an ounce of fat on him.

I was looking, and I shouldn't be, but I was, and I was doing the calculating in my head, and yeah. This guy was ripped.

He was mesmerizing.

And he had power and authority and he knew how to use both of them.

He walked into that room like he owned it, like he'd been there the whole time, like everyone and everything belonged to him and we had yet to learn that fact.

The room shrank around him.

The air electrified. It became more energized.

Bright and Wilson both straightened, their shoulders rolling back.

They weren't the only ones affected.

This guy didn't even look at me, but I felt his attention. I felt that if I moved even a strand of hair, he'd know. My insides were turned inside out because, whoever this guy was, I already felt owned, and I hated that.

My body was warming. A fire was in there, building. My throat felt parched.

I felt zapped, all my nerve endings already at the ready, and it was just because this guy walked into the room.

He nodded to both detectives, who dipped their heads in return.

A chair scraped against the floor. A click of heels and both detectives were gone.

The door slammed shut behind them.

The brevity of the situation hit me hard, right in the sternum, and I swallowed over a sudden lump in my throat. I wasn't sure if it was a good lump or a quivering one, but here we were.

It was me and him. We were alone in this room. And then another fact hit me square in the forehead. It hadn't been my father watching. It was this guy.

Who was this guy?

He'd been the one on the other side of that camera. I felt it, the hairs on the back of my neck standing upright. Tingles shot through me, sweeping through me, making me feel more. Just . . . more.

I wasn't sure if I liked this "more."

He looked at me squarely, and I was pinned in place.

Then he spoke. "My name is Kashton Colello, and I am an associate of your father's. No, your mother does not know about me, and yes, I am aware of who you are. I know what happened to you earlier tonight, and I am here to give you two options. You can leave with me, meet your father and your siblings, or you can disappear into a witness protection type of program with your mother." He paused, just one beat. "Leave with me, meet your father, or disappear with your mother." The corner of his mouth tugged up in a smirk. "Your choice."

A second.

Two.

I stared at him, standing by the table as he was sitting, waiting, and I felt slapped across the face.

It took me two seconds to know my response. That was it.

I stepped in, placed a hand on the table, leaned in, and breathed on him.

"Fuck. You."

I was given twenty-four hours.

I had a day and a night to decide. That was it.

Mr. Stick Up My Ass Kashton Colello hadn't even seemed insulted by my response. There was no reaction on his face before he nodded. "Fine. Your mother is outside, waiting in an SUV. We'll have you taken to a nearby hotel. You can decide tomorrow morning."

Decide.

I wanted to give him the middle finger, and just about did. I was raising my hand when he spoke again, his voice so goddamn cold. "There have been other attempts."

If I felt slapped by him before, those words punched me. Hard. Right in the gut.

He didn't wait to let me process it, saying, still so fucking cold, "They tried to take your father. They didn't succeed. Security doubled. They moved to your siblings. They came close twice. Security tripled." A brief pause. "They're going for the outliers now, the ones who aren't protected."

That was me. An outlier.

An outsider.

The outcast.

"They got the littlest one for ten minutes." He stood. "And this is what we know about these types of people. They *will* try again, and they do not care about the ex-girlfriends or ex-mistresses, so while your mother will be safe, you will not be. If you return to Brookley, the quaint small town it is, they will try again. If you leave with me, your mother does not have to have her life upended. She can return there, live her life happily but away from her daughter, while you give us time to search out your abductors and eliminate this threat."

And here we were, heading to a hotel.

We had two SUVs with us.

There was no word to describe this.

Everything was different.

I glanced over to my mom. Chrissy was gazing out the window, a slight excited smile on her face. When I got out to the SUV, she looked at me, but I only said we'd talk later. I might've growled it. Or grunted it. I didn't know. I was still peeved, so I had transferred from the Numb Train to the Not Giving a Shit Train. Either way, she just seemed relieved.

We were driving through downtown Chicago, so her eyes kept going up, her neck craning to see the tops of the buildings all around us.

I recognized the look in her eyes.

She thought everything would be fine now. She was relieved, more than anything else.

I twisted my hands together in my lap.

Brookley had her job. Bingo night at the local VFW. My aunt Sarah. Chrissy was a godmother to two of my cousins. My two uncles. My grandparents. Her younger sister. There was a family tribe there, and they all had their own friends, who were my mother's friends. Yes, there were issues and divides, but she wanted to be there.

My mom was tough. Hardworking. She never wanted a handout, refused them 102 percent of the time. She got into nursing school, dropped out for a year to have me, then finished the next.

I took that one year from her.

How could I take everything else from her?

"Oh!" Her hand grabbed my arm and squeezed. "Bailey."

We were pulling into a hotel parking lot. The Francois Nova. It was one of those skyscraper ones, a hotel that could've been in a magazine. I might have been impressed a day ago.

Now it was just the last time I'd see my mom.

For a while. That's what that asshole had said. He needed time. Things would get safe, and I could go back.

Right. I was going with that. It didn't make my insides feel like they're being ripped out of me.

"We're here," Chrissy said, just as the doors on both sides of the SUV opened and we clambered out.

We were surrounded by cement on a dark parking ramp.

Six guards stood around us, most facing outward, but one went to the door connecting the hotel to the parking ramp. He knocked once, and it opened.

Another two guards stood on the other side, along with a hotel employee. Make that two employees. A woman with her name pinned to her shirt, a pencil skirt, and hair pulled up in a tight bun waited for us. Another employee stood behind her, a bellhop. He was in full hotel uniform, even wearing white gloves.

The woman took us to our room, but it had to be inspected by the guards first.

My mom went inside, and I turned to look at the guards. They all watched me back, their faces impassive. I was going with my gut here. "You guys work for *him*, don't you?" I didn't know the setup, the hierarchies, but while my father might've been the big boss, I knew Asshole Kashton was their boss, too.

I didn't get a response. I didn't expect to.

"I'll let you know my answer in the morning, and not a second before."

Then I slipped inside, not feeling satisfied at all.

I checked the peephole. Two guards were outside the door. I'm sure they had one at each stairway, maybe even at the elevator too.

Chrissy came out from the bedroom. "This place is amazing."

Yeah. It sure was. Amazing.

She headed for the bathroom. "They gave us clothes . . . and what's this?" She picked up a small bag, unzipping it. "And toiletries. There's almost everything in here we need, but no . . ." She was sifting through it. "I'm going to need some Tums. With the wine I'm planning on drinking tonight, my reflux will not be pretty."

"They probably have some in the lobby. I'll get you some later."

I couldn't bring myself to interrogate her throughout the rest of the day.

Maybe I'd already made my decision.

Maybe I wanted to enjoy this last day with my mom.

Or maybe I was already tired, knowing that tomorrow we'd be ripped apart, and I didn't really know how long this would last.

Or maybe, just maybe, I didn't want to hear her excuses for the lies she'd told me all my life.

Nope. I just wanted a day with my mom. I was going with that reason.

We ordered in lunch. Ordered coffee. Ordered wine.

It was after dinner when I needed to get a breather.

I used the excuse to get her Tums.

The guards didn't want me to go, but I needed space. "Look . . ."

I was suddenly exhausted. "I'm going with a feeling that Peter Francis owns this hotel. Am I right?"

They didn't answer. Again, I didn't expect them to.

"That means you probably have the entire hotel scoped out with security footage. That you probably have a perimeter set up around the hotel. That anyone questionable or someone who raises red flags will be removed quietly, but quickly. Right?"

Still no answer.

"So the risk assessment is probably less than ten percent if I go to the lobby to get my mom some antacids."

Still no response. They just stared at me.

"Sixty percent of the adult population experience some type of reflux. That's around seven million people." I was quoting straight from the Healthline website. "I'm not asking to go buy a gun. My mom will be vomiting tonight if I don't get her some Tums."

Screw it.

I started down the hallway. "I'm going, whether you want me to or not." But they were right behind me, and I was right. There was a guard down the hall, by the exit door, and he was moving to take point outside the room I just left. My mom was safe.

The lobby was deserted when we got there.

A gold and red rug spread over a marble tile floor, with red and white chairs against the far wall. The front desk itself had a gold trim around the edges, and there were two sweeping stairways that led up to the second floor, separating around two large posts. The same red and gold carpet covered the stairs and the second floor.

The lobby was small, but intimate and grand. I wasn't surprised. Of course it would be, if Peter Francis owned it.

I started for the clerk but then saw a small shop across the lobby.

I asked the front desk clerk, "Can I get some antacids charged to my room?"

He started to nod, his hands going to his keyboard, but that's when everything stopped and went into slow motion. This was the second time today that something similar happened.

The hotel doors swept open and in strolled Asshole Kashton.

Like Bright and Wilson, the guards all stood at their tallest height, shoulders back, head up, hands slapped to their sides. The store clerk almost mimicked them without realizing. He was ramrod straight and the epitome of professionalism as he bobbed his head in one firm nod. "Mr. Colello."

Tension spread around this man.

Lovely. I was already tired of him.

He didn't look over, but he was aware of me. I knew it like I knew I had two hands. I just did.

"Is he in?"

The clerk's words almost tripped over themselves in his rush to answer. "Yes, Mr. Colello. We stopped allowing more guests as well."

Mr. Colello. That's what he called the guy. I could give him a different nickname.

Mr. Asshole.

Asshole Dipstick.

I could go on.

"Okay. Thank you."

I was standing across the lobby, inside two walls of shelves that made up their store.

He turned without pause.

His eyes went right to mine, not stopping or hesitating on the guards.

Those tingles from before were back, spreading through me, racing up and down my spine, and I felt heat in my belly.

I wanted him.

And I wanted him *badly*, and holy hell, I hated that. I hated feeling that, knowing that, and as his eyes darkened, I knew he knew it all, too. The side of his mouth lifted up. I wanted to curse again, because he knew exactly the effect he was having on me and he found it amusing.

A whole new wave of humiliation crashed over me.

I had never been affected by someone like this, ever.

He started for the elevator.

Relief hit me, but also disappointment.

I just scowled.

But nope. We weren't done, because the guard spoke up behind me. "Ma'am. We need to clear the lobby."

Which meant I was elevator bound too.

He was walking ahead of me. It was almost like he was a living, breathing weapon. He had an inherent athletic grace to him.

I stepped to his side, then moved another step behind him.

It was petty. I felt like everyone knew why I did it, but I did it anyway.

I was not beside him. *Beside him* meant something, like I was there to engage, like I was his equal. *Behind him* meant something else totally, like I was submissive to him, like he was the boss and I was another of his employees.

So I was behind him and to the side. I did not want to engage, but I was not submitting either.

And he knew it too.

His mouth curved even higher.

The elevator door pinged open.

He went in, moved to the side, and now his eyes were on me.

He watched me step in next to him and raised his head to the guards. "Stay. I'll send it down."

"Oh hell no." I started to step out, but his hand caught my wrist.

A zing of sensation went through me.

He pulled me back in, then tugged me to his side.

"What are you doing?"

As soon as the doors were closed, he let me go and stepped

back to lean against the wall. He smirked again, but his eyes were trained on my lips. "I'm not here for you. Relax."

My mouth flattened. "*You* relax."

The smirk moved to a grin. "You have attitude."

I looked away and tried to ignore the inferno his touch had lit inside of me.

FIVE

"You're the team manager?"

Why I blurted those words out, I had no idea. I was also noting he had hit the penthouse floor.

His eyes narrowed, and he shifted to the side. He lowered his head, his eyes still on me.

I was waiting.

And still, nothing.

"It's a joke. Most IT start-ups have a flat hierarchy now. The head guy in charge is now termed 'team manager.' You manage the team. Right?"

It was an insult. He was so not about equality and a positive work environment, which was the new push in IT departments.

And I was being passive-aggressive.

I didn't care.

"Why were you in the lobby?"

I couldn't handle those eyes. Still facing forward, I leaned my shoulder against the other side of the elevator.

"Antacids for my mom."

"You had to get Tums for your mother?"

I was pissed off, and he was here, and I didn't like him, and I was trying to ignore how my body was having the opposite reaction, so I decided then and there to unleash my frustrations on him.

I turned, facing him squarely. "Who are you? I mean, really."

A faint grin teased the corner of his mouth as he moved to

lean a shoulder against the back of the elevator. He was full-on facing me. "I thought I was the team manager?"

He was enjoying this.

He shouldn't be.

That made it worse.

"I know you're not a team manager. You said you're an associate of my fath—Peter's. You're up there in the power chain, but who? Head of security?"

His lips thinned, but I still felt he was trying not to laugh.

"A higher security person?"

He rubbed a hand over his jaw.

I tracked his hand the whole time, and I shouldn't have.

My mouth dried up.

"I'm a consultant of sorts for your father."

"You consult *for* him? *With* him? *About* him?"

A confused look entered his eyes as he eyed me back, studying me almost as intently as I was grilling him. "What are you doing, Bailey?"

Shit. The way he said my name, my blood was singing.

I averted my gaze.

We were nearing the top, and as we did, I began to hear music. It was getting louder and louder, the closer we got, until we were only a few floors away, and whatever he said, I could no longer make out his words.

We hit the top and I could hear only bass and the sound of a cat screeching the same word over and over again.

The elevators opened and it was worse.

He glanced to me. No good-bye. Or wave.

Not even a smirk.

Well then.

He just stepped out and started forward.

There was no hallway. It opened onto the actual room itself.

I couldn't help myself. I hit the button to keep the elevator door open and I stared, like curious nosy spyware. Pressed against the panel wall, I angled my head out, just enough so one eyeball could see.

He headed toward the main room, and like that, there was another burst of loud music, as if a door opened somewhere inside. A guy passed Kashton, heading to the other side of the room. Shirtless. A lean frame like Kashton's, but skinnier, his jeans were half falling off him. He had dark blond hair that looked greasy, spiked high, and he slapped Kashton on the shoulder as he went by him. He barely looked up before he was out of sight, and then he backtracked. Slowly. Foot by foot. There was no casual walk this time, until he was standing just in front of Kashton . . . staring right at me.

I hit the wall just as Kashton turned to look, too, and I let go of the button.

I knew who I had just seen. My half brother from Peter's first marriage.

Matt Francis was almost a regular fixture on the gossip sites. Rumored heir to Peter Francis's empire. It was reported that he had no interest in learning about cyber security or anything that has to do with computers. I ached for my idol, literally ached, when I first read that in an article. What son of a billionaire genius didn't want anything to do with his father's company? It was blasphemous.

His interests lay toward partying, being photographed with models, and more partying. The last scandal had put him in a huge exposé for Camille Story's largely popular gossip website. The girl was invited to all the rich and famous parties, gossiped on them, and somehow remained within their circles.

I'd only caught the last article on him because my last roommate sent me a link, the subject line gushing, "I KNOW YOU LOVE HIS DAD! EAT YOUR CYBER HEART OUT!"

I'd just moved back home after graduating, and I wanted to read up on him. He'd been in a car accident after flipping off the paparazzi. Exiting that article, I'd been jealous of him. It'd been an odd reaction. I'd admitted that to myself then, wondering why I was envious of this rich kid's exploits, but then I'd shrugged it off and went to make spaghetti for when my mom got off her shift.

When I got to my floor, my stomach was heaving all over the place.

Even my hand was shaking.

It was then, opening the hotel door, that I remembered.

I forgot the Tums.

SIX

Chrissy was rifling through the minibar when I got back from my second trip, Tums in hand this time. A pile of single-serving alcohol bottles was on the table, along with candy bars, sugar candy, and bags of chips. She popped up, a robe on, bare feet, and her hair wrapped in a towel.

"Hey, honey!" She saw the Tums in my hand. "Great! You got 'em."

She scooped up all the food and alcohol, leading the way to the bathroom. The tub was filled up, with bubbles almost overflowing. She had laid out a bunch of towels beside it, and she put all the candy and alcohol on the toilet lid.

"What are you doing?" I paused in the doorway.

She tested the water, then de-robed. Literally. Untying her sash, she held her arms behind her and stepped out of the robe. It fell to the floor behind her.

"*Mom!*"

I turned away.

"I don't need to see you naked. No one needs to see their parent without clothes."

She just laughed, and I heard the water sloshing around. "I got ready for a bath. How can I not take advantage of this? Do you know how many hotels have a claw-foot bathtub? None that I know of. This is so rare, and *ooh*, it feels so good. Do me a favor, sweetie."

"Are you covered by the bubbles? Is it safe to look?"

She laughed. "I've got the same parts as you do, just a different size. Every female should be appreciated. If we all looked the same, there'd be no fun in life."

"Seriously, Chrissy."

This wasn't a vacation, but back to my whole diatribe earlier, she thought it was. Oh, to hell with it. I snagged one of the wine bottles and sank down to the floor beside the tub.

I didn't know the time anymore, but drinks made the most sense.

Chrissy smiled at me, her head just over the bubbles and wine in hand. "Cheers, honey."

Yes. Cheers. We saluted each other.

She sipped her wine, next reaching for one of the candy bars. "Help yourself. I did a whole raid through everything."

My stomach was metaphorically on the floor. "Mom, we have to talk about what happened."

It was time.

"Oh." She waved that off. "Not now." Finishing her wine, she settled back, closing her eyes. "I know what happened was traumatizing, but you're safe and . . ." Her voice slipped. "Do you really want to bring up all the bad stuff tonight? We're in the lap of luxury here."

"Mom."

She opened her eyes again. Her mouth flattened. "Okay." She nodded, sitting back up, some of the water splashing over the side of the tub and wetting where my feet were. "Okay. You're right. You must have a million questions—"

Before she even finished, I started, "How?"

She choked a little before a knowing grin tugged at her mouth. "Bailey. If you don't know how a baby is made by now, then—"

"Mom." I wasn't amused. I let her see that.

She laughed. "Okay. Enough teasing. Give me another wine thingy. They aren't big enough."

I grabbed one that was on the edge of the toilet and handed it over. Her hand closed over my wrist instead, and she tugged.

"Ah!"

I'd been kneeling to give her the wine, and from my position, my side hit the tub before she pulled the rest of me into the bath with her.

"*Chrissy!*"

She was laughing. The water was going everywhere.

"Come on. Let's have a bath together. You and me. Mother and daughter."

I ignored her comment. Some days she was Mom. Others, she was the child. I tended to switch too, except I was never supposed to be the parent. That was her job.

I shoved up. Half the water was on the floor now. "Who's the child in our relationship now?"

"Oh, myself, for sure. That's a no-brainer."

I got out of the bath. My pants completely drenched. "I'm soaked."

She waved, her hand and arm covered in bubbles. "Put the robe on. Peter always was the best at planning for any *outliers*—his word, not mine."

Just like that, I sobered up.

It wasn't the *outliers* word, though it still stung. It was how she said Peter's name.

She said his name for the first time as if she knew him. It was a window to how they were when they would've made me. I hungered for more. I needed more, but I did as she suggested. I shimmied out of my wet pants and shirt, pulling the robe on and then ridding myself of the rest.

I was heading back to the bathroom when there was a soft knock on the door.

A guard was on the other side. "The vehicle will be downstairs at six in the morning."

Six a.m.

It was so early, but as my throat burned, it wasn't enough time. Not nearly enough time.

We were lounging on the couch.

My mother had gone through half the contents of the mini-bar, and she was groaning, rubbing her stomach. "I may be in pain right now, but I'm not going to regret this night. Not one bit." She was grinning, eyeing me. "How about you?" Her eyes grew concerned. "I noticed you've barely touched any of the food or drinks all night. You okay?"

Now. It had to be now.

It was nearing eleven, and I knew my mother would pass out within the hour.

I sat up and pulled a pillow to rest on my lap. It felt like a small amount of protection against what was coming.

"I have to know everything, Mom."

"Bailey." She sighed. "How about we have this conversation tomorrow? We can get coffee on the way back to the house and talk everything over at Carla's."

"Why Carla's?" She was a coworker, neighbor, and the closest person my mom had to a best friend.

"I'm assuming there's still damage at the house." She sat up, moving slow, and got up to start cleaning.

Now she cleaned?

She frowned at the pizza box. "You won't want any for breakfast?"

I shook my head.

She turned to the door. "I could offer the last few pieces to the guards outside. They must be hungry."

There was my mother.

She was stalling and evading. She was even avoiding. Let's

throw in some deflection while we're at it. It was my new favorite word.

I sat there, watching her getting up and starting to clean the room, and I knew I should be the dutiful daughter and help. I didn't. I couldn't bring myself to move from this couch. If I did, I wouldn't have the courage to keep pressing. She would increase her attempts, asking to cuddle or trying to talk me into watching a movie as she crawled into bed. Either way, we wouldn't get any-where, or *I* wouldn't get anywhere.

The guards turned down the food, so she shrugged and put the box in the garbage. She rinsed out the emptied little wine bottles and put them in the recycling bin.

All the candy wrappers went in the trash.

She went to the bathroom. I heard her moving around.

Ten minutes or so later, she came back. I caught the whiff of toothpaste and mouthwash as she returned to her perch on the couch.

Seeing I hadn't moved at all, she raised an eyebrow, then sat. Her shoulders fell down.

"Okay." Her head bobbed up and down. "Okay, Bailey. I'm all yours. What would you like to know?"

"Everything."

SEVEN

I never went to sleep.

My mom nodded off around three in the morning; she broke her eleven o'clock rule for me. I stayed up and watched her sleep. I didn't tell her I was leaving. It was all left in a note, and a part of me felt like a coward. The other part of me knew that if I told her, she wouldn't let me go. She might have moments where she acted young and carefree, but I knew Chrissy. She would've pulled all the mom tricks she had and somehow we'd be going into witness protection later. But I knew her. She would miss Brookley, so I outlined in my letter that, during this time, I would be safe. So would she.

And the other factor: I was going to meet my father.

A shiver of anticipation went through me as I dressed in a set of clothes from that overnight bag they had given me, and bent to kiss my mom on her cheek. She was breathing so steadily, deeply. I brushed some of her hair back from her forehead, whispering, "Love you, Mom." My voice caught on a sob, and before I could lose my will to do this, I turned and left.

Two different guards were there.

"What? You guys aren't superhuman? No twenty-four-hour shifts?"

Jokes. Me. My way of distracting from the complete suckage happening.

I was here all day, folks.

I grunted. I missed the other guards.

The ride down in the elevator was silent. It was eerie to walk across the just-as-silent lobby. The front desk staff had one person, the same clerk as last night, and he stared at me the entire time. No facial expression. None. A shiver went up my spine, raising the hairs on the back of my neck.

Why did I feel like I was walking to my death?

But then the front doors were opening. A black Denali SUV was parked, waiting for me. Two guards detached from the wall and moved ahead of me. One opened the back door. I approached, peeking in and not seeing anyone. A part of me sagged in relief; the other was . . . disappointed?

What was wrong with me? But it was what it was. I'd be taking this ride to meet my father alone after all.

Sliding in, I discovered I was wrong.

In a seat that had been converted so it was facing me sat Kashton Colello.

I ignored the spike in my pulse. That was still unwanted.

His eyes were hooded.

God. Why'd that make him look even better?

We stared at each other a moment.

"Team manager."

He grunted back, his eyes steady on me. "Outlier."

I deflated. Outlier. An academic word for "outcast."

Scooting to the far end, I hugged my bag on my lap and turned to watch out the window as the Denali pulled away from the hotel.

"Did you say your good-byes to your mother?"

"Was that my half brother last night?"

He didn't get to ask me about her. She was the last thing that would be taken from me, even if I was being taken from her. For those reasons, I clamped my mouth shut and pointedly turned to look out the windows.

"Yes, that was him."

I was brimming with questions, but not at the same time. Everything was overwhelming.

"He didn't know who you were."

I looked back. "Huh?"

"He asked who that 'hot chick' was last night."

"Oh." That was . . . awkward. And gross.

"I told him he'd meet you later."

"You did?"

And just like that, any dark amusement that might've been in his eyes was gone. "All teasing aside, there's a reason I'm riding with you today." He pulled out a folder and a phone that were on the seat next to him and tossed them to me. Opening the folder, my father's face stared back at me. It was the same photo that was used in a lot of the newspaper articles and outlets. Shifting to the next page, I skimmed, reading over a list of facts about him. The second sheet was an image of his wife, my—my heart squeezed—stepmother. The page after her was the same thing. A bulleted list of information that made no sense.

"What is this?" I held up the phone.

"You cannot use your old one. You can keep it, or just keep the SIM card, but it must remain off at all times." He nodded to the one in my hand. "That's your new one to use, and you will not be calling your mother on it. Flip to my page."

"Your page?" But there he was, right after my stepmother.

I pulled out his picture. It wasn't a professional head shot like the others. Kashton's image had been taken with a long zoom lens, showed him leaving a building with a phone to his head.

He looked hard and mean.

COVER: *family friend of Kashton Colello (called Kash by friends & family)*

Reason for visit: "Hard breakup." If further questioned: emotionally and mentally abusive, relocation needed, "a new healthier environment."

When/how did they meet?: Knows Kash through his father's family side. Neighbor to Aunt Judith. Were friends when Kash would visit 4–8 years old. Kept in contact.

Names she should use: Aunt Judith, Cousin Stephanie, Uncle Martin.

List of other names to memorize. Page 4

List of events/dates to memorize. Page 5

I was seething. "What is this?"

"You are not going to be introduced to the Francis family as Peter's bastard child."

Bastard child.

I flinched, feeling slapped in the face by that one.

"This is your cover while you stay at the Chesapeake estates."

"The Chesapeake." I grinned at hearing it again. The Yorktown estate would be the name of Chrissy's house.

"Mr. Francis—"

Another wince. *Mr. Francis* was no longer referred to as my father, not even Peter. Mr. Francis. Like he was—the cover clicked in place—like he was my family friend's employer.

Like I was beneath him.

Like I was nothing to him.

Kash was saying, ". . . named each of his estates, and you are going to be staying at his most secured estate."

If this was my cover, if I was going to be a lie, then I'd need to learn my part. "So I'm a family friend of yours?"

I was reading through the list of events and dates I needed to memorize.

I was expecting a response.

I got none, and looked back up.

For the first time since I had seen him walk into that room at Phoenix Tech—his presence commanding everyone's submission in the hotel lobby, the slight amusement he showed in the elevator, and even now, with how professional he was being—he was uncomfortable. There was no outward reaction from him, but as he remained frozen a second, not looking at me, not moving a muscle, I knew that I'd thrown him off balance with that question.

It was my cover.

I didn't understand why, but then he spoke, low. "There's going to be a level of curiosity about you because of your cover." He cleared his throat, returning back to his detached self. "Just remain vigilant in your responses. Since I'm a part of the Francis family, little is known about my past. I intend to keep it that way. Peter, myself, and others felt if we attached you to my family, you'd be questioned less."

One, I was not shocked. Two, the way he said "Peter" told me so much more. He spoke about my father as if Peter were *his* father.

"What *do* they know?"

"My parents died when I was young. I came to live with the Francis family after that. I've stayed in touch with family on my father's side and this was how you and I met." He added, "We thought this would give you an added layer of protection."

I frowned. "Protection? Isn't me being at this estate enough?"

"We're hoping, yes. But you'll be staying in my villa on the estates."

I—Huh? His villa?

"As in . . ." Alone? Was that what he was saying? "You and me?"

"You are coming to stay in my villa at the Francises' personal and most secured estate. There will be people curious about you, but you will be asked to remain in the villa as much as possible. You are to keep a low profile. So yes, staying in the home I use when I'm at the Chesapeake estates is ensuring another boundary of privacy." He paused, looking out the window. "For yourself and for the Francis family."

For the *Francis family*. I jerked back against the headrest.

There it was again. I was not a part of this man's family. He was making it clear.

Anger and hurt were grinding against each other inside, flipping over, squeezing my heart. Pain sliced down the middle of my chest.

I was there for my safety, nothing else. That was being made very clear, and I was starting to want to know my father less and less.

Consider myself checked. I was put in my place.

I was being brought to the estate for one reason only: so I wasn't kidnapped, so Peter Francis didn't have a child's death on his conscience, but I was *not* one of his children. I was a lie. I was a cover. I was . . . I was someone that didn't matter.

"When we get to the estates, you'll meet Marie. She's the only other person besides myself and Peter who knows the truth about you. She runs the estate and she'll be a helpful asset for you. If you need something, you are to go to her. Not myself. Not your father. Marie. Consider her your handler of sorts."

Kash and Marie, my babysitters, or hostage keepers.

Kash added, pulling out his phone. "Memorize the information. Your cover is the most vital. Matthew is already curious about you."

My heart flickered. He was?

Kash scrolled over his screen. "He'll be convinced you and I are having a torrid affair." His eyes lifted, those eyes pinning me in place again, searing me. "It's important that you maintain that you and I *only* have a friendship."

My chest pinched together. He saw my reaction yesterday. He knew, and he was cementing it down. Got it. Nothing except business.

"Why?" I asked. "You have a girlfriend or something?"

I didn't care.

But . . .

Did he?

Kash looked back to his phone, dismissing me. "If you are introduced as a love interest of mine, Matthew's curiosity will know no boundaries. As of right now, he keeps to his hotel with his own security team, but trust me when I say that we do not want your half brother wanting to know you. He has a tendency to expose anything he can, if the mood suits him."

I knew my place.

I was elevator music: annoying and in the background.

EIGHT

The Chesapeake was really Holy Crap City. The place was huge, and I was getting the gist of why Peter Francis had to name his places.

And yeah, I'm not using the *d*-word or the *f*-word.

If I was supposed to hide as his illegitimate bastard, well then, so was he. A bastard. And illegitimate to *me*.

After stopping at a huge security gate, we drove up a long winding driveway that went past two fountains. Not one but two. It was like we were in the middle of a golf course, with those types of fancy water fountains when you first pull up to the main lodge, except this place was bigger than a nine-hole golf course. And I knew that because I had to set up cyber security for Brookley's golf course back home. Crap pay but they wouldn't get hacked again. Not that they got hacked in the first place, because, small confession, that'd been me. I needed some quick cash. They needed better security. So I was really helping *them* out. See. Giver. Me. That was one characteristic they failed to add to my résumé—or so I was assuming. They only gave me a whole file on who I was supposed to be *pretending* to be.

"Since pulling past the gates, you have sighed, laughed, growled, and now you're glaring." Kash raised an eyebrow, looking so cool and collected. "Are you planning someone's murder?"

"Maybe." I gave him a meaningful look. "Yours?"

He only grinned back, his eyes dropping to my lips. Lingering. Darkening. "Well, that'll be fun."

The buzzing was back.

I ignored it. "So you live here too?"

He nodded. "I have a villa here, yes."

I raised an eyebrow. "And you're still not going to tell me what you do for my fa—" Damn. "For Peter Francis?"

His eyebrows dipped at my change. "You'll find out. Eventually. Until then, just stick to the file. You've memorized it already?"

I tapped my head. "Photographic memory up here, Jeeves."

I waited, but neither of us commented on where that came from. I loved my mom, but she had the opposite of a photographic memory. Show her something to remember and it's the first thing she forgets.

We were going past a smaller brick building, with three garage stalls on the side. It looked like the security headquarters. Two golf carts were parked outside of it. A sidewalk wove past it on the lawn, sweeping up to the larger and main house, which is where we were heading.

And . . .

We went right past it.

It looked like a mausoleum, or a small medieval castle. It had brick and stone on the outside. A grandiose doorway that probably stretched up three floors just by itself. The steps going up to the doors put the steps at my last high school to shame. There were pointed arches on wings that were setting out from the house.

Then we turned, driving around the main building and heading to the right of it. I glimpsed the backyard, which was just as impressive. A pool. A tennis court. A cobblestone patio that stretched out and had different levels to it. One section had a campfire section, swinging chairs set up around it. Another section had a large grill and kitchen area built into the rock. A third section was where the sidewalk met the back of the house. There was more back there, but we were too far away for me to see it.

A whole line of trees blocked my view from seeing what else was back there.

We parked and I turned around, and my mouth fell open once more.

It should just stay there. I could start sweeping, get paid as a maid while I was here.

Jokes aside, I wasn't fully gaping. On the outside, I probably had wide and alert eyes as I was taking everything in, but the mouth was cleaning floor on my insides.

The door opened, and I stepped out to see another mansion.

Villa was a *cute* word for this home. This was huge, just not as huge as the other one.

A cobblestone walkway led to the front, a whole white brick porch. A set of wrought iron doors opened to a front entryway, and there was another set of doors after them. And going through there, it was all man inside.

Sleek, dark gray trim. Granite floor that covered the entire first floor. The main floor had an open layout. I could see the living room with the fireplace that ran all the way to the ceiling. The wall across from me was mostly made up of windows, floor to ceiling. The kitchen had European shelving and a waterfall kitchen island. The backsplash was white rock.

Stairs went up to the next floor from my right. A walkway connected to another back section of the house.

"Did you just have that one bag?" Kash touched the small of my back, just one touch before he passed by and went to his kitchen.

I sucked in my breath.

He went to a pile of mail on his counter, picking up an envelope. I still hadn't answered, so he lifted his head. "Bailey."

"Hmm?" I jerked out of my trance.

I was a mess inside. Seeing everything my sperm donor had, knowing I had left my mom behind, knowing they wouldn't have let her come here—I was feeling some bitterness.

She was my mom. I had been his kid. If he'd given her a little extra, she could've—no, no, no! I couldn't do that. I wouldn't.

Thinking like that was toxic. Be glad for what you get in life. Be thankful and you never have to feel the pinch of "Why not me?" syndrome. That was poison if you let it take over.

"You okay?"

The back of my neck was getting warm, but I coughed. Why did he have to actually sound like he cared? All concerned and sympathetic. "Yeah. Yeah. So . . ." I was supposed to stay here? With him? I heard it before, but I hadn't fully thought about it. Him. Me. This house. Plus the whole secrecy about who I was. I was getting the distinct impression I was in *way* over my head.

"Will that be all, Mr. Colello?" The driver came in behind me, a suitcase in hand. "Would you like this brought to your room?"

Kash gave him a nod. "Thank you, Edward. You can leave that right there."

I knew an Edward once. Edward Vance. He was my seventh-grade math teacher. He was supposed to teach me algebra and instead I offered to figure out how he could get a tax refund bonus for extra credit. At the end of that year, he asked my mom out and they dated through the summer. That'd been awkward. I didn't need to hear how Edward Vance could take the van all the way home.

"Bailey?"

"Yes!" I checked back in. "Where's my room here?"

I was freaking.

This was post kidnapping.

This was post learning a huge fucking lie.

This was not-knowing-what-was-going-to-happen-in-my-future freaking.

This was just plain freaking.

Everything was hitting me all at once.

My stomach twisted up inside.

"Bailey." Kash was frowning at me, the mail down on the counter.

I clamped a hand over my mouth. "I don't feel so good."

His eyebrows shot up, and he was at my side in a flash.

Opening a door, he pushed me down to the floor. The toilet lid was shoved up, and then I let it rip.

Worst. Day. Ever.

Wait. Scratch that. I forgot about the kidnapping.

Second worst. Day. Ever.

NINE

"Well." I groaned, falling to rest against the wall behind me. "That was embarrassing."

Kash had stepped back.

I gagged. I dry heaved. It was like a premature ejaculation experience.

There was no follow-through, no meat to my girth.

I didn't perform. I *under*performed. Air. That was all that came out of me—and a small little snot that fell from my nose.

And, remembering it, I wiped it away, tucking my hand down. I was going to press it on the floor, but that was gross. Kash was here, watching me, and these were his floors.

"Here." He tore off a couple pieces of toilet paper and handed them over.

I took them, feeling that heat all over my body now. Embarrassing.

"Thanks," I croaked, unable to meet his gaze.

He leaned against the counter, folding his arms over his chest. "All of this must be a lot to take in."

I snorted. "A little?"

And another thing of snot came out. Gah. So embarrassing. I wiped at it quick, praying he hadn't seen that, but knowing he had. This guy had hawk eyes. He saw everything. I doubted there was much he didn't notice.

"Listen." His voice gentled and he slid down to sit across from me, his feet on both sides of my legs.

I should've scooted back, put some respectable distance

between us, but I didn't. His legs touched mine and I . . . couldn't bring myself to move away. If anything, my leg sagged a little bit against his.

I was sick. That's why.

He rested his head back against the bathroom counter. "You've been through a traumatic event." His eyes grew softer. "For what you've been through, I was . . . I could've been *softer* yesterday." His voice hardened. "You were forced to choose between a father you didn't know and your mother. It's a hard place to be in, and I do—"

If he said "sympathize," I was going to pinch his nuts.

I waited, but he only said, "You had a day with your mom, but given how fast everything has happened, I'd understand if you needed a night."

"You want me to pull myself together?"

He winced. "The family knows I have a guest coming. They know you're here, so they'll want to meet you. Seraphina is especially excited. She's texted me ten times asking when my 'lady friend' is getting here."

My throat swelled up. "How—how old is Seraphina?"

"You're trying to tell me you don't know?" He gave me a knowing look, his lips tugging up.

I flushed.

I tugged at the end of my shirt, smoothing it out. "You know about my brain." Not a question, a statement.

"Yeah." His voice softened again. "I know." And he kept on, his voice taking on an almost intimate sound, sliding behind my walls. "I know you probably read up on your father, read about his family, your family, but I don't get why you want me to say it. What does it mean for me to tell you how old your sister is?"

My throat burned.

How could I explain that? That it would make me feel normal, that I wanted someone to tell me about my family, that this one time, I didn't want to already know the answer before someone told it to me? Especially about her, about Matthew, about my other brother.

How could I say all that to him?

I jerked up a shoulder, looking away. "Just tell me about her."

"We call her Ser." His voice softened too. "She's twelve, and she'll be shy when she first sees you, but trust me, she's dying to have another female around, one somewhat in her age range."

"How old are the females around here?"

"Quinn is thirty-five. She married your father young, but Ser doesn't count her own mother. Most of the female staff on the estate are in their forties or fifties. When Quinn came into the picture, most of the younger females were asked to leave or were transferred to other estates, other jobs owned by your father."

Cripes. Quinn sounded like she had issues.

"They weren't fired?"

He shook his head. "They were relocated. Besides yourself, and a few staff members, the only other female allowed around Ser is Victoria."

I was going to ask who Victoria was when he continued on. "And then there's Cyclone."

"Cyclone?"

"Your little brother, and he's a handful." He laughed lightly before standing up, then paused. Looking down at me, his eyes darkened before he shook his head. "You look better, not so pale. Let me grab you something to drink quick. Don't stand up."

He left, and I rested my head back.

A little sister who seemed to lack female companionship, who was shy but excited. A brother who I had a feeling might be a terror. I mean, I doubted his real name was Cyclone. And Matthew. Even from the tabloids and gossip sites, I knew he was a handful.

That could've been me.

If I had known, if I had been raised here, it might've been me in the tabloids.

"Here." Kash came back in, a glass of water in hand. He held it down and I took it. Our fingers grazed against each other. I averted my gaze, and he stepped back. "I have to be somewhere."

He paused, and I lifted my head again.

Those eyes, they were locked on me. A deep look was in them, as if there was a storm going on in his head, as if somehow that storm had something to do with me, as if he didn't like that. Then, like before, he closed his eyes, and when he opened them again, gone. The storm was dead.

I didn't know what that was about, but I felt as if I'd just lost out on something, something big, something I might've desperately wanted.

A bunch of sensations twisted inside of me.

He cleared his throat, deadpanning, and yeah, I was completely locked out of whatever had gone on in his head. Again.

"Are you going to be okay here for the evening?"

"No freak-outs." I shook my head, a hard wave. "I'll be fine."

Kash gave me a doubtful look, and I couldn't blame him. I didn't believe myself either.

I amended, "I'll do my best."

"Okay." His eyebrows were dipped low, but his phone buzzed and he sighed. "I really do have to go." He pointed to the ceiling. "You can have your pick of the rooms upstairs. My room is on the main floor, but make yourself at home. Relax. Settle in. There's food in the fridge, or if you wanted the main kitchen to make you something special, just pick up the phone and dial one. It'll ring you through to the communications desk."

A communications desk.

For a house.

Yeah. Not normal.

He stepped farther back. "If an older woman comes around, it'll be Marie. Like I said, she's the only other one who really knows why you're here. You can trust her. Go to her for anything you might need."

His phone buzzed again. He cursed, reading whatever was on

the screen. "I *really* have to go." He stepped to the side, then stopped. "Oh. I called yesterday and you should have clothes upstairs for you. If they aren't in the room you want, just mention it to Marie. She'll have the staff switch everything for you."

One more pause, one more look back. "Do you need anything from me?"

I needed my mom. I needed all of this not to have happened. I needed a new father.

I forced a smile. "Not a thing."

"Okay." And he was gone.

Yes. Not a thing . . .

TEN

I was snooping. No shame here.

An hour later, I was in his bedroom. He had his own library in there, and his own balcony. Not to mention the bed. The bed! It was big enough for five people to sleep in it.

"We kill cats here."

I jumped as I was shutting the balcony doors, and whirled.

I thought it was Kash, but it wasn't. Someone else.

My insides instantly knotted, seeing who it was, recognizing who it was.

Matthew Francis leaned against the door frame, a smirk on his face, dressed like he was going to a nightclub. Low-hanging jeans. A leather jacket. A shirt underneath that was one of those where they bought them already ripped. His hair was messily rumpled, though I was sure there was hair product in it. The jacket added a little more bulk to him than I had noticed the night before, but he was still gangly.

"You kill cats here?"

His eyebrows went up. His smirk turned knowing. "So you are Kash's mystery guest, and you're already snooping around?"

I broke out a tentative grin. "Still curious about the cat comment." Splaying my hands out to my side, I tucked them behind me and glanced down.

It was a nervous movement, but damn. My brother was *talking* to me.

"I'm Matthew Francis. Kash works with my father." He was eyeing me up and down, dissecting me. There was frank curiosity and a slight flash of anger mixed in. He raised his hand up, a drink there, and took a sip. Hissing, baring his teeth from the burn, he coughed and then put his hand back down. His fingers transferred so he was holding the glass by the top of the rim, and his head went back up, resting against the door frame. "Kash is the king of secrets and mystery around this place, so the way I figure, you're either running from someone or something else is going on." He straightened from the doorway. "Which is it, little cat? I introduced myself. Now you introduce yourself."

My nostrils flared as I straightened to my fullest height. My head rose. My chin squared against his and I rolled my shoulders back. He took everything in, a flare of surprise in his eyes, but he masked it deftly.

"I'd imagine that if Kash wanted you to know who I was, he would've told you." I wasn't sure if that was the right thing to say, but I had a feeling if I rattled off his entire Wikipedia page he wouldn't be impressed. He would be suspicious.

I had the names and dates and lies to spew out. Aunt Judith. Uncle Martin. Cousin Stephanie. Bad breakup. Kash and I kept in contact when he visited them from when he was four year old till he was eight. There was nothing in those files about why he stopped, so I'd have to bluff there as well, but I would.

Kash had underestimated my brother. He was suspicious, enough to seek me out within an hour of being on the premises.

"I saw you at the hotel. You were in the elevator with Kash." He lowered his head until he was more normal. He must've bought at least a little of what I said. "If you were there and you were Kash's girl, why didn't he walk you to your room? If you really knew Kash, he never would've let you go to your room alone. He can be a protective asshole sometimes."

Damn.

I opened my mouth. I wasn't sure what I was going to spew, but it was going to be as much a surprise to myself as to him . . . and then someone else spoke for me.

"She's not my girl," Kash drawled behind Matthew.

Aw, shit.

I was busted by both of them, and looking at Kash, I gulped.

His eyes were glittering at me. His jaw was clenched. His mouth tight. The guy was pissed, and a wave of awareness crashed over me. This was like seeing him walking into that interrogation room for the first time. He must've been toning down his intensity since the car ride, but it was back in full force now. He was dangerous, and livid. Not a good mix. But his eyes latched on to me, burning me, before sliding to Matthew. That's where he stayed, and that's when I saw the arrogant bravado start to slip from my half brother.

Matt's head lowered an inch. He grew a little . . . self-conscious? Was that what I was picking up from him?

"What are you doing here, Matt?" Kash clipped out, strolling past him.

That was wrong, too.

He stalked past him, coming in, bypassing me. His eyes had moved to me, he watched me the whole time he went past, until he stepped into his closet. Coming out, he'd taken off his shirt and carried another one in hand. Tossing it on his bed, his hands dropped to his pants.

Oh, whoa.

I did *not* look away.

I should've. I could've.

I didn't.

No way.

He was cut and chiseled, and there were sleek lines of muscle all over him. Not overly, where it was too much muscle, but enough to give him a leanness. He was like a jaguar, one trimmed and poised to attack. His eyes flashed to me again, and I gulped before they skirted to Matthew and stayed there. He'd found his target.

"I asked you a question. What are you doing here, Matt?" He

let go of his jeans and shoved his arms in the shirt, pulling it over and down. It fit perfectly.

Shocker.

"I'm meeting your new friend. What's *her* name? She still hasn't told me."

"Because it's not your business," Kash shot back.

Matthew laughed, but I heard the unease in there. "First time you bring a girl here, and you think I'm not going to check her out? You nuts?"

"Right there." Kash's head fell back, his nostrils flaring. "First time. First. Time. You don't think I'd want privacy, even if she was *my* girl?"

Doubt filtered over Matthew's face, his eyebrows pinching together. "You're always shoving your way into *my* places."

Places. Matt had more than one?

Matt was still speaking. "You never give a shit if I'm pissed or not."

"That's different."

A snort. "How?"

"Because you're a dumbass that usually needs me to either kick your ass or someone else's ass around you. That's why."

I waited, expecting a retort from my brother. None came. He nodded, running a hand over his head and gripping his neck for a moment. "That's fair." A corner of his mouth curved up, and he went back to studying me. "But seriously. Who is she?"

Kash let out a sigh, grabbing his shirt. "She's a friend from the family. My family. Bailey Hayes." He bundled his shirt up in a ball and threw it at Matthew, hard. It was enough to smack against his chest from across the room. "That's all you need to know. Respect her wish. She ain't here on vacation."

My eyes darted to him, my body warming.

There was that protective asshole that Matthew commented on, but it was regarding me. I knew it was a lie. He was helping with my cover, but I couldn't deny that it felt nice to hear it. I almost wished it were true.

"How you going to handle Victoria?"

Victoria? Kash had mentioned her earlier. I waited to see what he'd say, but he only jerked a shoulder up, before unbuckling his jeans. "I'll handle her." He paused, raking us both with a look. "Can you both get out? I need to change my pants."

Matthew started laughing. "Now I know she really ain't your girl." He nodded to me, still smiling. "Come on, Little Mystery. If you're going to snoop in Kash's place, you're not going to find the right spots. I'll show you where he keeps the good booze."

My gaze skirted to Kash at the *snooping* word, but he didn't seem to mind. His head cocked to the side, his fingers waiting, holding on to his waistband, he looked annoyed. Trailing after Matthew, I tried to wrap my head around everything.

My brother was right in front of me.

He had caught me, questioned me, then tried to grill me. Now he was showing me where Kash hid his booze, which wasn't a secret place at all. Down the hall. To the kitchen. He wound around the island to the pantry, and that was where a whole row of bottles was shelved.

"Wow," I deadpanned, waiting in the doorway as he grabbed a few of them. "You're right. I never would've found those."

He shot me a grin, going past me and setting them on the island. "It's the only place with fun stuff in Kash's house."

He turned to me.

I thought he needed to go past me for glasses, but he didn't. He only leaned down, purposely getting in my space, and his eyes were hard. His words were blunt. "I don't know what the fuck's going on, but I know something is. If you actually did know Kash, you would've known he keeps all his real shit in his downtown apartment."

Oh.

Crap.

"Why do you keep thinking I was snooping?"

"You were."

Yeah. Well. "Why do you insist that I was looking for the 'real shit'? How do you know I wasn't up there because he has a freaking library? Did you see those bookshelves? Sue me. I like reading. Hide some books somewhere, and I'll sniff 'em out. Hidden talent of mine."

He straightened his back again, sneering in disbelief. "Whatever you say. You'd know he only uses this house when he's forced to stay on the estate, which ain't that often. Another fact I know you don't know about my boy, so why don't you cut the bullshit. Nerd aside, who are you? Really."

I let out a sigh.

Kash was padding barefoot down the hallway and starting to cross the room. He had changed into sweatpants that fell low on his hips. Matthew's back was to him. He didn't know Kash was there, and I frowned slightly, a brief flash of familiarity nagging at me. Kash walked so quietly, he was soundless.

He had covered for me in his room, but this was the real test.

A dark warning flared in Kash's gaze. I ignored it, meeting my brother's gaze, and I shifted back a step so I could think. "Fine." I made sure my voice cracked. "You're right."

Triumph flooded over his face. He narrowed his eyes. "Still waiting."

"But you're wrong about most of it. I don't know Kash that well, but I do know his family. I was neighbors with Judith and Martin." I paused, wondering, "You know them?"

He stiffened. "Kash doesn't talk about his family, hardly ever."

So he really was a mystery, even to them? Even if he grew up with them, as he said?

"I was good friends with his cousin, Stephanie." I didn't pause to ask if he knew her. I was betting he didn't. "And anyways, I *am*

going through a hard time right now. It's a bad breakup, okay?"
My voice wobbled. My bottom lip trembled.

Could I get a tear?

I tried. I did. Chrissy would've been all over that, but it wasn't
a talent of mine. Still. I was convincing, because my half brother
was looking at me with a mix of sympathy and guilt.

Good. He should feel guilty, for wasting away all the privileges
he got as Peter Francis's eldest son. Not going to be interested
in computers, my ass. He was insane. Peter Francis might be my
sperm donor, but I *still* would kill for an internship at Phoenix
Tech.

It was in my blood. Literally.

I turned, pressing into the island counter with my fingers. I
couldn't pick at it. It was one giant piece of stone, so I did the best
I could, rubbing the bottoms of my fingers against it. "I . . . I got
to a dark place, okay? Stephanie was alarmed enough"—I nodded in the direction of Kash's bedroom—"she called in a favor. I
remember Kash when we were younger. He visited for a few years,
but yeah, I've not seen him for almost twenty years. Don't matter.
Stephanie said I needed to get out of there, said I should stay here
until I was better. A change of environment would do me good."

I waited, holding my breath.

I didn't dare look up. My brother was sharp, seriously sharp.
He'd had one whiff of something not making sense, and this was
his second attempt at figuring it out.

"I feel like a dipshit."

My knees almost gave out from relief. He bought it.

Instead, I looked up, keeping sure my facial expression was
locked up. "Yeah?"

He rolled his eyes. "I don't know why I thought something
funny was going on. Kash never brings girls here, but I don't
know anything about his family. Who am I to interrogate you,
you know?"

Hell yes, but I only smiled. "It's okay. You're being protective."

He snorted at that. "Don't know why. If anyone doesn't need it, it's him." He was watching me again. The suspicion was still there. "But you'd know that much, right?"

A hand reached inside my spine and took hold of it, in a viselike grip. That's how it felt, because he was still testing me.

Enough was enough. I pretended not to see it and moved away. "Hmm, yeah. He always was when he was little too." Opening a shelf, I asked, "You know where the glasses are? If we're going to have a drink, we need a few of those."

Hearing a door close from down the hallway, Kash must've gone back. He was alerting us, or alerting Matthew. Walking out, he yawned and tossed his phone on the couch as he passed it.

I searched his face, but there was no indication he'd heard anything that was just spoken.

He was a good liar, too. His eyes lingered on mine for a second before taking in the sight of us and everything on the counter. "We're drinking? Didn't you get in enough trouble last night?"

I saw my brother tense up beside me. His hand gripped the neck of one of the bottles tighter. "One can never get in enough trouble. What'chu talkin' 'bout, Willis?"

Kash ignored the sitcom quote, padding into the kitchen and grabbing a tray of ice from the freezer. He slid it over the counter to us. "Fine, Matt. You want to have a few drinks, at least make them right, huh?"

It was later, after Matthew went to the bathroom, that Kash grabbed my wrist and pulled me to a corner of the room. He folded his arms over his chest, staring down at me, and standing close. Way too close.

Or that's what I was trying to tell myself.

"What'd he want?"

He was studying me, but his eyes were first on mine, then dipped to my mouth. And lingered there.

And stayed lingering there.

And still more lingering.

It was a sauna in here. Someone threw open the doors and hell's inferno had started.

I parted my lips, surprised at his proximity, but he wasn't moving back.

He needed to move back, or I'd do something we'd both regret. My hand was itching.

God. His jaw. It was so smooth, so square, so strong. I was itching to touch it, or maybe his chest. That shirt looked smooth. Or his arms, how they were folded tight over his chest and the muscles were bulging out. How there was a dip between them and—

He shifted closer, letting out a sigh and a hiss at the same time. "Listen."

My eyes flew to his, and I gulped because his were intense, *seriously* intense.

He placed a hand on the wall behind me, trapping me in, but it was just one hand. His eyes were still boring down into mine, then fell back to my mouth.

"This. You. Me."

I wanted to shift up on my tiptoes, getting closer. I didn't, but holy God, did I want to.

Then, suddenly, a barrier fell back between us. Not a literal barrier, but whatever was in his head. I felt the cold rejection almost physically. He moved back, his face becoming stone again, and I jerked back into the wall.

I never felt the impact.

He cursed, rubbing a hand over his face. "Jesus. What'd he want?"

I couldn't talk. A full three seconds. Crap, that rejection *hurt*.

I croaked out, "Nothing. Just trying to say I don't know you." My own guilt pushed up, storing the other stuff away. "Look, I'm sorry. I wanted to explore your house. I wasn't snooping as he keeps saying—"

Kash clipped his head from side to side. "I don't care about that. You're a stranger. There's no way I'd let you stay here if I had something of value in this house."

He wouldn't?

Yep. Wow. Another slap to the face. This guy was just doling out the punches left and right.

"Your story was good." He nodded in approval, shifting back from me when we heard the toilet flush. He raked me up and down. "You're a good liar."

What I was going for in life. My highest goal achieved.

Then he moved away, going to the kitchen as Matthew was coming back, and I had to kick myself. Why did I care if he thought I was a good liar? I was here to hide for my life. That was it.

When the threat was gone, I was gone.

ELEVEN

"Mr. Colello."

A woman was knocking on his front door. She had a shorter build, maybe around five foot four inches, with a stockier physique to her. Coming to the second-floor loft area, I stood there a moment. She had dark hair pulled back in a fierce bun. She wore a black shirt that resembled a scrub top my mother might've worn for her shift at the hospital. Dark pants. Dark shoes.

She was tough. I could tell. Her stockiness wasn't from being overweight. It was muscle. She raised her hand to knock again. "Mr. Colello."

"Coming," Kash called from his bedroom. A second later, he came out from under where I stood, pulling his shirt down over his shoulders. There was a rippling effect over his muscles from the movement.

My mouth dried up.

Kash was opening the door, stepping back. "Morning, Marie."

This was Marie?

A small churning of unease started in me. She was the only other person who knew who I was. Because, after last night, there was no way I was going to Kash for anything. Yeah, yeah. There'd been attraction. I couldn't deny that. But that was done with.

I was way out of my league with him.

By the end of the night, I was in awe, but also slightly horrified that this was the guy I'd be living with for the next few months. He had sealed the cover with my half brother to perfection. He'd been so good that even I was starting to believe him.

I went to bed having to remind myself that I didn't actually know Stephanie, and I never went shopping with her for a Thanksgiving tradition.

"Yes, she's . . ."

They both turned to look at me.

Crap. I didn't hide in time.

Marie had come inside, the door closed behind them. Neither smiled. Both just stared up at me.

I raised my hand, then remembered. "Is Matthew still here?"

He'd been the only one to get drunk last night, and when we went to our rooms, he'd been snoring from the living room.

Kash looked tired. "He took off around four this morning, said he wanted to feel like shit in his own bed." He motioned to Marie. "This is Marie, Bailey. Come down to meet her."

My legs felt like wood as I did.

This was real. After meeting this woman, another stranger, I knew what was next. Going to the main house. Seeing my other siblings, my stepmother . . . that *f*-word. Peter Francis. Meeting him. I wiped my hands over my pants. They were suddenly shaking.

"Miss Bailey."

The woman's hand was strong, just like I thought. She pumped my hand up and down with a clipped nod, and her dark brown eyes were hard on me. This woman was not one to mess around.

"Marie." I was already terrified of this woman. "How are you?"

She didn't respond, her eyes just went back to Kash, who'd been watching the exchange. He shifted back, his arms crossed over his chest. Raking me over, a troubled look in his eyes, he shook his head. The look cleared.

"Marie's in charge from now on. You sleep here. You rest, do what you need, but other than that, she's your go-to. Got it?"

"Got it."

Seriously. I fought to keep myself from saluting him. That was not mature.

"Uh."

Kash had started to return to his room, but paused and raised an eyebrow at my sound.

There those hands went again, jerking a little. I held them flat against my sides. "Is there a way I could get my old laptop?"

"Your computer?"

"It's like air to me. I need it." Did Marie know? "I'm a hacker, Kash. The fact I've gone this long without my computer is a miracle. Be glad I didn't find one of yours in the house and go to town."

Marie studied me, her head tilted to the side. I ignored her. Kash only narrowed his eyes before moving his head up and down in a stiff nod. "Yes. You're right. Peter's the same." He turned to Marie. "I'll have someone retrieve hers, but get her an extra desktop from the house in the meantime." He began to move again, then stopped. "You don't have work to do while you're here, do you?"

"I was working on a new security program, but no, not really."

And that was all he needed. He spoke to Marie again, speaking in that authoritative tone, like he was used to giving orders. "If there are projects you need done around the house, put her on it."

Marie's face sharpened. Heavy disdain lined her words. "Projects? Like what? Printing recipes for the kitchen staff?"

"Like writing code for a robot rabbit that Cyclone is working on. Projects like that."

A robot rabbit?

I perked up.

Tell me more.

I mused, "I thought intelligence was passed down through the mother."

Kash snorted, leaving for real this time. Disappearing down the hallway to his room, he called over his shoulder, "Who said anything about you being intelligent?"

I started at that. Frowning.

He just burned me.

I jerked forward, calling, "Don't be jealous, Colello, just because I could write a new program to lock you out of your own house and you'd have no idea how to get it fixed." I was smiling. I shouldn't have been, but I was. Then I turned to find Marie still studying me. Her eyes were harder than before, and that smile dropped immediately. "Hi."

Yep. They were slits now. "Don't you mess with Mr. Colello."

"We were flirting. Foreplay." I wiggled my eyebrows.

I heard another snort from in his room.

Marie didn't get the joke. She turned for the door again. "You go and get dressed. Come to the main house. Be there in twenty minutes. Do not be late. You hear me?"

Definitely don't piss her off. I nodded, knowing I already had. "Yes. Got it."

She harrumphed before leaving and I was alone, still in my pajamas from the night before.

"You're fighting it." Kash spoke from behind me. His hands were in his pockets and his head lowered. His hair was messed a little, giving him a dark and broody look, and it wasn't affecting me at all. That little tickle in my stomach wasn't from him.

Nope. Not at all.

I ignored it, and I also didn't pretend not to know what he meant.

He added, "We're not the enemy, Bailey. Those men who tried to kidnap you, they are. Don't forget that. I get you don't like how you're being introduced to the family, but it's unavoidable." His head lifted up, his eyes never leaving mine. "You'll see that too, eventually, and you'll be grateful." He indicated the door. "That woman is almost a second mother to me. You hurt her and you and me will have a problem. I don't have problems. I eliminate them. Got *me*?"

Well.

Crap.

I nodded. "Yeah." Then, "Are you sure my mother is safe?"

"Going after the mother would hurt the child, not the target. Peter Francis doesn't tend to care about his exes once they part ways. He doesn't do it to be mean. It's just how he is. His mind works in a different way. He's on to the next project." He began to step back toward his room, leaving me with, "I have a feeling you might be like that, too."

I wasn't.

I heard his door shut a second later.

I wasn't like my father in that way at all.

TWELVE

It felt wrong to walk into a stranger's home alone. I felt like I was invading their privacy when I went to the main house, but no one cared. No one questioned me. No one even paused along the way to ask who I was, why I was there.

The side door opened onto a hallway. Marble floors. Pure white walls. I heard people from one end and headed that way. Gold and crystal chandeliers hung from the ceiling. As I neared the door, people were hurrying back and forth.

"One more!"

"Tray's done."

"Watch out!"

Crash.

Thud.

"Oh no!"

Clap, clap! "Let's keep going. Not a moment's delay, people."

More rushing back and forth.

Coming to stand in the doorway, I couldn't believe what I was seeing. They weren't dressed like Marie, but they had a similar uniform. Their tops were blue with gold trim, matching the chandeliers, which were hanging above their heads in this room, too. They were in the kitchen, and when I say "kitchen," I really mean a cafeteria-like room used to make food for an entire company. This room was double the size of the kitchen at my high school.

I was pretty sure my mouth was on the floor.

Twenty-plus people were inside, whipping around in a frenzy.

Trays upon trays were being loaded, checked over, loaded onto a staff member's shoulder, and carried out a separate door. Even how the staff member approached the door was a ceremony in itself.

It was a three-person job.

The person would hoist the tray up, stand at the ready, nod to someone at the door. That person would look out the window, nod to another person, and wait for a signal before opening it. They would follow it through, stand, hold it open. The person with the tray would whisk through.

There were people at the grill. People at a separate stove. People dicing up other food, sliding it into containers, those containers being covered and then put into a line of fridges that lined one entire wall of the room.

"Oh, sorry." Someone bumped into me from behind.

I glanced back, seeing the cutest little boy standing behind me. Bright blue eyes that looked almost like teardrops. Wavy blond hair, and freckles spread all over his tan face.

This was Cyclone.

I was dumbfounded.

He'd been about to run past me, but when I turned to him, he skidded to a stop and stared up at me. He looked me up and down. "Who are you? Where's your uniform?"

He thought I was staff.

Well, maybe I was. "Hey, kid."

He frowned, his nose pinching up, then he thought about it and burst out laughing. "Kid. I like that. I'll call you Girl."

"Cyclone!" Marie hollered from inside the kitchen. She was coming toward us, waving. "Come here."

He saw her, gave me a wave. "Nice knowing you, Girl." He took off running into the kitchen.

"Cyclone!"

He was laughing as he weaved around everyone. Two people lifted up their trays for him. Another toppled over, the tray of food spreading everywhere on the floor. The tray itself shattered into pieces.

"Cyclone!"

About three people were yelling. One staff member was holding back a smile, and still more were just shaking their heads in resignation. The far door was shoved open and he disappeared.

"Marie!" One of the other women was coming our way, her face tight in anger. "He cannot come in here. He's messing up our entire operation. That tray alone cost over sixty dollars, not counting the food loss."

"I know. I know, Theresa." Marie stopped before she got to me. "I'll talk to Mistress Quinn, but you know Cyclone."

"Seraphina wasn't like that."

"But Matthew was." Both women shared a look. The other one groaned as Marie added, "He was worse, if you remember."

"Yes, yes." Theresa wasn't happy. "I know, I know." Her eyes caught on me and she stopped. She jutted out her chin. "Who is this?" She looked me up and down. "She doesn't wear a uniform, and I've not heard of any new staff joining us."

"She's . . ." Marie frowned at me.

I stepped forward, time to do my part. "I'm a friend of Kash—" I'd been about to say Kash Colello, but that wouldn't sell the part. "Kash's. He told me to look for Marie while he was working."

At the mention of Kash's name, a hush fell over the kitchen.

I'd been standing there, being invisible moments ago, but his name had everyone watching us.

"Coming!" someone yelled on the other side of the door. When the door person didn't answer, they yelled again, "Coming in—" The door was pushed open, and smacked into the door attendant, who was staring at me. "Whoa—agh!" The tray hit the person's back, and the staff member caught it, but not the dishes. Two more plates clattered to the floor, shattering.

Theresa whipped around, the spell broken. She threw her arm up. "Mick! Pay attention."

I was rooted in place, still feeling their attention as they got back to work.

Marie sidled up closer. I dropped my voice. "Why?"

For the first time since I saw her, a pitying expression graced her face. "Come with me. I'll explain a bit more."

Great. I couldn't tell my new family that I was family. I couldn't tell the staff who I wasn't, and Marie was feeling sorry for me. For some reason, I didn't think that was a good sign. What wasn't Kash telling me?

We moved farther down the hallway before I glanced back over my shoulder. "What was going on in the other room?" But I was more distracted that I had just met my brother. Cyclone. He said I could call him Kid.

Kid. Girl.

We were off to a good start. Then I realized he might never know who I was.

Pain sliced through me, cutting me deep, splitting me in half, and I had to stop a second.

"Come, come." Marie motioned me to keep going. "I'll answer all your questions in my office."

I followed.

I tried not to dwell on a sudden emptiness that took root in the middle of my chest. Down a hallway, another. We were weaving to a far corner. The sounds of the kitchen faded until it was only the sounds of our own feet on the floor. "Here we go." She paused before a door, punching in a code.

The door opened, and I was hit with the smells of cake and candy.

She waved me in, going to sit behind a desk that was piled high with paperwork.

This was obviously Marie's place, and after meeting her at

Kash's villa, I expected to find an office room that was pristine and clean. Instead, her own desk was filled with papers and files. A counter was in the corner, filled with goodies and candy. Vanilla cake on a platter. There was a large table in the middle of the room, where crafts had been started and left behind. A pile of beads were spread out over one end, with wires next to it as a bracelet, half made, was abandoned. In another corner were three gaming chairs on the floor. A PlayStation was hooked up beneath a television, the consoles resting on the floor between the chairs and TV. A bag of chips was scrunched down between two of the chairs.

She had filing cabinets in another corner, covered in picture frames.

A half wall jutted out so I couldn't see what was on the other side, but the back of a desk chair had been rolled out.

The room was large, more resembling an elementary school classroom than the office of someone who managed the staff at Peter Francis's estate.

"Come in, come in. Shut the door." She waved at me, impatiently.

I sat on the chair across from her desk, sinking into it.

She was watching me, already riffling through some of her papers, and the ends of her mouth were pulled in. I tried not to feel her disapproval, but it was hard. It washed over me like a hot wave of embarrassment.

She motioned around the room behind me. "That's for the children. They like to come in and spend time here."

"Cyclone and Seraphina?"

"Cyclone." She was nodding as she spoke. "Seraphina, if she can sneak away from Victoria or her mother. And some of the other women bring their children if they're sick or school is closed. The master and mistress are very accepting if the staff don't have day care options in case of an emergency." She waved around her office again. "They come in here. We call in a day care worker if there's enough children, but you are right." Her eyes paused on me, looking over a piece of paper. "It's mostly Cyclone, and if he has a friend over at times. His parents like him to have friends here. Seraphina too, but her friends prefer her own wing rather than in here."

Jesus. Wing.

I heard the fondness and pride.

She was proud of what she did at this estate, of who she worked for, or perhaps of what she did for the children. She provided a sanctuary for these children, and that was important to her.

She waved to the partition behind me. "There's a desk behind that. That's for you."

"Me?"

"As soon as Kash informed me you were coming, I had maintenance bring up a desk for you. It'll be your spot for when you are inside the estate home. I called after seeing you at the villa and they're bringing up a computer as well. It might already be there, but you can check later. Now . . ." She was done with her paperwork, putting it all aside and fixing me with a direct stare. "Let's discuss you."

I swallowed, not getting a good feeling from how she said that. "Me?"

"You." And she narrowed those eyes at me. "You are going to be a problem."

Those were the words every illegitimate daughter longed to hear.

And, feeling like a smartass, I smiled. "Please elaborate."

She fixed me with a look, her mouth flattening even further. She was not amused.

I tried to make my smile more sincere. "Pretty please?" Was that better? Then I just sighed on the inside. Kash was right earlier. I *was* fighting being here, but could he blame me? Could anyone? But that wasn't her problem. That was mine. That was my f— that *f*-word. She was just doing her job.

I sat up straighter in my chair and rolled back my shoulders. "Okay. Lay it on me. Tell me how to not be a problem for you, and I'll do the best I can." I bobbed my head up and down. "Promise."

Her mouth pursed together and she moved her head, giving me a side-eye. She blinked, slowly, and rotated her face to look at me square again.

"Okay." She laid her hands down on her desk, folding them together. "You want to not be a problem for me?" She didn't wait a beat. "You should go home, go back to where your mother is, and not contact Mr. Colello or Mr. Francis again."

I stand corrected.

Those were the words every illegitimate daughter longed to hear.

THIRTEEN

"Excuse me?" I pretended to clean out my ears. I hadn't heard that right, had I?

"You heard me." It was like she could read my mind. She fixed me with a steely glare. It wasn't a full glare, but it wasn't a stare.

"You will only upset this household. There is no place for you. If Mr. Francis wanted to include you in his family, he would've introduced you as his daughter, not this facade of being Mr. Colello's family friend. You are upsetting master and mistress, their children, and also Mr. Colello himself. He has enough to worry about. He does not need to add a stranger into the mix to babysit." She lowered her voice, but that only made her more terrifying. "If you should pack up and require a ride from the estate to return to your real family, I could set that up. You could do it quietly, and tonight, when Mr. Colello is in the city dealing with other aspects of his life."

Other aspects of his life? What all did he do?

"I thought Kash worked for . . ." Did I say "master" too? "For Mr. Francis. Does he not?"

Some of the steam cooled, but she was still chilly.

"Let's stick to what you need to know, and that's this: if you stay here, you will upset the balance of this family."

Right.

This family. Not mine.

Not me.

Them.

She kept on. "If you remain here, Cyclone will get attached. Seraphina will care for you. They are good children. Your presence is a risk. There is a possibility they could discover who you claim to be, and if they do, what then? You are under a guise. You are not here as a member of this family, nor will you ever be. This has happened before, where someone came under the facade of proclaiming they were Peter Francis's child. When it is discovered you are not, you will only hurt those dear children. Their hearts will be ripped out, all because Mr. and Mrs. Francis had the kind heart to bring you into their fold, even if Mr. Colello is insisting for your presence to be kept under wraps so they do not get attached."

Attached.

Guise.

Facade.

She thought I was lying. She thought I was a fake.

"You think I'm conning my biological father?"

My hand curled in on itself on my lap.

Her nostrils flared and, flattening her hand on the desk, she inched forward. "Mr. Colello would never allow that to happen, but it is alarming that you've been given free range of the estate."

She should've just shoved her fist into my throat. That's what I was feeling here. "You think I'm here . . . why?" *Think, Bailey.*

"Why do people usually claim to be a long-lost daughter of Peter Francis?"

She was so cold, mocking me now.

I flinched. "Right. Right."

Her mouth thinned. "Why else would you be restricted to being under my charge if Mr. Colello was not still investigating your claims? He assured me you wouldn't be here long."

I almost laughed at that. "He said that because I go to graduate school in the fall." I leaned forward. "For computer security. I'm a hacker, Marie. Don't you think that's a big coincidence, if you thought I was this con man?"

She drew up her chest, letting it lower again, then shrugged. "I think you underestimate the lengths some people will go to be claimed as a child from Peter Francis."

So she just didn't believe me.

Well, that was an easy fix.

"Right," I drawled. I didn't think anything I said would get anywhere, and on top of that, I wasn't sure if I even wanted her to believe me. Maybe there was a reason she was being so distrustful? Kash could've dealt with this when he told her I was coming, but he hadn't.

Maybe it was for the best? I mean, in a way, she was speaking the truth. I would be gone soon. She just didn't know the real reason.

And, at this rate, who knew if I'd even meet my father. It was day three and no one mentioned him being anywhere in the vicinity. I was given a desk in the staff headquarters, for God's sakes. I was not wanted here.

Fine.

I stood up.

"Where are you going?"

"Can you have the computer brought to Kash's place? I can do some of my work from there instead of . . ." My eyes skimmed her office and my heart sank a little. If this had been my home, if she'd been in charge of my family, I would've loved to spend time here. The room was warm and inviting, just not to me. My throat tightened up. "I'll remain out of the way as long as possible, until Mr. Colello's done with his *investigation*."

I didn't wait for her response. I left, and going down one hallway in the direction of where I thought I'd come in, I had to stop.

There were three hallways breaking off from mine, but no door. No kitchen either.

I was completely lost.

Karma was a funny bitch indeed.

FOURTEEN

I was going down hallway number 233.

Okay, that was sarcasm, but it felt like I'd been wandering this mausoleum for an hour. Part of it was my fault. I could find someone, get directions (I still couldn't get over that I would need to get directions in a house), but the point of sneaking out was to actually *sneak* out. Marching up to someone and asking them how to leave violated the whole point of my exit. Because of that, every time I started to hear voices at one end of a hall, I took the next hallway. It didn't matter if it led up, down, left, or right, and if I had to brake and back up, I did.

I did not need to be told anymore how unwanted I was here.

I was just trying to move along, convince myself it wasn't actually ripping out my organs to see I did have a family with siblings out there. They just didn't want me—the father anyway.

"How did you meet?" I'd asked Chrissy two nights ago, arms wrapped tight around my knees, my heart in my chest as I waited for her to tell me.

"Oh, baby." She had wiped a tear away.

And she told me.

They met when she was doing clinicals in nursing school. She was hired to care for someone who was dying.

Her eyes were closed. Her hand didn't move from that bottle. She held it suspended in the air, as if she had frozen in time.

Then, with a rasping gasp, she continued. *"I took care of his mama for a year, a full year . . ."*

She wouldn't look at me as she continued. He was married.

He was unhappy. They shouldn't have done what they did, but it was the last night.

"*The night she died, no one was there for him. His wife never came.*" Her voice grew hoarse. "*I was crying. He was crying. They came and took the body, and I went to him.*"

Another pause. Her eyes closed. Another tear fell down.

"*I'll never regret it. It was one night. His wife came the next day, and we acted like nothing happened.*"

That hadn't been all of it. There'd been more, but those were the words I couldn't get out of my head.

My phone buzzed in my pocket. Kash.

Where are you? Marie said you're at my house, but cameras aren't showing you.

Shit.

And wait—he had cameras on me?

Took a wrong turn about 823 turns ago. This house is freaking huge. I'm in a mall. An empty and deserted mall. Everyone's at the Gap.

Kash: *What?*

Me: *I'm lost.*

Kash: *You're lost?*

Me: *Yes.*

Kash: *Where?*

Me: *In the house.*

Kash: *What house?*

Me: *The big kahuna.*

Kash: *Did you ask for help?*

I grinned.

Me: *Why would I do that?*

Kash: *So you're not lost.*

Even through the phone, I could feel his irritation.

I was loving it. More foreplay.

Me: *What if I'm just lost in life? No one to help me with that one.*

Kash: *What the hell*

I paused. He'd stopped midtext. That wasn't a good sign, until my phone rang in my hand.

Double shit.

I answered, not even looking. I knew who it was. And before he could snipe at me first, I started in. "You need to understand that a girl in my position, with my background, there's not much I have."

He growled, "What are you talking about?"

"You see that you *don't* see. I don't have much here, on my end. I'm not that kid who saw too much, et cetera, growing up, but I did see one or two too many guys come in our home. I saw a couple that treated her right. I saw a few who didn't, and I learned how I wanted to be, growing up.

"Now, I can't say I know what morals Peter Francis may have, but I feel I can say with almost an eighty percent certainty that I got my morals and values from living with my mother. Chrissy tried. She really did. She's a hard worker. She was in her third year of nursing when she got pregnant with me. Took a year off to have me, then went right back. She finished while she worked, and I don't think she could've got more than five hours of sleep a week."

I was starting to ramble, but he was quiet. He was listening. No one was around, so I was going with it.

"So you see, when I'm here and I'm being told that I'm a lie, and I'm being told I should go back home, and I'm being told everyone would be better off without me, well . . . wandering a bit in a gigantic house is not that big of a deal. Not enough for you to call me with a growl in your voice, because I have integrity. And if you don't mind, I'm going to keep the last bit of it I have, and I'll find my way out of this house eventually without asking for help."

I didn't give him a chance to reply. I hung up, and I powered off the phone for good measure. Sticking it back in my pocket, I turned—only to reel backward.

I didn't know for sure, but since she was exquisite and had a sunlight-wheat color to her blond hair, which was swept up and pinned to the top of her head, I assumed that I was staring at Quinn Francis. She had clear cornflower-blue eyes, the same teardrop shape as Cyclone. High cheekbones that swept out, a chin that molded down to complete a heart-shaped face, and the plushest lips I'd seen in person.

She was stunning.

There were no other words, and she was gazing at me, not a whiff of anger, suspicion, or even warmth. There was confusion, as if she wasn't sure if I was real or not.

The image was completed by a soft-hue pink dress that had a scoop neckline, a layer of white lace, and a hemline that fitted just above her knees; the rest was the same hue of pink tulle that fell to the floor. There was no jewelry anywhere, even on her hands. My heart ached because I knew that my mother had kept up with Peter Francis, and if this was who my father had married, then my mother had compared herself to this woman. And there was no comparison. My mother would have won, hands down, for the mere fact that she was Chrissy Hayes, and no one could compete against Chrissy Hayes.

I readied myself, figuring she'd overheard me, and I waited to see what she'd say.

Her mouth parted. She was studying me up and down, all over, and damn it, I knew I was going to break first.

"I'm only here for . . . *you know*." She knew, right? How could she not? I jerked my gaze to the floor. It was so much easier this way. "And, uh, as soon as they catch 'em, the Arcane people, I'll go. I'm not here to upset anyone or disturb nothing." And I couldn't talk, either. Proper grammar be damned. "I was trying to find Kash's villa again and I got lost."

She continued to stare at me. Not a wrinkle marred her face, until thirty seconds later she pointed behind her. "Walk until the T, turn right, and keep going. There's a back door by the pool.

You can skirt around the fence and hook onto the sidewalk that goes past the golf course. Keep straight and Kash's villa will be in front of you."

Of course. That was easy enough. Chances of getting lost were 100 percent, but I was going with it.

"What's your name, dear?"

She didn't know my name? I considered lying, because integrity, but I heard myself answering the truth.

"Bailey." And because no one could compare to my mother, I added, "Chrissy Hayes is my mother."

I slipped away after that, but I wasn't sure if I imagined that soft gasp from her or not.

I didn't stick around to check.

FIFTEEN

I was frothing at the mouth. Literal drool was sliding out.

Getting back to Kash's place, finding it empty, and finding a desktop left on the kitchen table was a eureka moment for me. My hands were almost shaking from the anticipation of my own little office put in place in my bedroom, and knowing I could disappear in mere moments.

I had to set everything up first.

Finding a small table in the basement, I hauled that sucker up two flights of stairs. The chair was next, which was a bit of a struggle. I was tired from the desk. The chair, easier, but it had wheels. That meant back twisting, and the last time I had worked out was never. Once I had both those in place, the table and chair pushed up against one of the corners, the computer was third. That was just placing and plugging. I'd deal with a Wi-Fi connection, but that was the last and final moments before hackerdom.

Necessities. I needed them.

Headphones, preferably a headset with a thirty-six-inch cord. They were the cheapest on the market, but they were the best sellers for a reason. The fancy ones stopped working after six months or so. Then snacks and drinks. A normal all-dayer/nighter, I'd want coffee or energy drinks. Energy drinks were preferred, but after raiding Kash's kitchen, I saw he wasn't a fan of the stuff. That was something I needed to note to ask for later. Until then, coffee. Lots and lots of coffee.

Snagging a bag of chips, some candy, I was ready to go.

Everything was spread out around me. The snacks had to be on the table. The drinks on the left side, mid-keyboard location. The snacks were just beyond the screen, left side as well. I needed the mouse on the right.

And last, clothes.

I was going the comfy route. Soft athletic pants, a tank top, sports bra, and my hair pulled back in a messy bun. It was the best uniform.

After that, the internet connection.

Pulling up the networks, I could guess which was the main security one, the one Kash might use as his own, and a few other aliases. Who knew the landscaping department for my father had its own internet connection. The kitchen staff, too.

Skimming down the line, I clicked on Hotboi2012. Gut was telling me that little Cyclone had his own network, and as I right-clicked on that bitch, I was right about another thing. He hadn't secured it. I was able to connect the backpath.

I shook my head, *ts*king, "Little boy, little boy. You've got some things to learn still." I took his IP address, because he let that sit out there all unattended. Anything I did, they'd think it was him. That didn't feel right. Crap. I was moving the mouse before I thought about it, and I clicked into the network I was pretty sure Marie used. I'd use her IP address, even though I had plans to hack her. I'd just deal with it.

Once I was connected, I sat back.

A satisfied smile on my face.

I got to work.

Mrs. Quinn Francis was first up, just because she was the last person I saw. She wasn't a soft target, and it wasn't long before I got into her social media accounts, saved half her emails to my online drive, and went through her private messages. A nagging voice was whispering that this was wrong, but I shushed them. They weren't that damn loud, and it'd been way too long since I'd been around a computer.

The next target was still soft—or the next three targets. All of my siblings.

I only skimmed their stuff. By then the voice was speaking up a bit louder and I had a little twist in my stomach, thinking of going through little Cyclone's emails. But damn, that kid had a lot of them. I wasn't surprised, if he was building a robot rabbit. I found his computer and saved that file to my phone. The rest went to my online drive.

I was going to help him. That's what I was telling myself.

Seraphina was up, and I didn't see anything interesting there. Conversations with her friends. Complete files dedicated to male models. One of her friends had a mean girls book, and clicking through, I saw that the little shits were vicious to their classmates. Christ. They rated each person based on clothes, hair, manners, associations, personality, and intelligence. There was an overall cool level assigned at the end, and—surprise, surprise—only the girls who were moderators for the file got the highest cool score.

I went down Seraphina's own rating and paused at her overall score.

She got a ten for clothes, for hair, for manners, for associations. She got a four for personality and a six for intelligence. Her cool level was five.

I reared back at that. She could see this. This was on *her* network. Those girls did that to her, knowing she would see it.

I hadn't met my sister, but by God, blood stood for something with me. All those little bitches just got on my medium-core target list.

I didn't snoop in Matthew's social media accounts and emails. Those were all I could find on him, but I was assuming he had a remote computer at his own place.

There was one more family member, but I paused. He was the big bang. He was the ultimate hit, and because of that he was saved for last. Now it was time for my hard target: Marie.

Hacking into the Chesapeake administration network, it

didn't take long for me to find Marie's files. From there, I tunneled my way to her personal computer. If she was there, she could see someone had access.

Going through all of this, I'd lost track of time. I knew it was longer than I thought, because I recognized the stiffness in my back and neck. My ass was protesting, and I hadn't gone to the bathroom in—I had no clue, but my bladder was screaming at me.

I shoved it all down and got to work.

I took all of Marie's files. All. Of. Them. And there was no voice telling me this was wrong. That woman had hurt me. I didn't care, at that moment, if she meant well. She had filleted me, saying I was a fraud. Well, honey, let's see who the fraud is after this evening—

Shut down!

My screen froze, fritzed, and it began to shut down immediately.

No, no, no.

I was scrambling, my pulse picking up.

They found me. That was fast. I was good—damn good. I could cover my tracks. I went through back doors they didn't know were there. Unless . . . Fuck. I gulped. Unless my father himself wrote his own security measures, but who actually did that? He was too big-time now.

Still. My screen was flashing at me now. I had only seconds to erase my final trail.

Four.

Fuck, fuck, fuck.

Three.

I screamed, shoving back the chair and typing faster than I had in ages.

Two.

"No!" I was up, and I yanked on the cord, cutting the connection, and once that was done—I couldn't move.

What had I just done?

I raised a hand to my forehead, feeling the sweat up there. I'd been in the zone. I'd been doing things I hadn't even realized I was doing. Shame was spreading through me at an alarming rate, and I fell to my knees, my mouth gaping.

What had I done? Oh my God. What had I done?

I was hurt. I took it. I digested it. And then seeing my stepmother had been too much for me, knowing my mother would've compared herself to that woman. I'd been blind in my need to strike back.

I hadn't—I hadn't been thinking. Walking from that house, feeling a bombshell going off in me, I only reacted. I needed to do what I did, and the computer was it for me.

But damn.

My hands were trembling. My knees too. I couldn't even get up.

They would know it was me. There was no way they wouldn't. One alert to Kash and he would know immediately.

I looked around. I had to get out of here. Where, I had no clue, but I had to go. Now.

Pushing to my feet, I grabbed some clothes from the closet and stuffed them in a bag. I had shoes and sneakers already on. Purse. My wallet. I had a few essentials with me. The phone, I took it out and gazed at it mournfully. I'd miss the guy, but that was the easiest way to track me.

How to get out without them realizing?

Cyclone said there was an event going on. I'd just go and hitch a ride in someone's trunk. Once I was gone, I'd figure it out from there. On the bright side, I could see my mom again.

I couldn't believe I was doing this, but after the security breach I just performed, they couldn't keep me here. They wouldn't. I'd punched a hole the size of a fist in their system. They shouldn't have found it right away, but it was there.

Looking at the clock, seeing it was almost six by now—the time had gone by that fast? Wow. But when I was in the zone, I could lose entire days.

Didn't matter.

It was time to go.

Six steps. That's how far I got. I glanced back to make sure the door closed, but I didn't complete that last step before I hit a hard chest and two hands grabbed my shoulders. The whole *Uh-oh* voice went off in my head, and I looked up.

Blistering and furious eyes glared down at me. Yep. I should have listened to that voice earlier.

Kash clipped out, "Inside. Now."

I was going to jail.

SIXTEEN

"She hacked into all of our hard drives! *All of them!*"

I was sitting outside an office in a separate section of the estate, and I could hear Quinn Francis screaming from inside. After meeting her in the hallway, I wouldn't have imagined this side of her.

But there it was.

Kash was saying something.

"I don't care!"

I winced. To give her credit, I thought most of this was the mama bear coming out. She was upset when she talked about her files. Her voice rose another decibel when it came to Seraphina. I heard Matt's name mentioned and it went up again, but when she got Cyclone's . . . Full. On. Screaming. I couldn't tell if it was because he was the baby or because he was her favorite. My guess is that it was a mix of both.

". . . get it all back."

"You're damn straight you'll get them all back," she snapped. My chair wasn't even right next to the door. There was about five yards separating me from the door, and when someone walked inside and I glimpsed her, I saw that she was completely on the other side of the room. Her heated level was impressive. She had to be close to boiling.

Kash was talking again. I couldn't make out the words. He was being more discreet, but I could hear his own frustration. Judging by how he'd handled me when he caught me, he was as pissed as she was. He was just keeping it together. After sitting here, I knew another reaming was coming, once he got me alone.

That was, *if* he got me alone again; if they reported me or kicked me out, I was sure Kash Colello would find time to kick my ass. I had a gut feeling that if anyone did any of his charges wrong, he annihilated them.

I let out a sigh, resting my head back against the wall.

There were two security guards standing at the ready, one at each end of the hall. It was because of them that I wasn't paying attention until I heard, "A friend of Kash's, huh?"

Aw, not good.

Matthew Francis was coming my way, his hands in his pockets and his eyes fixed right on me. He was dressed in trendy skinny jeans, a black long-sleeve hooded shirt, and a baseball cap pulled low over his forehead.

I didn't know what lie to go with, so I kept silent, watching him warily.

Instead of sitting, he grabbed the chair next to me and turned it around so he was facing me. He sat down, straddling it, and folded his arms over the back, his head leaning forward to scrutinize me better.

I looked down.

He was studying me way too intensely.

"Bullshit," he breathed out.

"What?" I looked back up.

His nostrils flared. "I say bullshit. If Kash walks out of that room—"

"*I don't care whose daughter she is, I want her gone!*"

"You don't have the authority to make that demand."

It wasn't Quinn's scream that startled us, though the scream took precedence. It was Kash's calm retort that had both my brother and me rearing back in surprise.

We could hear her gasp from inside.

"No offense," Kash snapped, "but her placement isn't up to you, Peter, or anyone else. It's up to me, me alone. And I say she stays here."

"Kash—"

"Enough, Quinn." He was walking to the door. His voice was getting louder, clearer. "I'll get her to erase everything she took, but she stays where she is. That's final."

"Kash! Do not walk out that door, not like that, not after what she's done. Kash—"

He shoved open the door, took in the sight of me, took in Matt's presence, and raked a hand through his hair. "Fuck me." Then he was off. He snapped his fingers, pointed at me, and barked, "Follow. Now." And he didn't stop.

Matt hopped up from his chair, hurrying after us. "Hey, Kashy. How's it going?" He snickered under his breath, shoving his hands back in his pockets.

"Not now, Matt."

Coming up to the door leading outside, Kash turned, grabbed for my arm, and used his back to slam the door open. It was one of those that could be pressed and shoved open. He pulled me with him without missing a beat, and once we were outside, he urged me next to him. His hand came to the small of my back, but once he saw that I was keeping up with him, his hand fell away. He leaned forward a little, his shoulders hunching forward, and he shoved his hands in his pockets almost the same way Matt had as he walked toward me in the hallway.

My brother wasn't walking that way now. He jogged to catch up, moving past us and turning to dart backward. His eyes were dancing, sparking even, and half of his mouth was up in a grin. "So. Can we talk about the elephant on the estate here?"

"Matt," Kash warned. "Don't start."

Ignoring him, Matt smirked at me. "Can we make this all official? Is she my full-blooded sister or half-blooded? What are we talking about here?"

"Matt," Kash growled in warning.

Matt got too close to Kash, veering over, and instead of going around him, Kash lifted up a hand and pushed him aside. All without breaking stride, just like inside.

Laughing, Matt started walking sideways, his long legs crossing over each other. "Come on, Kash. She's here. No one comes here. What she did, the secrecy about who she is . . . I might be going out on a limb, but it's obvious who her father is. I'm shocked more haven't figured it out." Matt narrowed his eyes on me. "She looks my age, so sometime around the end of Dad's divorce coming through? Maybe in that whole middle time after I was born? I heard there was a five-year period where it was just messy between the two. You know, my mom suffering postpartum and Dad just straight cheating. Nasty, nasty time for both of them."

His mom suffered postpartum?

"Stop, Matt. I mean it." We were nearing the sidewalk just outside of the villa. I didn't know how we got there so fast, but I was guessing Kash knew some shortcuts. Coming up to the door now, he led the way. Opening it, he went in first, stepped back. I ducked inside, and he had a hand out, stepping behind me to meet with Matt. "I said no." His tone returned to the authoritative command he used when talking to Quinn earlier. Without another word, as Matt stepped back from reflex, Kash stepped inside, shutting and locking the glass doors.

Matt's mouth dropped open. "Come on! Are you serious?" His hands went up in frustration. "Come on!"

Kash hit a button on the wall and two curtains flew down, shutting Matt out completely from seeing inside. Then it was just him and me, and he turned that furious gaze on me.

My stomach slipped to my feet.

This was not going to be good.

"I'm sorry—"

He shot a hand up, his other rubbing at his forehead. "Save it."

I did. Closing my mouth, I sank down on one of his couches and saved it.

His hands went to his hips and he continued to look down at the floor. He hadn't moved from the door, and when he started, his voice was low. "You have no idea what I was in the middle of when I got the call two hours ago. There was an online security breach. They found it and began tracing it back to the location it was coming from. We've had breaches before, and just shutting them out isn't usually what we do. We like to eliminate the risks completely. That's what they did. But while they usually move faster, get a location quicker, they were stalled because this hacker . . . this one had put up security walls behind her. Behind 'them.' That's what they called you, these computer specialists that are some of the best in the world. They work for your father, who *is* the best, and I quote, they said, 'These guys have to be a team collective. They're moving fast and at the same time putting up firewalls behind their tracks at a speed that no one person could manage.' Not one person. A team. And one reported to me that this must have been in the planning for months, not at the fucking sudden whim of a pissed-off child—"

I shoved to my feet. "I'm not a child!"

"You're acting like one!"

I had no comeback. He was right. So I just sighed. "I'm out of my depth here. I'm—"

"I get it. I do!" He started to pace now, his head still bent forward, one hand rubbing at the back of his neck.

The exhaustion came off of him in waves now. Exhaustion and frustration. It was then that I took in his clothing. Black. All black. Black shoes. Black pants. Black long-sleeve shirt. All. Black. Familiarity teased me. There was something, something about him, about how he was standing, about his voice, about his clothes . . . I couldn't place it, though.

"Christ, Bailey!" He stopped, his head up and his eyes blazing at me, piercing me. "One day. One fucking day and you rip through their online security like it's candy. Like it's Halloween and all you have to do is put on a costume, knock on a door, and you get the treats handed to you. One person. One *fucking afternoon*! It took them three hours to locate you. Three hours. Your walls were so good that they had to keep shutting down their own programs because your viruses were that good. This is one of the best in the world, and you crumbled them to their knees in a day. Not even a day."

I hadn't realized I'd done that much damage.

"I'm sorry." My voice was a hoarse whisper as I sat down.

"What were you thinking?" He stepped closer to me. "Did you want attention? Your dad's not here. He's in New Zealand. Did you want payback? You said people had said some messed up shit to you—was it *them* that you wanted to hurt? You went through your siblings' social media, their emails. You downloaded a copy of Seraphina's online journal. Why would you do that? She's in tears. Tears! I heard her crying when Quinn called me. She's humiliated by whatever you found in there.

"Marie—" He stopped, taking a deep breath. He started again, calmer, but only slightly. "Marie said she's completely wiped out of her computer. She said it's all gone. You took everything and you left a blinking middle finger icon as her wallpaper. It pops up every time she tries to put a password in."

I mashed my lips together at that one.

It wasn't funny.

It wasn't. Nope.

I started coughing, remembering how I had laughed to myself when I programmed that in. Hearing it from Kash now, it was so totally not funny.

But it was. It was hilarious.

I coughed some more, pushing that tickle away. No good would come if I let that out.

"Yes. I . . ."

Kash snorted. "You don't even sound remorseful. You sound

like you're about to apologize for being thirty minutes late for cur-
few. I'm not your father. This isn't a situation where you merely
get grounded. The shit we have on you, you could do prison.
It's that bad. Your father has files on those computers. National
security files. You launched an attack that could've compromised
those files. I say the word, give my go-ahead, and your father's
lawyers could make this go all the way in the black. You could be
hauled off and never see your mother again."

I felt the blood draining from me. That tickle was replaced
with fear, real fear, the kind where I felt a cold trickle of sweat on
the back of my hairline.

He was right.

He was so right. I knew the laws. I knew the risks. I knew my
father had job contracts with the government. I'm not playing in
the little leagues. I messed with a professional, a big and powerful
professional who may or may not have any sentimental feelings
toward me. He probably had none, to be honest. I was a risk to
his empire.

Then I asked, "He's in New Zealand?"

"What?"

"There was an event here earlier. I thought—"

"It was a charity brunch. Quinn does a lot for nonprofit orga-
nizations. But no. Your father wasn't in attendance."

Oh.

I swallowed over a lump in my throat.

Why did I care?

I shouldn't. I mean . . . yeah, why did that bother me so much?

Kash sighed. "You wanted to get your dad's attention?"

"No." I said the word quickly. Too quickly.

"It's okay if that's what you were doing."

God.

Another wave of embarrassment rode through me, crashing.
He was right. I was acting like a child. I was almost twenty-three,

and I had acted out like a rebellious teenager. It was the equivalent of drinking too much, taking drugs, racing cars—what some wealthy kids might've done. Not me. I crashed their internet. I basically walked up to their house, and instead of knocking like a normal person, I set it on fire.

"I'm sorry."

Kash was silent a moment.

"I am." I smoothed my hand out over my shirt before looking up again.

He was standing a few feet from me, his arms crossed over his chest and his eyebrows pinched together. He didn't believe me.

I said it again, "I really am sorry. I . . . I wasn't thinking. And you're right. I was told to go back where I came from, in essence, and I reacted. I was mad, and hurting, and I lashed out in the way I *can* lash out. I am truly sorry."

His chest rose slowly. He drew in some air before letting it back out, just as slowly. He shook his head. "I know. I can see that." His eyes softened. The lines around his mouth smoothed out. "Look, they won't be told who hacked into their privacy. They won't know it was you."

"Matt knows."

"Matt knows nothing. Matt will know what I tell him to know."

He said it so swiftly, with a hint of violence, and that familiarity was whispering at me again. How he said those words, that cold look in his eyes . . . What was bugging me?

"You need to put back what you took, and you need to delete what copies you made. By now, the team's got most of your bugs out of their systems. You will go in and remove the rest."

"Go in? What do you mean?"

Not . . . No way. He gave me a meaningful look.

My eyes widened. "You mean go into their security room and use one of their computers?" I didn't know if I was salivating at the chance to see what they were working with on their end or dreading it because they would see me in person.

"Quinn wants you removed from the estate. I won't allow it. But you will not be free to walk around any longer, not until you've earned trust back."

"Trust? Whose trust?"

"*Mine.*" His eyes were heated again, smoldering at me. "You will earn my trust. After removing your viruses, you will be stripped of computer privileges—"

"You can't do that! I need to work on my graduate project. I—" I surged to my feet.

"Watch me." He met me, surging right back at me.

I didn't move. Neither did he. We were almost touching, staring back at each other, both angry, heated breaths coming in and out, and I was suddenly hot for a whole other reason.

God's sake.

I needed to look away. I did. I couldn't.

I wanted to reach out. I wanted to touch him, and my gaze fell to his chest. I could see how his shirt molded to him, hugging him so perfectly, and I could desperately imagine the feel of him against me. So strong, firm. Earlier, I had thought there wasn't an inch of fat on his body, and now I was salivating, wanting to test my theory.

Kash broke first, stepping back. His voice came out ragged. "Your punishment is this: You will remain in this house. You will only walk on the grounds with a security guard, and when I feel you can be trusted, you will earn your freedom more and more."

"My God," I bit out, but I wasn't sure if I was reacting because of the punishment or something else. I stepped back, drawing more air. I needed to clear my head, because it was swimming.

"Prison," he said. "You could be made to disappear and never come back. That's a drastic measure, but in a way, it'd clear up your father's problems a whole lot easier for us. You need a reality check of what I'm saving you from. Quinn wants you gone. She doesn't give a shit about keeping you protected. I'm doing this. Me. You'll do as you're told and you'll do it without an attitude or, so help me, Bailey, you can get fucked in a thousand different ways here. None of them pleasurable. Deal with it."

Really. Those exact words.

Okay.

That burned.

I wanted the entire summer with my computer. I wanted a head start on my graduate project, and I couldn't do any of that now. I had screwed up, but damn, it was going to be a hard one to swallow.

He started to move away, and then he stopped. He was half turned toward me, his head tipped back, stormy eyes taking me in.

"You never asked who noticed your breach in the first place."

My throat swelled up for some reason. "What do you mean? I thought their system would've caught me."

His phone buzzed in his hand, but he ignored it. "You disabled their alert system almost right away. It was one person who realized you were in the system. If he hadn't, who knows when they would've realized you were there. Quinn and your siblings didn't know you hacked them until they were told to check their accounts. They were in, doing their own thing at the same time you were in there, taking their things." He paused, his eyes narrowing slightly. "It was the same person who shut you down, too."

I felt it. The burn was back. It was spreading from my throat, to my stomach, to my feet. Traveling all the way down my legs, setting every nerve on edge.

"Who was it?"

A look flared in Kash's eyes. Menacing, a warning, but there was something else there. I wasn't quite sure what it was. And he said, "Your father. He's the one who caught you. You got your wish."

A beat.

He looked at his phone.

"Your dad's coming back. He's on the plane right now."

SEVENTEEN

Adrenaline was high.

He was coming. My childhood idol. The guy who was my sperm donor. I went through varying phases of excitement, fear, loathing, anger, impatience, and back to excitement. No matter the home front, no matter how he had hurt my mom—

And *eeek*. Ground to a halt. Hold up.

He hurt my mom.

That stomped everything.

Once I remembered that, dread took hold of me for the night and through the next day. But I was on pins and needles, expecting a guard to knock on the door at any moment.

None came.

The phone didn't ring.

Kash had to return to where he was before the whole hacking incident, and even he didn't text.

Nothing. I was on radio silence. Or I was on prison silence. I was in *isolation*.

The entire first day, I was waiting. Just waiting. Waiting to meet my father. Waiting for Matthew to sneak in. Waiting for Kash to show up and scold me for something. Waiting, waiting, waiting. That transitioned to a little less waiting the second day.

Boredom hit me that afternoon. Drastic, dull, soul-consuming boredom. I even took a trip to his garage to see what parts were there, if there were extra wires lying around. Maybe it was time to build a robot to keep Cyclone's robot rabbit company, and once that thought hit me, I remembered that I had saved his entire file. It was one that I saved to my phone, not to the computer or internet. My phone, the one thing I still had access to. It'd been an automatic response when I saw it. I knew I'd want to read it later on, maybe even before bed. That was my version of night-time reading.

Kash didn't say I couldn't—

No, he actually did, but would he really be that pissed if I peeked ahead, trying to help Cyclone? I could hide that I read it? He said no Wi-Fi. Technically, my phone didn't have Wi-Fi anymore. It had satellite connection, but I was honoring our agreement. He said no computer stuff. It was hard. It was painful. But I was sticking to it.

So that night, I curled up on the couch and started reading.

I kept reading his file, all through the night, until I realized it was three in the morning. Three thirty-two, to be exact. Putting it away, feeling my stomach growling, I dismissed both and headed for bed. Cleaning up, brushing my teeth, I pulled on some pajamas and crawled under the covers . . . only to reach for my phone again. There. I saw a text that I had missed somehow.

Clicking on it, I saw it was from Kash.

Cameras show you're being good. Did you tamper with the feeds?

I snorted out loud, then wiped the grin from my face. I wasn't supposed to find that funny.

I'm being good. Reading on my phone, if you want to know the specifics.

Buzz from him.

Someone will come to the house tomorrow just after seven in the morning. You'll be taken to the offices to finish cleaning up your mess.

A second buzz from him.

Go. Clean everything. Go back to the house.

A third buzz.

Your father had to stop in DC for something, fyi.

Oh. That—

Nope. That didn't matter to me. He had hurt my mother. That's all I cared about now.

Okay.

I started to go back to my reading, but then I texted again. I couldn't help myself.

Me: *You broke the cardinal rule.*

Kash: *What's that?*

Me: *You didn't ask what I was reading. You can't have that many books in your library to not be a book lover. You should know that rule.*

Kash: *I already know what you're reading and you lied.*

I almost dropped my phone. How did he—

And it hit me. I forgot for a moment. Cursing, I typed out again, almost punching the phone.

Me: *Not fair. Not right. No privacy.*

Kash: *You lost that privilege.*

A second buzz.

Kash: *Earn it. Earn. It.*

I didn't have a response to that, and after I didn't text again, he didn't either. Sighing, curling up on my pillow and tucking the cover to my chin, I folded my arms over it and brought my phone back up.

I read almost the entire file that night, finally stopping around five in the morning.

It was the doorbell that got me up in the morning.

It was who was ringing that bell that *woke* me up.

Peter Francis stood on Kash's doorstep.

Kash said "someone."

Well, someone it was.

I had hoped, but a part of me assumed it'd be a guard. Nope. My da—Peter Francis, I mean.

It was actually him.

I wouldn't pass out. Nope. No way.

My heart was pounding, and holy hell; my hands were all sweaty. When did they get like that?

I remained quiet because this was his show. He showed up. No doubt he was pissed, and here I was. The outlier child, messing up his cyber security, and he had to fly all the way back just for me.

I should've been overjoyed.

Okay. I kinda was.

This was my father. Holy shit.

Back to the sweaty palms.

He'd been my idol, growing up. That awestruck doesn't go away. It's in the blood, but I was fast remembering my circumstances, and that I was still not wanted here, so that was helping with the fangirling going on in me.

Still. Quiet. I could do that.

I swallowed.

He was staring me down, studying me. I was studying him right back. Dark hair. Blue tint to it. Hazel eyes like me.

I had his brain.

This was my sperm donor. That was for sure.

He was taller in person.

I knew his stats. I knew his weight, 190 pounds. His height at six feet exactly. He probably shaved once a day, and there were some whiskers showing, so I figured he'd skipped it this morning.

And he was one of the most powerful men in the cyber world.

I was about to hyperventilate here.

"Are you ready?"

That was it. Those were the first words my father ever said to me.

Was I ready?

I blinked. I couldn't have heard that right. "What?"

He stepped back, moved aside, and gestured to the main

house. "Kash said you would fix everything, since you could do it the fastest. I'm going to watch you while you do it."

Watch me.

He was going to walk me there, watch me, and then what?

"Really? That's all you have to say to me?"

He shifted again, his head down, and he tightened his mouth.

"Some of your breaches are time sensitive. You broke them. Kash is right. You're the best one to fix them. I could, but it would take me longer."

This was Kash's idea? I thought it'd been Peter's.

Peter was moving forward, but then stopped. He was waiting for me. He didn't look back at me again but was still pausing. It was obvious. I got the unspoken message, and with a heavy sigh, I walked with him.

My heart was sliced in half.

As we walked, pieces of me split off. I was leaving a trail behind me.

He was here for work. For *time-sensitive* shit. Because I could fix everything faster than he could.

There went another piece, just thinking of that.

We kept going and my mind was racing.

I should make him explain everything to me.

I should confront him about Chrissy, about how he left her, why he left her. Why everything. Did he know about me? Did he not know about me? If he did, why didn't he reach out to me? Talk to me? Even send a card? Something. Anything.

Why wasn't I good enough?

What was wrong with me?

Why didn't he love me?

All those questions were ricocheting in my brain, but at the same time I was memorizing everything about him.

I was walking next to my dad. Whether I would like him after this or not, love him after this or not, hate him after this or not, this was a day I would always remember. It would be in my brain, and not because of my photographic memory. This was a day that any child in my shoes, either forgotten or left behind, would remember until the day their heart stopped beating.

He wasn't dressed how a business dad would dress—or maybe he was. He wore khaki pants. A dark blue warm-up jacket. There was a white collar underneath, so he had a nice-looking white shirt, one that could be a polo.

He had a Rolex Daytona on his wrist. Rose gold band.

A wedding ring.

His shoes were Nike sneakers.

His hair had been combed to the side. There was a part from where his fingers wove through it, brushing it over. His face was tan. His hands tan. He spent time in the sun, maybe from golfing. I didn't know. I remembered a magazine article that said he enjoyed rowing.

Who rowed around here?

Well, maybe he did.

I was still going with the golfing though. His house was in the middle of his own personal golf course.

He walked with a slight bounce that pushed him further, to go faster, and as if sensing my scrutiny, he shoved his hands into his jacket pockets. His head went down. His shoulders bunched forward, and he picked up his pace.

He wanted to get this done with.

He wanted to be done with me.

We went past the main house, around to the side, and to that building with the three garages I had noticed when we drove in. As we drew nearer, the back door opened. A guard came out, holding the door for us.

No words were exchanged. The guard didn't even make eye contact.

Peter moved forward, leading the way.

I paused, just on the doorstep, and looked up at the guard. I don't know why I did that. Maybe I wanted to memorize him, too.

Or maybe I wanted one more second to remember this morning.

Seven in the morning.

A slight chill in the air.

The sky was a pewter gray.

I heard the sounds of birds. Ducks. Others chirping.

I felt mist in the air. Knew it would rain later.

This morning was the day I walked beside my father.

This was what I wanted to memorialize, because once I went in there, when I sat behind a computer, I wouldn't think about this again. I would get sucked into that world and all of this would go away, so I drew a breath in, waiting one beat, knowing everything was committed to my long-term memory, and then I went inside.

He was waiting for me, a funny look on his face.

I ducked my head, avoiding his eyes.

He opened a door, and going through it, I was in the main control room.

This was my world, my haven.

The main computer was already booted up. He waited at the door, and there was no reason for words after this.

I sat down, got up close to the computer. There were headphones at the ready, and once I started, someone brought me coffee. I didn't ask, and I knew it wasn't him, because it was a slender wrist, but I drank it. I kept working.

It took an hour to put everything back for Cyclone's files. Thirty minutes for Matt's. Forty-two minutes for Seraphina's. Forty-one minutes for Quinn's. I hated it, but it was another full hour to return everything for Marie.

I never hacked him.

What they wanted from me was done. I restored everything and I could've pulled away from the computer, shut it down, and returned to Kash's villa.

I didn't.

My fingers were already typing before I thought about it, but I did other stuff. I reinforced their firewalls. I put in a new surprise security program. It would be there if someone got through again. And then I started writing code that would close the holes I had used in the first place.

I secured Cyclone's IP address.

I put in a double lock on the whole system, and I even put in a small system that would sniff out anyone like me and send a preliminary alert to the entire security system.

During all of this, he stood behind me. I knew it because I could feel him. There were moments I forgot he was there, but a sixth sense kept pricking at me, and I knew that was his scrutiny. He never wavered the whole time, so I just worked through it.

I went through four cups of coffee and two energy drinks.

When I was done, I shoved away from the computer and had to dash to the bathroom. My bladder was bursting to be released. In the stall, I did the math. I'd been working to repair and then make his system better for six hours. I had started after seven. It was almost two in the afternoon.

Why did I do that? Why did I help to better what he did for a living?

I didn't want to know the answer or think about it, but I couldn't help myself. Approval. I wanted his approval. And I tasted my own shame at realizing that.

He had cast me out.

I shouldn't want his approval or anything. His acceptance. Nothing. He obviously wasn't going to give it or he would've said something before we walked here, or on the walk.

He was quiet the whole time, but still . . . A thought was pricking me again. He was behind me for six hours and watched everything. Who would do that?

He never drank anything. He never ate anything. I would've noticed, because while I hated it, I was still keenly aware of him.

He never left the room to use the bathroom, phone. Nothing. There'd been no sounds of him texting.

That was something. Right?

Had to be.

Had to mean something that he stood and watched me work and never left, not once.

Or maybe my hope was starting again, and I needed to squash it. Yes. That was it. I had to eviscerate that. It was his job. My job. He wanted to see what I could do.

That's why he watched me.

Yeah.

Bitterness spread through me. Pain tore at me. But that made the most sense.

Business. His business. That's the only reason he never moved while I worked.

Leaving the stall, washing my hands, my feet were moving like I was walking in slightly dry cement. It was hard to trudge through it. Then I was in the hallway and he wasn't there.

See.

I was right.

But I was done, so I could go back to the villa. Heading for the exit, I heard their voices as I neared the door.

"Fuck, Dad. This is what you were doing today?"

I reached for the door handle.

"Settle down, Matthew. I wanted to see her skill level in person."

I paused and waited, my breath held.

Both were irritated. Both were snapping at each other. But Matt's voice held an extra edge while Peter's held something else . . . maybe confusion?

He kept going. "She's got a gift. It's unbelievable. I wish you had that gift."

Matt snorted. "Of course. You get your system blown to pieces and you're already reveling in how great she did it. You're standing here telling me what a fuckup I am at the same time. Nice, Dad. Nice. Super loving father you are."

"You're putting words in my mouth, but you're right. I don't need a son that parties all hours of the day and night, has one job to do and still can't get his life together. Kashton does your job for you half the time—"

A harsh laugh from Matt ripped through the air, ripped through me even.

"God. Jesus. You think Kash only does *my* job?" His tone was mocking now. Biting too. "We both know he runs half your businesses."

"One!"

I jumped back from Peter's sudden bellow.

"One job! One goddamn hotel to manage. You're not even managing it. You have managers to do that. They are supposed to report to you, but I've sat next to Kashton while he gets the reports from them. One hotel to overlook and even that you've fucked up. Whose son are you?"

The cold chill in that last question. It pierced me.

I wasn't the only one. Matt was silent. I almost started forward, then I heard him. He sounded beaten down.

"You're right, Dad. I'm the fuckup here. And yet, of the two of us, I'm pretty certain I'm the one waiting for her because I share blood with her."

He didn't say anything else.

Neither did Peter.

He was just silent.

Kash: *How'd it go?*
Me: *It went.*

EIGHTEEN

The next night, I was lying in bed. Not sleeping. Trying to sleep.

Trying not to think about the day before, how when I pushed open the door and stepped out, I saw both of their backs, leaving. A guard was there waiting instead, and he showed me back to Kash's villa.

I stayed there the day, not thinking, not feeling, not admitting how crushed I was. The afternoon passed. I ate some dinner, but that's all I was hungry for. Drank a hot cup of tea, then settled into bed.

The alarm pierced the air.

A red light flashed in the house.

Fear catapulted me upright, and then I stopped. I was paralyzed, my heart and chest in my throat.

Someone had broken in.

The door burst open and I was freed from my paralysis.

I launched myself out of bed.

I didn't go at the person. My fight-or-flight instinct was fully functioning. I was running, and it didn't matter where, because that's all I was focused on. I must've looked straight out of *The Matrix*, because I jumped straight up in bed, and before I came back down to where my feet made contact with the covers, I was already trying to run. My feet circled in the air for a split second, then I hit the mattress again and I was off, like Speedy Gonzalez.

The intruder came at me, but I ran him over. Literally. He came to the bed, and that was the time my feet made contact with the bed. I bowled him like he was a pin and I was the bowling ball, and I didn't stop.

He made a sound, yelling my name, but no way. No way, Jose. Of course the intruder would know my name. They broke in for me. They sure as shit hadn't broken in for Kash or for introductions. Slamming down on the floor, my heart in my throat, I tore down the hallway, the stairs, and I was sprinting for the door when the person recovered enough to come to the second-floor landing.

He yelled out, "It's me! Matt! Stop!"

Matt?

I wasn't stupid. I still wasn't stopping. But I looked over my shoulder just as I rounded the corner and I got a glimpse of him, his hand outstretched toward me.

Gah.

My feet were pounding the pavement. Stop? Keep going? If I hadn't almost been kidnapped once, maybe I would've stopped, because that seemed the rational thing, but it happened once. No way was it happening again. I was heading down the sidewalk as a barrage of security guards were running to meet me. They came from everywhere. Back. Front. Left. Right. I wouldn't have been surprised if a few popped up from underground.

"Ms. Hayes!" One was yelling at me, a hand toward me while he kept his gun pointed downward.

"Ms. Hayes." That same guy was almost to me. He was slowing down. They were all slowing down—well, the ones who were surrounding me were. I couldn't stop. I just couldn't. My brain was not commanding my feet, so I slammed into one of them. They caught me up, and that's when I looked over my shoulder again. A group had separated from the others and was approaching the villa. Their guns were out, and they weren't making a sound. They were doing a bunch of hand signals to each other as a few were touching their ears, getting their commands that way.

I just couldn't stop. I couldn't stop moving, fighting, running. Because of that, I almost ran up the side of the guard holding me, and he grunted, tightening his hold. "Stop, Ms. Hayes. Stop. We have you. You're safe."

I couldn't comprehend what he was saying, and I couldn't stop.

He cursed, grunting.

"Take her out of here. Take her to the house."

The guard nodded behind me. I knew I needed to stop, but I wasn't used to fear like that. Fear that told me that if I stopped moving, I could die. If I stopped moving, they could take me again. If I stopped moving, Rafe, Clemin, and Boots could get me again. Arcane.

I couldn't stop moving. Ever.

And because of that, the guard needed a second man to help hold me as they carried me, holding me up so my feet were in the air, still trying to run. I looked like I was trying to ride a bike. That's how I was when they carried me inside the mansion, past a group of staff who had congregated in the hallway. I recognized the room a split second before the door opened and there stood Marie, her eyes wide, her face pale, and her stocky body not letting them pass.

"Move, Marie." The guard wasn't waiting for her. He barked that order and she had a split second before jutting aside for us. He deposited me on the floor and I was off, but by then my brain had more control over me. Just my heart was pounding, and I had to walk off my nerves, so I immediately began pacing the large table in the middle of the room. Round and round again. Round and round.

I never stopped, not after the two guards started to leave and I croaked out, "Don't leave. Please." Or after Marie settled in, just watching me. I wasn't paying her attention anymore, or the guards who remained after my request. One was in the open door, guarding us, and the other was just watching me.

I just kept going.

I had no idea how much time passed before we heard

movement in the hallway again. More guards were coming toward us. They paused. There was a conversation at the door, then the one guard shifted aside and Matthew stepped inside the room.

"Bailey?"

Nope. I wasn't having it. I kept walking around that table because it was the only thing that was making sense in my life at that moment. The table. It was long and rectangular shaped and the perfect thing to walk around, so that's what I was doing.

"Bailey." Matt's voice softened. He was cautious as he approached me. "Stop. You can stop."

He reached out as I made a pass by him, and I shoved his hand away. "Don't. Do not!" I stalked past and went for another circle.

"I know what happened to you."

That made me slow down, but I still couldn't stop. Feeling helpless and powerless made you need to do something, anything to push that feeling aside. It was the most terrifying thing a person could experience.

I couldn't endure that again.

Matt's voice dropped low, breaking. "They tried to take Cyclone once, too."

Oh, God.

Cyclone.

Kid.

Matt spoke as I kept pacing around the table. "He was four and he doesn't remember it, but it was the most traumatizing day of our lives. They got him. They actually got him for a few minutes. Then Kash found 'em and he tore them apart. Those kidnappers are in prison now and they'll never be free. And they're in the kind of prison where no one knows it even exists, that kind. My dad made sure of that. Kash made sure of that." He paused, hesitating. "There's been two other rings who have tried to take us. Both times, Kash caught them. He stopped them, and he'll stop who's tried to take you too. I promise."

I didn't know I was crying till then, till my hand raised to wipe something tickling my cheek. Feeling the tears, I looked at my hand oddly. I didn't cry. Hayes women did not do tears. What was this wetness?

My eyeballs were sweating.

Kash. I needed to talk to Kash. I didn't know why. I wasn't questioning it. I just needed him. He had texted earlier in the day, but I hadn't had the heart to reply. Now he was all I had the heart to hear from.

"Where's Kash?"

Matt paused, frowning. "You want to talk to Kash?"

I jerked my head in a nod. "Please."

I had stopped. I hadn't realized that, either. There was a whole bunch I wasn't paying attention to, but that was the point of walking, of getting numb. I wanted to turn off the world. That's how it worked. Once I felt safe, I'd come back.

I was still waiting.

"I'm sorry I scared you. I didn't know." Matt was speaking closer to me. He had a phone in his hand. "I wanted to talk to you, but when you reacted . . . I knew what happened to you. I'm really, really sorry, Bailey. Truly sorry. Cyclone gets nightmares. He doesn't remember what happened, but it's like his mind does, or whatever part where dreams still remember. Not that often, but maybe once or twice a year. I've heard them. They send chills down my back when I hear 'em. I feel sick thinking about what could've happened. I am so sorry. So sorry." He kept repeating those last two words as he gently, slowly, and so tenderly stepped in so he could hug me.

Once I was there, he felt my heart racing and cursed before hugging me tighter.

"Why haven't you come to us sooner? God."

I hugged him back, and I saw the faces watching us. It was almost too much to take in. The guards. Marie. Theresa was behind Marie. And still farther, down the hallway, I saw Quinn holding Cyclone's hand. A younger girl was next to her, her hand over her mouth. They shouldn't have been able to see us, but somehow an opening had formed. The guards shifted to the side, almost like they weren't sure whether to stay or to leave, and that was how we were on display for more than twenty people in that hallway.

I just closed my eyes.

I wanted two things.

I wished I had come to them sooner.

And I wished that it was Kash holding me.

"No one overheard me that didn't already know," Matt was saying into the phone, with Kash on the other end. He was walking in a circle, his hand pressed in his other ear to help him hear. "I know. I know. . . . No. Trust me. No one heard. I mean, Marie knew. The guards knew. Well . . . shit. Theresa knows now, too, but that's it. Theresa is Marie's daughter, so it's cool. She wouldn't say anything anyways. No one else could've heard."

He raised his hand to get one of the guards' attention. He motioned to the hallway, saying over the phone, "Theresa needs to sign that NDA, just in case. It's a specific one about—" He nodded to where I was sitting.

If *sitting* was even the appropriate word to describe how I was.

I was half crouched on the floor, half curled in a ball, and half resting on the balls of my heels, bouncing in place. It would be a killer on my leg muscles tomorrow, but I still wasn't feeling any pain. Slowly, over the last hour, the shock had started to subside, but there was still a healthy amount with me.

Everyone had been told to leave, urged to return to their beds.

The guards were outside, so it was just Matt and me in the room when Kash called. I was waiting till the report was done.

"Okay. . . . Yeah. Okay." Matt paused, nodding his head. "Yeah, yeah. I will. Okay."

He turned to me, staring at me, listening to Kash, then nodded again. "Here she is." He held the phone out to me.

I took it, feeling foolish in one second and grateful in the other. I should not be like this, needing to talk to him, but I was. And I was weak enough, scared enough, not to fight it. This time.

I moved across the room. "Hello?"

His voice was low and raspy. "Are you okay?"

A rush went right to my knees. I didn't know why, but I was suddenly gripping this phone like it was my lifeline and biting my lip to keep that perspiration from sliding down my face even more. Seriously. Embarrassing.

I croaked back, "I'm—" Bite. Breathe. I could do this. My voice didn't need to tremble. "I'm fine. Yes."

"Why don't I believe you?"

I half laughed at that. "If it's any consolation, I don't believe myself."

He was quiet. "Then why are you pretending?"

"Didn't you know? That's why I'm here. To pretend."

He was silent again. Then a soft sigh came over the phone. "I can't get away from where I am or I would."

Why was he telling me that? It shouldn't matter to me.

"Bailey?"

God. Why did he have to sound so concerned? It was breaking me. There was more sweating happening. I tried to talk, but only a whisper came out. "I'm—I was just scared."

Fuck it.

Bending my head low, I walked to the wall and rested my head against it. My back was to Matt, and I whispered, my voice breaking, "It was like before, when they burst in. I had a second's notice before—" I couldn't speak. My throat was closed off, and those tears were strolling back down my cheeks.

"Breathe, ba—breathe, Bailey." He was so soothing, tender almost.

My chest swelled up and the tension eased, just a bit.

He continued. "You had a traumatic thing happen to you. There's going to be residual effects; this is just one of them. You will be fine. I promise."

I was gripping that phone so tight, holding on to it like it was a life jacket. "You promise?" God. I hated crying. Hayes women did not cry. "Yell at me."

"What?"

"Yell at me." I groaned, clasping my eyes shut tight. "Please. I need a distraction."

He laughed. "If that's all you're worried about, I think you'll be fine." He was silent a second. We both heard my sniffling. "I have to stay where I am for a while. Does that make you stop crying?"

I bit my lip. It did, but there was an ache in my chest. Why was that fucking ache there?

"Bailey?" he prompted.

I wanted him to come back, but that was ridiculous. Instead, I said, "Stop spying on me all the time. It's creepy."

A chuckle from his end. "You sound better. Matt said your phone's probably at the villa. Call me when you get in."

"Why?"

"Just do it," he snipped at me—and just like that, I relaxed.

We were on firm ground again, ground I was familiar with.

"Yeah. Okay."

I handed the phone back to Matt. He spoke a few more words before hanging up. Turning to me, regarding me with raised eyebrows, he asked, "What would you like to do now?"

We both knew I wouldn't be sleeping.

I took a deep breath and considered what I needed to know to feel safe.

I needed to know the lay of the land. I wanted to know all of the security measures they had in place, physical and cyber, and I wanted to gauge any holes myself.

"Tour."

Matt said, "Tour it is."

NINETEEN

They had a bowling lane.

A pool with a waterfall. A tennis court. I already knew about the basketball court, the nine-hole golf course. I knew about the water fountains, but there was one inside the house as well. A movie theater room. Cyclone had a room where his friends could play air hockey, foosball, a pool table, a basketball hoop that I'd only seen at arcades. Seraphina had her own friend room, too, with a modeling stage, a photo shoot area, a selfie booth, and a rotating closet with clothes for dress-up. There were three makeup tables along the wall.

Matt didn't take me to Quinn's section of the house, but he stopped in his old room. Besides having his own entertainment area right outside his room, like the others, complete with a sectional couch that spanned the entire room and a movie screen against one wall and full-length bar against the other, his room was relatively normal. A desk. A large bed. A bathroom. That was it, besides the walk-in closet and his own entrance. The other two didn't have that.

I was overwhelmed. Seriously and totally overwhelmed.

This wasn't a life I could've had. There was no way I could stand with these people, with everything they were given. That was not what Hayes women did. We worked. We hustled. Hayes women kept going, no matter what happened to us.

Hayes women persevere.

Matt must've sensed my anxiety. His eyebrows went up. "Whatever's going on in that head, don't worry about it. I know I give Kash a lot of shit, but the guy's saved my ass almost a dozen times. If he says you're safe here, you're safe here. Don't get scared because I was the dumbass who broke in."

He was mistaking my silence, but on that matter, he was right. I took in his room. "You guys have . . . a lot here."

The tour took a long time, and to be honest I wasn't paying much attention to time. I knew it was early morning by now because the sun was starting to show through the windows. If Matt was tired, he never let on. He was patient through the whole tour.

He nodded, leading me out to sit in his entertainment area. Plopping down on one of the couches, he threw his leg up on the table in front of him. Leaning back, his arms spreading over the backs of the corner he was in, he frowned at me.

I followed at a more sedate pace, curling up in the far corner. I was tempted to pull a pillow over my lap, but I just toed off my shoes and pulled my knees up, hugging them to me. I gazed back at him, resting my chin between my knees.

He seemed about to say something, when a soft and feminine cough came from the hallway, just past the doorway that connected Matt's "wing" with the rest of the house. Quinn stood there, not in a ball gown like the other day, but still looking just as exquisite. She wore a soft cashmere bodysuit. The front crossed over her body, connecting with a tied sash at the waist. There was a lace bodice underneath, but she was very classy. Her hair was swept up in a French side bun, and like the other day, there was no jewelry at all. She had a clean, simple, natural look to her, but I knew her makeup was as good as if a professional had done it for her.

Crap. This is how she looked so early in the morning?

No way could I hang with these people. I'd still be walking blind, trying to find the coffee pot, and probably knocking into everything and everyone in my way.

Before she spoke, I saw two heads pop up from behind her.

Cyclone's grinning mischievous gaze sparked back at me, right before he pushed forward, shoving his mom aside as he darted ahead. "Heya, Girl!" He ran around the couch, launching over the table to tackle Matt. "Heya, loser asswipe!"

He was wide awake too.

When did these people get up? Was this normal?

Matt's arms shot up, catching his little brother. "Oh *really*? I'm the loser asswipe?" He laughed, rolling Cyclone to the cushions beside him and starting to tickle him. "*I'm* the loser?"

"Loser!" Cyclone laughed as his legs were flailing in the air. He landed a good solid kick to Matt's face. "Whoa! Sorry. I'm sorry, Matt."

Matt jerked back, a hand cupping the side of his face, and he turned away.

Silence. Total silence.

"Matt?" Cyclone's eyes were wide with fear.

A sniffle came from behind Matt's hand before he jumped back on his little brother, pinning him back down and tickling him with no mercy. "Gotcha, you little punk. That's what you get for kicking your older brother. Huh? Huh? Am I right?"

Cyclone was trying to wrestle, but he was no match for his older brother.

Quinn wore a fond expression, with a resigned patience there, too, as if this were a common occurrence.

It was then that I noticed that Seraphina had stepped farther out from behind her mother, more to the side. They were holding hands.

Seraphina looked almost exactly like her mother. Same cornflower-blue eyes, same honey-blond hair, but with a touch lighter streak to it. It couldn't compare to her mother's, but Seraphina's hair was wispy, with a bit of natural volume and frizz to it. She had some flyaway strands that couldn't be contained in the braid her hair had been put in. Similar high cheekbones and a heart-shaped face with a pert little chin. She could be a model. Long arms and legs that she was still growing into, but she didn't have the teardrop eyes her brother and mother had. She must've taken after her father, like the rest of us.

The rest of us.

That was the first time I lumped myself in with them, as if I were one of them.

But I wasn't. I was the outlier.

"I can see we weren't the only ones up early this morning. I think we're all a bit 'feisty' from the lack of sleep." The same fondness, shot through with a frustration, too. Quinn raised her chin up as both her boys paused in their wrestling, which had taken them to the floor by then. "Matthew, perhaps you and . . ." Her eyes darted to mine. "Kash's friend could join us for a late lunch later today? Seraphina has her lessons at three, remember?"

Matt scoffed, grabbing Cyclone and lifting him to his feet as he stood. "I did not, dear Mother, realize my being here may upset Seraphina's precious lessons in how to be a lady."

Quinn wasn't amused. Her mouth pinched together.

Seraphina giggled, looking down at the floor.

Matt smirked, still holding his brother captive. Cyclone was trying to kick out of his hold, but not enough to actually be set free. "I'm surprised Victoria is coming today. Does she not realize that Kash isn't here?" His smirk dropped to a meaner glint. "She'd be wasting her time."

Cyclone stopped kicking.

I could see from the angle that Seraphina's eyes had widened, but she kept her face pointed downward.

The only one who moved was Quinn herself, and it was when her eyes narrowed. "Be nice, Matthew, or I won't be, either." Her gaze slid my way and her threat was evident.

Cyclone watched her too, and his head popped up. "Why'd you be mean to Kash's friend? She's Kash's friend." He said it like it made the most perfect sense in the world, as if he had been asked if his name was Cyclone or not. The whole tone was a resounding "Duh."

"Yes, well . . ."

Seraphina looked up now, watching her mother with those same big eyes. Her mouth opened, just a centimeter.

Quinn took in both of her children's gazes and her face clouded over. She cast me a tight closed-mouth smile. "Seraphina's been asking to meet Kash's lady friend, and Cyclone has talked about you as well. Both are eager to get to know our mystery guest more. Would you like to sit with us for our lunch later today?"

I gazed at her.

She was really beautiful, and it took a second before I realized she was addressing me. And waiting for a response.

My gaze fell back to Seraphina and I saw the curiosity there. It was banked, hidden behind a few walls of her own, and some shyness, but I saw it. I felt it, too. Her and Cyclone. I wanted to get to know them both—and Matt.

"Yes." My voice was hoarse for some reason. I cleared it, speaking clearer. "Yes. I'd love that, actually."

Seraphina shyly grinned. Cyclone snorted.

Quinn said to Matt, "We'll be in the family room at one then." Her gaze fell. "Cyclone, let's go and get you dressed for the day."

He looked down at his outfit, a yellow polo shirt and khaki shorts. Mumbling, as Matt lowered him to the floor, he followed her out. "I thought I *was* dressed. This is what Marie put out." Seraphina trailed behind, and all of them disappeared around the corner. "Do I really have to change? What's wrong with these clothes?"

I couldn't hear her response.

Matt walked to stand next to me, both of us watching where they had gone. "You ready for that?"

My response was automatic. "No."

He looked at me.

"But those are my siblings."

I wanted to know them. No Quinn, no Victoria (whoever she was) would deter me. "We have to dress for this thing?"

Matt snorted. "God no. That's just Quinn. You scare her. You're not like . . ." He was searching for the right word. "You're not like the rest of us. You're not scared of her. Maybe that's the best way to say it?"

"She terrifies me."

He laughed, starting ahead. "Don't let her know that. Come on. We've not slept. I doubt Quinn did either, but we've a few hours of downtime before lunch. You want breakfast?"

I gave him a look

He laughed. "Right. Let's watch a movie and see if we can not think, at least, until lunch then."

We turned down another hallway.

Theresa was coming out of a room, took one look at me, and her eyebrows rose almost to her hairline. She made the sign of the cross over her forehead and chest.

I was thinking I'd need more than that sign, but okay then.

TWENTY

Matt had two drinks down before Quinn showed, with Cyclone coming ahead of her and Seraphina following at a more sedate pace.

The movie hadn't helped.

I'd been restless the entire time.

Matt went from drinking coffee to now drinking alcohol. I couldn't blame him.

I was used to my little cousins trying to act cool and subdued. There was none of that with Cyclone. He was just himself.

It was refreshing. And Seraphina just seemed kind, excruciatingly kind.

Cyclone launched himself into the chair next to Matt, panting slightly. He smiled at me before turning to his older brother. "When'd you get here, Matt? What was going on last night, with all the guards and Miss Bailey in Marie's room? Is she going to die? Is everyone okay? Mom said everything was fine, Miss Bailey was cold and she just needed a hug to warm up? Is that because Kash isn't here?" A breath. A pause, and he wasn't done. He slid to his bottom on the chair and started with me. "How'd you and Kash meet? Why isn't Kash here? Did you guys have a fight? Are you the kind of friends like Mom and Dad? Do you kiss, then walk away from each other? I thought Kash was with Dad?"

Oh, sweet Jesus.

The kid really was the Tasmanian Devil.

No one else seemed perturbed. A cool smile came to Quinn's

face as she lowered herself to the seat across from me and next to Matt. Nodding to one of the servers, who brought over a drink for her, she replied, "I don't think Miss Bailey is that type of friend with Kash. I think she's the kind like Victoria is with our family."

He frowned.

Matt shook his head.

Cyclone said, "But Victoria is always hanging all over Kash."

Matt coughed to cover up his laugh.

My eyebrows went up.

Seraphina was watching her little brother as if she'd been given sour lemonade to drink.

The only one unaffected was Quinn herself. She barely blinked, no joke. "Maybe we can focus on eating instead of asking twenty questions?"

Cyclone. "But why? Marie told me to always ask questions if I don't understand something." He pointed at me. "I don't understand who she is. If she's Kash's friend, why isn't he here? If my friends are here, I don't go and leave them alone. Marie said that's bad manners." His head popped up farther. "You said that's bad manners too, Mom."

Matt cleared his throat, sliding out of his chair. "I need something stronger than this. Excuse me."

I wanted to go with him. I wanted to hide under the table like I was the ten-year-old.

Instead, I moved to face Cyclone better. "So, have you ever known someone who was sad about something?"

He nodded, his eyes so rapt as he listened to me.

"Well, that's kinda what I'm going through." I hated lying. *Hated* it. And still, I was so damn good at it. "So I used to love someone, like your mom and your dad love each other, but that person decided he didn't want to be with me."

Cyclone was still silent.

"And there was a reason I couldn't stay where I used to live, because I'd see him. He was around a lot, and a friend of mine is Kash's cousin. She suggested I come here to stay with him. That's what is going on. Kash is here for me, but he still has to do his job."

I was talking to him like he was younger than ten. I got that. But sometimes when something's confusing, that's the best way to handle it. Strip it down to the bare bones and go from there.

And because I didn't want to get sympathy from my little brother for a lie, I distracted him. "How are you doing with the robot rabbit? Has your dad helped you with your switchboard at all?"

It worked.

His eyes grew wide, wider, and the widest. He whispered, awed, "You know about switchboards?"

"I do."

"How?"

That was it. Hook, line, sinker. The rest of us didn't even need to be there as we ate because Cyclone was shooting question after question at me, all about robotics, engineering, switchboards, and what kind of wiring would make the most cohesive connection. I could almost see the rest glaze over in boredom, but no one was protesting.

Matt seemed to be getting a kick out of the whole conversation. He kept watching Cyclone, me, then swinging his head to Quinn and smirking. By the end of our last course, which was just two spoonfuls of sherbet with a mint leaf over the top, Seraphina was yawning. She lifted her hands to rub at her eyes. Quinn caught one, stopping her.

"Don't mess your eyes up, darling." She swept the table, lingering on me, then Cyclone. "Honey, your own tutor is coming as well. You have just enough time to go to your room, have a play or a nap, before Benjamin arrives."

Cyclone's nose wrinkled up. "I want to work on my robot. Can Bailey stay and help me?"

I was Bailey now, not Miss Bailey.

I felt a nice tickle in the back of my throat at that one.

"No." Quinn was no-nonsense, standing from the table as Theresa came in to start collecting the rest of the dishes. "Benjamin travels a great distance to teach you German. He's very expensive, so we don't want to waste his time. Seraphina, sweetheart . . ." She ran her hand down Seraphina's hair, tucking the end of her braid over her shoulder. "Victoria will be here soon. Are you ready for your lessons of the day?"

Seraphina, who I still hadn't heard say a word, snuck a look at me, then nodded at her mother. "Hmm."

"Pronounce your words, dear." Quinn cupped her daughter lightly under her chin. Her tone was disapproving, but the smile was all love. "That's the basics of being a lady in our society. The world will expect you to use your words. Understand?"

She squeezed softly.

Seraphina smiled, whispering, "Yes, Mother. I understand."

"Good." Her hand dropped, but her smile spread bigger. "You'll do amazing."

"Thank you, Mother." Another whisper.

Quinn nodded to me, that smile dimming. "It was lovely to have you for lunch. I assume that Matthew will see to you from here now?"

Matt stood, his gaze a little dark and locked on his stepmother. "But of course, Quinn. Being such good friends with Kash, and coming here in her time of need, she's practically *family*." He paused a second. "Just like the Bonhams."

Quinn's eyes snapped to his, and she froze in place. Her face took on a haggard look, then a blink, and she was smiling again. "Drew and Amanda Bonham are wonderful friends of ours. I don't think Miss Bailey will be the same. She'll return home before long."

Where was the popcorn?

A slow grin spread. Matt added, "Yes. I'm aware how close the Bonhams are with you, and you never know with Bailey. *I* won't let her down."

I waited. Seraphina and Cyclone paused too. Quinn and Matt were at an impasse, but Quinn forced out a wry chuckle. "Yes. Of course. I'll see you both later, hmm? I'm off to a charity meeting." She turned, a bit clipped in her movement. "Seraphina, let me know when Victoria arrives, would you?"

"Of course, Mother."

Quinn left the room.

Tiny arms wrapped around my waist. Cyclone tipped his head back, looking up at me. "We have family movie night when Dad comes home from his trips. Kash comes too, sometimes. Would you come without him, if he didn't?"

He was inviting me to family . . . Emotion ripped through me. "Of course I will." My little brother asked, so I was going to make it happen. I grinned back down at him, hugging him. "If you need help with your robot, you can ask me. I'll see if I can help."

"Thanks." And he was off, running from the room. "Bye, Matt!"

Matt chuckled, coming to stand next to me. "The kid's in love with you."

Another small hand fitted in my hand, and that warmth skyrocketed to something deeper. Seraphina wasn't looking at me. She stood at an angle, half turned away, but I heard her whisper, "It was nice meeting you," before she squeezed my hand again, just so softly. I tried to form the words, but she disappeared from the room almost as quickly as Cyclone had.

They were like air, there on the inhale and gone on the exhale, and I wanted to keep breathing them for the rest of my days.

That lunch. That squeeze from Cyclone, the hand-holding from Seraphina—it was all worth it. *They* were worth it.

"Thank you." I ran a hand over my face.

"So." Matt regarded me with a cautious half grin. One of his hands went into his pocket, and the other raked through his hair. "What's on the agenda now?"

"You telling me about the Bonhams."

TWENTY-ONE

Me: *Who are the Bonhams? Matthew won't tell me.*

    Kash: *Headaches.*

    Kash: *Why?*

    Me: *There was a weird exchange between Matt and Quinn today.*
He won't tell me. And you won't let me go on the internet.

    Kash: *You're a menace.*

    Kash: *Bonhams are a trap door. Don't step on it.*

    Kash: *Night.*

    Me: *Sigh. You're boring.*

    Me: *Night.*

TWENTY-TWO

Me: *I want to know about the Bonhams.*

    Kash: *Trap door. And I'm not supposed to be texting.*

    Me: *Why?*

    Kash: *Nosey too.*

    Me: *I'm bored. An idiot took away my internet.*

    Kash: *Smart guy.*

    Me: *You made me laugh. That doesn't compute with the dick image I have of you.*

    Kash: *Dick image?*

    Me: *You know what I mean.*

    Kash: *Um . . .*

    Me: *Stop flirting.*

    Kash: *Who brought up dick image?*

    Me: *I'm not laughing.*

    Kash: *Cameras say otherwise.*

    Me: *Dick.*

    Kash: Go to bed. Text me when you wake up.

    Me: *Only if you tell me about the Bonhams and why you can't be texting.*

    Kash: *Don't text me in the morning.*

TWENTY-THREE

Kash: *I'm coming back tonight.*
    Me: *Who is this?*
    Kash: *Bailey.*
    Me: *Bonhams. Why you can't text, but are texting.*
    Kash: *You're tenacious.*
    Me: *Tell the truth. Autocorrect had to help with that word,* didn't it?
    Kash: *Let's talk about my dick image again.*

TWENTY-FOUR

He never told me about them.

Matt only said he didn't care for them, and I let it go. Shocking. But the main reason I let it go wasn't because both of them refused to elaborate; it was because I had three glorious days.

I got quality time with my siblings. There was minimal time with Quinn, who it turned out did charity work as a full-time career. She had events in the mornings, meetings in the afternoons, and banquets in the evenings. Miss Victoria came around once a week, I learned, but she hadn't been back since that one day of our lunch, so I hadn't met her. After the bit I'd learned about her, I wasn't sure if I wanted to meet her, but I also wasn't letting that overshadow anything.

That first night after our lunch, I had dinner with my siblings. Marie and Theresa joined us, along with an older man named Barney, who turned out to be Marie's husband.

Marie and Theresa were a lot nicer than the first time I had met them, and the rest were relaxed. There were no rules, no pressure to be a certain way, eat a certain way. They could pick at their pizza if they wanted, or scarf down a whole bowl of mac and cheese. After that first night, I caught Marie eyeing me with guilt. Matt told me later that our "dinners" were an unofficial secret. It wasn't that whenever Quinn wasn't around they ate like that, but over the last few days, I got their routine. If Quinn wasn't around, they still ate healthy two out of three meals of the day. There was a healthy snack, too, but the evenings were laid back. Burned pizza was one of Seraphina's favorites.

And the whole secret part was that no one told Quinn.

I loved it. I loved it all.

We were hanging out in one of the media rooms, three boxes of pizza on the floor and the latest superhero movie on the screen, when Matt's phone buzzed.

I was curled up in the corner, my favorite place to sit.

Cyclone was lying next to me, his head in my lap. Seraphina was sprawled on the floor, her head propped up on her hands and her feet kicking back at the end of our couch. Marie had started to watch the movie with us but then left thirty minutes in, saying she'd be back the next morning.

Quinn was at another charity event for the evening.

The buzzing started, and Matt declined the call. No one paid him much attention. This had happened over the last few days. He had an active social life, but he'd been spending most of his time here and staying at Kash's villa with me. He slept in Kash's bed, and I was in mine.

But tonight the buzzing just kept going.

Buzz.

Buzz.

Buzz.

After a full twenty minutes of his phone going off, Seraphina sat up. "Just answer it! It's so annoying."

He laughed, reaching for the phone just as it started again. Hitting a button, he was speaking into it, "Yo. What do you want?" He sat up straight. "Oh, hey. . . . No. It didn't come up that it was you—

"Oh. Okay." He looked up at me, alarmed.

I started to sit up straighter, so did Cyclone. All three of us were waiting, but Matt got up, his phone to his ear. He left the room and we could only hear fragments of the conversation.

"Yeah? . . . No. I mean, it's a movie. . . . She's here. What? . . . I've been there. Yeah. . . . Why? . . . Oh. . . . For real? . . . No shit, huh. . . . He is?"

Suddenly his voice got louder, clearer. He was coming back.

Cyclone scrambled off the couch, grabbing the remote, and the movie was turned off. The screen went to black and he moved to the wall, hitting the switch so the room was bathed in light.

Matt came to stand in the doorway, his phone pressed to his ear. Seeing the screen off, he lowered his hand and took all of us in.

He swallowed stiffly, his eyes finding mine. I saw the worry, and my chest started to grow tight.

He murmured, his mouth curving down, "Yeah. . . . Yeah. I will. . . . Thank you. Yeah."

Ending the call, he scrolled through something on his screen before his eyes darkened and he put his phone back in his pocket.

Then the fakest thing I've witnessed in a long time happened.

He plastered a huge bright smile on his face. "Guess what, guys?"

Seraphina scrambled to her knees. "What?"

Cyclone was hanging off the end of the couch. He thrust his arm in the air. "Dude, just tell us!"

"Dad's coming home." Matt looked at me. "Tonight."

"*What?*" Seraphina jumped to her feet, lighting up.

"When?" Cyclone was right with her, shooting up to start jumping on the couch.

"Uh . . ." Matt checked the time on his phone again. "In like an hour. You guys are supposed to hurry and get ready for bed."

"What?"

"Why?" Seraphina asked right after Cyclone's whine.

"Because your mom's planning a whole night of movies. So if you wash up, clean your teeth, get in your pajamas, you pick the first movie to watch with Dad."

"*Yeah?*"

"Really?" Seraphina asked

Matt was tense as he clipped his head up and down. "Yep. Go and get ready, then come back in here with your blankets. Your mom said something about a sleepover even."

Cyclone jumped off from the couch. "Yes!" And he took off running down the hall.

Seraphina hurried after him, but stopped, turned, and came back to give me a tight hug around my neck. "Thanks for tonight. It was a lot of fun." Before I could reply, she hurried from the room, yelling over her shoulder, "Bye, Matt! Love you."

"And then there's the two of us, until Kash gets back also." Matt regarded me, a deep sigh leaving him. He slid his hands in his front pockets. "How's it going?"

He was coming back.

Not that I cared.

Not that I'd been waiting.

Not that I'd been looking forward to seeing him again.

I had done as he asked, called him once I got my phone again. That set the precedent. We talked the next day. We texted in the morning, in the afternoon, in the evening. Good times. And there were also the good night texts and good morning texts.

I disliked those the most.

Yep. Detested them. Loathed them.

Why hadn't he told me good morning today?

I didn't care. Not one bit.

I was lying. I was a caring fool.

Then I noticed Matt's silence and began looking on the floor. "What are you doing?"

"Looking for the shoe you're about to drop."

"Ha ha." He rubbed at his forehead, ignoring my lame grin. "I'm sorry. I actually took two calls just now. One was Kash, letting me know about Dad, but the other was Quinn. She . . ." His hand dropped. "She asked me to make sure you weren't on the property when my—when Dad gets home."

I reeled from that one.

"He's been in DC working on a big project, and I guess it was a tense time for him. Something happened. She thinks it'll be better if he doesn't add anything extra on his plate."

Right. Extra. I was the extra.

Backward.

I was feeling shoved out of the house. One by one, all the doors were closing in my face until I was so far out that I was outside the gates. That's what Quinn just did.

I was getting kicked out.

"I see." I looked down at my lap. There was a slight tremor with my hands, so I stuffed them between my legs, stopping it.

It was fine.

I mean, it's not like I expected to see him again.

Or hoped to see him again.

He hurt Chrissy. I drew that in, remembering, hardening. He hurt my mom.

"She doesn't even want me in Kash's villa?"

He hesitated, before slumping down on the couch next to me. "No. Not even there. Look, it'll be fine. I tend to have a whole security team on me when I leave, and since Quinn would rather both of us"—he nudged me with his shoulder—"not be here . . . I can't help but go at her sometimes, so I was thinking we can head downtown to my place. I have a place. You'll be safe. Kash has given me the safety approval before."

"Francois Nova?"

He nodded. "It's where I normally stay. I moved out of this house years ago. We could go there. A few of my friends are heading to a new nightclub, if you wanted to go there too?"

"Friends?"

Another nod. "I could go for a night of debauchery, to tell you the truth."

It sounded wrong somehow. "I don't know, Matt."

"Come on. It'll just be one or two friends. I told you, Kash is good with it. I've got the whole security team and everything. And it won't be anything big. These guys are cool. Might do you good to meet a few of the girls, if they're there." He stopped, rolling his eyes. "What am I saying? If there's a new club opening, they'll be there." His shoulder bumped mine playfully. "Maybe it's time to meet a few of the gang."

"You have a gang?"

He stood, making up our minds for both of us, and catching my hand, he hauled me with him. "One thing you need to learn about this world: we might live in an exclusive club, but it's a *small* exclusive club. And once it's out who you are, everyone's going to want to get their hooks in you. Might be a good idea to meet them one by one, in small doses, and when they don't know who you are."

I wasn't fully following his theory, but I didn't have a choice. Quinn wanted me gone, and Matt was doing her bidding. He was just going with me.

I nodded, giving in. "Should I pack a bag then?"

"Nah." His mouth twitched in a half smirk, and he threw his arm back around my shoulder as we headed out. "As long as you have your phone, you're good to go. I'll have everything at my place."

"I.D.? You have women's clothes at your place?"

"When you go with me, you don't need I.D." He just laughed. "And being rich gives you the luxury of being prepared for anything. Come on. Let's go forget about family 'stress' by getting wasted."

It wasn't what I'd normally do.

I was in.

TWENTY-FIVE

You're not wanted.

We want you gone.

You're too much of a problem.

You'll just disturb everything. You'll upset everyone.

Here I was, sitting in the back corner of a booth, a DJ playing blaring techno music, neon lights flashing, fog being pumped through the club, sipping drink number I-had-lost-count, but I couldn't get those thoughts out of my head.

You're not worth it.

You're not worthy.

You're nothing.

I was trying, seriously trying to block it out. I couldn't.

Matt walked in front of me when we arrived. He was right. No one stopped us or carded us when we went inside. He didn't even need to go to the bar, though that's where he was leading me. A girl in a skimpy leotard for a uniform, holding a tray of shots, met him halfway, and he kissed her cheek as he snagged one shot for me, another for him. Before moving ahead, he grabbed two more. I declined my second, wanting to pace myself. Not Matt. He threw both back like a pro.

Then we went to the bar, but only for Matt to motion to a private box. The bartender nodded and we were sitting there for ten minutes, when two of Matt's friends showed up.

Chester and Tony.

Chester was taller, looking like Prince Harry, and more slender than Tony, who had dark, combed-back hair.

They looked like Ivy League bad boys. Wealth. Privilege. Superior. All of that emanated from them.

The club was packed, since it was nearing eight on a Friday night, but not to those guys. Not to Matt. All three got the same treatment coming in. Eyes tracked them. I didn't know who the parents of Chester and Tony were, but I had no doubt they were someone.

That was an hour ago.

Since then, it'd been a parade of girls coming over.

The first one came over, an alluring smile on her face as she sat on Matt's lap. The two had been whispering, nuzzling, kissing since. Her hands were on him, his hands weren't on her. He sat on the outside of the booth, with one arm draped over the back of the booth.

I was sitting farther inside, but the booth was huge.

Chester had moved in beside me, but four people could've sat between us. Five minutes after the first girl came over, three more showed up. They didn't sit on anyone's lap. They stood at the end of the table, talking and flirting with the two guys. To their credit, neither Chester nor Tony seemed to be doing much flirting. They were aloof, but still conversing. The girls were the ones trying to flirt, drawing them in.

And me—no one said a word to me.

Not my brother. Certainly not the girl he was making out with. Not his friends. And the only thing I got were cold snubs from the other three.

So it was me and my drink. An hour passed that way.

"Francis."

One of the friends gestured past the walkway. He spoke in a slight break between the beats, so Matt heard, his head lifting from the girl's neck.

Three more girls were walking up to where we sat. The girl in the lead had rich, dark auburn hair that fell past her shoulders, grazing the tops of her arms and chest. Doe-like almond eyes.

This girl was stunning. Tall. Slender. She had the height and frame to be a model.

One of the other two was shorter, around five four, with dark hair that had a small bounce to it. She had a heart-shaped face but a little more filled out. Her eyes, though . . . they stood out the most. They were hazel, a green tint to them. The third girl was blond. She was the same height as the first but wasn't as slender. She had a few more pounds, enough to actually have curves, and I knew, by glancing at the guys, that she was the one they liked the most.

They stopped, paused, and waited for their presence to be announced. These girls weren't acting like the other girls. These three were different.

They expected attention.

And they got it, as Matt sat farther back from the girl on his lap, a name escaping him like a frustrated sigh. "Victoria."

Victoria?

As in the Victoria who hung over Kash, who was mentoring Seraphina? *That* Victoria?

She swung those eyes to me and raised her nose up a fraction of an inch. "This is the houseguest Ser was talking about the other day?"

Fuck. It *was* her.

Double fuck.

She wasn't stunning anymore. She was gorgeous on another level. There was no way anyone could compete against her.

I mean, not that I was. But anyone else, no way. Anyone who was trying.

Matt skimmed me with a look, a coldness in there that I was surprised to see. "Back off on this one, Vic." He guided the girl off his lap, and as she stood next to him, a pout on her face, he leaned forward to rest his arms on the table. His gaze was solely locked on Victoria now, and he lifted his top lip in a half sneer. "No fucking with her." He raised one eyebrow. "You got me?"

No one spoke.

No one moved.

No one breathed.

Her friends' mouths opened an inch. Their own eyebrows rose at a slower pace, but they waited until Victoria's mouth mashed together and a glare was directed toward me. If she'd had superpowers, I would've been incinerated right then and there, but she turned as a strangled growl left her. She stalked right back down the walkway before turning toward another booth of guys. Seeing them, Chester nodded. "Mattson and Atchins are over there." He scanned them. "Don't know the rest."

Tony grunted. "Do we care? Mattson can suck my dick."

Just like that, the matter was settled. What the matter had been, I had no clue, but it was decided. The guys went back to the girls in front of them. Tony stood, his hands finding one of the girls' hips. He raised his chin up toward Matt. "We're going to move more private." His eyes flicked to me, back to my brother. "You want to come?" They landed on the girl Matt had been making out with, still standing next to the booth. Matt's arm had wound around her waist, pulling her against his side.

Chester scooted to the edge of the booth, but he didn't stand.

Victoria's two friends were still standing at our table. It was clear they were waiting to be addressed by the guys.

Matt glanced to me, his eyebrows up in a question.

I didn't know what "private" meant, so I just shrugged and reached for the drink Matt had had a waitress refill ten minutes before.

"Nah." Matt tugged his girl back to his lap. "We're good here."

"Gotcha. See you around, then."

Tony tapped the girl on the hip and she led the way, moving off in a seductive sway. Her two friends gazed at Chester a second, but he only shook his head and flicked his fingers at them. "I'm not interested. You all can go and make sure my boy's taken care of, hmm?"

They flushed, getting what he was saying, and hurried off.

One muttered, "Asshole," under her breath, searing him with a glower.

He didn't care, rolling his eyes before addressing Victoria's friends. "You still here?" He paused a beat. "Why?"

The blonde sucked in her breath. "You're such a dick, Chester."

He lifted up a shoulder, lounging back against the booth so his head rested against the cushion and his feet were stretched out past the table. He idly scratched at his neck. "That seemed to turn you on last night, Fleur."

She shook her head, pointedly turning away from him. "Matt."

My brother had gone back to nuzzling the neck of the girl on his lap. He didn't lift his head, but he did stop in his ministrations.

"Matt."

He groaned, looking up now. His eyebrows moved together. He wasn't happy. "What?"

She tried to act impassive under the heat of his annoyance, but shifting on her feet, she dropped her gaze. "Where's Kash? Victoria's worried about him. He's not been gone this long, not for a while."

That got Chester's attention.

He sat forward, leaning, resting his arms on the table as Matt had been when the three girls first approached. "That's why you stayed back? To ask about Colello?"

Matt grinned, a dark amusement lining that smile. He rested his head back against the booth, watching this play out and enjoying it in an almost cruel way. "She stayed back to do Victoria's dirty work. Didn't you, Fleur?" Then it was as if he grew bored with this new toy. His eyes flashed his annoyance and he sat forward, reaching for his girl again. "Go away. Stop being Vic's bitch and asking about Kash. If Kash wanted her to know, he would tell her. Says enough right there."

"Matt."

His head snapped up again, his nostrils flaring. "Fuck. Off. What don't you understand about that?"

Chester stood, almost lazily. "Come on." He hooked his finger around her hand and tugged her behind him, heading down the walkway. "Let's go get some shots."

Glaring one more time at Matt, she followed behind, her other hand resting over his.

The last friend remained, looking almost bored.

"What?"

She lifted up a shoulder. "Nothing. Just . . . you know the real reason she's over here." Her eyes, like everyone else, darted to me and held there.

I got it then. Or I thought I did. Chester and Tony might not have cared about who I was, but these three did. The other girls hadn't. They weren't in the "club," as Matt had first explained, but Victoria, Fleur, and this one were. I was here. I was in the booth, and it was obvious I wasn't here to be a sex play toy to the guys. Since Matt was sitting on the outskirts of the booth, that meant I was someone to them. They just didn't know who I was.

Matt had already pushed back at Victoria about me, and he'd pushed hard, but the other was crucified as well. I had a nagging feeling that her asking about Kash wasn't really asking about where he was, that there were other levels mixed in, other dynamics playing out underneath those words. I wasn't sure what, but I'd have to learn if I was staying—

What was I doing?

I was sitting here acting like I was a part of this world, but I wasn't.

I was here because of a threat, but after, I was back to my mom.

Matt, Seraphina, Cyclone. Could I go back to not knowing them?

Pain split down my middle, tearing me apart.

Matt was watching me, his head lowered. "You okay?" I felt his concern, and my God but it was too much.

It almost unglued everything I had just shoved down and I felt tears coming to my eyes. Blinking rapidly, I jerked my head in a nod, but motioned to get out. "Can I—I have to go to the bathroom."

Matt didn't move, not at first. "Bailey."

"Pee, Matt. I have to do it, here or there. I'd prefer there." I wasn't looking at him. I couldn't. He'd see I was hurting, more than he might've suspected right now. I couldn't hold it back. I didn't know why, but the wall I had tried to erect was gone and I was raw, exposed in that moment. I couldn't be like that, not here, not among these people. This was the worst place to be bleeding out.

When he still didn't move, I dropped my voice to a raw, "Please."

He made a soft sound. A break in the music was the only reason he heard me, I heard him, but it was enough. He stood up, carrying the girl with him and setting her on her feet as I rushed past them.

He reached out for me. I was expecting it, and I ducked my arm and shoulder down, evading his touch. Then I was off. I didn't know where the bathrooms were, but it didn't really matter at that point. I just needed to get away. It was hurting too much, knowing I'd have to leave those three, knowing I'd be forced to leave them.

I shoved through the crowd, only stopping to gape in some much-needed fog, when I knew I'd been swallowed up. No one from that world could see me, and, still feeling the bite of tears at my eyes, I started forward.

I wandered the club.

There was a guard on my tail. I saw him a few times. I knew there were another two who had accompanied us into the club, but once we got inside, I hadn't seen them. They'd been blending in with everyone, but once I got to the higher floor, and as the crowd lessened dramatically, I saw the guard.

He clipped a nod to me, remaining a few yards away. Coming to an empty table, one in the corner by the exit door, I slid in. I just needed to get away. I needed to wrap my head around things, and only then would I be able to put that wall back up.

The guard didn't come forward. He held back, folding his arms in front of him as he took point and watched out for anyone coming and going. Where I was sitting, though, no one was doing that. I had gone as far up as I could and as far inside as I could. I stayed there until I lost track of time. I assumed Matt asked where I was, because the guard took his phone out. It was lighting up from someone calling, and he was only on it for a few seconds before he put it back into his pocket.

Two staff members came in through the exit door, breezing past me without a second look. I didn't think they even saw me, though they saw my guard. Both staff paused, checking him out, before walking past. One paused and said something under her breath, but the guard only smiled and shook his head briefly. She started forward, only then looking back over her shoulder and seeing me. Her eyes widened, and her mouth opened, but she kept going.

A few minutes later, she came back with a drink in hand.

I watched, expecting her to offer it to the guard, but she didn't. She sent him a coy smile, going past and holding it out to me. "Compliments from the bar."

"Really? What is it?"

"One of the girls said you were sitting in the VIP earlier. She said it's the same drink you had down there." She touched my shoulder lightly, a small smile on her face. "Have your Mr. Tall, Dark, and Delicious nod to me downstairs if you want another. I'll be watching."

I was momentarily stunned, then nodded. "Thank you."

The small gesture of kindness was appreciated.

The guard came forward when she left. He took the drink, testing it first. I waited, and after a few minutes he nodded. "It's fine." He handed it back to me. "You can drink it."

Thanking him, I sipped the drink, and by the end of it, I was ready to head back. This time, as I went, I got a different reaction. People watched me. They moved aside. Eyes tracked me as they had watched Matt cross the club, and his friends. I got that same reception. It was an unsettling feeling, until I glanced over my shoulder and saw that my guard was closer than I had realized.

I was pondering that when a hand came out of nowhere.

I was yanked down a hallway. It happened so fast, I couldn't react.

A door was opened. I was dragged inside, then a decisive "Stop!" barked out and the door was slammed shut behind me.

The light was never turned on.

I had no idea where I was, but it didn't matter. I felt him, whoever he was, in front of me. He placed two hands on either side of me, trapping me in place, and as I was frozen, he bent over me. I felt his breath, warming me, teasing me. His body pressed in. He was crowding me. He wasn't plastered against me, but I was flattened as much as I could be against the wall, still feeling his heat before he spoke into my ear.

"What the *fuck* are you doing here?"

TWENTY-SIX

I was jarred.

It was abrupt. It was harsh, and it sent me back to *that* night.

I was in that dark room, but I wasn't. My mind was back there, in my mom's house, in my room. A hand was over my mouth in my home again.

I was remembering . . .

"Stop fighting and pay attention."

Who was here?

"Bailey." A sharp rasp. "I asked you a question."

I was feeling pulled down, down. I was falling. The smell of that room again, feeling a cold breeze from him as he pressed against me. The sound of his silent footsteps as he caught me before I could run, as he pushed me to the wall.

"They're going to think I raped you, and you'll cry."

"Bailey."

I looked to the side, but it was just darkness. I could only feel him, sense him. He had trapped me again. A fog was clouding over my mind, dragging me still down, back into my memories.

I didn't want to go there, and a whimper left me.

"Bailey." Softer this time.

A hand slid to the back of my neck. His forehead touched mine, and I felt his chest. My hand raised there, touching him, holding him back.

"I will not let them hurt you. Got it?"

"Your house. Your territory. Your only shot of living."

I sucked in a sharp breath. A hand moved on my neck—not Chase's hand, but a different hand. Kash's hand.

Kash was here.

I was not there.

I was safe. Here. With Kash. Not. There.

His thumb stroking back and forth, sliding up into my hair. A whispered, "Bailey," before he moved even closer, his head falling beside mine. His cheek against mine, holding there, steady there. Never leaving there.

I sucked my breath in at the reminder of that night.

"Shh."

A gargled cry had slipped from me. I was moving my head back and forth. It was hard to breathe. Harder still. An invisible pressure was pushing me down. The room was closing in on us.

I grabbed for him, my hand splaying out. Up. Over his strong chest, over muscles that I was faintly registering, over tight shoulders, around a rigid back.

He held still over me, above me. His head lifted back and he was watching me. I couldn't see his eyes, but I felt his gaze.

I choked out, "Kash?"

His arms folded around me, tugging me the last bit of space and holding me against him. He buried his head in my neck, his body slightly trembling. "I'm sorry. I didn't think. I didn't mean to scare you." He breathed out against my skin. "It's okay. You're safe. You're safe. It's just me. It's Kash."

A light turned on.

His hand came back. He was cupping both sides of my face.

His forehead was almost touching. His eyes boring into mine. A fierceness in there that had me pausing, waiting.

"Tell me you're okay." His hands tightened on my face. "Tell me, Bailey. I need to hear the words."

My mind was spinning. Different thoughts were coming at me, snapping at me. They were quick and harsh and terrifying.

I paused, my heart pounding.

I sucked in a shuddering breath. "I'm fine." I said it faintly, but I was. And I said it stronger, clearer, because I meant it. "I'm fine. I'm sorry. I just—"

His hands were sweeping back my hair and he shook his head, his forehead moving on mine. "You're fine. I grabbed you fast. I wasn't thinking. It's me."

His arms moved more around me, and I could feel his breath. His lips were so close to mine, but then he was talking. "We can talk later. I promise. But first . . ." He moved back again, the same glittering fierceness coming back. "What the *fuck* are you doing here?"

"Oh." I rested my head against the wall, my insides sagging in relief for the moment. "Matt said you called, said Peter was coming back also. Quinn wanted me gone."

His hand had tightened as I spoke, until the last part. "The fuck?"

I didn't know what to say, so I only lifted a shoulder up and down. "We have security on us . . ."

"I know. That's how I found you. I flew in thirty minutes ago."

Thirty. Whoa. He had come straight here from the airport.

"We've been trying to locate the Arcane team after their last attempt. They went underground after losing you."

That was—wow. That was just wow.

"Their last . . ."

Last.

And then, "Their *last attempt?*" Now my eyes were blazing. "What haven't you been telling me?"

A sad look had him dropping his hand, but he didn't move away. He closed his eyes, standing toe to toe with me. Chest to chest. Forehead resting on mine, and he said softly, "This was their third try."

I hadn't heard that right.

No way.

I couldn't have.

Right?

Third. Try.

Third. Attempt.

This.

This was what it felt like to have the world fall from under your feet, because I dropped.

I was mad. I was pissed, but I was also light-headed.

Seriously light-headed.

My knees buckled and my body went down, but Kash caught me.

"Whoa. Bailey." He grunted from the surprise and swiftness of it, but then he was swinging me up in his arms.

"No, Kash."

"Shh." He shifted me, cradling me, and his one hand smoothed back some of my hair. He pressed my head to the crook of his neck and shoulder. "Come on. I'll take you to my place."

I couldn't process what was happening. My world had been turned upside down for the final time, and I was out.

The booze might've helped.

I felt him move, kicking the door. It was opened from the other side.

"Wha—"

"Call ahead. I want my car brought to the rear. We're going out that way."

Kash was carrying me through the nightclub.

"Mr. Colello." An anxious female, maybe a staff member? "Is everything okay? Should I call for an ambulance?"

"No," Kash clipped out. "I need a clear path to your rear exit. That's it."

"Yes, sir. Certainly, sir."

She rushed off.

The guard veered in close. I heard him say, "Matt is looking for her. He's worried."

"Matt?" Every inch of Kash went rigid underneath me.

"I meant Mr. Francis." A pause. "Sir."

"You'll tell him I have her, and escort him to his own place."

"And when he asks where you're taking her?"

Kash stopped again, rounding with a snap. "Excuse me?"

The guard sounded apologetic. "You know he'll ask, sir. He'll come around to look for her too."

Kash's voice rumbled from his chest, and he started forward again. "Tell him I have her and I'm taking her back to the estate."

"And are you?"

Kash stopped and pivoted back once again.

The guard added, "Sir."

"How the hell is that any of your business?"

He waited.

No answer.

I lifted my head up. The two were in a stare-off. The guard took me in, and his features tightened. He dropped his face, saying, "She's cared for, sir. By others now."

"Fucking hell." Kash's arms tightened under me, his hand digging into my thigh. "You'll relay my message to Mr. Francis, then you're relieved for the night, Helms. Don't come to work for three days. You and I will have a meeting before you're back on duty. Or, I swear to God, I will drop you right now."

I frowned. My head was pounding. I didn't understand the animosity, but Helms dipped his head in an abrupt nod. "Yes, sir." One step back, his eyes flicked up to mine, and he was swallowed up by the crowd. He had stood out before, following me from the upper level. Now he hid.

"What was that about?" I tried to ask. My tongue was heavy, and I mumbled out two of the words to sound like "Whahsssthadabout?"

Kash shifted his hold on me, lifting me higher so he was back to holding me up with only one arm. He said, roughly, "Nothing. Lay your head back. We'll be there in a few minutes."

"This way, Mr. Colello." That same female from before.

I saw it was the girl who had given me the free drink. She was extending her hand toward a back hallway, a clipboard in hand, an earpiece in place. She met my gaze for a second, swallowing, and looked away.

All these people clambered under Kash. No one had spoken against him, no one—until tonight, and he got suspended from his job for three days.

A shiver went through me.

Feeling my reaction, Kash was moving down the hallway, but he turned so his eyes could catch mine. His face was right there. One move and our lips would touch. One brush. He frowned, his eyes dipping down to my lips, staying there.

"This way, Mr. Colello." The same girl. She slipped past us, opening another door.

No one was down here, until we turned into the second hallway. Voices echoed across from us. We were in a kitchen area. Kash was following her, walking us through a maze of hallways and doors.

He held me until she opened the last door, a cool breeze from the night greeting us.

"Mr. Colello."

"Mr. Colello."

Two voices greeted us, both male.

A door was opened. Kash ducked, holding me, and placed me in a backseat. He shifted me over so I was in the middle before he climbed in next to me. The employee had followed us, and she waited off to the side.

Kash dug into his pocket and pulled out some money. He held it out. "Thank you for your discretion."

"Of course, sir." She stepped forward, took the money, and her eyes slid to mine again. "Feel better, miss."

I sank down onto the seat, my body molding to it, and my eyelids were closing again. Quinn's rejection. The drinks. The shock of Kash showing up.

I wanted to sleep for days.

The door still hadn't shut, and Kash was saying something short and clipped to the woman. She dipped her head down, stepping back. "I'll see to it myself." Then she was gone, going back into the club. The back door was shut. A front door opened. A driver got in, and we were off. There was a car in front of us. As it turned, we turned. As it slowed, we slowed. There were other guards in there, or so I was assuming.

Kash waited a beat before turning to me. He took one look, and all the tension lifted from him as well. He reached for me at the same time I went to him, climbing into his lap.

I had missed him. I mean, I hadn't missed him.

I was letting him hold me. Yeah. I was doing *him* a favor.

It wasn't long, maybe twelve minutes or so, until we pulled into a basement garage of an apartment building. When the SUV stopped in front of some elevators, Kash nudged me. "Bailey?"

His arms felt so warm, so strong. Sheltered and protected. That's what I felt, along with a whole host of butterflies and tingles that I knew I shouldn't be feeling. My blood was on a slow boil, getting warmer and warmer the longer I stayed in his lap. It was so hard, my eyelids felt like a pound of cement were on them, but I forced them open and tipped my head back to look at him.

Then I paused.

God.

Beautiful. Dangerous. Mysterious. And I was in his arms.

My tongue swelled up. A whole host of sensations were sending my body on vibrate. Gone was the exhaustion, in that mere look, as his eyes were smoldering down at me. I felt zapped, as if he had touched my chest and gave me an electric jolt.

I was breathless too.

Unthinking, unable to think, my hand raised, and I touched his cheek. "You're back."

He stilled, blinking a second, then a slow grin spread—and holy hell. That smile, in that moment, in the way he was looking at me, holding me, and my heart was stampeding out of my chest. My whole blood just *wooshed* over itself, a wave crashing hard on me, and I was sputtering in its wake, in *his* wake.

I wanted him.

"I came back."

The world went away.

It was only Kash and me, and his eyes went to my lips, holding there. I was yearning for it, for him. I wanted to feel his mouth on mine. I wanted to feel more, so much more, but his mouth first and foremost.

I was lifting up.

He was leaning down—

His phone started ringing.

Just like that, the spell was broken.

Kash's entire body turned into a cement block. He drew in a sharp breath before turning his head away from mine. He warned, darkly, "Someone needs to be in the hospital or a body bag, otherwise I'm going to be putting them in the hospital or a body bag myself."

An awkward cough as we waited. Then, "It's Mr. Francis. Matthew. Sir."

"What is it?" Kash clipped out, a savage growl right behind it.

"There's a *problem* at the penthouse."

"Fuck."

Exactly.

I hated it, my entire body was protesting, but I was sitting up. Feeling me move, Kash helped deposit me beside him. He turned his back to the guard, looking at me straight on.

"You want to come with me?"

There was no real question there. "Hell yes."

I was suddenly awake, so awake I didn't think I'd sleep again.

He closed his eyes, groaning again before shifting back in his seat. "Take us to Matt's."

TWENTY-SEVEN

We pulled up to the front of the Francois Nova. As soon as the SUV paused in front of the circling glass doors, Kash didn't wait for his guard. He opened the door and whisked me out of there. The doorman just barely had time to nod a greeting to us.

Once in the lobby, I felt the attention from everyone in there. It wasn't locked down like it had been when we were there before. Hotel guests. The concierge staff. The front desk attendant, who I saw was the same as when we had stayed. His eyes were wide, taking us in. Kash was moving so fast that the guards had to run in to get ahead of us. Kash dropped my hand but linked our index fingers. He turned, heading to the elevators. A guard got there just in time, and the doors opened so we didn't have to wait. Kash dropped my finger, his hand going to the back of my elbow.

Once we were in, the guard came with us.

As we rose to the penthouse floor, his thumb began rubbing the inside of my elbow.

Good Lord. It was doing all sorts of things to me.

The doors opened. We arrived, and raucous laughter, yelling, cheering, and bass-heavy music hit us full blast. Something illegal was being smoked, too.

"Come on! Drink it. Down it."

Kash's eyes narrowed.

He let go of my elbow, striding forward. The guards went with him, though they didn't look like they were there to protect him. The room opened to a wide living room. Kash motioned for one of the guards.

The guard walked to the entertainment console and the music was cut.

"Hey!"

Matt was lounging on one of his white leather couches, his pants unzipped and pulled down to show the top of his hip bones. He was shirtless, his hair ruffled, and he was holding a joint. He was in the process of bringing it to his mouth for a drag when the music cut. It took a full second before that filtered in, and he turned, looking, looking, then lighting up when he saw Kash.

"Hey! It's Kashy. Hey, Kashy."

His eyes were dilated, and he couldn't even sit up. He was sluggish. After he couldn't get up on the second attempt, he just let gravity pull his body back down into the couch. His feet never moved, outstretched on the floor. The girl sitting beside him only had on a bra and panties. Nothing else. And she wasn't the girl he'd been necking with at the club.

The rest of the room was filled.

Chester and Tony were in similar stances, but on a back couch in the corner. And unlike Matt, who didn't have a girl actively sucking his dick, theirs were out. There was Matt's club girl. Her lips were guzzling on Chester's dick. The girl sucking Tony's dick might've been a staff member from the club. I wasn't sure. I wasn't looking too close.

A few other girls, in varying states of dress, were still dancing, hair extensions in the air, bottles of booze waving around.

"Jesus Christ, Matt." Kash stepped further into the room, taking everything in. "We just left the club twenty minutes ago."

Matt's smile was sloppy drunk as he reached for a beer on the table by him. "I was getting fucked up before we left the club." He frowned, remembering something . . . something . . . something—and he searched, finding me. "Hey! It's my sis—"

"Stop!" Kash cut him off, taking two steps to his couch. He grabbed the joint, stuffed it out, and knocked the beer out of Matt's hand. "Everyone out. Now!"

The girls whined.

Kash motioned to his guards. "Get 'em out."

There was no arguing with him.

One girl was still swinging her arms around. Now she was tripping. She was falling backward, and she fell right into the pool that extended out from Matt's room and went over a glass-bottomed patio, so it looked like you were swimming over the edge of the building.

Water splashed all over the floor, but then she was up and smoothing her hair back. Her vodka smashed on the floor, and her bra had fallen off from the impact with the water. Two inflatable boobs stood straight out. "Whooey." She laughed, falling back to float on her back. Her arms stretched out in the water. "This is nice." Her eyes were closing.

Kash motioned to one of the guards. "Get her."

The guy waded into the water, starting to pick her up and pull her to the edge. She stiffened. "Hey. What? Who are you? No! What are you doing? No!"

She was twisting around, or trying.

He ignored her, carrying her to the edge and lifting her up. Another guard was there, a large towel in hand, waiting for her. And with a quick *woosh*, the towel was wrapped around her and she was picked up, being carried out.

Matt's girl started to slide to her knees, but Kash wrapped his arm around her waist. He picked her up.

"Hey! Wait! What—"

Kash kept that arm around her waist, holding her like she was a two-year-old having a temper tantrum. Kicking. Flailing. Wriggling around.

"*Hey!*" she screeched.

"Kashy." Matt rubbed a hand up his stomach, scratching at his chest, and yawned. "That's not cool. This isn't cool at all. Wait. Where's my sis—"

"Shut up. Stop almost messing up."

Kash yelled from across the room, as a guard took the girl from him, carried her to wherever they were taking these people.

"What?" Now Matt was clueing in, blinking rapidly, and starting to try and sit up.

Kash was crossing the room, back toward Matt, but he snapped his fingers, pointing at Chester and Tony's couch. "Out, both of you fucks."

"Hey," Chester started to growl, but the guards were back. They snatched up the girls.

I tried to avert my eyes in time, but to no avail. Two semihard dicks were in the air. Neither Chester nor Tony moved to cover them up. Tony seemed confused about what was happening. Chester was trying to get up from the couch, but like Matt, he kept falling down.

"I'm going to fuck you up, Colello." That was what he resorted to.

Kash ignored him, ducking down to Matt.

I never would've imagined it if I hadn't watched it with my own eyes, but in two moves he had lifted my brother up as if he weighed nothing. Tucking his shoulders against Matt's chest, he pushed one arm behind Matt's back and tucked him in, standing back up. My brother was dangling over Kash's back like a doll.

"Agh—ugh."

The pressure to his sternum must've been enough. Matt opened his mouth and the vomit was starting to spew. Kash grimaced, but ignored that too. He nodded to his guards, who were approaching Chester and Tony with large buckets of water. In two seconds, both had been thrown at the boys.

They shot to their feet, cursing, sputtering, and glaring.

The dicks were still waving around. Now their jeans slid to the floor. Chester bent to grab his, trying to shake off one arm, but he took a step forward, got tangled, and down he fell. Two guards yelled and rushed to the rug that Chester had fallen on.

They had him rolled up, just like they'd done with the pool girl, and he was hoisted over both their shoulders and taken out.

Tony was the last one, and he stood there, glazed over. "Wha—where'd everyone go?"

The guards waited for Kash's command, but as he carried Matt to a back room, Kash turned. "They went to the next party. Tuck it in and get out, Cottweiler."

"Huh?" But, shrugging, he grabbed his pants up.

No one had shoes on. No one had a shirt on. And they all left that way. The guards were picking up their clothes when Kash yelled for me.

"Back here."

I'd been gawking. I couldn't help it. This whole scene was something I never could've imagined, but there it was. Proof my brother's partying ways weren't made up in the tabloids.

"Bailey!"

"Coming." Making sure I didn't step on glass or—gross, there was a condom there—anything I could get an STD from, I found Kash and Matt in a back bathroom. Matt was kneeling at the toilet, puking. Kash was leaning against the bathroom sink. His hands were resting on the counter's edge, one foot crossed over the other, and he locked me in with a hooded gaze.

"Hey." I was hesitant here. I wasn't sure of my place.

"Hey back." Motioning to Matt, he added, "I'm going to have to stay and get him sober. Do you want to stay or would you like a ride back to my place?"

"I . . ." I wasn't sure what I should do.

A rather nasty gurgle left Matt, his back arching from the force of it.

I sighed, leaning against the door frame. "It doesn't feel right, leaving."

"This isn't your mess. Trust me. I'd suggest finding one of his guest rooms and curling up, but I can't promise they haven't already been used tonight."

I winced at his insinuation.

"Shit, Kash. Twenty minutes."

That's all the time they would've been here, if even that.

Unless Matt left me at the club . . .

"The rooms are probably safe. Looks like they used his main room for the partying."

Matt paused in his puking and looked up. Sweaty, pale, and a green tinge coming to his face, he smiled up at me. "Hey, it's my sister. Kashy, it's my sister. Look." He tried to pat Kash on the leg and point, but Kash shifted out of Matt's reach. Swinging in the air, Matt didn't register, and he beamed back up at me. "I'm so happy that you came to party with me tonight. Next time will be better. Promise."

When I said he beamed at me, I meant he was smiling stupidly at the wastebasket. He reached out, patting it. "You're a good sister. Smart, too." Then he moaned, going back to resting his head over the open toilet.

We were still there five minutes later, when a guard came to the door.

"Everything is picked up."

Kash nodded, running a brisk hand down his face. "Have staff clean everything, bedrooms too."

"On it." He indicated Matt. "A guest complained from three floors below about the music. Hotel staff didn't want to deal with it, called it in to one of our guys right away. That was the call. He barred them from the room so they weren't sure what was going on in here."

Kash scowled. "Guards should never be barred from a room. That defeats the purpose of why they're paid."

"Agreed." He flinched. "I'll talk to my men tomorrow."

"You'll suspend those that fucked up. Helms as well. I told him to take off for three days."

"Sir?"

"There should be no emotional attachments. They're hired to do their jobs, that's all."

The guard was confused, but he dipped his head down. "Yes, sir." He hesitated again. "Orders for the rest of the night?"

Kash's gaze had fallen to me, holding there. He asked the guard, "Quinn didn't want her at the estate?"

The guard stood up tall, reacting to his question. He coughed before answering, "Uh. Yes. Those were her orders."

A storm was brewing. Something uneasy passed in the air. The guard felt it. I felt it, the hairs on the back of my neck standing up. Even Matt paused, confused, as he turned to look at us again. He mistook the tub for us this time, and nodded, his eyes glossing over before he turned back to the toilet.

"Sir?"

Kash snapped out of his thought, shaking his head. "Normal rotations. I'd like an on-call nurse to come up. She'll relieve us from Matt."

"Yes, sir."

The guard left immediately after.

Not a word was spoken over the next hour.

Kash moved to grab some water for Matt, but returned to half standing/half leaning against the counter by the toilet. I slid down to the floor, hugging my knees to my chest, and after thirty minutes, I rested my head on my knees. When Matt took a breather, Kash would hand him the water with instructions to take only a few sips. He'd take the water when Matt was done, hand him a washcloth to wipe his face, and take it back before Matt lurched over the toilet again.

Judging from the almost bored expression on Kash's face, I had a feeling this was normal. For them.

Once Matt stopped, Kash and a guard carried him to his bed. He was gently laid down, which surprised me. Another guy might've just tossed Matt in, but Kash and the guard didn't.

He was propped on his side. The water on the stand. A fresh washcloth next to it and a towel folded up. Kash put the garbage right underneath Matt so he could lean over and vomit if he needed. At the same time, the guard was positioning Matt's head so a towel was underneath his face, over the pillow and bed. His knees were bent forward.

When they were done, they stood back and studied him.

The guard glanced at Kash. "Leave the pants on?"

Kash grunted. "I'm not taking them off." He side-eyed the guard. "You game?"

"Is that part of my job description? Undressing a detox patient?"

For the first time that night, Kash's mouth flickered in a grin. It was grim and still dark—his theme since he got to the club that night—but it was there.

Oh boy. My heart jumped at the sight.

But Kash was saying, "I think we're good. Go get the nurse."

The guard left, and Kash pulled up the sheet over Matt. The room plunged into blackness, and a second later we could hear Matt's deep and even breathing.

A hand found mine, our fingers linking, and Kash tugged me from the room.

A nurse was standing in the hallway, coming from the living room. She paused, taking us in. Her eyes enlarged at the sight of Kash, but she didn't say anything. A faint blush came to her cheeks. I didn't blame her.

He stopped, giving her instructions to check on Matt.

Then we were leaving. Kash went to the elevator. And just as when we were leaving the club, the SUV was waiting for us. We ducked in, slid in, and the vehicle took us to another underground parking lot. We got out, repeated all the same motions, until the doors opened up to what I knew was Kash's downtown home. This was the one he mentioned before, where he kept all his stuff that he wouldn't trust around a stranger.

I was tongue-tied, realizing what he'd just shown me by bringing me here.

Kash trusted me. When had that happened?

He dropped my hand when we left the elevator, waiting for
the doors to slide shut again. The guard went back down, and
Kash was keying in some sort of code. A green light positioned
above the frame clicked over to red, then Kash turned and took
me in.

His hair was messed up. There were rings under his eyes,
around his mouth. He was exhausted, to put it bluntly. But those
eyes were wide awake and filled with lust. They were nearly black
as he started for me, stalking to me.

One foot in front of the other.

I braced myself, excited, thrilled, and so scared. He paused
just before touching me. "We weren't exactly friendly before I left.
That was a week ago. Since then . . ." His gaze moved up and
down me, inspecting me, making me feel naked before him. He
whispered, moving closer, his hand coming out to touch my shirt.
"Things have accelerated tonight. I need to know you're okay
with that."

It wasn't framed as a question. Or a request.

I licked my lips, my mouth suddenly drying up.

Jerking my head in a stiff nod, I wrung out, "So okay with
that."

His hand fisted in my shirt and he pulled me to him. And
tipping my head back, raising my lips—his mouth was on mine.

TWENTY-EIGHT

Fire.

I expected hot and commanding and that's what I got. My arms around his neck. My legs around him. The perfect pressure, and I was whimpering.

Flames enveloped me. Every inch of me was blazing.

Then he was gentling his kiss, soothing the pressure until the lightest and most tender graze whispered over me.

Goose bumps broke out over my skin from that last kiss. Holy hell.

I was panting.

He was pulling away.

And then—I was waking up.

I woke up. It was dark out. My head was foggy, but bits of a conversation were waking me.

"Yes, we did. . . . No. . . . No." A pause. "She is, yes."

I lay back down. God. I had been dreaming about last night, about that kiss. The first kiss. Holy crap. That first kiss had been epic, and I wanted to forget, then experience it all over again. Please. Could that happen?

A harsh exclamation from the other room. "You want to see her, come and see her."

Reality dumped over me like a bucket of cold water. Kash was talking to my father.

Man.

Lying there, after that had happened, the last few days, and those words just crept back in. *Idol. Father.* Then, *That guy who hurt my mom.* And somehow in the last three days he'd become *father* again.

I expelled some air, blowing a strand of hair off my forehead. It went up, paused, and landed back down. Story of my life. Up, up, up, hold, and slam back down. Okay, okay. I was being a bit dramatic, but Quinn's eviction notice stung.

Fuck it.

I sat up, scooting to the edge of the bed, and listened in. It was easy enough to do. Kash had left his door open a crack. Just a crack, but enough. He would've heard me if I got up for the bathroom, and the only other course of action would be to fall back asleep, but I was awake. In fact, I was wired awake. I had enough energy bouncing in me to go on a full all-nighter on the computer—and just like that, I was missing working on my code fierce.

"You might want to remember that it was your wife who asked for her to be removed from the premises. . . . Yes. Not me. Your wife." Another beat of silence on Kash's side. "Gladly. I'd love to have a conversation with Quinn. . . . What? No. For fuck's sake, Peter, think about what you're saying." He drew in a sharp breath, pausing.

I could see him through the crack, and as if he felt my eyes, his head lifted. His body went rigid, then he came right for me. I didn't have time to hide or even fall back and pull the blanket over my body, even with my feet still on the floor.

He was there, pushing open the door, and everything in him softened. He took me in, those same eyes warming.

"Peter," he murmured, the bite leaving him. "Peter." Nope. It was bit, just a little. "We'll talk later." He didn't say good-bye, just hit the End button and tossed his phone onto an ottoman in the corner.

Folding his arms over his chest, he leaned his shoulder against the door frame. "How are you feeling?"

Memories of last night hit me.

We kissed. We did more than kiss, and Kash was a phenomenal kisser. He was a phenomenal everything. How he touched me. How he whispered to me. How he made me feel loved, worshipped, satisfied.

My face was heating up, just remembering, and also remembering how I had wanted more. That was a theme by the end of the night. I just wanted more, but we didn't have sex. After making me groan and moan for two hours, Kash eased back and shifted so he was holding me.

I fell asleep like that. I wished I had woken, just to experience his arms again. Seeing them now, remembering how firm they felt, my mouth was watering.

"I'm good." My voice came out hoarse.

The corner of his mouth lifted up, as if he was reading my thoughts. "Good. I need to check on Matt. Security called that he's at another party. We're supposed to collect him and take him back to the estate. Apparently Quinn is worried about her stepson."

"*Another* party?"

"This is Matt. If he's bored, if he's upset, if he's unhappy—he parties." That grin faded. "Look. We didn't talk about Quinn last night, but you have to know that if you want to be in this family, it'll be a fight. She's not going to make it easy for you. None of them will, except Seraphina and Cyclone."

Oh. We were going serious.

"Matt's been nice."

"Matt's been playing with you."

My mouth opened. "What?" No way. "That's bullshit."

His eyebrows went up. His words were hurting me, but he didn't care. He was putting it out there bluntly. "It's true. He thought you were a new toy of mine, and he wanted to mess with you like a cat does with a mouse. Then he got wind of your computer skills and put two and two together. But if he's acting like he cares, he's lying. He's playing you."

"Why would he do that?"

Damn. That was burning more than I wished it had been.

Liability. That's what I was. No feelings. Right? I could do that.

I was already failing.

"To get at your father. Peter's been after Matt to do more with the company. He doesn't want his oldest son to be a fuckup—Peter's words, because that's what he thinks of Matt. He doesn't mean it how it comes out, but anyone who's not doing computer work is a fuckup. Only reason he's off my back is because I can physically hurt him if I want. Your dad is . . ." He shook his head side to side, choosing his words. "He's like a conceited, glorified nerd with power. There's a nerd in him, but it's mixed with all the other crap that makes him hard to deal with sometimes.

"Matt is not a nerd. He's never been a nerd. He's smart, but he grew up with social skills and getting pussy and—you know the drill. You saw it last night. Peter doesn't understand his kids. Not Seraphina, who has a heart of gold and is shy, or even Cyclone, who *does* get the computer stuff. The similarities end there. Cyclone has ADHD, and as soon as he starts one thing, he's off to another. And now Peter is learning more about the daughter he didn't have in his life, and he's not liking it. Matt's going to capitalize on it. He's loving that he's the family member in your ear. Gives him something that Peter wants; it'll make him back off your brother. Or that's what Matt thinks."

Another one-two punch. Complete with a roundhouse to the face.

I was done, and down for the count.

Jesus.

"Thanks for that." I cut my eyes to the side.

"Hey." That word had me looking up before I could catch myself. Kash's mouth was pressed in a line. "Peter's not liking himself right now, because you're the kid who's like him the most. And he really hates that you spent the night here with me." A smirk tugged back at those lips. "And he really, *really* hates that he can't order me to stay away from you, because I'm the one protecting you right now. He thinks you're a kid still."

I bristled at that. "I'm not a kid."

"You're a woman, and you're hot, and you're smart, and you have a sarcastic side to you that I want to come out more. I like your fight and I like your sass and you gotta cement up those walls if you want to hang in with this world. They're all wolves, Bailey. They're not nice like your mom. They're not Mrs. Jones, who called the police at seeing a mysterious vehicle sitting in your driveway. Yes, I read the police notes. They're not going to look out for you. The kids, maybe, if they were taught that way. They're not being taught that way. And Matt, he's too angry at your dad to see that beneath the layer where he's using you, he actually is starting to care about you." He frowned. "But don't expect him to tunnel down and start acting all nice like. It's not in him. It's not the world they come from."

They.

Not we.

All his words were making me feel raw, but I focused on that one word. "Aren't you one of them too?"

He paused, his eyes moving away for the first time since seeing I was awake. "I'm half in, half out. I come from a whole other dark and twisted world that makes your father's world look like it's made of cotton candy. And no . . ." He shook his head, seeing I was about to ask another question. "That's it for sharing time. Get dressed. We gotta go collect your brother. Again."

Well then.

Consider me yanked up by the bootstraps, a firm pat on the ass, and sent on my way.

I went to the bathroom, then saw my newly washed clothes folded and waiting for me on the counter, alongside a cup of coffee, and some of that annoyance dissipated.

Only *some* of it.

I didn't know why Kash even told me what he had, if he was telling the truth about Matt, or how what we did together would play out, but this was the Kash from earlier. Or maybe this was the Kash he had to be when he was in work mode? Maybe? I didn't know. I just knew I liked the Kash from last night. That Kash—my gaze paused on the coffee—was the kind to bring me a cup of coffee before I even asked.

Who was I kidding?

I was in *way* over my head.

TWENTY-NINE

We found Matt in a similar state as the night before, surrounded by his friends, in a tent set apart from the rest of the party. Instead of a nightclub, it was a day party.

Matt's eyes were glazed over and his head flipped up when he saw us. "Hey. Look. It's my family."

Kash frowned. "You vomited for a full hour last night."

"Yeah." Matt hiccupped, smiling wide. His eyes were dilated. "Thanks for the IV drip. Your nurse hooked me up and it made me feel good enough, I thought, *Why not?*" He started laughing, Chester and another friend joining in. "Am I right? Right, Nuts?"

Chester stopped laughing. "Shut up, dickhead."

Matt just laughed harder. So did the other guy friend.

Chester shot him a dark look. The friend didn't care. Even the girl laughed.

I was trying to remember her name. Fleur! It was Fleur.

How'd I forget *that* name?

Chester shot her a look too. "Shut it, PussyPedal."

She gasped. "Ass!"

He lifted a shoulder, smirking. "Karma, honey. Karma."

"Kash! Kash!" Matt was ignoring his friends, stumbling over to Kash. Slapping a hand on his shoulder, Matt didn't notice the look that Kash gave the hand. He was waving a tequila bottle in the air again. "Guys. You all have no idea what Kash does for our family. No idea."

"And they won't, because you're done."

Kash nodded to the guards, and like last night, they went

into motion. The girls were herded out of there. Nuts, Pussy-Pedal, and the friend were next. Kash plucked the bottle from Matt's hand and tossed it outside the tent. It fell, spilling on the ground, but then was snatched up right away. A guard was walking away with it.

"That's the second time in eighteen hours that you've threatened to spill secrets."

It took a second for me to register the quiet warning from Kash, but once I heard it, chills traveled over my spine. I snapped my gaze to him, and there it was. It wasn't prominent, but it was simmering and it was deep.

Kash was furious.

Matt scoffed, his eyes still wild. "Whatever. What secrets? I don't know anything. Dear old Dad doesn't share shit with me. You don't, either. I don't have a clue what's going on." His head was swinging around, swinging, swinging, and it caught on me. His eyes narrowed.

It was then that I saw it. The mean streak in Matt, the one Kash had warned me about last night.

"Except her."

His eyes were calculating now, a bitter hint just underneath.

"I know her secret. Quinn hates that I know." He took another unsteady step toward me, and as I moved back, the hairs on the back of my neck standing up, Kash moved an inch so he was between us. His movement was slight, but it was there.

Matt kept on. "And Dad." He threw his head back, a shrill laugh ripping from him. "God. It's the best. Dad hates that she's here. Hates it." He looked back and his eyes narrowed once more, a cruel giddiness showing. "You think you had it bad, Bailey? You didn't. You had it good. A loving mom. None of the bullshit we deal with. Yeah, yeah, poor little girl whose daddy abandoned her. Right? That's what you think in your head, but you're so wrong. *Wrong.*" His nostrils flared. "You had it good. Like you won't be secured for life with that brain of yours. Fuck.

I bet you could write a program that'll make millions in just a day. Not me."

He leaned toward me, but Kash had inserted himself almost completely between Matt and me. His arm went up. My brother still leaned forward, hate flooding his gaze, the drunkenness and wildness dissipating. "I'm the dumb one. I had the dumb mom. Not this one." He clamped a hand on Kash's shoulder, who stiffened underneath it.

Matt wasn't done. "Not Seraphina or Cyclone. Shit. Quinn might be a cold prude, but she's still smart. You know?" He paused again, thinking, and laughed to himself. "No, no. You wouldn't know, would you? You don't know anything about us. Nothing. You know our name. You know your daddy, what the magazines and websites and shows tell you about him, but you don't really know him. There's so much you have no clue about. No clue."

He was fading. He turned, his eyes downward now. "She doesn't. Does she, Kash? She has no clue about you, about your family, about—"

"Enough," Kash said. "You have two choices. Walk out there with us, or get carried out."

"Why?" Matt's nostrils flared as he took one large sniff.

"Mama Quinn wants a family day." Kash's words were short. "All of us."

Matt rolled his eyes upward. He swung a hand out again, gesturing to me. "Not her. She's not included, and you know it. What are you going to do with her?"

"Her" was standing right here.

"She's coming with."

Matt studied Kash, looking at a face I couldn't see because Kash was still mostly in front of me, and whatever he saw, he began laughing. He slapped his knee. "This'll be good." He bobbed his head, mind made up. "All right. You don't have to knock me out. I'll come willingly. Anything for those fireworks." His eyes swung my way on that last word.

I wasn't getting a good feeling about this.

"Let's go." Kash stepped farther back, his arm extending toward the tent. He wanted Matt to lead the way, and noting it, Matt mumbled, "Yeah, yeah." His hand fisted in his hair a second before falling to his side as he headed for the tent's entryway. Hearing the end of our conversation, a guard opened the flap, and Matt was able to step right through.

He didn't wait, veering in the direction of the cars. He had to right himself a few times before walking into someone, but Kash commanded, "Flank him." And the guards left us alone, hurrying to close ranks about Matt. They steered him toward the cars.

I was waiting, but Kash didn't move to follow. He was watching Matt's progress, still from inside the tent. The flap was being held open by one remaining guard.

Not knowing what was going on, I started forward.

Kash caught my arm. "Hold up."

"What is it?"

I wasn't feeling good about this—or, well, about any of it. Matt was mean, seriously mean. Hearing about it, being warned about it by Kash, hadn't fully prepared me for what I saw just now. It was like walking on a bed of embers. I had no idea where to step to go forward, and I was starting to become wary about Kash, too. It seemed there were even more secrets he was hiding.

He closed his eyes for a second, rubbing at his forehead, before he looked at me. There was exhaustion in there, but also the same wariness I was feeling. "I need to know how you're doing."

"With what?"

He nodded behind me, his hand going into his pocket. "With Matt. His attitude. With what he's spilling, or insinuating." A new light shone from him, bright and yearning, and before he blinked it out, he stepped close to me. His head dropped so he could see me better. Only a few feet separated us, so he also dropped his tone and I could still hear. "Matt is more bark than bite, but his bark can hurt. I've witnessed it before, and he's doing it again. These guys . . ." He looked past my shoulder, his gaze hardening. "They don't grow up wanting things. They grow up being bored. They don't have normal worries like the rest of us."

Us?

"And because of that, they like games and they like toys and they like to get their kicks from places they shouldn't." His eyes found mine again, a warning in them. "Matt's not intending to hurt you, but he's not being considerate, either. He won't see how he's battered his toy until it's destroyed. Then he'll feel bad. Then he'll stop and think on what he shouldn't have done, but not till then. It's been his way since he was a child."

A heaviness came to my shoulders, pushing me down.

I thought about what he was saying, but I wasn't worried about Matt. I really wasn't. My brother didn't have the capability to destroy me.

Kash, on the other hand . . .

"Matt's nothing more than a spoiled little grown boy," I said. "There's good and bad in there, but he needs to learn to make the good more than the bad." My tone was dry, because that wasn't my job. It wouldn't be my job. "I can handle him."

"But?"

Kash moved even closer.

"I asked you once if you were head of my father's security." I tipped my head back as Kash finally, finally closed in. One foot gone. Six inches melted away. He was there, right there in front of me, and his eyes were looking right into me. "You said you weren't. Did you lie to me?" I remembered what else Matt had said. "Matt said *his* mother was dumb, but not yours." I waited, seeing the wariness flare forward in his eyes. I kept on. "What about your father? Your mother? What was your family like?"

Kash didn't answer. His gaze remained locked on mine, and I couldn't see anything.

He locked me out, and after thirty seconds, I started to swing forward to the tent's opening. I took one step before that same hand took my arm and pulled me back. His arm wrapped around my waist and he maneuvered us to the side, out of sight of anyone looking in. He pulled me against him, and his head dipped down.

"My father was a good man, but he was simple. And my mom . . ." He stopped, his jaw clenching. "The Francis family consider me family. I grew up with them. I slept in their home. But I am not one of them. I'm a whole other different animal." He paused, rubbing a hand over his face.

Secrets were popping up. Anywhere I looked, it was a secret trap door to history I was being warned about.

Taking Kash's hand, I squeezed it. "I can adapt to anything. Us Hayes women are known for that talent. Whatever comes, I can handle it."

Yes. Matt had a mean streak. Everyone did in this world.

Yes. I was missing Chrissy and my old life something fierce.

Yes, there were reasons I wasn't going anywhere. I had three siblings to love and to know.

Kash . . .

But there was one thing none of them knew, either. Not fully. Not really. Not yet.

Me.

THIRTY

I was ready. Battle hat on. War paint applied. Figuratively.

I was prepped and ready to destroy anyone or anything coming at me—except water. I wasn't prepared to be soaked by a water balloon the second I stepped out of Kash's car.

"I got Bailey!" Giggles and shrieks were heard as, looking up, I had a one-second glimpse of a pale/red streak running back behind the gate that surrounded the pool. I could hear Cyclone yelling, laughing so hard he could barely get the words out. "I got her, you guys. Bailey's soaked." And then, "Banzai!"

"Cyclone!"

"No, Cyclone!"

"*Ahh!*"

A slap was heard all the way out here, before being drowned out by a massive amount of splashing. Chairs were shoved back. Feet were heard running. Kash and I looked at each other before we both took off sprinting, but when we got to the open gate, Cyclone's head was above the water and he was laughing. The tips of his ears were red, matching his swimsuit. He pointed at all of us standing on the edge, looking at him. "I got you all good."

"You just belly flopped hard." Seraphina was glaring at him, her little hands in fists at her side.

He lifted his little shoulders up, floating to his back. "It's all good. I can handle the pain." He looked at Kash. "Right, Kash? What's a little pain here and there?"

Everyone winced at the redness already showing on his tummy.

Kash drawled out, "Not stupid pain. A belly flop is stupid pain unless it was an accident."

"It wasn't an accident." Marie was gritting her teeth. Her arms were crossed over her chest, her cheeks reddening to be almost as bright as Cyclone's shorts. "You get in here, little boy. Enough running around for you. You hear me?"

He looked ready to argue, then began dog-paddling to the ladder. Just as he got there, another *woosh* sound was heard behind us as someone yelled out, "*Cannonball!*"

Quinn was standing on the opposite side of the pool, a couple standing with her. All three of them scrambled out of the way just as Matt came in, his clothes still on. He jumped high, tucked his knees to his chest, and splashed everyone.

Most of the water hit the couple next to Quinn.

The woman screamed, but she was laughing. "Matthew!"

The man schooled his features tight, disapproving. They were dressed in regular clothes, as was Quinn—not for a pool party. The woman was still laughing as she stepped away from the pool.

Quinn moved forward, her face sharpening. "Foresight, Matthew. The Bonhams and I are not dressed to get wet. Notice, next time, please."

Wait. What? That was them?

He only smirked, holding the woman's gaze a second longer before looking to Quinn. Kicking back, he said, "I did." Then he tucked back into a somersault, his feet kicking up and splashing Cyclone.

Quinn's mouth was pressed tight. She looked ready for battle. But Cyclone jumped from the ladder *on* top of Matt when his head came back up, and it was on after that. Matt was searching, and he lunged forward, grabbed Seraphina's hand, and toppled her into the water. She screamed, making a mad grab for Marie, who reached for the person next to her, who was Theresa.

All three of them fell into the pool.

During this, Quinn and the couple moved inside. The woman

glanced back, a look on her face that I couldn't quite place as she watched them all in the pool.

"Okay. That's enough. No more Mr. Nice Marie. You, Matthew, are going down," Marie growled.

Theresa had come back to the surface as well.

Marie looked at her, both on the same page, and together they pounced. "Matt's going down! Anyone can help."

"*Yeeeah!*"

Cyclone had crawled up the ladder, but at that war cry he jumped in the water, trying to cannonball his brother. After that, chaos. Complete and total chaos, and I loved it. I was grinning ear to ear. I had to be. I couldn't stop myself.

This. Right here. Fun with siblings—this is why I was here. I didn't care for the real reasons, but if I were one to believe in a higher power, I did in that moment. Gratitude bloomed in my chest, filling me up, and I was a step away from blinking back tears. Good tears.

I was an only child growing up. Me. Chrissy.

I had family near Brookley, but Chrissy was prideful and stubborn. Hella stubborn. No family member was taken up on their offer. Anyone who watched me had to be someone who came into Chrissy's life on her terms, not through family. And while I loved going to school with my cousins, my mom's way put distance between me and them. We didn't know at the time, but we felt it. It felt wrong to yearn to eat supper at my aunt's house when my mom was working the second shift. And when I grew old enough not to have a babysitter, it was me and my computer.

Computers were endless.

There were friends in there, lives in there, daydreams I could create, and it was mine. No one told me who I couldn't or could see. No one put restrictions on me. That was my domain. But this, standing by this pool and hearing Cyclone laugh as Matt pretended to toss him at Seraphina—I was absorbing every possible bit of this domain.

I would continue to, until I was told to go.

"Kash! Bailey!" Cyclone was paddling toward us. "Come in."

I wanted to. God, I wanted to.

Then I felt a hand on my arm.

Looking up, I saw Kash was looking behind me. His glance went rigid before I looked.

Peter Francis stood on the sidewalk that attached the pool area to the area beyond the gates. Behind him, the pathway led back into the house, and it looked like he'd just stepped out as an afterthought. Dark navy dress pants. Loafers. A white-buttoned dress shirt, with even the neck collar buttoned up. He was holding a phone in one hand, a file of papers in the other, and he was standing half turned to go back to the house.

Peter cleared his throat, his eyes still on me. "Kash."

I hadn't looked away.

A second cough, his eyebrows pulled down, and he forced his gaze to the guy behind me. He held up his file. "A word inside?"

There it was. Another meeting of the guy who had helped to form me.

He called a name that wasn't mine.

He asked to see someone who wasn't me.

He turned and went inside, and I was trying to deny how the world caved in on me.

Kash remained beside me, his hand still touching my arm. "You okay?"

I forced myself to nod. I so wasn't, but there was no way in hell they were going to see that. Plastering a smile on my face, I used an old trick I had used when Chrissy would ask if I was happy and I didn't want to hurt her feelings: I thought happy thoughts. Central processing units. Motherboards. A hardware upgrade. Each one made my smile a bit more genuine, and I nodded. "I'm fine."

He didn't move.

"Really, Kash." How to reassure someone 101: offer physical

touch. I touched his arm. Ask how you can help. "Unless you need me?" Offer a gift as well, which I couldn't. So I went down the list. Direct eye contact. A genuine smile on your face, head tilt to cement the look. And lastly, I squeezed his arm back, just a bit.

Then I waited.

His eyes narrowed.

I had a feeling he saw right through my bullshit, but damn, give me an Oscar.

"Yeah. Okay." His mouth flattened. "I'll text you the code for the house, if you need it for some reason."

"Huh?"

He was moving past me. A look back over his shoulder, he smirked at me. "We're staying here tonight."

My eyes got big. Oh. I hadn't expected that.

He saw my surprise and a ghost of a grin teased me before he nodded in the direction of the pool. Leaning in, he said, for my ears only, "I don't give a shit what Quinn wants. I'm here. You're here. That's how it goes. Have fun with them, don't have fun with them. I don't care. Just make sure no one pushes you around."

No pushing around. I bobbed my head up and down as he disappeared from the pool area. I could do that. No problem.

Matt was giving me a look of pity. Marie wasn't looking; her eyes were fixed on Cyclone, who was swimming around her. Theresa was pretending to fend off a splashing Seraphina, though it was more like a dribble coming at her.

Right. I could do this.

Claim my place. That's what Kash was basically saying. Right?

Battle ready. No one was going to push me away or evict me again.

"Bailey." Seraphina had stopped splashing to tread along the deep end of the pool, a hand on Theresa. Her smile—I melted at that smile. She was waving, water dripping down her forehead, and her cheeks were glowing. "Jump in! Matt did, with his clothes."

It struck me later that this was the moment when I was the one to choose.

I wasn't forced somewhere. I wasn't told to leave or coerced to play. I could stay or go. I could've made up some excuse, lame or not, and disappeared to Kash's house. He wouldn't have judged me. No one would have. And I got that when Marie and Theresa both looked up after Seraphina's request. Both had warmed to me during this last week. Marie never said the words, but I saw it now. Finally. There was a welcome in her eyes.

In that moment, I could do what I wanted.

If I jumped in that pool, it was because I was choosing to stay, to continue a relationship with my siblings.

There was no question.

I jumped in.

THIRTY-ONE

Kash joined us an hour later.

He'd changed into swim shorts and sprinted in, doing a full body flip in the air before landing right between Cyclone and Matt. I had no idea how he did it, but he aimed his splash to get Matt right in the face.

I didn't care, because it. Was. Awesome.

Scowling, Matt wiped a hand to clear the water, and then a new battle was on. Matt lost. He lost bad. He'd launch at Kash, who'd evade him, either swimming around Matt or ducking to the side or jumping out of the pool and then get him all over again. After twenty minutes of this—with Cyclone trying to help, but he really only paddled one way then to the other and then he'd turn around all over again, and with Seraphina cheering from the side—Matt couldn't stay mad. It was humiliating, but in the best way. He was no match for Kash.

Kash was half fish.

"Did you have fun, earlier today?" Kash came to my bedroom, his hands in his pockets, as he gave me a hooded look.

"I did, yeah. You?"

We'd come back earlier to shower and change. Quinn had a charity event that Peter was meeting her at, so it was a laid-back sort of dinner again. That meant chicken nuggets or pizza for the main course. I'd just finished changing into leggings and a white top. The top was light enough to be transparent, so I had on a white tank underneath. I wasn't going for dressy, but both shirts had my back exposed, and I was feeling enough of the girly-girl ways to look nice for Kash.

Reaching behind me for a hair tie, I turned back. Kash's eyes were on my ass.

My body heated, and I looked down as I reached up to pull my hair up in a messy bun. I was feeling the butterflies again. I hated those things, but I hadn't felt them in so long.

"You look nice."

He hadn't answered my question.

I lifted my eyes, seeing that his had darkened—and, oh boy, the butterflies fled to all my extremities. I was in for a world of hurt. I just knew it, but I couldn't stop it. He was looking at me that way, I was feeling how I was, and there was only one way we were heading.

I didn't know those secrets he harbored, but I had a feeling this was a rare moment in my life.

I was now here for four people.

"You okay?"

"What?" I tried to remember. Oh, yes. He said I looked nice. "Thank you. You look good too." Because he did, deliciously. Charcoal-gray sweatpants, riding low on his hips, and a white T-shirt.

My blood was heating.

"You're not human."

The words were out before I caught myself. I cringed, hearing them. "I mean—" What *did* I mean?

The ends of his mouth tugged up and there was a faint amount of amusement in those eyes, but he only propped his shoulder against the door frame. His head tilted to the side and he raised an eyebrow in a "Come on" motion.

I groaned. "I mean—" Again. Fuck it. I faced off against him, or I felt like I was. "Why do people in this world deem you as important when the media has no idea who you are?" I motioned to him. "You're hot. Like seriously fuck-my-ovaries hot, and you live with Peter Francis's family. You have a supermodel wanting to date you. How is it that you're not on the gossip sites with Matt? How is it that you say you grew up with this family and you're working to help find the Arcane group who kidnapped me?" The dam broke in me. "You put yourself as an 'us,' when you're not. You're not like me. You're not normal. You're like them." I gestured beyond him, beyond this room. "You're powerful. How do you have the power to tell my biological father what to do? And he listens to you."

I—I had more.

Who was he to make me feel alive? safe? protected?

Who was he to pick me up?

Who was he to make me feel things I shouldn't?

But I couldn't ask any of those. If I did, game over. I'd be giving him everything in me, and I couldn't do that. Everything else had been stripped from me.

I turned away, hugging myself. The tighter I grabbed the back of my arms, the harder I tried to hide.

"Bailey." A soft request from him.

My heart ached. Even that sound from him dug through my pain and pulled on that organ I needed to live. I started shaking my head. I couldn't look at him anymore. I did, I was done. Not now.

I was too exposed.

My insides were twisting around. He wasn't going to tell me. I knew him. I blurted out all those questions for no reason. He wouldn't let me in. He wouldn't share, and I was slowly dying of embarrassment.

I needed to get out. Now. I needed to get away from him.

Retreat. Back up. Run!

"Anyways." Thank goodness, my voice came out chipper and upbeat, so not what I was feeling. I shouldered past him. "I'm hungry. You ready to go?"

I got two steps. His hand touched my arm. I tried to pull free, pretending it wasn't there, but it only tightened, and he drew me back to him. Not all the way to him. Oh no, because that would've helped. I think? Maybe not. He pulled me just enough so it was still mortifying as he was looking down at me. I could feel the concern from his eyes, even though I wasn't looking. I looked, and I'd fold. It was taking everything in me to keep from lifting my head up, so I kept my eyes trained on his chest.

He shifted closer.

So not helping.

His hand began running up and down my arm, soothing, feeling nice, and the flutters were back. Damn it.

"Look."

No. If I did, I was a goner.

"I know things are in a weird place between us."

I wanted to scoff. "Weird" was putting it mildly. But I kept my lips pressed tight. No sound came out.

He tugged me even farther in, until my head was against his chest. That hand moved to my back, and his other arm wrapped around me, resting on the small of my back. He began rubbing up and down.

Did that have to feel so good?

He rested his chin on top of my head, then turned so it was his cheek instead. "I know you have questions about me. I know last night was intense." His arms tightened around me. "I know there's a lot of other shit happening right now. Just, trust me?" He pulled back. His finger was under my chin, and he tipped my face up. Our eyes met. His hand moved to cup my cheek and his thumb smoothed over it. "I want to get these assholes, and then you and me, we'll figure everything out. Okay?"

I didn't know what that meant, but he was so fierce. I whispered back, "Okay."

He dipped his head, his lips finding mine, and I gave in.

I was gone.

THIRTY-TWO

"We are never going to find these kids."

I elbowed Matt later that night, tiptoeing through the mausoleum. Why I was tiptoeing, I had no clue. The seeker in this game didn't need to be secretive, but there we were, at nine at night. After two large pizzas, after *Ferdinand* had been watched, after Marie and Theresa went home, after the night nanny was on duty, Kash had the brilliant idea to play hide-and-seek.

Seraphina and Cyclone squealed and took off.

And two seconds after they were gone, Matt rounded on Kash. "Are you kidding?! You grew up here too. This place has a million hiding spots. And we're trying to get them to bed."

Kash gave him a smug look. "Relax. What do you think happens to a hyper kid after pizza, swimming, a movie, and he has to stay in the same position while waiting to be found? He falls asleep." He smacked the back of Matt's head. "You're *it*."

"Hey!" Matt glared, ducking his head down, but Kash was heading down another hallway. "Hey! Where are you going?"

"Hiding." Kash didn't look back, jogging and turning another corner.

"We are really screwed if we have to find that guy."

Kash's idea was solid. I tapped Matt's wrist, jerking my head forward. "Come on. Kids usually aren't too brilliant about where they hide. Under beds, behind doors, behind a post."

Matt snorted, trailing after me. "You've never played this game with a little genius."

I started to laugh, but then stopped. He was right.

"Yeah. See." Matt was reading my face. "This was a bad idea. It'll take us hours to find 'em, and how do we know if they're still alive by then? They could be hiding in a freezer. Or—"

I clamped a hand over his mouth, and on the echoes of his voice, there it was. Giggles.

Hearing it, Matt's eyebrows shot up.

Turning. Turning. Pinpointing where those giggles came from. Bull's-eye.

Then I crapped myself. The laundry chute.

"Oh my God!" Sprinting to the wall, I flung open the cupboard that led to the laundry chute downstairs.

"Cyclone!" Matt lunged for him.

He was wedged inside the chute, his hands and feet braced against the other side so he didn't fall. "Aw, man. Seriously? You guys found me too quick." And with a quick grin, just as Matt's arms started to go for under his arms, he let go.

"*Cyclone!*"

We heard a "Catch me later, losers!" all the way down, until a thud.

"Curt!" Matt yelled down.

I was right next to him. "Cyclone!"

I couldn't—*ohmygodohmygodohmygod*—and then Kash hollered up, "I got him."

"Fuck's sakes. How'd he know?"

Kash answered Matt. "Little punk found me one time hiding in the same spot." He was laughing. "I hadn't fully filled out by then. Can't believe he remembered."

I couldn't get air in for a full beat. Then I lost it, curling my hands over the edge and leaning down, "Some of us are human, Kash! We can't scale buildings and jump over fences and we don't keep all our limbs if we fall down a two-story laundry chute."

Matt's lips pressed together.

"I'm fine, Bailey! I mean it." Did he have to sound so happy, too?

I replied to Cyclone. "Just be safe!"

"I will. Promise, promise, promise."

Matt whispered, "That's the ultimate promise in this house. He'll be careful."

A second later, from Kash: "We're going to hide again. Come find us."

My phone buzzed in my pocket. It was Kash.

I had security send me the footage. Seraphina is already asleep in the movie room. Go and have a drink with Matt in the bar. Be there as soon as Cy falls asleep.

Relief flooded me. I nudged Matt, showing him. "This is why adults should always have a plan in every game." Then, "You guys have your own bar?"

How had I missed that in the tour?

It was an actual bar. A long, sleek counter ran down the length of the wall.

Matt went behind it, pouring a drink. He slid it over to me, nodding at one of the stools. "The most family time we've had has been this week." He leaned back against the wall, pointing his drink to me. "Because of you."

"You serious?"

He nodded, slowly. "Why do you think Ser and Cyclone took to you so fast? Marie stays longer. Theresa sticks around. I'm here. Kash was around today. It's all been you."

"You called him Curt before. Is that Cyclone's name?"

I knew, but I wanted to actually be told that. It seemed like information that should've been spoken, not read on a computer screen or in a file.

A second nod.

He was studying the bottom of his glass now. "Yeah. Quinn used to call him that. 'My little Cyclone.'" His mouth tipped up. "Name stuck because, you know." He looked up now. "The ADHD stuff."

I noted, not knowing if I should, "He's her favorite. It's obvious."

"Yeah." His voice faded. He was looking back into his drink. "She's hard on Ser."

"Yeah."

A sad grin at me. "You. Me. Them. Different moms. Dad got around." His frown deepened, became more prominent. "I don't know why he's not claiming you. It wouldn't be a surprise. He was with my mom, cheated on her with Quinn. Well . . ." He glanced to me before returning to that glass. "Cheated with yours, too, apparently. It's been Quinn. She had Ser, and a couple years later, Cyclone. Funny thing is that he and Quinn were struggling. She went off with her family, then came back with Cyclone."

I was quiet. I didn't know what to think about any of it, the cheating, or anything.

Matt laughed abruptly.

His jaw clenched and his fingers tightened on his glass before he tipped his head back and drank the whole thing in one go. He never hissed. I was waiting. I'd watched as he poured the alcohol in there. It was almost all liquor. Then he motioned to my glass. "Want another one?"

He wasn't waiting. He turned and began to pour himself a second drink.

I didn't answer, just waited for him to finish and turn back to me.

He did, but he didn't look at me. Instead of the glass, his gaze was fixed on the bar. His thoughts were elsewhere, that was obvious. "It was kinda messed up."

"What was?"

He jerked his head up and jerked it back down, his eyes glittering in anger. "I overhead Peter talking to Kash one night.

Quinn wanted to have another kid, but he'd been cheating on her. Quinn knows Kash's family, actually, but that's why she left. Because of the cheating. It ended how it was supposed to be, I guess. Quinn always wanted a boy." He looked up now. "She got what she wanted, huh?"

I was hit with a wave of anguish. Not mine. Matt's. It was so clear and so powerful that he couldn't mask it. He was struggling to. His hand kept tightening, loosening, tightening again around his glass. I kept an eye on it, wondering if he was going to shatter it.

"*Another* boy." His voice cracked. "She didn't want a nine-year-old from another woman."

"Matt." My heart sank for him.

"She wanted a *baby* boy. A boy to match her perfect little girl." Without warning, he threw his glass across the bar. It hit the wall and shattered. Matt just stood there, watching the liquid start to spread over the floor. His jaw kept clenching. His nostrils were flaring at the same time. "Fucking bitch. That's what she is." Suddenly, he looked over, piercing me with that same anguish that almost knocked me off my stool. "Watch yourself with her. She doesn't like you. She doesn't like having you here, and she might be gone all the time, but she knows what's going on. She knows you and Kash have something going on."

Crap.

"She doesn't like that, either, I bet you. She'll do something to get you out of here. Don't know what, but something."

"That's enough." A snarl came from the doorway.

Kash was there. "Nothing's going to happen to Bailey."

Matt laughed, the sound harsh. "That doesn't mean shit with Quinn. You know it. Bailey can see it. Ser and Cyclone, they can feel it. Ser—Jesus, Ser. She's terrified of her own mom, her mom that dotes on Cyclone more than she does her. Seraphina's expected to be perfect. Always put together. Quiet. She's supposed to have the popular friends, girls who are outright bitches. Have you been around when they come over? They're horrible to Ser, and Quinn loves it. She gets off on it, I swear."

"Shut up."

"No. No, man. It's time something happened." Matt flung a hand in my direction. "Quinn's going to take all the goodness in my sister and she's going to gut her. She'll take it out and fill her with nothing. We'll be lucky if she doesn't di—"

He stopped, just stopped.

He blinked.

No one said a word. No one stopped him.

Then his eyes grew bleak. He rubbed a hand over the back of his neck, his head folding down. "We're so far fucked up. We're ruined, Kash. All of us. We're too damaged." He saw me and blinked a few times, focusing to see me better. "You should get away from us, before you become like us. Get lost, Bailey. I mean it. For your own good."

He moved past Kash. He started for the door.

"Where are you going?"

Matt paused, shaking his head. "Does it really matter?" Then he headed out.

I flicked a tear away, my throat closing up.

"His mom killed herself."

What? That was a punch to my system. Matt . . .

I wanted to go after him, hug him until he healed, no matter how long that took. I'd hug him for years if I had to.

Kash moved to the stool beside me, sitting with his back to the bar behind him. "Report says car accident, and technically that is how she died. Report doesn't say that she directed the car at a tree, or how security cameras across the street show her staring ahead. There was nothing wrong with her. She was like a statue. She turned that wheel, sat back, undid her seat belt, and pressed down on the accelerator."

I sucked in a breath. My gaze flicking back to where Matt had gone.

"He doesn't know about the footage, just that she wrote a good-bye note to him and she was dead. Death by tree." Kash was looking too. "He's smart. He's always known, without asking. It's something we don't talk about."

I was aching. For Matt. For Seraphina. For Cyclone. For Kash, too.

As I moved my hand to his, I wasn't sure what he'd do.

I wasn't expecting him to flip his hand over and slide his fingers between mine. I wasn't expecting to suddenly be pulled into his arms, his head burying in my neck. And I really wasn't expecting him to press a kiss there. "I will never let *anything* happen to you. No one."

My legs parted and he was between them. Just holding me. I was holding him back.

We stayed like that.

Minutes could've passed. An hour. I didn't know. I didn't care. Until we heard footsteps on the ceiling above us and Kash stiffened.

He cursed under his breath. "They're back."

Which meant we'd leave. I was starting to understand this family's dynamics. Understanding, yes, but not liking it. How could I?

We were going past the kitchen, our hands entwined, when Peter appeared in the doorway.

Kash stopped. I stopped.

Peter seared me with his eyes before switching to Kash.

He clipped out, "Matthew took off in the Lamborghini. He'd been drinking."

Another look my way, and then he disappeared.

His words echoed in my head first.

Worry for Matt hit me second.

And third, I was seared.

Peter had walked away from me again.

I should have been used to it by now.

THIRTY-THREE

Kash called the security team on Matt, and we were pulling up outside of a dark mansion two hours later. It took us that long to get his location.

"Where are we?"

Kash flashed a quick grin at me, pocketing his keys. He had chosen to drive us himself, in a sports car. Two SUVs pulled in behind us. I recognized the guards.

"We had a team following us?"

Kash had skimmed a look over me before focusing on the road again. "There's always a unit on us. They might not be in the car with us, but they're around."

The house wasn't in a gated community. That felt wrong, but the road was isolated. I didn't see any other houses along it, just forest. Tree after tree blanketed both sides of the road as we drove here, giving us an isolated feeling. The house itself was three stories. The driveway wasn't long, but three cars were parked in front. I recognized a Lamborghini and assumed that was Matt's. The others were just as expensive looking.

Kash walked ahead of me, pocketing his keys and phone. He took my hand, leading me up to a fence. He gazed up at the camera perched on top of it and, without saying anything, pushed a button. The gate swung open for him.

Strobe lights lit up the backyard. Low bass filled the air. The smell of bonfire and marijuana was strong, too. But the view. Man. The view was spectacular. This was why this house was built here. A drop-off opened up to a valley filled with lights from each of the homes nestled along the side, and the river at the bottom had bobbing boat lights.

Lush green lawns spread out until the drop at an edge.

Neon and sparkling crystal lights lit up the entire backyard.

I was getting another glimpse into a world that was so far from the one I grew up in.

Kash led me forward, circling around to the back, and we turned the corner of the house. A couple was in the pool. His lips moved down her throat.

Kash walked past without a second glance. Like it was nothing new, like it was something he saw every day.

Going through the rest of the house, we saw other couples. All having sex.

Kash tightened his hold on my hand as he opened a door that led to the basement. The bass we had heard outside was louder here. We were headed right to its source, and a sick feeling overcame me.

I didn't know what we were going to see down there. Kash did. His face was rigid and masked, and that told me enough. But I kept with him.

More couples. More orgies.

This place—Matt was here. And he was hurting and he was here and there were drugs and I didn't know what state we would find him in, until finally, finally, Kash pushed open a back door.

Matt's pants were undone. Shirtless. A girl was bent over in front of him and he was thrusting inside of her. Another girl was beneath her, her mouth on the girl's breasts.

There was more movement in the back.

As my eyes adjusted to the darkness, I recognized Chester, Tony, and the other guy from the tent earlier. All three were nailing a third girl.

Kash flipped on the main light.

No one reacted.

Well, that's not true.

Matt looked right at us, and even through the glaze, I could see the ugliness. He didn't stop thrusting. He grabbed her hips and pounded even harder until he came.

Once he was done, Matt pulled up his pants, coming toward us. "You come for the show?" He passed us by, going into the hallway.

Kash didn't follow, not right away. His gaze was on the girls on the bed. His jaw clenched before he swung his head my way. His eyes met mine, and a look passed between us. He was trying to warn me, remind me again. Kids who grew up wanting nothing, who had the power to get anything.

They could use people for their games.

Anger was building in me. They didn't know how privileged they were.

Kash saw it coming. "Bailey."

A growl erupted from me. I couldn't, I just couldn't. Storming off, going blindly through the house. Down the hallway, through the room, up the stairs, through the door, and I was lost again. Kash's fingers curled over my arms. Taking the lead, he tugged me the rest of the way. My head remained down now. I didn't want to see what else was happening, where the moans were coming from, what was being snorted.

Matt was outside, waiting for us.

This world—I didn't want it. But if things had been different, I would've seen this long before now. I was reeling, feeling like I was half stumbling.

Someone called out, "Francis. You leaving?"

Matt snorted. "Got in trouble. The 'rents found me."

Someone else asked, "Who's the girl?"

Kash's hand tightened on me, and he didn't pause in his stride.

"Wait!" Their voice picked up, excited. "Colello? That you?"

A female gasped.

"Kashton Colello? Where?"

Kash picked up his pace.

"Kash!"

He ignored them all. Not pausing until we got to the cars, he held his hand out. "Don't fuck with me. Not now."

Matt rolled his eyes but dug into his pockets and tossed his keys to Kash. Kash caught them and almost immediately tossed them to someone approaching from the street. It was the security team.

Kash pointed to the back of our car, and Matt got in. He pulled the door shut, yawning. "And to think you almost missed all this fun. Right, Bailey?"

But he wasn't looking at me. I was watching him in the mirror. His head was turned, watching a small group of people who had gathered at the gate and were watching us in return.

A harsh, clipped laugh from Matt, and he held his hand up against the window. "Look at them. Fucking trash." He extended his middle finger, still laughing.

The vehemence in Matt's tone, the superiority. My stomach curled in on itself again.

"Who's the girl?" a guy shouted, gesturing to me.

Matt raised his voice. "Kash doesn't give a fuck about you guys. Go and finance your own shit. You're beneath us."

Kash was reversing the car.

I expected a reprimand, something, but he said nothing. He remained quiet.

Matt let out a sigh, a last biting laugh leaving him. "You don't have to say anything, Kash. I have your six. My turn, dude."

His turn? For what?

THIRTY-FOUR

Kash paused the car at an intersection, his head bent forward.

When he turned left, Matt burst out laughing. "He doesn't trust me to be alone at my own place, and he doesn't want to spend the night with you there. I can't go to his place. He doesn't want that, either, so we're going back to the estate." He laughed to himself, speaking to himself, "The fucking Chesapeake. Our dad is lame."

If he was expecting a response, he would be disappointed. No one spoke. There were things to say, but it wasn't the right time. After a while, Matt's deep breathing was the only sound in the car. Maybe I would have fallen asleep, if it had been a normal night, but it wasn't. I was wide awake, and when we slowed at the gate, it let us in.

After he parked, I didn't wait for Kash. I got out, heading for the villa.

He called after me, coming around to Matt's side, "Wait for a guard."

I didn't. "I'll be fine."

"Bailey."

I slowed, half turned toward him.

Damn him. A soft request and my knees were melting.

He added, almost gentle, "Wait for a guard."

I waited, but I was gritting my teeth as I did. A car pulled in behind us and three guards got of their own vehicle, another two getting out of Matt's Lamborghini. Kash nodded toward me. "Two with her. The rest with Matt." They broke apart. Three bent in, and Matt was shifted in their arms. They all carried him inside.

I was going to start ahead, now that I had my two bookends, but the main door opened. My father stood there, a deep frown on his face as he took in Matt. He was wearing a robe, a phone in his hand. Shifting back to give them space, he was putting his phone in his pocket, but the screen lit up.

"Kash." He called for him before looking.

Kash was already there, following behind Matt's guards. He stepped inside and the door was mostly closed, left open only a crack. I couldn't hear them. They were all the way up the front steps of the house. I could only make out Kash's face as Peter's phone was held between them. A second later, the door opened wide. Kash slipped out and approached me. He slowed down.

I saw the regret a mile away.

"I have to go and check on something." He nodded behind me.

Quiet footfalls were heard. The guards were moving away, giving us privacy.

"You okay?" His mouth dropped. He rested his forehead to mine, our favorite place.

"No."

A corner of his mouth lifted. "At least you're honest."

I took hold of his shirt, not looking into his eyes. I focused right at his chest. "Who are you? I thought you worked for my father, then you were raised by them, and now all those people . . ."

I didn't want to see the lies, the walls, the reservations. I needed him open.

I continued. "Those are people who have money, wealth that I couldn't even fathom before coming here. They were clamoring for your attention." I gripped his shirt tighter. "I need to know. I need to know who you are."

I couldn't tell him I was sinking. I was so past sinking.

He raised his hands, cupped my face and tipped it back. Right before his mouth closed over mine, he whispered, "I will tell you everything."

"When?"

"Tonight. When I get back." He waited a beat. "Or tomorrow. Matt's going to be handled, and you and I can go to my place downtown. I want alone time with you anyways." He sucked in some air. "I need alone time with you."

Those lips opened over mine, and I stopped questioning. I couldn't. Lust. Desire. Need. All of those and more, so much more, rose up in me, and I was panting by the time he pulled away.

A second kiss. A second whisper. "I'll come to you tonight, later this morning."

The guards walked me back to the villa. They went in, had me wait just inside, and once the house was secured, I went to bed.

I didn't think I could sleep. I kept replaying everything. The house. The people. The sex. The drugs. Matt's cruelty.

"You're beneath us."

I cringed.

How Matt talked to those people, how his group had been in the farthest back room of the house, as if others weren't allowed in, weren't good enough to join. At how he hadn't been shocked to see Kash at all.

How Kash knew right where to go.

What have I gotten myself into?

THIRTY-FIVE

I had fallen asleep.

The sheet lifted and I startled.

A hand touched my hip, sliding over my waist, and I felt the bed dip under his weight. "It's just me." Kash pulled me back to him, lining up his entire body against mine, and he kissed my shoulder. "Go back to sleep."

He tightened his hold on me.

Another whisper. "I've got you."

Another kiss.

And I slept.

I woke up hot. Like *hot* hot. I was panting. A mouth was on mine, kissing, licking, tasting. As I gasped awake, Kash was above me, his hand on my stomach, his mouth on mine, and he was claiming me. Legit possessive alpha claiming. A growl worked up from his throat and he lifted his head, rasping out, "Is this okay?" His hand trailed down my neck, moving south, moving, moving, trailing all the way down and moving aside my tank top like it was nothing. "Please tell me it's okay."

He shifted against me, his erection right there, and *hard*.

Desire slammed into my senses and I gasped from how violent my need for him was. "Yes." I mewled. "God yes." Moving to my side, I wound my arms around his neck, and his mouth was back on mine.

I was already a mix of writhing and boneless.

He was taking from me again, his mouth opening over mine, his tongue sliding inside, and I met him. I matched him, almost clawing to get closer. His hand moved to my thigh. We were both on our sides, pressed smack against each other, and we were both needing. Just needing. My leg moved between his and his hips rocked against mine. There. We paused. Both hissing from the touch. Molten desire speared in me.

I needed him now.

Not yesterday. Not an hour from now. Now.

"Kash," I moaned.

"Bailey."

All rational thought fled me.

Impatience and urgency were two very prominent themes happening inside of me now. I slid my hand to my stomach. He was shirtless. So much the better. I rolled my body against him, salivating at the feel of his muscles. They were tight and taut and pulsating with the control he was using. He was holding back.

I suddenly didn't want him to hold back. Ever. Most certainly not now, not when I was aching, throbbing. I moved against him, grinding, and he hissed, his hand clamping on my thigh.

"Fuck, Bailey." He gasped, his forehead going to mine, his eyes searching for me. "I want to . . ."

I heard his hesitation. I shook my head. No hesitation. There was no place for that, not in this bed. I started to tell him that, my voice completely wrecked, when he shifted our positions. He rolled me swiftly to my back and rose above me. Pushing my legs apart, he settled between me, and then rocked against me. Once more. Deliciously. Agonizingly. So. Fucking. Slow. I whimpered, biting my lip. My hands formed into fists, and I pushed them against his shoulder.

"Kash, please."

He swooped down, his mouth catching my whimper.

He caught it and answered back with his own growl, but he didn't move faster or harder. He held himself up, his arms braced on the bed beside me, and gazing down at me, holding my eyes, looking deep in me, he pushed against me.

He was wearing boxer shorts.

I was wearing sleeping shorts.

Why the hell were they both on?

I wanted to push at them, rip them off, but he chuckled, his mouth opening over mine again. "Not here." A soft kiss. "Not when there's two guards who can hear us." A hard kiss. "This weekend." A harder kiss. "At my place downtown." The hardest kiss, and I caught the back of his head before he could lift up again.

"Fuck yes." I lifted up, holding him in place, and kissing him. I was claiming him.

All those girls at that house last night. Hell no. All those orgies happening. Fuck no. They wanted him. Victoria. Her friends. Whatever was going on there. No, no, no. Just no. A primal thirst had opened inside me, and I wasn't shutting it up. I was letting it out and I was reveling in it.

Kash was mine. I didn't care who tried to take him from me, or who *would* take him from me. He was mine right now.

Mine. Just mine.

And for the next hour, he showed me how much I was his, too.

THIRTY-SIX

The whole reveal never happened.

Kash was supposed to tell me everything. He didn't.

I woke late the next morning and Kash was gone. He left a text on my phone.

Emergency. I'll be back when I can.

I didn't know what the emergency was. No one shared, and no one else acted like they knew. And over the next few days, Kash was gone. Matt left, too, so it was me, Marie, Theresa, and the kids. Quinn was at her charity meetings/functions. My father was around. I heard his voice one day when I was on my computer, set up in Marie's office. After Kash left, I asked to be let back on, and Marie was okay with it. The fact that it was her who gave me the okay wasn't lost on me. Ironic. Or karma. Either of those, but I was eternally grateful to her.

Working on that computer saved me, because those few days turned into weeks.

Kash was able to return, but only at night, and he'd be gone the next morning. I knew this because he'd wake me up while sliding into bed. If he didn't wake me that way, he woke me with his mouth on me. He would roll on top of me and take me to new heights, night after night. Or it *was* night after night, until it became every other night. Then every third night.

I missed him.

I loved spending time with Cyclone and Seraphina. I loved being able to work on my security program, and a small part of me was even enjoying the brief moments when my dad would

enter Marie's office to talk to her. I knew she let him know I was
behind the wall partition, because he'd get quiet right away and
leave. But after a week of this, she stopped telling him. I never
moved.

I sat suspended until he would leave.

He'd come in for a general report from her. He wanted to
know how Cyclone was during the day, what projects he spent
time on, his dietary habits even. He would ask about Seraphina.
He would ask if she had heard from Matt. He got the layout of
how the staff was doing, who was complaining, who was doing
well. He liked to praise the ones who worked the hardest, and he
would watch the ones Marie said weren't working. After a week,
one of those was let go. After two weeks, a second one was let go.

He even asked about Quinn, wanting to know when she left,
what charities she had mentioned to Marie.

She told him what she knew. Marie never hesitated or lied.

The only two people he never asked about were Kash and me.

It stung at first. I mean, how could it not? A father that I was
foisted on. He was gone the first few weeks, then here, and still
not talking to me—or *about* me even. But then again, maybe he
asked when I wasn't around? Maybe he knew I was there? Maybe
that's why he continued to ask her those questions, knowing I
was there, wanting, in a weird way, to build a connection to me?

I didn't know.

He just didn't ask about me. That's what I knew.

A month passed, and another couple weeks after that.

More days spent with my siblings. More nights with Kash. It
was now nearing the end of July, and I was missing Chrissy.

"Heya, lonely sister, but one that's so much more mature
than me."

Matt dropped into the chair behind me with a collapsing sigh.
His head fell back, his mouth opened, and a full groan left him.
"It's fucking hot." He rotated in the chair, casting a beady look
at Marie, who was sitting at her desk. "I know you like it hot, but

would it kill you to put a fan in here?" He gestured to me. "At least for Bailey's sake. There's a whole sweat line going down her back."

"There is?"

I shot him a look. "Dumbass. I'm fine."

"Doesn't matter, because," Matt stood, saying to me, "I came to rescue you."

"Rescue?" I was still pissed at him. We had never talked about the sex club night.

"From Victoria and the German tutor for Cyclone. They have lessons in an hour, and I know Quinn is intending to ask both of them to stay for lunch."

Marie piped in, "Mistress Quinn is still here?"

He nodded at her. "She pulled in when I got here. Called from the car to invite me for lunch."

Marie hurried out of the room, the door slamming in her wake.

Matt smirked at me. He raised an eyebrow. "Want to tell me why you lied just now? I can see how uncomfortable you are, and this room is hot-like-a-sauna hot."

More shifting around. I didn't like this, not a bit.

"Spill it." He was scowling.

I turned back to the computer monitor. "I just don't want to be a nuisance. To anyone."

I was turning the computer off.

Matt had fallen silent.

If he had come in to rescue me, I knew he wasn't going to make me stay for that lunch. Not that Quinn would invite me. She'd been avoiding me as much as I had her, and it wasn't the first time since I was here that the tutor and Victoria were at the estate.

They came once a week.

Marie would pointedly suggest I fix something on her computer, or Theresa's monitor, or would say they would bring me something to eat in Kash's villa.

No one had mentioned their visits, and while I caught the tail end of Victoria leaving once, I hadn't brought them up, either.

I turned back, standing up. Then, catching Matt's face, I froze.

He was pissed. Seriously pissed.

"What?"

"Why do you think you're a nuisance?"

Oh God. Where would I start? "Matt . . ."

"Bailey," he ground out.

He was waiting. His other eyebrow went up.

"Look, it's nothing. For real. I don't want to bug Marie. That's all."

He waited, still studying me.

I was waiting too. I didn't want him to push this. It felt wrong to complain to him about his own family, because it wasn't just Marie or Theresa that I didn't want to bother. It was everyone. Well, not Kash. I liked bugging him. A lot. Every night. Multiple times a night. An itching was forming under my skin, and I knew that wouldn't go away until Kash came again. It'd been three full nights since his last visit. I was addicted to him, needing the feel of him against me to keep going.

I mean, we barely talked.

I mean, that wasn't going to fly all the time.

But, I mean, it was Kash. He was my fix.

"You sure that's all it is?"

My knees almost buckled from the relief. "Yes. That's all."

He still wasn't happy, but he was relenting. The look faded, and his smirk showed again. "Want to get out of here with me?"

I hesitated. "Where? I know what parties you go to, and Matt . . ." I didn't want to swim in his depths. "I can't handle your crowd. I'm not like that."

"Like what?" But he was grinning. He knew what I meant.

"The orgies. The drugs. No, thank you."

"I know." His eyes flashed in an apology. "Look, I've been

embarrassed. Really embarrassed. What you saw that night, or the other nights. I'm sorry, Bailey. I am. Seeing how you were looking at me, at everyone." His foot moved back and forth on the carpet. "Kash reamed me out the next day."

He did?

"I woke up and the night came back to me in patches. Jesus, Bailey. You saw me fucking some random from behind. That's—yeah." A strangled laugh slipped out. "That's pretty high up on my list of embarrassments." His eyes caught mine. "But I wasn't high that night. I was the other night, but not that night. It feels weird. I just usually start out with people being disappointed in me, you know."

He was trying to be funny.

"Hey." My throat was closing up. "I'm not judging you. Don't think that."

"Still." He shoved his hands deep in his pockets. "I want to make it up to you, and trust me, me getting you out of here before Cyclone and Seraphina insist you join the Trio of Terrors is one small way of making things right again. I got a friend who's in a polo tournament today. You want to go?"

I wasn't sure.

"It'll be all classy and shit. Wine. Hats. Dresses. Guys who dress up like they've got sticks up their asses. The whole shebang. And if you don't want to hang out in the club area, I know the place the tournament's at. We own a barn there, and there's a loft we can sit in. I won't let anyone up there, if you don't want them."

I was weighing my options.

Stay. Work on the computer. Do something I loved? Or go to this polo place, where I was pretty sure I didn't like any of Matt's friends? If I stayed, Cyclone and Seraphina could make it awkward, if they insisted I join them for lunch. That meant enduring Quinn and Victoria—who, even though she had said only one sentence to me, I already knew hated me.

There was no dilemma here.

I groaned. "What do I wear to this getup?"

Matt's smile flashed wide. "There's my sister I love."

I let out an abrupt laugh.

Sister. Love.

I felt faint. He could've tipped me over, right then and there.

THIRTY-SEVEN

We were heading down the road when the phone in Matt's car went off. We had a car ahead of us, with security, and an SUV behind us, but he had wanted to drive himself. Hitting the button to answer the phone, he said, "Talk to me."

"There's an issue at the field." It was one of the security teams.

Matt frowned. "What's the issue?"

"There's two problems. There's press, and your loft is being used."

Matt's head reared back an inch. His frown deepened. "I figured there'd be press, but I was hoping to enter the back way and let Bailey stay at the loft. Who's using the loft? It's supposed to be off-limits unless we give the say-so."

"According to the field manager, your father gave the say-so."

"My dad? He's there?"

"No, but he gave them permission."

"I want those people cleared. I can't bring Bailey there unless it is."

There was silence on their end, until, "Maybe you could go another day?"

Matt's scowl was immediate. "Fuck that. It's horses, and sticks waving in the air. Yes, there's press, but no one that's a risk to Bailey. We're going; that's final. Tell the manager to clear the loft. We'll be there in twenty minutes."

I was more distracted by the press comment. "You think Camille Story will be there?" I hadn't thought about that, but she'd been known to go to events like this. And she loved reporting on Matt. A lot. She had a thing for him. She never came out and said it, but that was my theory. The stats of her stories on Matt compared to those on others was disproportionately in his favor. Almost a landslide.

His answering growl confirmed my question. "I hope not. She's a pain in the ass."

I was starting to enjoy this. "You guys ever sleep together? Because she reports on you a lot—like *a lot* a lot."

Silence. Again.

My eyes widened. "Are you for real? You did Camille Story?"

He was moving in his seat, adjusting and rolling his shoulders back. "What? She's hot. And I was wasted."

"She never reported on that."

Screw *enjoying.* I was loving this.

I asked, "Did you reject her? Is she one of the girls that she says you bang for a night and then toss 'em out like garbage?"

"No." A beat. "Maybe. I don't know. She took pictures of my dick. She was going to post them on her site, but Kash found out and slapped her with a lawsuit that would've bankrupted her four times over."

"Kash does stuff like that?"

"Kash takes care of us. Either physically or with this shit. He scared the crap out of her. She backed down, signed a contract that she had to destroy all of those pictures—and he got her first site shut down because of it."

"Oh, whoa." I remembered when she disappeared for a month.

"We have to watch out for her if she's there. She's scared of Kash, though. He's the reason she posts only half the crap she wants to. She can't afford to run across him again."

Really.

What more could I find out about this guy who was crawling into my bed?

I couldn't stop myself. The need to know was too high. "Who is Kash to your family?"

Matt glanced at me.

"I mean, what exactly does he do? How'd he grow up with you guys?"

"He hasn't told you?"

I shook my head, slowly.

Matt's eyelids shuttered closed for a second before lifting to continue watching the road. He spoke tightly. "I think you should wait for that conversation with him."

Damn it.

"But Bailey."

"Yeah?"

His tone softened considerably. "Kash takes care of us, and that's not because he's paid. He took that role on himself, and even I don't know the reasons. I'm just saying, he's complicated. If he tells you everything, then you'll know more than any of us."

"You don't even know?"

"I know some. I know . . ." He bobbed his head to the side. "I know what I'm allowed to know, I guess I should clarify. Kash is . . . like I said—"

I finished for him. "Complicated."

"Yeah." His hand tightened on the steering wheel, and then we were slowing down. The turn signal was put on and we were going down another road. This one wasn't as empty as the others had been. Cars were lined up along the side of the road, and the farther we traveled, the more compact they were becoming. They weren't normal cars, either. They were rich ones. Bentleys. Navigators. More than a few brand-new Audis. A couple Rolls-Royces. Range Rovers. Porsches. A Bugatti, even.

"Who plays in this tournament?"

Matt spared me a grin, slowing the car again, as the rest of the traffic had backed up to where we were. We weren't moving, so he sat back, his wrist resting on the steering wheel, and he went to switching on some music.

A knock came on the window.

It was one of Matt's usual security.

"The manager said we can pull around and come in through the back entrance, but the loft isn't available. Your father gave specific permission to the party occupying it to have it for the whole day. She's tried to get in touch with your dad, but he's unavailable right now."

Matt swore. "What about Kash? He can override those orders sometimes."

"We've been, uh"—his eyes darted to me, then back—"trying to get in touch with him ourselves, about another matter. His phone was turned off."

Turned off. That's not a big deal.

Right?

But there came those nerves again. It wasn't a common event for me, but I had reached out to him a few times over the last few weeks. A simple text, and every time, Kash had replied right away. Sometimes he could call.

He'd never had his phone off.

"Shit." Matt leaned back, scowling. "There's no point in coming if—"

The guard's phone went off and he showed us the screen. "It's the manager. Hold one moment." He answered it, moving away. We didn't wait long before he came back. "She said the party left on their own. They've moved to another location. We're cleared to go in."

We couldn't move, but within ten minutes a caravan of vehicles was leaving the tournament, going past us. They went past us at a slow pace, and I recognized a couple movie stars. A pop princess was in one of them.

"Holy whoa." Trying not to gape here.

Failing.

I was gawking.

"Those were probably the guys in the loft. That girl's manager knows Dad." Then he flashed me a smile and jerked forward in his seat. Now that we had the go-ahead, and now that the line was starting to inch forward, Matt's mood got dramatically better. He'd been relaxed and normal, but now he was becoming restless. Impatient. I was recognizing the hyperness that he'd exhibited before. His words were more clipped. His smile was on edge.

We were pulling ahead.

The first security team was paused. One of the parking attendants spoke to them and they were waved forward. We were led onto a back road, going around the field, the main building where most of the crowd seemed to be gathering. A barn was farther off, at the southern end of the field, and seeing a patio hanging off the end of it, I was guessing that was where Matt was taking us.

We bypassed more cars, all the people drinking and mingling beside the field. The back of the main lodge was beautiful. Everything was, and I was glad that I had listened to Matt when he picked my outfit. He had chosen a pair of black capris and a white tank top that crossed my chest. It was lace and frilly and I felt exposed in it.

It was perfect.

Noting all the dresses, I gave Matt a look. "You told me I didn't need to wear a dress."

He grinned. "My sister does not need to show off her legs. To anyone." He shrugged, turning onto another gravel road, which was leading straight to the barn. "Besides, we're just hanging in the loft. Anyone who comes over won't care. They'll just be happy we're allowing them in there."

"I thought it was just you and me hanging out today?"

"Hmm?" But he was distracted.

Two large barn doors were being pulled open for us. A myriad of staff were running around inside the barn, bending to pick things up off the ground.

I leaned forward, my hand resting on the dashboard. "What's going on?"

"Cars don't usually drive into the barn. Scares the horses. But we're making an exception today. They're making sure it's clear for the tires. Nothing will puncture them."

It seemed a lot of work, but we'd come this far, and with this whole caravan we had going, we'd attracted a fair amount of attention.

I asked, wondering to myself, "What do they all think of this?"

"This?"

"Of us." I motioned to the barn.

Matt shrugged again, making a dismissive face. His mouth moved to the side before speaking. "I don't know. Who cares? It's not like anyone will get close to you. We have an army around us." He winked at me before pulling all the way into the barn. This was the Matt when he was high, when he was raving in the tent, or at an orgy party.

I was recognizing him now. Dread crawled up in me, digging a hole.

We parked in the middle of the barn and waited. Most of the guards came in with us, checking the barn, and waited until the staff were asked to leave. One guy was arguing, but a guard was handling him. The last few were walked out and the doors in the front and back were both shut. The guards took position as Matt was getting out.

My door was opened by a guard, so I got out as well.

We were led past a few of the stalls to a door. It was opened and we went up the stairs, stepping out onto the second floor that spanned the entire length of the barn. It was a full apartment.

Then the doors were being opened below.

Matt's car was driven out, and we could hear the staff returning.

Matt said to me, "Don't worry. No one will come up here. We have security all over the barn." He nodded to the two who took point just inside the room, standing by the entrance.

"Is that the only way up here?"

"Yeah, unless someone tries parasailing in from the deck." He motioned toward the open patio area. "But even they'll be shot down, and we got the guys behind us. They'd rush the interloper." He patted me on the arm before moving toward the bar. "You're good to go. Let's drink and relax, yeah?"

I was slower to move forward.

This didn't feel right. There were too many people around. Then again, Matt had been the one who took me to the night-club that night. Kash hadn't been happy I was there. After that, Kash was the one who took me to the other two events, but those had been house parties. We were in and out, no lingering around.

I glanced uneasily at one of the security staff.

He noticed and approached. "Ma'am?"

"You guys haven't gotten ahold of Kash?"

He was frowning. "Ma'am?"

I lifted a shoulder, skirting around the rest of the loft to him. "I . . . Just . . . He'd want to know I'm here, right?"

Understanding cleared and he nodded. "Yes, ma'am. We'll continue to update him with our location. We always do anyway. It's protocol."

"Oh." My head perked up. "That's good then."

"Yes, ma'am." He nodded forward. "You can relax, have a good time, as Mr. Francis is doing right now." I caught the slight grin on his face and looked ahead.

He was right.

Matt was getting a drink, already flirting with the bartender. The female bartender.

She was flirting right back, until she saw me. A nice frosty layer cooled her smile, until Matt said, "This is my—" He caught himself. "Distant cousin. Family. Extended family." He rolled his eyes, pulling me to his side. "Come on, cuz. Let's have a shot." He beamed at the bartender. "Shots for both of us. You, too."

After that, the bartender warmed up to me, but she was friendlier with Matt.

When another bartender came up to relieve her, an hour later, she stayed, sitting on Matt's lap the rest of the time.

I settled back.

The whispering should've alerted me. It didn't.

There was movement in the corner and I looked over, seeing the first bartender standing up. Her hand was in Matt's, and she was leading him off the couch.

"Hey."

Whoa. I stopped. I was feeling that third glass of wine. The barn had started to move. The horses. Where were the horses? There'd been horses in the field in front of us a moment ago. But then I heard sounds beneath us. The horses were coming in. A match was done. Horses were being led in and out. Watered. Fed.

It'd been like this the whole time we were here. Another match would start up. But Matt.

I looked for him.

He was gone.

"Matt?"

He was in the corner, whispering into the girl's ear.

He came back over, leaning down. "You mind if I sneak off for a quick romp?"

"What?"

He was smiling at the bartender, a dirty look in his eyes.

"I'll be quick."

I snorted. "I wouldn't lead with that with the ladies."

He flashed me a grin. "Seriously. Do you mind? You have the guards. Only a few will go with me. I won't be long."

I looked over my shoulder. There was a sitting area behind me. A long table. Three couches in the other corner. A kitchenette against the wall—with an island, even. Then a hallway, and I was assuming there was a bathroom and a bedroom, probably more than one. "Just go back there. Why do you have to *leave* leave?"

He made a face. "Because that's gross. Embarrassment aside

from last time, I don't want my sister to actually hear me get my rocks off." He nudged my shoulder. "Come on. I'll just be a bit. I'll go over to the main lodge. There's rooms for this thing, and I'll stay, say hi to some friends, then come back."

It wasn't a good idea. Not at all. I wasn't going to say yes.

"Bailey." He crouched down, peering at me intently. His voice was coaxing. Soft.

Damn him.

"You're supposed to stay here."

"Please." He bumped my forehead with his, grinning. "She's got me all worked up. I'll go have my fun, then come back. We can take off after that if you want."

"Food."

"What?"

I was so not happy with this, but he was going to go anyway. I might as well get something out of this. My stomach was rumbling. "Food. I want food. I haven't eaten today."

"Why didn't you say something?"

I shrugged. "Because you gave me wine? I don't know." I hadn't said anything because I didn't want to be a nuisance, and I still didn't, and I knew that's why Matt was going to do what he wanted here. Because I didn't have the balls to stand up and insist we leave. The same reason I didn't speak up when I started to have a bad feeling about coming to this place.

"Please, please, please." He whispered, "I promise to take you anywhere you want for dinner, once I get back. How about that? Or we can order food in, have a movie night at Kash's? Bowling? Pool party. Anything. I will owe you. Promise."

I hated promises. They were always broken.

But, lowering my head, I moved it up and down, enough to indicate a nod, and he whooped. His hand squeezed my shoulder. "Thanks, Bailes. I'll be right back. Promise, promise, promise."

Then he was gone.

Bailes.

Gah. I liked that he gave me a nickname.

The guards went with him, and two others rotated up. I recognized them as the ones normally assigned to me. Standing, I went to the banister and watched as Matt and his bartender walked around the field, heading toward the main lodge area. Three guards tailed them.

"You said you were hungry?"

"Hmm?" I turned. The other bartender had approached, a friendly enough smile on his face.

"Your stomach is growling." He nodded to me. "I can actually hear it."

"Oh." I pressed a hand, feeling the rumbling. "Yeah."

He was smiling. His eyes were smiling.

My head was clouding up and my vision was tunneling, but if I had some food in me, and water, I would sober up. I'd be okay then.

He offered, "I can make a call to the kitchen, have them send something over. Would you like that?"

I waited a hot second. "Hell yes."

He laughed, moving back behind the bar, taking my glass with him. "I'll top this off for you, too."

That's when the guard moved forward, a phone in his hand. "Miss Bailey?"

"Yeah?"

The bartender was pouring the wine, not watching us, but sound traveled. He could hear us.

The guard held out the phone. "Mr. Colello's on the phone for you."

I couldn't squash down the tingle that went through me at hearing Kash was on the phone. Taking it, I tried not to hop up too quick. The floor would've rushed me.

The bartender was bringing over the wine as I put the phone to my ear. "Hello?"

"Where are you?"

The wine was held out to me.

I took it, trying to keep my hand clear of his, but the bartender moved his finger at the last second. It grazed against mine. My eyes went to his. A seductive gleam was there, a faint grin on his face, and taking my look as permission, he rubbed his finger against mine more gently, and way more suggestively.

I jerked back. My wine splashed, hitting my face, the phone, my top.

I gasped.

"Oh no. I'm so sorry." The bartender and guard moved at the same time.

The bartender was going toward my top, the towel that he rested over his shoulder already in hand, ready to help dry something. Me. My shirt. I didn't know. But the guard growled and hip checked the guy. He literally bumped him back. The other guard rushed forward.

Kash was saying something on the phone. "What's happening?"

I was burning up. My face. My neck. My ears. I was embarrassed.

And I could only stare in terror as both guards wrestled the bartender to the ground.

"Stop!" I ran forward, holding the phone, ignoring Kash. I went to one of the guards, pulling at his arm. "Stop. Let him up. He was trying to help. I did it. I jerked back and spilled the wine."

"Bailey!" From the phone.

I put it back to my ear, saying, rushed, "I gotta go. There was a thing."

"A thing?"

I hung up, thrusting the phone at the guard.

Both stepped back, letting the bartender get back to his feet.

I was there, patting him on the arm now, the chest. "I'm so sorry. So sorry." Why was I doing this? I was the one still wet. I felt bad. That's why. "Again. I'm so sorry. They're just—"

He was easing back from me, putting a safe distance between me and him, and he nodded. "Doing their job. I got it." He held his hands up, moving one step at a time until he was behind the bar. "I'll . . . uh . . . I'll be doing my job." He was the face of professionalism now. Cold and detached. Not the flirting guy from seconds earlier. Clearing his throat, he kept eyeing the guards behind me. "I'll, just, call in that order, ma'am."

Great.

Not that I cared, but there was another person who thought I was a pariah. It shouldn't matter. I was telling myself that, as I went back to the couch I'd been sitting on. The next match was starting, with new horses, ones that looked fresh under their riders.

It was okay I was an embarrassment.

I mean, who was here that cared? Matt was gone. I was good. All by myself.

I didn't need any company.

I should've stayed at the estate. At least there I was starting to feel comfortable. I wasn't treated as an outcast. I mean, an outcast who was being protected, but still. The sentiment stuck. If I went over to that lodge, I didn't know those people. I never would know those people.

Those people . . . I was watching them and seeing a commotion starting. I leaned forward.

What was happening?

A large crowd had started to form, moving from down the driveway and going slowly toward the lodge, then behind it. People were running to the other side, catching up with the crowd, until a car was breaking free from the group.

It was coming toward me.

I stood, knowing, feeling, not daring to hope, and went to the edge of the banister so I could see better.

Unlike when Matt and I waited to pull in and everyone had to empty the barn so we could get out in private, Kash folded out of his car. He tossed the keys to one of the guards, his eyes lifting and finding mine. Hands in his pockets, he ducked his head down, ignoring a few guys who had tried to call out to him. Some of the stable staff lingered outside the barn, confused as to who Kash was, and then I heard him coming up the stairs.

Well, I didn't hear him. One didn't hear Kash. But I felt him. I knew he was coming.

One of the guards went to the door, opened it before Kash got there, and in he strolled. His gaze locked on me and was not moving away.

He wasn't moving away. He was coming right at me, no pause, no slowing down. It seemed like it took three steps for him to be across the room, and then he grabbed my arm and was pulling me with him down the hallway. He didn't spare anyone a glance, just pushed open the back bedroom door, dragged me in, and closed the door. He locked it before he turned.

His gaze pinned me in place, narrowing, and he leaned back against the door.

He drawled one word. "Explain."

And I gulped.

THIRTY-EIGHT

God.

I was itching to feel him, but he was staring at me, angry.

His voice was seemingly laid back, but he wasn't. He so wasn't. His body was tense. His eyes stormy. His hair was messed a little, sexily messed up. His jaw was clenching every few seconds as he waited for me to answer, and the air was electrified. I felt the pull to go to him, hard, and it was taking everything in me to remember he wanted me to say something to him.

Explain.

I frowned. "Explain what?"

He pushed off from the door, stalking toward me. My body veered backward, but my legs stayed and I was captivated by him.

He dropped his voice low, sending a sensual tingle straight between my legs. "Explain *what*? Explain why you're here. Explain why you're alone. Explain where the fuck Matt is. Explain, Bailey. Explain so I don't leave here and rip the head off someone I consider like a brother." He stopped, breathing down on me, inches from me. I felt his heat, warm and intoxicating, and I was having a hard time circulating my own air.

I wanted *his*.

"Oh." I reached out, my hand touching his stomach, and holy God, he was tense. He was tight, and I could feel the control it was taking for him to restrain himself. It was rolling around in him, his stomach muscles vibrating, and it only got worse under my touch. His eyes were closed. His face bent down toward mine.

I said it softly, not knowing it was coming out. "I missed you."
Three long nights.

His eyes opened, anguish and need and frustration and torment
all looked back at me. The hairs on the back of my neck stood up.
My heart paused, literally paused.

He wrapped a hand around my nape, tugging me to him and
closing the distance. As soon as we touched, I felt centered.
Settled.

The world made sense, just for a moment, if only for that
moment. Everything going around and around. Everything making me confused. Family. Years of loneliness. Love. Yearning.
Wanting a father, now wanting my mother. Not knowing where
I came from, as if I didn't know where my roots anchored me to
the ground.

All of that. Gone. One touch from Kash and I felt right.

"Fuck," he whispered. His hand slid to cup the side of my face.
"You're not supposed to be here. Not without me. Never without
me. And I got the call where Matt took you, and I am trying not
to kill him right now." His hand was gentle, his thumb starting
to rub over my cheek. He did this. He cradled me in the palm of
his hand, and every time, I fell a little bit more.

I didn't even stop myself this time. I let myself go, because it
was so good to see him, hear him, feel him.

"He apologized for the party, then brought me here because
Victoria's at the house. Her and the guy giving Cyclone tutoring
lessons. Matt said Quinn was going to have lunch with them, and
Cyclone and Seraphina would've begged me to sit there."

Kash didn't move.

Not an inch. But his arm did. His bicep muscle bulged up a
full second, held, then relaxed. He expelled more air. "Shit. He
was right, but wrong. Victoria is *here*. She texted, asking me to
meet her here. But he was right about Quinn. Her and Victoria
together would've been a nightmare."

Victoria was here?

My pulse jumped. I didn't like that.

"Kash." I slid my hand down his chest, lingering over his stomach. He went still under my touch, not even breathing. "You said you would explain things." I looked back up. "It's time you did that."

"I know." He sighed, but his arms slid around me, and he hugged me to him. He said into my neck, "I will. I promise. It's a lot for you to know." He lifted his head again, his eyes flashing dark and sensual promises. "I'll beat up Matt, then you and I, we'll go to my place. I'm back for a while now. I can explain everything."

Call me weak, but I was stupid happy he was back.

I nodded. "Okay."

His eyes paused on my lips, hunger showing, and he groaned. His hand came up. His thumb touched my bottom lip. He liked to do that. Then he forced himself away. Catching my hand in his, he entwined our fingers and said roughly, "Let's go."

I felt the bartender's eyes as Kash led me back out to the main room.

Kash stopped, telling our security the plan, and then we were off. I wasn't sure what to expect, but we were moving at a fast pace. Down the stairs, out from the barn. We were heading back across the yard, and people were noticing. All the guards, except the three that went with Matt, were with us. They fanned out, surrounding us.

Kash moved a little behind me, a hand on my nape as we walked forward.

"Colello!" A guy was cutting over, running to us.

Running? Really?

He had a hand in the air. "Colello! What's the word on you taking your father's place with Phoenix Tech after all these years?"

Kash's hand tightened on my neck, just a smidgen. He ignored the guy.

Another guy joined him, and soon more and more people.

They were press, along with the regular partygoers who'd come to enjoy the tournament. One woman yelled, "Kash! We partied together at Noi. Do you still have my number?"

Another: "Who's the girl?"

Still another: "Your grandfather's made it known he wants you back in the family. What's your response to that?"

"Kash! There are rumors you were helping the government in trying to go after your grandfather. Is there any truth to that?"

"Should we expect regular appearances on the nightclub scene?"

We were almost to the main lodge. A staff member came out to meet us. She was held off by the guards, but she waved her badge. "We sectioned off a room for Mr. Colello and his guest."

The guard looked back.

Kash dipped his head in a nod, his mouth tight and closed. He guided me forward as we got to the lodge. A whole wave of people was on the deck above us and coming to stand around the front sitting area with tables and tents. They were all watching us, some curiously and some surprised.

We were led right under the awning of the deck, all those people shifting to watch us, and into a back hallway.

One girl shifted to the front, a drink in hand. She smiled, though it didn't travel to her eyes, and she leaned down. "Kash!"

He paused for this one, looking up.

I was gritting my teeth. It was Victoria, and she was looking just as stunning as ever. Her hair was shining from the sunlight over us, and her lips moved into a more seductive smile. "Invite me down. I'd like to talk to you."

He growled, his head jerking back down. "Not now."

"But—Kash!"

We were inside. The staff member guided us to a back sitting room. A bar was in a corner. Couches. Chairs. A television on one wall. Shades were closed, with light shining underneath, and we could hear people on the other side. Someone knocked against the window. That was behind the shades. Laughter pealed out from the other side.

"This is the best we could do under the circumstances." She motioned to the shades. "Those are patio doors, but we locked them and they're covered. As long as you're relatively quiet, they won't know you're in here." She hesitated, her hair coming out from her bun, giving her a harried look. "Would you . . ." She turned. There was no one at the bar. "Would you like a staff member to come in?"

"No." Kash's hand fell from my nape, but touched the small of my back. "Thank you."

She nodded toward a phone on the wall. "Just pick it up if you need something."

Kash waited until she was gone before he turned to his guards. "Where is he?"

One guard started for the door. "I'll take you to him."

I started to go with, but Kash's hand rested on my stomach. "Stay. You'll be safe."

All the same questions that I'd had for the last month and a half were still in my head, but I nodded to him. He and the guard left, and it took only five minutes before he was back. Alone. The storm was in him again, but it had upped to a hurricane. An angry hurricane.

Kash looked capable of murder.

He blew into the room, coming right to me. His hand wrapped around the back of my elbow. "Let's go."

I didn't ask where Matt was. I didn't have time.

Kash was walking me back out into the hallway. The guards were in front of us and behind us. We could hear yelling as we went through the back, the kitchen, to a back door, and we were out. Kash's car was there. He guided me around to the front, opened the door for me, a hand to my back as I got in. Then he was moving around to get behind the driver's side. An SUV was in front of us and one was behind us. The guards piled in both.

I waited until we pulled away from the lodge. "Where's Matt?"

"He left," Kash growled, slamming on the brakes as some people darted out from the side of the lodge. Laying on the horn, he turned the wheel to ease around them. Staff from the lodge ran outside to try to barricade the people back.

This was insane. They were acting like Kash was royalty, and he'd been in hiding for years.

I couldn't even process all of that, so I fixated on what I could. "What do you mean Matt left?"

He left me?

The SUV in front of us began to pick up the pace. Then we had to pause as we pulled out and onto the road. Once there, Kash was done waiting. There was a pocket of space where he could pass, so he punched it forward and zipped around the front SUV. We really were off after that. We couldn't get away fast enough, and he was up to fifty, sixty, seventy. The road widened further and Kash really let it go. We were past eighty in the next three minutes.

"He left you to go fuck someone."

"He told me he was going to the lodge."

"No." Kash was so cold. "He told you that to keep you there, feeling all fine. Thought you'd be safe at the loft. The little fuck took off somewhere else."

"He left with the bartender girl?"

Kash spared me a quick look, his top lip sneering. "No bartender. Unless he took her with him. No. Matt's fucking a married woman. He went to her house. You were his alibi if he got caught."

It was as if Matt was here, picked up a paddle, and slammed it against my face.

"What?" No. That couldn't be.

"Believe it," he clipped out. "I'm going to hurt him."

I felt like I'd just ingested a full piece of tree bark. "Was it all a lie? The lunch? Victoria?"

Kash didn't reply right away. He looked through the corner of his eye, his lip flattening. "I don't know. The lunch was probably a truth he twisted. Matt has an ability to do that."

My head was pounding, but I fell silent the rest of the way.

We were on the outskirts of the city, and Kash was maneuvering the car around others on the interstate. We were rounding, heading into the suburbs on the southern edge. Slowing down, he took an exit, and the size of the houses maybe shouldn't have surprised me, considering the estate, but they still did. I think I had stopped considering the estate as a home. It was just that—an estate. People lived there, but it was more than a mere home. And these buildings, they were large houses. A few were big enough to be considered mansions, but most were just large, though large enough to impress me.

The sports car slowed and pulled in to a home that had a tower of glass extending up past three floors. The home itself had a rectangular shape on one side; the tower attached this to another section of the house. I was guessing that the main rectangular shape was where the living room and kitchen were, with the bedrooms and the rest of the home in the other section. Matt's car was parked in front of a four-stall garage, alongside a sleek-looking Mercedes Benz. It was brand-new, the chrome still sparkling. The license plate had a pink frame.

Kash pulled up behind Matt's car, blocking him in, and was out. I thought he'd head inside, but he came around to my side. I was opening the door before he could get there, but he took the handle and held it open as I got out. Shutting it for me, he locked the car and pocketed his keys as we headed for the front door.

"What's the plan?"

Kash gave me a look, his hand coming to the back of my hip. He was pulling ahead, once we got to the front door, and that's when the guards showed up. Behind us and in front of us. Just as we were approaching, a guard came to the door from inside the house, his hand to his earpiece. He looked at Kash and me, saw the others who were pulling into the driveway, and nodded briefly. He opened the door for Kash, saying, as we went past, "Third floor. Back right."

Kash took the stairs two at a time.

I was following at a slower pace, stunned by everything happening. His guards had sold Matt out, but Kash was the boss. And as I saw Kash get to the third floor, he looked back to me. I was coming to the second floor. I waved him off. I was going, mainly because I wanted to see Matt's betrayal for myself, but I didn't want another visualization of my brother thrusting into some woman.

I was just getting to the third floor when I heard it.

A woman screamed.

Matt started yelling, "*Get the fuck out! What are you doing? Kash!*" More yelling. Something thumped on the wall, then the floor.

I heard feet pounding on the ground.

A guard was outside the door, watching me come, with a lidded expression.

Oh, joy. That wasn't good.

"*Help! Max!*"

The guard looked in, stared a second, and turned back to watch my approach.

"You little fuck." That was Kash. A savage curse ripping from him.

Another thud.

The woman began screaming again. "Oh my God. Don't. What are you doing? Don't hurt him!"

The sound of fists meeting skin came next.

I winced but forced myself forward. I was moving at a much slower pace, though. Then, deep breath, I was in the doorway.

The woman was holding a bedsheet to her front.

I recognized her. She was the Bonham wife, from a couple that was friends with Quinn. She was naked, her entire side was exposed. She didn't see me, her eyes wide in horror.

Matt went to the floor, but he was trying to fight. He rolled to his feet and windmilled his feet up, thrashing everywhere. I wasn't sure of his intention with that move.

It was almost humiliating to watch.

Matt tried to punch back. Kash easily deflected and hit him even harder. My brother was bleeding from the face, and he finally quit, collapsing to the ground with his arms and legs spread out.

Standing over him, not even breathing hard, Kash saw he had stopped and stepped back. He grabbed one of the pillows, dropping it on Matt's stomach with extra oomph.

Groaning, Matt could only get one eye open. "You dick."

"*You're* the dick," Kash shot back. "You left her at that loft."

Matt paled.

"Oh."

"Yeah." Disgust and disdain laced that word. "You're lucky you can still walk. You don't use her, then leave her. Ever."

"What? She has guards. She's fine."

Kash was looking at me.

Matt stopped talking, trailing, looking up, and finding me. He said, "Oh no."

A frustrated sound roared from Kash's throat before he stepped away from him. "It's taking everything in me not to beat you senseless. Get the fuck up."

Mrs. Bonham—I didn't know her first name—was staring at me now, but I avoided her gaze.

Just felt wrong to have violated this scene, but I had to see. Matt didn't deny what Kash said. It was true. With how long it took us to drive here, knowing Matt had intentionally used me, lied to me—how long would I have been there?

A tear fell, but I brushed it away. I wasn't going to cry over this. "How were you intending to make this okay? Were you go-ing to try and cover your tracks?" What lie would he have used, when he finally came to get me? But I saw the guilt flare, then shame, and he turned his head. He literally looked the other way.

He wasn't coming back for me.

I was in the room, heading for him, when I growled, "Are you serious? You would've left me there? *All day?*" There was a hys-terical note coming from me. It didn't sound like it was me, but it was. I heard it. I was cringing at it, but I couldn't stop. I wasn't even conscious of making the decision to go into the room, but as soon as I started, I wasn't stopping.

"Answer me!" A guttural cry from me.

A guard was inside, coming behind me. He had an arm around my stomach, but I shifted, pivoting. I was running at Matt.

Kash cursed, moving to block me. He stepped over Matt and caught me up just as I would've kicked my brother's face. With my momentum and the abruptness of how he caught me, I was in the air. Gravity was pushing me up, somehow, but Kash was moving away. He didn't let me go over his shoulder. Tucking his head into my side, he wrapped one arm around my back, anchoring me to him, with the other behind my waist.

I was yelling over his shoulder as he carried me out.

"Huh, Matt? You piece of shit. You were going to just let me figure it out for myself? How long? *How long?*"

Kash grunted, but clipped out to the guard, "Get him fixed. I want him taken back to the estate. I'll deal with him tomorrow." He carried me out to the hallway. The guard moved in front so I couldn't see Matt, but the last image I had of him was his face turned the other way. The woman, who the fuck cared about her? I didn't, but our eyes caught for a second. The same horror hadn't faded, and I had an urge to give her the middle finger. I didn't.

Kash set me down before we started down the stairs.

My legs buckled. He caught me, then hoisted me back up, just how he'd been holding me. He carried me all the way down, and by then I was moving around. "I can walk. I'm fine." So he let me go, but when I started back up the stairs, a quick laugh hit my ears as he settled himself directly behind me. He walked me outside. I was being herded by his arms and hips.

I broke away once we were outside. "Is he for real?!"

Kash wasn't responding. He kept a hand to my elbow and steered me to his car.

"I can walk on my own." I ripped my arm away.

"Still." He stopped, making sure he was behind me so I couldn't make a run to the house.

Giving up, with one last curse, I turned, storming to his car. I got inside, slamming the door behind me.

Kash stood on the sidewalk, his gaze latched on to me. His head was lowered, his hands going to his pockets. A security guard approached him, and they spoke before Kash got into the car. We didn't talk as we drove out of there.

I wasn't paying attention to where we were going. I was stewing.

Then I noticed the large buildings.

"Where are we going?" We were downtown.

"My place."

"Why?"

He slid me a heated look. "Because it's time you know everything."

THIRTY-NINE

"You know Calhoun Bastian?"

We'd just gotten to Kash's downtown place and I was starting to take it all in. The last time had been fast and hot. I hadn't had time to really look at his place, and I was currently gaping at how sleek and modern and masculine it all was. Shiny cement floors. Dark leather couch—the good leather, too. The tight stuff. A big mural of a mustang on his fireplace.

He had a fireplace. I pointed at it. "Do you actually use that? Is that safe?"

He leaned back against his kitchen counter, his hands in his pockets, his head down and his eyes lidded. He always gave me that look, and damn but it did things to me on the inside. My little heart flipped over at the sight.

His hair was messed again, too.

"Did you hear what I asked?"

"Huh?" I rewound and nodded. "Yeah. He's the sixth-richest man in the world. How do you know him?"

He stared at me. Long. Hard.

There was no joy in those eyes, his darkness coming forth once again, and the back of my neck prickled. My heart flipped again, sinking. What he had to say to me wasn't good. I just knew that much.

Then he said, "He's my grandfather."

More gaping.

I couldn't . . .

Holy shit.

Still more gaping.

"That guy? But he's . . ." Evil. That was the best word.

Kash looked at the ground, his hands coming to rest on the counter behind him. His elbows were splayed outward. His knuckles were white. "He's acquaintances with dictators, third world leaders. He knows six branches of the mafia. He's done business with all of them. His friends are murderers, and that's the *best* way to call them." A swift intake of air. "He also has two daughters, one that's dead and one that might as well be. He has two grandsons, myself and my cousin. And he's the biggest narcissist I've ever met."

His head lifted and I almost stepped back from the agony looking at me. Pure torment and anguish.

"He declared my mom dead to him when she married Joseph Colello. He didn't have much. My father's side of the family are middle class, have a shit ton of pride, and are just as stubborn as my grandfather. When my dad brought my mom around, they saw the torture she'd been through. They witnessed, because that's what it was. That's what my grandfather did to her. He would say he would kill her sister if she didn't leave my father. He'd send her videos of my aunt being raped. They saw all of that, heard all of that, and that's only the stuff I can handle telling you. There was more. There was worse. All the while, he never came and forced her to return to him. He couldn't do that because, in his twisted mind, that wasn't *her* coming to *him*. He had to beat her down, destroy her completely. That's the only window she got to remain where she was, and that's when she had me."

I felt faint. "Kash," I murmured, wanting to go to him.

I did. I started. But he clipped his head to the side. Almost a savage motion. "No," he growled. Half his hand was white now. He was starting to breathe hard, harsh, through flared nostrils.

I could feel his grandfather's hate. It was in Kash, coming out of him.

And I ached. I wanted to go to him, comfort him, push it

away, protect him from his own family. I wanted to do what he'd been doing for me this whole time.

His voice was low, raw. "My grandfather is the most powerful man I know, and he wants me to return to his side." His eyes zeroed in on me. "This is where all that ugliness connects to you." A pause. His chest lifted, held, then lowered.

He closed his eyes but remained absolutely still.

"My father met yours when Peter Francis was young and starting to build his empire. He wasn't quite there. He needed more capital, and he needed investors. My father invested. Because he got in early, yours gave up enough capital so mine was the primary shareholder. Until he died."

"What happened?" I moved forward now, feeling as if I had to break through a vortex around him. I moved closer. Inch by inch. Kash looked like a cornered animal. I needed to approach with caution.

Still raw, his voice dipped. "When my parents died, those shares weren't sold or diluted. Your father kept them, and he's been acting in representation of me. I hold those shares."

I reared back. "You said primary shareholder? Is that . . ." Dear Lord. Did he own more than . . . I swallowed tight.

A hard glint showed in his eyes. "I own more of your father's empire than even he does." He showed his teeth, the smile not a smile at all. And he pushed off the counter now. "I also have an inheritance from my mother that would make me the tenth-richest man in the world. My grandfather fucked up. He killed the wrong daughter. He took out the one who was smart, who knew how to invest, how to use the money she inherited from her parents, who had his talent for making money. She did it all under his nose. He never knew, until he did." A pause.

"It says my parents died by carbon monoxide poisoning from an accidental malfunction at a cabin. Those reports don't detail how the head of my grandfather's security booked a plane ticket to Aspen on the day before my parents were there. That there's camera footage of him driving the very road to their cabin, or how he booked a late plane ticket out of Aspen the night they died." Black humor lifted. "They went peacefully, and I've no doubt that was at the request of *him*. Because he loved my mother more than he did my aunt. It was his weakness. He could hurt my aunt all day and all night, but my mother—he respected her. It's why he never forced her to join him. But letting her live free of him? He couldn't do that, not when he found out how much wealth she had accumulated, because he wanted it. He still wants it."

"Oh, God. Kash."

I needed to touch him. I needed to help him.

I was in front of him, my hand raising.

He caught it, almost violently. I was about to touch his chest, when he moved like a snake, latching on to my wrist, and held me there. I was transfixed, my arm in the air, his hand holding it there, and we both stared at each other.

A primal look flared. Deep. Primitive.

I felt it in me, answering him. I was burning alive, awake. I had to touch him, and I tried again. Stepping in. Nothing. He held me in place, not letting me move an inch, but he didn't look away. He couldn't. He was staring at me like he was starving for me.

"Because my mother was estranged, she had documents saying that in *any* circumstances, I should go to your father. I was never adopted, but they fostered me. If Peter adopted me, my grandfather wouldn't have allowed it. His ego wouldn't have been able to allow it. Your father raised me when he couldn't raise you." His nostrils closed, his eyes were smoldering. "I'm the reason you weren't brought into the family."

"What?" A hole was punched inside of me.

"When your mother told Peter about you, he told her there was danger in growing up as his child. Your mother made the choice to raise you without him. Your mom did that. Not Peter. And it was because of me. He was worried my grandfather would try to hurt Peter through his children. A bastard child for a bastard child. That's what he thinks of me. A bastard child. So, you're not alone in that category."

I felt sick.

I tried to pull away, but he didn't let go of me.

"There've been kidnapping rings who have tried to ransom the others. That happens sometimes, when someone is as rich as your father, but the one who got the closest was with Cyclone. I destroyed them. Word got out who I was, where I came from, who I have been hiding from, learning to fight, learning how to protect myself all my life, and those hostage attempts stopped. Until you. I had your father wipe out everything on the internet about me.

"We don't know a ton, but we do know some. Arcane was sent by someone who knows my grandfather. We don't know if he actually sent them. We haven't been able to find that out, but we know there was a middleman, someone who reached out to my grandfather's networks and who was the one to hire Arcane and his team. My grandfather blames your father for my mother's desertion. His pride doesn't let him consider that she stayed away because she loved a lowly middle-class investor, but a genius tech billionaire—that is someone he feels is worth being his adversary." He tugged me closer, his hand moving to mine, and I felt him spread my fingers wide.

Palm to palm.

I could pull away. I didn't.

I turned, looking at him through our fingers aligned together.

Pain so stark I felt it cutting off my own legs stared back at me. He was looking at me like I was his lifeline, and I was feeling the string. He was reeling me in, one tug at a time.

He dropped his voice low again, almost a whisper. "I am not a good guy. I have grown up with the threat of my grandfather over my head. He could take me away any second. He could have me killed any moment. And I *hated* that feeling." His eyes were growing cold, dead. "So I became worse. You asked me why some people know me but there are no pictures of me on the gossip sites. It's because of your father. Any image of me that goes up is taken down within seconds. He wrote a program for it. I couldn't fight my grandfather if everyone knew who I was. My world is in the shadows. Your world, your family's world, is in the spotlight."

Another tug. Another inch.

Our fingers entwined.

He was staring at them instead of me. "I wasn't there when they tried to take you, but I'm here now. I'm not leaving. I won't let them take you."

A last tug. The last inch.

His hand left my hand, sliding up my throat, circling, cupping the back of my head. His fingers moved through my hair. He applied pressure, his forehead finding his favorite spot. Our eyes were so close, too close. I was seeing inside of him.

He sighed. "I've been playing with him, toying with him thinking I was returning to the family. All I was doing was stalling. I'm of age. He wants me under his control, and I'm running out of time. I was supposed to take my father's place as shareholder, and my inheritance will come to me in three months. When all that happens, there's no more hiding. The world will know everything about me, and it'll be game over. He'll know I'm not joining him, so he'll send someone to kill me. It's a matter of time."

"Kash," I whispered. It was because of me, but I couldn't fix it. Any of it. It was too much above my head. I was out of my league. Kash was way out of my league. "What can I do?"

"Be with me."

FORTY

He added, "If just for the night."

A whisper filled with so much yearning, I felt a pang in my chest. Like I was the one dying, and I answered without thinking. I stood up on tiptoe, lifted my mouth, and we were kissing. Our lips to each other.

The night. One night?

I couldn't do that. I'd need more. I already needed more.

His lips touched mine, tingles spread through me, warming me. I surged up, getting caught up in him, just him, and he bit out a growl, tightening his hold on me. I was lifted. He was turning. I was put on the counter behind where he'd been, and he shoved my knees open, stepping in. His mouth never left mine. It only opened more, demanded more, commanded more, and I was melting into him. I was hanging on for anything, and he tipped my head, angling his head for a deeper kiss. His tongue slid in.

I moaned.

He caught the sound, answering with a deep groan of his own. His hands shifted down, smoothing down my back, sending sensual sensations in his trail, all the way to my ass. He gripped me there, pulling me in hard to him. And I felt him. He was hard, pressing against me, and we both paused at the feel.

Both moaned.

"Bailey," he growled. "*Fuck*. You feel so good."

All those nights he crawled into my bed, tasted me, touched me, kissed me, licked me. He made me come, his fingers sliding inside of me, sometimes his tongue, and I would gasp, then explode, and in the mornings he would be gone. He never let me reciprocate. He had been waiting, and I was half worried he wouldn't let me this time, let himself, but as he began grinding on me, I knew what he wanted.

I was burning for it. My skin was buzzing, goose bumps all over. My blood was boiling, washing through my body, warming me until I was at a dizzying heat level.

"Now." I pushed my hips against him, jerking back so I was pushing off from the cupboards.

His hand clamped on my hip, and he caught me, rocking with my motion. I was going hard, desperate, and a guttural sound left his throat as he opened his mouth, moving down my throat. Kissing. More tasting. More licking.

He knew every inch of me, had explored there for hours at times. He knew how my pulse would flutter when he lingered over my carotid or swept down the arch of my throat. How my body would jerk and kick up when he would pause between my breasts. Tonight, though . . . Tonight he didn't have the control of those nights. Tonight he was hungry and just as wild as me. His kisses were harder, more primitive. More crazy. His lips closed over my nipple as I kept my hips rubbing against him. He was pushing back, pushing hard into me, his body arched over mine on the counter.

"Fucking hell," he gasped. "You're fucking gorgeous."

This was—He was in me. He was under my skin, and what we were going to do next meant something. There were words I wanted to spill, but I didn't know if I dared. I didn't know if I could. We hadn't gone there. But then he groaned, his eyes black now, and he bent down. His mouth found mine in the gentlest but most soul-consuming kiss I'd ever felt. I opened for him. There was no resistance in me, just hunger.

Just need.

I whispered against his lips, "I want you."

Another groan, and he bent over me, his knee settling between my legs. His hand went down my back, shifting so it was under my hip, and he lifted me, carrying me to the bed.

He crawled over me, holding himself above me, and he dipped down, his mouth meeting mine again. I met him halfway. A kiss. A second. A third. We kept kissing, tasting each other.

He moved back, taking his pants off, his boxer briefs next, and he sprang forward.

My eyes opened wide at the size, but I knew it was like that. I had felt him pressing against me for so many nights.

He caught my look, a grin appearing. "Don't worry. I'll make you feel good. I promise."

"That's not what I'm worried about." I'd never want someone else. He would ruin me, but he didn't ask, and he reached for a condom. Sliding it on, he paused, his eyes twinkling. "Next time, you put it on. That'll be a different sort of fun game."

More groaning. He was going to be the death of me.

Then he was on the bed again, his fingers making quick work of my pants. He tugged them off, my underwear next, until I was stretched out for his viewing pleasure. He paused, taking me all in, and he nudged my legs wider, bending quick to press a kiss there before moving over me. I felt him line up, and he paused, our gazes holding.

"Ready?"

"*God* yes."

At "God," he pushed in, and I arched, my back leaving the bed, my breasts pushing against his chest. I was so full. He paused before moving even further inside of me.

I was seeing stars.

I was *feeling* stars.

He began to move, and I couldn't hold it in. The sensations. The lust. He was moving slow, taking me deep, pulling me, pushing me, owning me, and I was holding on for my life. He began to move quicker. I was with him, my hips rocking. I raked my nails down his back and he gasped into my neck, his head rearing up.

He paused, rasping out, "Slow or rough? You choose."

His hips pressed down on mine. He swiveled them, grinding inside of me, twisting both ways, and I could barely breathe.

"Choose." He said it softly, falling to place a lingering kiss on my throat. "Or I will."

I couldn't choose. I was shaking my head, just needing him. "Both."

"Oh, you're getting both, but you choose the first one."

I felt it building, and feeling it coming up, erupting out of me, I cried out, "Rough! Rough, please."

He grunted, his hand coming to my hip. He pulled out till his tip was just inside, then he thrust in, and he thrust in hard. He picked me up, his hand under my ass, gripping me, and he went fast, he went rough, until I was seeing those stars all over again.

"Kash!"

Still he kept going. Still he didn't stop.

Then he held me still, arched over me. He moved in and out of me, seamlessly, gliding. It was spreading, moving. He was building a whole new level of frenzied fervor underneath the throb I was already feeling. He was entwining both of them, threading them together. And he paused again, gripped me, and lifted me up. He shoved us both back so the headboard was behind me, his knees on the bed, and I was pinned in place as he continued to plunge into me.

I felt it from the base of my spine.

He was helping it, taking me, bending over me, and his mouth latched onto mine as my climax ripped through me. I screamed from the onslaught of it, his lips claimed me, and a moment later I felt him erupting, just on the heels of my climax.

He held me until we'd both stopped shaking, and then he slid out gently. Climbing off the bed, he disposed of the condom, but he came back, pulling me to him.

"Kash?" I looked up, my head resting against his shoulder. "I don't want just one night."

His eyes darkened with lust—and another emotion. "Then it won't be just one night." He bent down, his lips finding mine, and it wasn't long before he moved and lifted me again, and this time I rode him.

FORTY-ONE

I padded barefoot out to his kitchen.

We'd woken twice during the night. Kash reached for me the first, and I had pulled him in the second time. There'd been a third round this morning, in the shower, and I was fully sated. Completely sated. I almost couldn't move this morning.

I was sore, but it was worth it. More than worth it.

Glancing at the clock on the wall, I saw it was just past eleven.

Kash was at the stove, shirtless, and I had to stop and gawk. No one would blame me. He was standing, half turned away from me, paused in his stirring as he read something on his phone. His shoulder muscles were standing out. His spine flattened in as the rest of his back was corded and—was this an addiction? My mouth went dry at the sight of him. His sweatpants low on those hips. Those same hips that had been moving against mine, in and out, in and out, rotating, going deeper.

His eyes flicked to mine.

I flushed, caught ogling him, and I ducked my head down.

He grinned, putting his phone down. "How are you feeling?"

"Good."

He watched me as I moved farther into the kitchen, going to the coffee machine. He asked, "You're not sore?"

I turned, glanced at him. I felt bad saying it.

His grin grew, turning rakish. "You can be sore. I'd imagine you would be. I should apologize, but I'd be lying. I'm not sorry, not at all. Last night was amazing."

I took out the coffeepot. "This morning, too."

His eyes darkened, skimming down my face, lingering on my lips, traveling all the way until I could feel his gaze on my ass. I was wearing his shirt, nothing underneath, and the sight made him happy. Lust had started to form.

Pouring myself a cup, I turned, blowing on it a second. My back rested against the counter. I shook my head. "And you're right. I am sore. I'll need at least an hour to heal."

He laughed, turning back to the eggs in the pan. "You like 'em hard?"

I'd been taking a sip, then sputtered at that. Shooting him a glare. "Har har."

He still chuckled, then grew serious, motioning to his phone. "We have to go to the estate today. I have to deal with Matt later."

"Can it be *later* later?"

He studied me a second. "You're needing a break?"

"From them." I waved to his phone. "Matt. Yes. Most definitely." Gazing around, I asked, "Can we have a skip day? Is that a thing?"

"You want to hang here for the day?"

I half joked, "Can we hang here forever?"

His eyes darkened again, somber, and going to my lips. "We can stay here, yeah." He crossed the kitchen, dipping down for a light kiss. He murmured, "I was thinking you'd like to check in on your mother today, too."

I pulled back. "I can do that? We can do that?"

He nodded behind me, at his laptop. "You can use that to check in on her if you want. Your mom had a security system installed. I'm assuming you can figure your way in to see her? It has your father's program to erase your trail, though the bad guys already know you're with me."

Bad guys. Right. His grandfather.

I suppressed a shiver, heading over and grabbing his laptop to take to the couch with me. Putting my coffee on the end table,

I folded my legs and pulled his computer onto my lap, a pillow underneath.

Now *this* was heaven.

Kash shirtless. Coffee. Me in his shirt. A night of hot and intense sex. And a computer.

I was almost purring.

Opening it, I saw he already had it ready for me, and it didn't take long for me to find her security system or to hack in. I was surprised at the security cameras; they were everywhere except—I had to snort—except her bathroom. Of course. Her toilet time was precious. Zooming around, I found her in the living room, snuggled on the couch, a blanket over her. She was lying down. The television screen on channel four, the late morning news on.

Then I noticed the popcorn bowl of tissues on the floor. How she sat up. How she wiped at her face with the back of her arm. How she stood and looked like an eighty-year-old, not the forty-five-year-old she was. Her skin was pale, gaunt. Her eyes were sunken, her cheekbones the same. She reached to pick some of the tissues, and she wavered, her hands shaking.

Pure horror settled in my bones.

She was not good.

I whipped around to Kash. "Did you know this?"

He frowned. "Hmm?"

"I thought you had men watching her. Weren't they seeing this and reporting it?" I motioned to the computer, my finger pointing.

I was angry. I was livid.

"Kash!" I yelled, when he took too long to answer, turning the stove off and coming over the back end of the couch. His frown deepened as he saw what I saw, and he didn't respond. "Kash."

He ignored me, picking up his phone.

Moving to the bedroom, I heard him. "Who's watching

Chrissy Hayes right now?" Then he shut the door and I could only hear the sounds of an argument on the other end. I couldn't make out the words, but it wasn't long before it quieted and he came back in.

He stopped in the open doorway, staring starkly at me, cradling that phone like it was a barrier between us. "I'm sorry."

I was on my feet, his computer dropped on the couch. His shirt grazed the tops of my thighs. "What'd they say?"

"She's not eating. She was devastated when she woke at the hotel. No one reported to me, and I was distracted." His eyes wavered, the ends of his mouth tucking in. He was cringing.

A wave of shame flooded me.

I was distracted too. This wasn't just on him.

I sat, my legs numb, folding underneath me. I cradled my head in my hands. "I should've asked. I should've bugged you. I . . . was . . ." I'd been focused on the possibility of a new father, siblings for the first time. A new family.

A sob was wrung from me, and then Kash was there. He was lifting me, sitting me on his lap. He wrapped his arms around me, his head folding over mine.

He whispered, "I'm sorry. I am. I'll make it right. I will."

"Kash." He couldn't, unless he told her where I was. "I thought she knew I was okay?"

"She was supposed to have been told. I'll figure out the breakdown. I promise." He brushed some of my hair from my forehead, kissing me there, then my cheek, finally my lips. "I'm so sorry." He ended, resting the side of his face against the crown of mine.

After a moment in silence, he jostled me a bit. "Tell me about your mom."

I sat up, giving him a look. "You probably know everything."

He grinned. "But not from you. I want to know from you."

It felt odd to talk. While I was growing up, not many people asked for my free thoughts on someone or something. I was asked where Chrissy was. I was asked what school I was going to. I was asked what scholarships I was trying for. I was asked who my friends were, what grade I got. I was asked questions to put me in a category so others understood me, but questions like this were far from normal, and that made me feel embarrassed. There'd been a drunken mistake in college, and a clumsy kiss when I was lonely one night, but that'd been it for guys. And I hadn't had close friends growing up. My cousins were the outgoing ones. They were popular, going to parties. I'd been the "brain."

Maybe another reason I migrated toward the computer.

I understood that world. The outside world, not so much. This world.

I was suddenly feeling tongue-tied.

Kash noticed, his eyebrows going up. "What's wrong?"

"All that's happened. I just realized you're my first *guy* guy." If we were even that, and I was really shy now. What if we weren't? I was so late to the game here.

"Hey." I'd looked down. He tipped my head back up. "You said not just for one night. In my book, that makes me your guy. Got it?"

"Got it," I whispered, and I knew he could feel the heat radiating from my body.

His thumb spread over my cheek. "Tell me about your mom. I want to understand her through you."

So I did. I told him she was a Gemini, how she took that to heart. She had the "mom" side that was strict and prideful. No help from anyone who might have strings attached. She had learned that lesson somewhere along the line. I had to go to school, go home right after. She didn't like not knowing where I was, even if she was working the second shift. She'd call the landline by four every afternoon to make sure I was home, and would call on each of her breaks so I didn't have time to sneak out and get kidnapped—her words, and the significance was now just setting it.

"Oh my God."

"What?"

"She knew. You're right. She knew. She was worried about me being taken." My chest tightened. "I thought that was just something every mom worried about, you know, just being a mom."

"That *is* something every mom worries about." He was watching me intently. "Just had an extra meaning with her, that's all."

"Yeah."

"Tell me about the other side to her."

He was prompting me, still gently. He didn't want me to sit and stew so my guilt would flare up. I was here. She was there. She was hurting, and I'd been the cause. But after he said my name again, I told him about her other side.

"Single moms, young moms, they don't want to grow up sometimes. That was her too. I mean, she was. She was grown up. But in other ways she wasn't. I was the one who didn't want to party on New Year's Eve, and she did. I didn't like to go trick-or-treating. She did. She's everything I'm not, honestly. Ditzy at times with social things, everyday life things. Money, parenting, work, that stuff she's great at. Everything else, not. But she's fun." I was grinning before I knew it. "She got tipsy one night at the VFW and she was playing peekaboo with me from outside the house that night. I thought it was so funny.

"She likes adventures. You know that story on the news, of the woman who drank wine out of a chip container in that discount store, riding around in the cart? That's something she'd do. She wasn't reckless. She'd be smart about it. But yeah, she liked doing silly things like that. Like getting pulled on a sled behind a lawn mower because we couldn't afford any other way to do rides like that. Or building forts in the living room and sleeping there for a few nights. Ghost stories. Sneaking up on her friends when they'd go camping and scaring them. Things like that."

I was missing my mom. I was missing her a whole lot.

And after I finished talking, when the tears rolled down— the good but missing kind—Kash picked me up and carried me to bed.

We stayed there the rest of the afternoon.

FORTY-TWO

I could feel the bass through our feet.

Once we stepped inside that nightclub, the same one Matt had brought me to so long ago, the dry ice assaulted us. The difference from that night to this one was that I was walking inside with Kash. My hand held with his. He was leading me. We came in through the back way, greeted by the same worker who had helped us last time.

She nodded, a ghost of a smile on her face.

"Welcome, Mr. Colello. Ms." She still didn't know my name, and that was partly my work, partly my father's. His program was still at work, and every photograph of Kash that hit the internet disappeared after minutes. Even the print news referenced Kash but not me. There were pictures of me, but no name printed. They apparently didn't know who I was, and I had to wonder how long that would last.

Knowing who Kash was, exactly, told me what a feat that was, for him to remain as mysterious as he was. He explained that it was partly because his grandfather had never publicly announced him or his relation, and Kash had never stepped up to take over his father's shares. Once he did that, his privacy would be gone. He'd be firmly in the spotlight. I understood why he kept to the background as much as possible, but with his association with my father's family, I also had to wonder how realistic that would be. It was only a matter of time before someone got a picture that couldn't be deleted, no matter how magical my father's program was.

So the worker not knowing my name was partly because the ones who'd gotten pictures of me didn't know who I was. There'd been one, but I had hacked her and deleted everything she had of me, Kash, and Matt. And there'd been an entire file on Matt.

Camille Story was still interested in Matt, if I had to go by the amount of information she had on him.

I hadn't told Kash I did that—or anyone. I wasn't sure if I should, but glancing around, taking note of the attention we were drawing, I figured I should. Everything came around. I believed in that. So yes, I had to tell him.

He was leading us toward the same back VIP section that I'd sat at with Matt before, and like that night, Matt was at the same booth. He didn't have a girl on his lap, but he was sitting in the back, his arms spread out over the top of the booth beside him, and two girls were pressed to either side of him. One was toying with his shirt. The other's arm was under the table, toying with something else.

Matt's gaze was trained on us, and he wasn't happy. His top lip sneered up. Nope. So not happy.

I slowed, but Kash tightened his hold and kept going. Judging from the locked jaw on his face, he wasn't happy either.

I was starting to recognize some of Matt's friends. Chester was there, nuzzling into a girl's neck, but not the other guy, who had been talking to Matt, or so I assumed, because he had an arm up behind the girl next to him. She was toying with his shirt, but he turned to watch us come in, too. There was light curiosity from him. Anger from Matt. And fear mixed with caution in Chester's face, when he sensed something was happening and lifted his head from the girl's neck.

The four girls didn't look over. They didn't even seem to know that other people were there. They kept doing what they'd been doing: flirting, teasing, and rubbing, judging by the girl whose hand didn't move from Matt's lap.

Once we were within earshot, Matt drawled, his eyes sparking,

"Well, well, well. Look who finally decided to have a chat with me." His eyes were mean. "You're usually on top of me, Kash. You're slipping. It's been a good two days since you beat the shit out of me."

His bruises were still there, but fading.

I winced, seeing them.

Chester and the other guy were enjoying this. Both seemed eager, and they leaned forward, resting their arms on the table.

Matt didn't move. Not an inch.

His eyes switched to mine. The ugly glint was there, but as I met his gaze and raised my chin, it faded. A glimmer of regret flashed briefly, but then it was gone. And with it, some of the fight lessened too. His shoulders went up and down, smoothly, and he broke free, leaning forward to match his friends' positions.

"And you . . . I am actually sorry." He grimaced. "Again. And again. And again." All the fight was gone. His shoulders slumped down. He mouthed a swear word, then motioned to the girls. "Leave. Go."

They didn't move quick enough, so he growled, "Get lost! Now."

Chester scowled. "What the fuck?" But he slid out, letting the girls out. His, too. The other one looked up at the third guy, and he nodded to her, dipping his head in the direction of the bar. She stood up and he smacked her on the ass, then cupped it. "I'll come find you. Don't go far."

Her eyes danced, and a seductive tilt formed on her mouth. "You know it."

As soon as the girls were gone, Kash lifted an eyebrow. He was glaring at Matt.

Matt sighed, rolled his eyes. "Nuts. Dick. You guys, too."

"What?"

"Dude."

Matt waved them off. "This is a family thing."

Both stood, glaring.

Dick's glare was less, and he hotfooted it after his girl. Chester stood, moving into Kash's space, but one turn of Kash's head and the guy scrambled out of the way.

The corner of Matt's mouth tugged. "The guys are all chicken-shits. Scared of you." He nodded to Kash, who stepped back, motioned for me to slide in on Dick's side, and got in behind me. He could scope out the club, but his body was angled toward us. A passerby would think he was focused only on talking to us, not on watching them. The maneuver was so innate and smooth that I wasn't sure he was even aware of it.

Then all got quiet.

Matt was glancing between the two of us, a slight frown marring his forehead. "Should I be the protective bro—"

"Shut up." But there was no heat in Kash's words, and Matt's grin only deepened. "What were you thinking? Boning Amanda Bonham? She's married."

Matt shrugged. "Doesn't act married in bed."

"Her sleeping with you doesn't change the fact who her husband is. He can make life difficult for your father."

Matt guffawed. "Right. Dad can roll over him in two seconds. You know it. You can roll over him in less." He skimmed me, nodding in my direction. "Bailey could probably take him down with an afternoon behind the keyboard. He's a weasel shit. He's *nothing* to me."

Kash only flattened his mouth.

Matt jerked forward, new fight coming to him. "He's in over his head. He owes the banks too much, and his new company is tanking. Besides, his wife has been cheating on him for years, and not just with me. When he finds out, he'll find the rest. I'll be the least of his worries. I know his two business partners got pokes in there, too, long before me. There's rumors of a Christmas party, if you get my drift."

Kash wasn't amused. His eyes were hard. "That only means he's desperate. He can latch onto the latest, a privileged prick of a tech golden boy. Guy that desperate won't sit back and think rationally about who else surrounded his wife. You get *my* drift?"

They were at a standoff.

Matt growled, falling back against the booth. "Fine. Whatever. I won't pick up when she calls."

Kash ignored that, pulling out a phone and sliding it over the table. "Now."

"What?" He was looking from the phone to Kash. His eyes widening. "No way."

"Now, Matt."

"Kash—"

"Goddamn it. Now. I'm not fucking around with this. There's too much else at stake. A scandal like this can have blowback." He motioned to me, his eyes not moving from Matt. "You know who else that can hurt. End it. Now."

Matt was snarling, until Kash referenced me. Then the snarl softened into mere regret, and he closed his eyes. Raking a hand over his face, he shook his head. "What a fucking mess. Fine." He took the phone, typing in her number and a text. Seconds later, he threw it at Kash. "There. Done." His glare was back. "You happy?"

Kash took the phone, pulled up the history, then pulled up a different number. He handed it back. "Now actually text the phone she uses and not a dummy number."

Matt froze.

Even I was surprised.

"You—" Matt grabbed the phone, saw the new number, and blood drained from his face. "How'd you get this—"

"Do you actually forget who your father is?" Kash jerked forward. He was close enough to be heard, but he dropped his voice low. There was a promise of violence under his words, being held back by a veiled line of restraint. He was done. That was obvious. Only Matt seemed still defiant, until Kash ground out, "I only had to give him a name, that was it. He pulled up everything.

Texts. DMs. Private messages. Emails from three fake accounts. We have it. So fucking end it."

"*You went to my dad?*" Matt's top lip turned white, it was stretched so tight.

"No. I gave him a name. That was it. And before you jump down my back for being a snitch, I *had* to give him the name, because Bonham is a threat to your father, your sister, and you now. It was for security reasons. Not to give him the name would be reckless and stupid. Unlike your dick, I'm not a moron."

"Jesus Christ, Kash. Sometimes I really hate you."

"Feeling's more than mutual right now, but you'll be loving me the next second you need my ass to help you. You know it. I know it. Everyone goddamn knows it."

I'd been watching the back-and-forth, but at Kash's mention of security reasons, I waited for a beat. It was now.

I jumped in, holding a hand up. "Camille Story."

Both looked to me. Both quieted.

I waited.

They didn't say anything until Kash said, "Explain."

I flushed, remembering another time he'd said the same phrase to me. But, pushing forward, I told them what I had done. Including the hacking. Including finding all the files on Matt.

"I deleted everything so she wouldn't notice it was gone until she went looking for it."

They were both silent a moment when I was done.

I fidgeted.

That was okay, what I'd done? I mean, maybe not in the grand scheme of the cosmic universe of morals and stuff, but she would've hurt us. Hurt Kash. Hurt Matt. In a way, I was just doing what they were doing for me, and what I'd done in the past. I was protecting people I cared about. In that way, I'd done nothing wrong. Karma was on my side.

I still eyed Kash, who hadn't turned away from me.

What was wrong?

Then he said slowly, "She had your name?"

I nodded, just as slowly as him. "Yeah."

"And how much information did she have on Matt?"

"A lot." Scanning through it in my head, I added, "She knew about the Bonham woman."

Matt jerked at that, rearing backward as if slapped. He hissed out, "What the fuck?"

Kash narrowed his eyes, still on me. "Tell me everything she had on us."

He waited as I went over it all, and he listened. It took a little while, long enough that a server came over to offer drinks. Matt waved her off as Kash ignored her, listening to me. When I was done, both wore decidedly different expressions than when I'd started.

Unease.

A little bit of panic with Matt, and a darker hint of anger from Kash, one that was riddled with intent to do something not good. I picked up on that unease, but it was about Camille Story. I had enjoyed reading her gossip blog, until finding out more about her run-ins with Matt and then finding how extensive her research on him had been.

"She had a picture of you," I told Kash.

"Me?"

I nodded. "I don't know why it wasn't deleted . . ." I was reexamining it, and that was wrong. I did know. "She diluted it. She ran it through a program and turned it into a sketch, not even a picture anymore, but it's of you. His program wouldn't have flagged it."

Crap. That was smart, and that had taken planning.

I added, "She knows about the program that wipes out your image."

Which meant there could be more, kept offline. That wasn't good.

"Shit." That was me.

"Shit." That was Matt.

And Kash, he didn't say anything. His jaw just firmed, and I knew he wouldn't be with me tonight. He'd be going somewhere else.

FORTY-THREE

I knew it was only a matter of time before Kash slipped away.

I didn't know if he'd have me go with him, take me to the estate, home, or where. Or if he'd have the security team take me instead. I just knew two things: he was going to where Camille Story lived, and I was making the most of my time with him.

We didn't do couple stuff.

This whole thing with us, it came out of nowhere. We hadn't been normal, but we were a we. I knew that much. Kash was possessive of me, but in a good way. The way a girl loves, the way that fills her up, making her feel special and loved and protected.

That was me, and that's what Kash was doing when we were offered a private box suite and took it. Pressed high above the club, higher than even where Matt was again sitting with his friends. I could look straight down. Glass was under our feet, the opposite side a mirror to those below. We were out on a deck portion, and a button could open it up, let us hear the music better, feel it.

We were feeling each other just fine.

Kash was behind me, his arms around me, his body pressed against me, and his mouth exploring my neck. He nibbled up, licking me, and a jolt of lust tripled in me. I felt zapped by electricity. My blood simmered almost beyond a light boil by now. A hand swipe down my front. Touching between my legs, exploring, pressing, then retreating and moving back up and tunneling under my top. His other hand slid up the side of my leg, going inside my dress. He'd specifically asked me to wear this, and I now knew why.

Access.

My back was exposed, and as his hand moved below, so did his mouth.

He draped kisses down my spine, and I surged upward, gasping and holding. My back was arched. My breasts pointed upward. He had made sure, bringing me to dizzying heights already before moving to a slower and more controlled pace.

As he pushed against me, I felt how much he wanted me.

He wouldn't indulge. I knew Kash by now. He would drive me crazy, make me fevered and blind, and then his hand would slide up the inside of my dress, then into me, and he would send me over the edge all over again.

Tantalizing. Torturing.

I was a mess as his mouth sucked, paused, explored more, and then proceeded to drive me into a pitch.

"Kash, Jesus!"

He didn't answer, but his hand splayed out in front of me, anchoring me to his mouth as he was sucking the small of my back. His tongue was doing magical things.

I tipped my head back, a full-body groan left me.

I felt his chuckle against my skin, more than heard him, and he knelt all the way down.

Oh, God.

I knew what he was doing.

"Kash," I was starting.

"Shh." Low and soothing, he turned me around, pausing to look up. I caught the twinkle in those eyes and could only hang on as he was lifting my dress up. His head ducked in, and I felt his tongue a second later.

I was prepared.

I thought I was prepared.

That's what I was telling myself.

I wasn't prepared.

I so wasn't prepared.

I gasped, my legs shaking, and he kept kissing me. His tongue moved in, sweeping, circling, and making me pulsate with pleasure.

I was going to drop on him. How embarrassing, but I was. My knees were shaking. I wasn't going to be able to endure this. And then he sucked on my clit as he dipped two fingers into me, and he had me soaring all over again.

I buckled, but Kash was ready for me.

He stood, his hand still inside me, and caught me. A hand clamped to my back, he held me in place, plastered against him. He waited until I was done quaking.

My entire body was jerking.

A soft kiss to my neck. A second one feathered to my jaw, then a lingering kiss on my lips.

He was claiming me.

I was his.

I was a complete muddled mess.

I shook my head. "You—not fair."

A rakish grin. "Trust me." Another kiss to the corner of my mouth. "You will be paying me back later tonight."

God yes.

That meant he was coming back to me, after whatever he had planned. Kash wouldn't say it if he didn't mean it.

Please mean it, I suddenly thought. *Please, please mean it.*

I was worried about him. And oh boy, if I was starting tonight, about a blogger's place, how would I handle the rest? His grandfather was Calhoun Bastian, for fuck's sake.

He ran a hand down my face, tucking a strand of hair back and frowning just slightly. "What's wrong? You just tensed." He mock frowned at me. "You're not supposed to be tense. That was the whole purpose of coming up here."

A different thought hit me.

"You don't think they have cameras in here?"

He grinned, his teeth flashing. "If they do, I have a feeling they're going to have a hack tonight."

Damn straight they would. Still. I eyed over his shoulder to the corners. I bet they did.

He dipped down again, his breath hot on my skin. "I asked them to turn them off."

Oh. Relief.

Then . . . "How do you know they actually did?"

"Look up."

I did.

"Is there a red light in the corner?"

Red. Red. Red. I was looking everywhere. I shook my head.

"They turned it off."

That was good—very, very good. Then I could indulge some more. I lifted a hand, trailing it up his shoulder. Moving in, I grazed my nose against his throat.

I felt his rumble. "What are you doing?"

"Maybe I want to make you lose control too?" I looked up, enough to flash him my whites and wink before I moved my hand to his front.

"Bailey." A gentle warning.

I didn't care. Biting my lip, I was exploring, and I was loving it.

I dipped my fingers inside his shirt, between his buttons, and he sucked in his stomach. "Goddamn." He grunted, grabbing for the railing behind me. "What are you doing?"

"Returning the favor." I glanced up, our eyes met for a second, and I lowered myself below him.

"Bailey."

He was hanging on, breathing harshly.

Good. That was so good.

I ran my hand over his pants, and he groaned, his body surging toward me. He was hard, straining against his zipper, and I was loving this. It was addicting, making him feel good, making him shudder from a mere touch, and pulling down the zipper, I reached in to bring him out.

"Fuck," he whispered.

I looked up. His head had fallen back. I couldn't see his eyes, but I saw his throat moving up and down.

Then I moved, my lips opening, and I encircled him.

"God," he hissed.

I moved my lips over him, my teeth gently touching him, and he jerked in my mouth. Delicious. Dark. That's how I felt, pleasuring him right back in this private box, in this club that had secrets in every corner. Here we were. My man and me. I was making him feel good, just as he had done for me, and I was loving every bit of it. Moving my mouth, angling for a deeper suction, I was bringing him how he had with me. I was leading him, taking him with me, and I could feel his stomach starting to tremble from the strength it took for him not to come.

I wanted him to come.

"*Fuck*, Bailey."

He finished, but I still held him. Lowering his head, looking at me, there was a gentleness regarding me, and it made my heart squeeze.

He shook his head, catching me and lifting me. He didn't help me stand. He picked me up, and I latched onto him. Like a damn koala. That was me. Legs wrapped around him. Arms holding on, and my head to his chest.

He walked me back to a couch and sat, me on top of him.

It was a bit later, after he had splayed me out on the couch and was bending over me, his mouth moving in another slow and torturous exploration, when the light flared on in the room.

I yelled, but Kash flattened his body over me, covering me, and growled, "It better be life-or-death."

A voice sounded from the door, strained. "It's Mr. Francis." And then said, "Something's wrong."

That was enough.

The tension lifted, and he clipped his head in a nod. "A second. Please."

"Of course, Mr. Colello."

The light was switched off. The door closed.

And silence.

He expelled a strong burst of air, lowering his head and pressing his forehead to my neck. "I'm sorry." He smoothed a hand down my side again, sitting up and helping to cover me.

I was quivering but moved my head up and down. I croaked, motioning, "Go. See what's wrong with Matt."

He frowned. "You sure?"

Another motion up and down. "Yeah." My voice was hoarse. "Leave the guards. They'll bring me down. I just need a second." I might've needed more than a second.

"Okay." He leaned in, kissing me before pushing himself up. "Don't take too long. If something's wrong, we'll have to go before press finds out."

"Okay." My hand was weak as I tried to smooth out my hair.

Kash stopped, turned back. He took in the sight of me and grinned. That grin was everything. It held so much promise, but also fun. We'd been fooling around up here like high school kids. Maybe doing more than what we should have at that age, but it was still fun. It was a respite from all the other worries, and I wanted more. I just wanted more. That's all I was feeling and thinking then, and when I gave him an answering grin, he turned and headed out.

Promise. I saw it in his eyes, and I couldn't wait to hold him to it.

I was excited to head back to his place tonight.

Standing, I found a small bathroom off the entryway, and

after using it, I tried to smooth out my appearance. I looked totally and completely laid.

I laughed softly to myself, trying to make my dress look normal again, and I headed out.

Three guards waited for me, and like the trek before, all eyes were on us as we joined the rest of the club. I ducked my head down to avoid seeing whoever was there. I had seen a few nasty looks before and I didn't want to see them again. I didn't want to feel nasty or to let their problems take away what had just happened upstairs.

It was beautiful up there.

It was special, important.

I was still telling myself that when suddenly I heard a shout. Someone screamed.

People began running.

The guards closed in around me.

A woman sprinted past us, and she was hip-checked out of the way. She would've hit me just from her mad dash to the front of the club.

The front of the club . . .

This wasn't good.

Matt. Kash.

Where were they?

I started picking up my pace, then I was running as well. The guards moved with me, but they slowed the whole group down. People were folding in around us. They didn't care about me, they cared about whatever was happening in the front.

I felt my phone buzzing.

Pulling it out, I saw it was Kash.

I answered, shouting, "Where are you?"

The shouts and screams from inside the club deafened me. I couldn't hear him, just barely making out a shout. Then he hung up.

We were still trying to push our way out. I grabbed for a guard. "Matt and Kash. Where are they?"

He didn't answer, just took my arm and helped me to keep going ahead.

My phone buzzed again. Kash.

Outside. Now.

I showed the guard my phone and he nodded. He already knew, touching his earpiece.

Kash let me know, making sure I was in the loop, but he must've been in communication with the security team. As we got closer, everyone was trying to pile out.

If enough people started panicking, there'd be shoving. Stampeding could happen.

It was like a bottleneck effect. Only a few would get out unharmed.

The guards must have had the same thought, because suddenly we were changing directions.

A worker was waving us out, the same staff member who had helped Kash and me leave through the back door last time. Her eyes were panicked, but she was trying to keep it together. Holding a door open, she motioned us in, and once we got past the door, the hallway was empty. We could hear more shouting from the back kitchen area.

"What's happening?"

She was hurrying down the hallway, but spoke over her shoulder. "We're not sure. Matt Francis collapsed and began convulsing. We have an ambulance en route. Mr. Colello is with him."

"But that wouldn't have started the rush out there."

A turn.

Another turn.

She said, as she pushed through a side door, "There were popping sounds. Could've been gunfire or fireworks. We don't know. That's what set everyone off. Mr. Francis's ambulance . . ." She trailed off, stepping out into an alley.

We all saw the flashing red and white lights together.

My heart clenched up. Matt. Matt was in trouble.

I started for the ambulance.

A guard was with me. "Miss Hayes, no."

Yes, I know. It wasn't safe.

Fuck being safe.

My brother was hurting.

"I'm going." I shoved past them and began running.

"What—what's going on?" the staff member asked.

I heard the guards running behind me, and I pushed to go faster. I just had to get to the ambulance before they got me, but they were there. I barely got a few feet away. One touched my arm, and I whirled around. "No! I mean it. No! I'm going to that ambulance and I will scream bloody murder if you don't let me."

They stared at me. One clipped his head. "Stay in the circle."

I nodded back. Decision made. We were going.

They started first, and I caught sight of the staff member. She was coming with us. I paused. "What are you doing?"

She hesitated. "Mr. Colello told me to take care of you."

I frowned.

But then we were heading to the main street again. Time for questions would have to be later—and once we got there, I was thinking it'd be much, much later.

Paparazzi were lined up on the streets.

Flashes of light went off as we rounded the alley corner. The ambulance was sitting in front of the club. The doors were open, people were streaming out. And in the middle of all of that, a stretcher was being loaded up.

"Matt!" I began running again.

Kash was off to the side, talking to a cop. His head snapped up at my shout, and a storm quickly clouded in. He was heading to cut me off, a hand up. I started before he even could. "I don't care. I have to make sure Matt is okay." I dodged around him, but it wasn't Matt on the stretcher.

"What?" I was confused.

A girl stared back at me, oxygen on her and a sheet covering her. She was sweating, tears on her face, and pale. Really pale. She was terrified. A guy was next to her, holding her hand, and at that moment the back door was shut. The paramedic walked to get in the front seat, and they pulled away.

"Where's Matt?"

Kash had my arm in his hand. He ignored me, speaking to the guard over my head. "You were supposed to take her back."

"She wouldn't cooperate."

Kash's hand tightened on my arm, a reflex to that answer. He growled, "You're supposed to make her." His eyes cut to the staff member. "What are you doing here?"

"I'm not on duty tonight. I came in because you asked." She motioned to me. "You said to watch her for you."

His jaw clenched.

He nodded to the guard. "Call for the car." He said nothing to me, drawing me away from the crowd and back to the alley. It wasn't empty anymore. Others had followed us, and they were streaming out, sprinting past us. Some were bloodied. Most sweating. Crying.

But all were scared.

Kash's hand slid down, catching mine, and he tugged me away. We went down another block and turned into a second alley. This one was empty. The guards were on their phones. All of them. The female staff member was still with us, and Kash turned to scowl at me.

"I don't care, okay?" I bristled, ready for a fight. "They said Matt was in trouble, then the riot started. I'm already worried about my mom. I've already lost enough. Not . . ." I quieted, a tear falling. "Not Matt too. Not him too."

His eyes gentled, but he still didn't talk.

A guard came over. "Car's coming down this back alley.

Streets blocked off up there. The cops were quick to respond. They're trying to contain the crowd."

Kash let out a curse, running a hand down his face. "This was a nightmare. Was that gunfire we heard?"

The guard was back on the phone, then shook his head. "They don't know yet."

The staff member approached, looking up from her phone. "Some workers found empty firework shells in the mens' bathroom, in the basement. That's probably what it was."

"Timing's suspect." That was Kash.

He wasn't happy. He wasn't happy at all.

But a car was coming down the alley, an SUV to be exact, and we moved aside as it stopped before us. Kash opened the back door. I started to get in, but Kash held me back. He motioned to the girl. "Get in, Torie. You're with us then."

He urged me in after, and followed to slide next to me.

Torie? I glanced at her.

As if reading my mind, she flashed me a grin. "Hi."

Okay. "I'm Bailey."

Another grin from her. "I know. I work at Naveah. Kash warned me a girl might be coming in with Matt Francis. Asked me to watch out for you, so I did."

"You told Kash we were at the club that night?"

"I did, but he already knew." Her eyes trailed past me. "I'm assuming your security notified him almost immediately."

Kash didn't respond to the slightly veiled question. He was on his phone.

His phone began ringing and he grunted into it. "Can you contain it?" Silence. He was listening. "I don't know. . . . I said, I don't know. I stayed back for her." Pause. "We're going now. . . . Yes. She is too." Another beat of silence.

That jaw clenching again. It was sexy, but *scary* in this moment.

His eyes closed. He took in some air, then his voice dipped low—eerily low, but still sexily low. "If you want to start telling me how to keep your *daughter* safe, you and I are going to have a whole new level of problems." He was quiet. "You got that?" He didn't wait, saying right away, "We're two minutes away. You want to know how she is, you ask her yourself. You want to know how your son is, you come ask him yourself." And he hung up, dropping the phone in his lap and turning to look out the window.

I was stunned.

That was Peter on the phone. Peter asking about me, then asking again. They got into a spat. Over me. Me. His daughter.

I was getting squeezed on the inside again. Pressure was pushing in from all angles.

"What needs to be contained?"

Kash's shoulders lifted up, then down, before he said, so quietly, such a contrast from the anger that was literally spewing from him, "Press got your name. Word's out." And then, "They know you're Peter Francis's daughter."

FORTY-FOUR

Camille Story was the one who broke the news.

And that was after I had hacked her. She had a whole offline file of everything. Smart. And annoying. But it almost didn't matter, because that night all that paparazzi got pictures of me standing by the ambulance, Kash's hand in mine. Peter's program to delete Kash's picture crashed. It was overloaded that night, so when Kash said word was out, word *really* was out.

On him.

As I sat in the waiting lounge, while Matt was being worked on by the hospital, I was seeing what I could do. And after an hour I had to come to the conclusion that it wasn't much. I only had my phone with me, and Kash's picture was everywhere.

He was the big story. Not me.

Press already knew about his image. There'd been articles posted about Kash, but I had to guess that it wasn't as much as they wanted to publish. Writing an article on Calhoun Bastian's grandson would've made me fear for my life, too. I wouldn't have had the nerve to write the story, so I almost had to give respect to the ones who were reporting on him.

I had to assume they already knew who Kash was, since someone having a picture that doesn't load for years is kinda big news. It makes you wonder who the hell that guy was. Now the world knew, and after the first few stories were posted, the rate of more and more posting was astonishing. Calhoun Bastian couldn't go after all of them. Safety in numbers, that sort of thing.

So, in a way, I was almost not news at all.

My boyfriend couldn't say the same.

He was news. He was huge, big news. And we were already seeing the result of the news spreading like wildfire. We'd been asked to leave the main general lounge right away, not because of Kash but because of all the guards. We were getting enough attention from that, but then we were asked, twenty minutes ago, to leave the second private waiting lobby for a third, way more private one.

I was pretty sure we were in the doctors' lounge.

Thirty minutes into our wait, when we were still in the second lobby, Peter and Quinn had arrived. The atmosphere in the hospital switched again. They came in dressed to the nines. Quinn was wearing a formal dress, with sparkling cleavage and diamond earrings. Her hair was pulled up in a twisted side bun, more diamonds added among the strands for decoration. Peter was in a tuxedo, shiny black shoes, and was even wearing a tailcoat.

There'd been a nervous excitement that had slowly built and built, but put this couple on the scene and I wasn't surprised when a guy walking with them screamed "hospital administrator" to me.

Shit was serious now.

The nurses kept stopping in, checking on us, their eyes going to Kash and staying. I was pretty sure all the nurses actually working on Matt weren't the ones coming to see how we were doing. That was all extra. And I knew this because *those* nurses were working. These weren't.

Waiting on Chrissy had meant that the hospital was almost a second home to me, growing up. I knew how the staff and shifts worked there. But all that stopped once the administrator was there. Nurses came in, saw him, saw the reproach in his gaze, and stopped coming in.

When Peter and Quinn entered the waiting room, Kash didn't go over to them. He remained in the seat next to mine.

I was surprised at that.

Both Peter and Quinn noticed, too, and Quinn's eyebrows furrowed a small bit. Peter's face was kept blank, his eyes darting to me as if reassuring himself, then he focused on what the administrator was saying.

It was another twenty minutes after their arrival, after they were given coffee and anything else they wanted, when the doctor breezed in through the door.

We all moved.

"We were able to diagnose the poison your son ingested."

"Poison!" Quinn sucked in her breath.

Kash stepped back, a harsh hiss from him.

Peter and Quinn both frowned at him.

The doctor frowned at them frowning at him and kept on, "It was touch-and-go for a while, but once we were able to identify the poison, we administered an antidote. Your son has since stabilized. We have an IV drip giving him saline, and extra oxygen. We want to make sure all his body functions and organs don't have any lasting damage, but the last set of vitals we got were good. They were very good. We want to monitor Matt for another night, make sure everything is fine. We'll have him moved to a more secure floor, too."

"Thank you, Doctor," Quinn said. "Can we see him?"

"He's sleeping, but once we have him in the room, a nurse will come to get you guys."

Peter was staring right at Kash, who was on his phone and moving away from the group. He was speaking in a low voice, one that he was using on purpose so none of us could hear what he was doing.

He was making plans. Without us.

I didn't like it. Someone had hurt my brother. I wanted in on the revenge, but that was ludicrous, right? Kash would handle it—that's what he did.

Then Peter cleared his throat.

He ignored the doctor, speaking over another question Quinn

was asking, and spoke right to Kash. "You're in the spotlight, Kash."

Kash stiffened, looking back. He spoke into the phone: "I'll call you back. Move on my orders until you hear from me."

He put the phone in his pocket and raised his head up, looking almost defiant. There was a big "fuck off" look in Kash's eyes, though. He wasn't being defiant. He was furious. He was being Kash. This was what he did.

"It was Bonham. He was picked up on the club's security feeds, leaving a few minutes before Matt collapsed."

Quinn gasped.

Peter's frown deepened. "Bonham? But—"

"The wife," Kash grated out. His glance skimmed to Quinn before returning to Peter. "Revenge."

"Oh dear Lord. Are you serious?"

"What?" Quinn was looking between the two. "What's going on?"

Both men ignored her.

Peter was saying, "That's insane. He would've known the enemy that I'd be for him."

"The man's at the end of his run. He knows it. The wife was the last straw." Kash's eyes narrowed. "He was desperate and not thinking."

"Jesus." Peter turned away, a hand going to his forehead. He was thinking. "His wife now? His home? There are children—"

Kash cut in. "Already called the police. They have units checking the home."

"They had a cabin. I had a meeting set up at the end of the week with Bonham to discuss the board he's still on. He asked to push it back. Said he would be up north at a cabin till then."

Kash looked at me, and then I got it.

I could do this. I could help this way.

Taking my phone out, I was already looking. "I'll get the address."

"Here."

An iPad was held out to me.

It took a second to put two and two together. The hand holding it out to me was . . . my father's. He waved it again. "You can work faster on this than your phone."

He was right.

I snatched it up, moving to the chairs. I'd process that later. My dad giving me his iPad, having it at the ready, letting me do my thing.

It wasn't a computer, but I got the address within minutes

"Got it!"

Kash was at my side, phone in hand. He read it off to whoever was on the other side.

"It'll take a little bit of time, but I can turn off his security program. Or at least get the codes, if they need them."

Kash gave me a look, saying into the phone, "Yes, Detective. You can reach me at this number. Thank you." He put the phone away and doubled his look. "An officer of the law just heard you offering to illegally hack a security system."

Oh.

Not good.

"Oops."

He shook his head, exasperated, but bent and kissed my forehead. "Only you. Only you." I heard the amusement from him, and that lessened some of the anxiety in me.

We waited another twenty minutes before a nurse came to show Quinn and Peter to Matt's room. I wanted to point out that Matt wouldn't have wanted Quinn in there. If he had a choice, I would've been the female he would've preferred, but Kash just gave me the signal to keep quiet. He held back, then said he was going to seek out the doctor again.

He wanted to check one more thing.

Torie had been waiting with us until then. Kash told her she could go and she did, saying good-bye to me and letting me know

I could call on her for anything. I appreciated that. I did. She'd become a quick friend, and at this point, I was being loose in my classification of friend. She was it, for the moment.

It was an hour later when we were told that Matt's prognosis was good, better than good. We could all go home and let Matt sleep the night through.

As soon as we got the report, exhaustion hit hard.

That was when we heard the shouting. Kash was walking with me, down a hallway. At the same time, Peter and Quinn were just coming off an elevator. They saw us. There was no surprise, so they must have planned to leave with Kash and me.

But then a stairway door burst open and I heard, "I am going to see my daughter whether you want me to or not! She's mine! I saw her on the news, heard the story, and this hospital is the closest to that club where patients would be sent. Doesn't take a genius to figure out that she's here, and I know she is. Call it mother's intuition."

A blond head was walking into the hallway, talking to two hospital staff behind her. Another nurse was behind them, looking aggrieved, and from down the hallway, hospital security was heading our way.

Then that blond ball of fury looked my way, and I swear I could see steam rising from Chrissy Hayes's head.

"There you are!"

My mother had arrived.

FORTY-FIVE

Chrissy Hayes hadn't arrived. It was *Christina Kathryn Hayes*, and she wasn't messing around.

I was lectured on the way out of the hospital. I was lectured in the car ride back to the estate. I was lectured as she followed me into Kash's villa, only pausing once to comment on how breathtaking the home was. She avoided looking at the mausoleum, even sniffing and wrinkling her nose, but she hadn't paused in her lectures.

Not one word. Not a beat. She never missed one.

She kept on even after Kash returned from talking to Peter.

He sat on the couch. Chrissy didn't stop.

I was an imbecile.

I wasn't thinking.

I was being ruled by childhood hopes and dreams.

I was being selfish.

I hadn't been thinking. That was a favorite of hers. I heard it sixteen times. Yes, I started counting.

How could I have done this to her?

Hadn't I known better?

She birthed me. She hadn't needed to do that. She could've kept me in her stomach for all of eternity. I ought to be grateful I was pushed out of her vagina. What a wonderful vag she had. I had ruined it, for a couple years. It was never the same.

What would my grandpa and grandma think? Had I thought about the other family? My cousins were missing me. (I was pretty sure they had no idea I'd been gone.) Apparently, Cousin

June got married and everyone wondered where I was. She was humiliated. (She didn't know that I knew Cousin June went to Guatemala on a mission trip.) I had missed the county fair. I never missed the county fair. (I missed it all the time.) I had missed bingo at the VFW. I wasn't around to be the caller for the nursing home bingo tournament. (All not true. I never went to them in the first place. Elderly playing bingo were scary. Mistakes were for the weak.)

There were bake sales.

There were football games. (Football hadn't started.)

There were basketball tournaments.

Softball. Baseball. Every single sport imaginable that I had never participated in, watched, or followed. I missed them all this past summer.

A pinball something. She didn't know what it was, but I missed it.

The words should've been hurtful, but I knew she didn't mean them. She was hurt and she'd been scared and she was rambling until she could deal enough to really talk to me. Everything else: air. Just air.

Kash listened to it for a while, waiting for a break so he could introduce himself. There was none. After an hour, I signaled that he could go to bed. His relief almost had me going with him, because I wasn't relieved. I was envious. If I'd gone with him, Chrissy would have just brushed her teeth, still talking, changed into her pajamas, still yelling from the bathroom, and then crawled into bed with us.

She would have. That was no exaggeration.

Kash came back out from the bedroom in pajama pants and a white shirt. He bent down, kissed me lightly, the mint smell from his toothpaste lingering, and murmured, "You going to be okay?"

"Save me now."

He chuckled, though we both knew I wasn't joking. Running a hand down my hair, he asked, "Want me to stay?"

I did, but I knew he had things to do in the morning, and since Chrissy was still talking, I knew she wasn't going to end until she passed out. That could be four . . . tomorrow afternoon.

I shook my head, my shoulders slumping. "Nah. I'll probably pass out while she's talking. It'll be fine."

"You sure?"

He was wonderful. I held his hand and nodded again. "I am."

Another kiss, another hand smoothing down my hair, before he headed up the stairs to my room. We had been using my room all this time because he had crawled into mine. I hadn't gone to bed in his. Now I was thinking that was foolish.

"Kash."

He paused on the landing above us.

"Let's sleep in your room." I motioned to my mom. "She can have mine."

"You sure?" He tilted his head to the side.

"Yeah." His bed was bigger. He was closer to the door, in case something happened. I was sure. And I wanted to curl up and snuggle in with sheets that held him, just him. His smell. His feel. His everything. My room wasn't my room anymore.

He came back down, mouthing "Come to bed when you can" as he passed by.

As soon as his door shut, Chrissy stopped talking.

My head whipped to hers. "You're done?"

Her eyes were on the room Kash had just disappeared into. She watched it for a second, then a new look found me. A determined look. A look that told me she wouldn't be pacified, and I had better come clean about everything or I'd be grounded until I was sixty.

"Is he your boyfriend?"

That was a real question. Now we were starting. "What?"

Her eyes narrowed. "He's your boyfriend."

"Mom." I shifted on the couch, tucking my knees against my chest.

She added, ignoring me now, "You have a very hot boyfriend."

"Mom!"

"Hot. Wealthy. Famous boyfriend." She looked at me now. "He's powerful."

I began rubbing at my forehead. "Mom."

"Not him." She grunted, lifting a shoulder. "Well, him too. I was talking about his grandfather."

Oh God. I really wanted to disappear now.

"Mom, please." I was shaking my head. "Not now. Not after tonight."

"Why not now?" She leaned forward, her arms resting on her legs, her focus totally and completely on me. "Because your half brother is in the hospital from overdosing at that fancy dirty nightclub?"

"Is *that* what the news is saying?"

"They're saying a rich, entitled boy took drugs at a nightclub and is in the hospital. He's not the big news. It's you and your boyfriend. Your boyfriend, mostly."

I looked down, hugging my knees tighter to me. I wanted a shield against this whole conversation. "He was poisoned."

She was quiet a beat. Then, "They know by who?"

Crap. The answer confirmed the disdain that was dripping from her voice. I just shrugged. "They're not sure yet."

She snorted a laugh. "Always knew when you were lying. Can't pull one over on your mother."

"Really?" I shot upright, my feet straightening back to the floor, and I twisted around on the couch to face her more squarely. "You had no clue I was going. You were all excited about spending a free night in a lavish hotel."

"You're right." Her voice raised. "I was." She shifted, so her body was facing me squarely. "I thought I raised you better!"

I shot to my feet. "He knew about me."

Those crystal-blue eyes stopped, then closed.

Her fight vanished. She seemed to shrink back into the couch.

I kept on. "You made the decision to keep me away. Not him. Not me. You. And you lied about it all my life."

She cursed, soft and quiet, then stood up. "Let's talk about this tomorrow."

I blocked her from leaving. "No way."

Then she threw at me, rearing back, "You think you know everything, but you're wrong. All of this doesn't have to be. You don't have to be here. The kidnapping attempts aren't real. It was all a hoax, an act to get you here."

What?

There was a crazed look in her eye. Her hair was a little undone, more than normal. A vein was sticking out from her neck, pulsating at a rapid pace.

I'd made my mom lose it.

"Mom." I had done this. I couldn't believe I'd done this.

I reached for her, but she turned away, her shoulder jerking back, rejecting my touch.

"No."

She folded her arms over her chest, her back to me, and bent her head down. She was settling in. When she got this way, it was useless to try to reason with her. I would have needed a sledgehammer—the drink *and* the tool—to make any headway.

I debated, and then decided. Screw it. I was going to try. I had to try.

I said it all to her back. "The attempt was real." I laid it all out to her. She hadn't been in the room with the cops. She had no clue how bad it had been. I told her about the guy who was my ally. About the supposed rape. About Boots, Rafe, Clemin. About Arcane. I told her how I had yelled for Mrs. Johnson.

I told her how scared I'd been.

I told her that I couldn't remember the whole night, and that was the only thing I couldn't remember.

I told her about the other attempts.

I told her everything, all the sordid details, and she seemed to shrink into herself with each word I spoke.

About my decision.

About seeing Kash in the interrogation room, then the elevator.

About leaving her that morning.

About coming to this new and huge home.

About meeting Cyclone, Seraphina, Matt. About Marie and Theresa. About seeing my father for the first time.

I told her about the first day, the second, the third. I told her how I couldn't go on a computer.

All of it. I left nothing out, except the sex.

And I ended by saying, softly, as I moved so I knew she could feel my words on her back, "And I'm pretty sure, not completely, but fairly certain, to a one-hundred-twenty-percent sure, that I'm falling in love with that boyfriend you mentioned." A deep breath. A painful breath. And I released the rest. "And I'm terrified because, while my father ignores me and Matt lies to me, I don't know how Kash can hurt me, but I know that if he does, he could shatter me. Shatter, Mom."

She turned then, big fat sobs rolling down her face.

"Oh, honey. Come here."

And then I stepped into my mother's arms, where I should've been the entire time.

FORTY-SIX

Chrissy was up before any of us the next morning. She marched over to the main house and had a word with Marie. Somehow, the two had a hashing out of sorts. Neither would tell me what they spoke about, but they did let Quinn and Peter know that my mother was staying.

They didn't ask. They informed.

There were other words shared. I wasn't allowed in on that conversation, but I got the gist of it later. Chrissy said it was for the parents. Quinn, Peter, my mother, and Marie were all included. Kash and I weren't. Not that I was champing at the bit to get in there, but I knew they were talking about me.

My mom had been *not* happy when I mentioned the part about Peter ignoring me, so I was guessing she wanted to deliver an ass chewing, and I was guessing Marie wanted to be witness to it.

An hour later they came out and the decision was announced.

My mother was here to stay.

Quinn left moments after that for a charity meeting, and the other bit of business was next dealt with. Seraphina and Cyclone were told about my mother, and then about me. No one could have been prepared for their reactions. Cyclone started sprinting around, pumping his fists in the air, his head back, chanting, "Yes to the matriarchy!" Seraphina dissolved into tears.

I'd been nervous about how they would react. Having a fun friend was one thing; having a sister was a whole different thing. At the first sight of Ser's tears, I almost dropped to the floor. Kash grabbed my arm, holding me up until Seraphina had wiped enough tears aside and came to me. Those thin little arms wrapped tightly around my waist, and she buried her face into my side.

Her words, though. Her words cemented everything.

"I'm so sorry," she whispered, her nose pressed into my shirt.

"Honey." I exchanged worried looks with the rest of the women in the room. Quinn was noticeably absent. No shock there, and something I knew my mom had noted, pressing her lips together.

Unwinding Seraphina's arms, I knelt down so we were face-to-face. Or closer to equal level, because now she towered over me. She'd had a recent growth spurt that I was just catching on to.

"Ser? What are you sorry about?"

"How you must've felt." Her eyes were decidedly not looking at me. She was biting her lip. Her head folded low and she was bunching her shirtsleeve over her hand, tucking back some hair that wasn't there. Her hair was perfectly swept back in a bun. Looked too tight for her head, to be honest.

"Felt?"

Her head lowered even more, almost falling to my shoulder. I could barely make out her next words.

"Us not knowing. You . . . We love you already." Her eyes lifted, meeting mine. Tears lined them. She was still whispering, but with renewed vigor. "You being our sister, now we can love you more. Should've loved you like that from the start. We didn't know." Her eyes fell to the ground again. Her voice hitched on a sob. "I'm sorry we didn't know."

She felt bad for me, for them not knowing.

Done. Everything was done for me then. I had fallen in love with my siblings before, but now I was even more in love. Chrissy and I were never leaving. School be damned. Well, not school and life in general, because I couldn't only be here.

She sniffled, and I promptly lost my resolve.

I was never leaving this little girl's side. Bring us bunk beds, because I was moving in. To infinity and beyond infinity.

"Oh, Ser." That's all I could get out. A huge slobbering lump formed in my throat, blocking me from talking and doing anything else. I just gathered her close, and I didn't think I could let her go. I managed to break out, "You loving me the way you've already been is more than enough. I'm not going anywhere."

We were both blubbering messes.

Chrissy was wiping at her nose.

Marie was blinking over and over again, then turning sharply to wheeze.

The men . . . I had no clue what they were doing. Kash was in the room, behind me somewhere. Cyclone had quieted. And Peter was there too, but like all the other times, he was in the background and still being quiet. Since my mom had arrived he hadn't looked at me, but why would I expect otherwise? Past behavior predicts the future. Well, future meet the same. He was being the same.

Then Cyclone launched himself at Seraphina and me and the moment was done. He hugged us both, kissed us both on the cheeks, and tipped his head back again to yell out, "*Pillow fight!*"

And it was on.

Whack!

He got Marie right in the face.

Chrissy went for him, a pillow in hand. Seraphina was giggling, shrieking, trying to help Marie get him back. When they began advancing on Kash, he gave them a look, arched an eyebrow, and they took off.

We could hear Cyclone yelling down the hallway, "*Theresa! We're coming for you!*"

Seraphina was still giggling right with him.

I looked up, but Peter had disappeared.

Chrissy saw, too, and I swear, if she'd been holding a balloon, it would've deflated from disappointment. Marie took it all in, then slapped her hands to her legs. "Right. Okay." She said to my mother, "You come with me. We'll find you a room on the estate somewhere."

And that was that.

Kash and I went to visit Matt the next hour.

Kash had gone earlier in the day, giving me time with Chrissy, and I knew he was checking up on the Bonham situation. He didn't share details when he took me with him later, and seeing how weak Matt was feeling, I didn't say anything to add stress to what he was already going through. Instead, I told him all about my mother's arrival, and he was grinning by the end.

Coughing, he rasped out, "I can't wait to meet her. Seems like I'll love her."

He probably would, and I wasn't sure if that was a good thing. "The two of you will be like two peas in a pod. Troublemakers."

He barked out a laugh, then winced. "Don't make me laugh." He looked to Kash, his lip lifting. "Can you imagine me taking Bailey's mom to an orgy night?"

I was horrified. "God, no! Please no."

Matt started laughing again, then began coughing, and a nurse came in to make sure he was okay. Kash thought it was time we headed back, and Matt was already closing his eyes by the time we were to the door.

There were conversations we didn't have, and I felt the weight of them heavy.

They were with us almost as soon as we left the estate for the hospital, including how Kash was handling that he was firmly in the press.

The attention he got at the hospital affirmed all of the media.

I hadn't looked online or watched television, so it was easy to forget. Not when we got to the hospital. All eyes turned to him. His face was on the television, even, and what was worse, no one stood to turn it off. They kept it running as we checked in to see Matt. Kash didn't really need to; he had checked in earlier. They knew his name. But the new day staff needed my name for the visiting sheet. All the while, total silence in the lobby, except for a baby crying and the reporter discussing the rift in Kash's family and how Peter Francis had taken him as a son.

I felt the pinch of tension in my shoulders as we left. Kash's hand went there, smoothing over me, like he could feel it. I was thankful, once we were past the prying eyes back there, but it hadn't really gotten better. Nurses quieted, watching us as we walked past. One nurse was coming out of a room as we walked by. She startled, saw Kash, and startled again, saying loudly, "Oh my *God!*" Her colleague hushed her, and both retreated back into the room they'd been leaving. The door was slammed shut behind us.

Then it was the elevators.

Waiting, we heard the whispers.

Getting on, we heard the looks. Yes, *heard* the looks. They were speaking volumes. A few business guys stood taller. A nurse was blushing. Another was eyeing Kash like he was candy. An elderly couple looked stricken to be in the same elevator as us.

It was like that going up to see Matt, and like that leaving, except word got out.

As soon as we hit the front lounge, press were outside.

Kash sighed, the first time I had heard it that day, and touched my arm. "Hold up." He was on his phone, having a car service brought around.

"Where are the guards?"

"I thought there'd be an even bigger spectacle if they came with us today." He was regretting that decision, I could tell.

A hospital staff member came over. "We were sent for you. You have a car waiting by a side exit."

Kash frowned but confirmed with his phone, and a moment later he nodded to her. She led us through that lobby, through those hallways, past the nursing desk again, and through a whole other department. We were taken out to the emergency room drive-up. A black sedan was waiting for us, pulled up so an ambulance could park behind.

"Your car?"

"We'll get it later. I can send someone for it."

"The estate, sir?" the guard in the passenger seat turned to ask, the driver already pulling out into traffic.

Kash nodded, his eyes closing. "Yes, please."

He looked so tired, the reason having nothing to do with sleeping. I ached for him, and so, reaching for his hand, I laced our fingers together.

He let out a sigh and squeezed my hand once. We rode back home that way.

FORTY-SEVEN

We were a public relations nightmare.

That much was obvious from how the publicist looked stressed. Instead of worrying about Cyclone and Seraphina sneaking in to eavesdrop, the entire group had transferred to a Phoenix Tech building downtown a few days later. Matt was deemed healthy enough to travel, and so here we were. We were around a conference table. My father. Kash. Matt. My mother. Even Marie. The only adult not present was Quinn. Peter was there to speak for her, and she had a luncheon to attend.

I'd started to zone out anytime someone mentioned where Quinn went. She was either doing charities or she was at a luncheon *about* a charity.

I honestly felt it was an excuse for wealthy socialite women to socialize, gossip, and wine.

I mean, I would have, if I was built that way.

I wasn't. I was glad where I was, and in that moment, I was sitting between Matt on my right and Chrissy on my left.

When we came into the room, Kash had gone somewhere else to speak with someone. He'd slipped in just moments after the publicist team marched in.

The head lady was a shorter woman, blond hair in a blow-out framing a round face, eyeglasses perched high on her nose, and makeup on point. She was maybe around five three, with a more muscular build. She wasn't petite, but she wasn't overweight. She was solid, and as she went right to the front of the conference table, I saw her calf muscles.

The woman worked out in her spare time.

I was inspired by her. Slightly.

The rest of her team followed at a more sedate pace. A lanky guy with glasses, brown hair. Another two younger women, maybe a few years older than me. They were eyeing Matt, but also sending a few furtive looks to Peter as well. Matt was the only one who winked back, getting a sly grin in return. An older woman was with them, but she stood in the back with a stern face. Matt accidentally included her in his wink, and I swear he got a small growl back from the woman.

I liked her already.

I was also scared of her.

The older woman gave Kash an evil side-eye when he came in, but he gave her no attention. He walked to the end of the table and took a seat. He and Peter sat on the other side, three chairs between them. Just after, introductions were made. The head publicist was named Martha. The guy was Colin. Sly-grin girl was Coral. The other one was named Mia. Older publicist woman was named Poppy.

I *really* liked her now. Poppy. What a name.

Still scared, though.

She and Marie exchanged a heated look, extending into a stare-off, until somehow both slowly edged their heads up. A shared look of respect passed between them.

Chrissy was eyeing everything, like me. One eyebrow slightly raised, chin down as if no one knew what we were doing, and half turned toward the front of the room. Matt was still eyeing the sly girl but trying to get the other one to join in.

Glancing across the table, I saw faint amusement on Peter's face as he watched my mother. Kash was not looking at anyone. His eyes were sharp, tired, and frustrated. They were trained on the windows behind Martha, but as if feeling my attention, they shifted to me. I felt a zap, like I always did when our gazes met. He gave me the slightest of grins before looking to Martha.

"Okay. Well." Martha clasped her hands together, rubbing, those pink nails flashing together before she dropped them to her hips and braced her shoulders back. She stood up, a full inch from that gesture. "Let's do this." Her gaze swept over the entire table and her team. "We have multiple fires to extinguish here."

She started with the smallest, reporting that a few articles were posted about the pending Bonham divorce proceedings. The guy moved fast.

She added, "But that story has not been linked to the smallest of our own pile." Her eyes flicked to Matt and held. "Thanks to Mr. Colello's employee at Naveah, no leaks came from the night-club connecting Bonham's appearance and Matt's incident."

Matt snorted at that. "Incident. Nice." His mouth thinned. "I was poisoned. The fucker—"

"Matt." A soft warning from Kash.

Matt swung his gaze over, and Kash met his with a not-so-soft glare.

A small breath out and Matt nodded. "Fine. Great." His tone was biting, and he jerked his chair to face forward, noticeably not in Kash's direction.

Peter was looking between the two, his eyebrows furrowed with a small amount of concern, but he didn't say anything.

Chrissy, on the other hand—her hand shot up. "I have a question!" She was loud about it, too.

Martha was about to proceed, but paused. "Uh. Yes. Miss Hayes."

"It's Ms. Thank you." Chrissy didn't give her time to digest that. Her elbows rested on the table and she leaned forward. "What's your plan of action when it comes out what Bonham did? Because it's a matter of time. Court reports can be public, and I can see Bonham wanting that to happen, just to be a pain in the ass for Matthew."

"Uh," Martha said, "I will handle that when we get to that, but until then, the next biggest problem for us to cover is Matthew himself." Her head clicked to the side, focusing on Matthew. "There's a fair amount of stories focusing on your drug overdose at the club." She glanced to Peter, then to Kash. "It's not as many as there would've been without the other two stories breaking, but it's enough to worry about." She paused. "Enough where it could come back and bite Matthew or yourself in the rear."

Peter nodded, straightening in his seat. "What are your suggestions?"

"Now, we have two other, bigger problems happening at the same time." Her eyes lingered on me, then Kash. Her words were for Peter. "Your daughter and Mr. Colello." Then she frowned, noting where I was sitting and where Kash was sitting. She coughed before proceeding. "There are images out there of the two touching—"

Kash's gaze sharpened. "Excuse me?"

See. She'd been all gung-ho, hear me roar woman. Now, under Kash's attention, hesitant little lamb. Made me feel all hot and bothered.

She cleared her throat again, glancing down, tapping the table with her nail before swinging her head back up. "There are pictures of you and Miss . . ." She glanced to me, then my mother. "Hayes." A pause. "In an intimate setting."

Oh God.

Matt was grinning at me.

Floor, pull me down. Let me melt and disappear.

"What pictures?" Kash's voice was clipped.

She nodded to one of her staff members.

Joy. It was the sultry one.

She slid the pictures to Kash first. His jaw tightened, then he slid them toward me.

My mom leaned over to see.

"Whoa." That was Matt.

"Honey." That was my mom.

Me. I was dying. Again.

The picture must've been taken just as Torie stepped out of our private suite. She was to the side, moving away. The door was starting to swing closed, and Kash's body was on top of mine. Our feet were entwined, and he was starting to sit up. A good amount of flesh was seen from just under him, along with my shirt pooled at my waist.

No boob or even side boob was showing. Hallelujah.

Still. I was embarrassed.

Kash was on his phone, and as it buzzed, he slid it over to me. I caught it, reading a text from Torie.

I'll have security look, but maybe your girl could find them faster?

I typed back on his phone.

Kash: *This is Bailey. I'll look after this meeting.*

Torie: *Look now in case there's more going out.*

I sent him the phone back. The entire meeting was on hold, waiting for us. Kash read the text, then nodded to me. He stood up. "We're leaving."

"What?" Martha piped up, her eyes widening.

"Bailey's tech skills are needed, and at the earliest." He nodded to the photographs. "Those should've been brought to my attention the second you knew about them."

"But—"

Peter stood, going to a corner of the room. He picked up a briefcase and brought it back, opening it again. "Excuse me, but I do think this will allow my daughter"—he paused, his eyes moving to me as he said that word—"to do what she's going to be doing and we can all remain here." He pulled out a laptop, opening it for me. "This meeting is needed, Kash. You should stay."

I didn't wait for Kash's response. I was already up and moving around the table.

Peter was pulling out a mouse and a pair of headphones. I almost purred like a cat, and I was soon going at it.

I was trying not to focus on it, but I was having a moment. Again.

It was in the back of my mind. I was trying to push it back there, way back there, but I was on Peter Francis's laptop. His personal laptop. The memory size alone had me blinking in shock, and the speed of his bandwidth—more melting moments for me. The good kind, the nerdy tech hacker kind. Plus, this guy had been my idol growing up. Finding out who he really was, how he'd been ignoring me, that put a damper on that, but there were years of history of idolatry there.

Years.

I could feel Chrissy's attention on me, like a hawk, but I had to ignore her.

It was quick work to get into Naveah's security feeds; Torie's passcode helped. I just had to sift through their history. Some had been deleted. I was making a mental note to look where those disappeared to and who did that, but then I found our footage.

It was the same footage as the picture. There'd been no person there. Whoever released that image worked at Naveah.

"Thank God that other camera was turned off." I dropped my voice low.

Kash nodded, his jaw rigid again. He peered over me to Peter. "Can you run accounts on your staff?" His eyes flicked to me, then to Peter.

I was pretty sure Kash was asking Peter to break the law. I could do it, look into bank statements of the club's employees, but that wasn't the bomb being dropped here. It was the fact that Peter owned the club. Though, was that really a shock? He owned the hotel Matt lived at, and I knew he owned a good amount of the city.

Peter nodded, his own jaw tightening. "I'll make inquiries." Without asking, he took the computer and he was off to work.

I was gawking. I was a stalker. I was a fan.

I was openly drooling over everything he was doing. Again. He was moving on his computer at a speed where I barely had time to identify what screen he was on before he was moving to the next. Then he was pulling up some dark web stuff, and I almost fainted right there.

Kash's hand found my leg, and he anchored me to him.

I looked back and found him watching me, a small tug at his lip. Without thinking, I sagged against his side.

"Um . . ." Martha was talking.

I looked.

Everyone was watching us. Some were confused. Some were hostile (Chrissy, Sultry woman), and some were grinning. That was Matt and Marie. The gangly guy was perplexed. His bottom lip folded down and he was itching at his forehead, pushing his glasses up.

"As I was starting to say, I feel some of the fires can be extinguished by a joint interview with Matthew and Bailey."

Peter paused on his typing, looking up. "Hmm?"

"What?" Matt barked.

"Yes." This was the part she didn't want to handle. Those shoulders squared back, and her whole demeanor of take-charge boss lady made more sense. She was going to push us to do something we didn't want to do.

An interview? Me? With Matt?

Did she not know about the kidnapping attempt, or *attempts*, since Kash told me it had been the third?

I expected Peter to say something, but he only slid his eyes to Kash and gave a firm nod. This was Kash's ballpark, and he wasted no time.

"No."

"But—"

"No." He was speaking clear and concise, but no heat. He was being kind to her, not barking like Matt. "There will be no interviews with Bailey. You will put out what you need to through lawsuits. Matthew can be interviewed, but there'll be no mention of

Bailey or his relation to her. You want help? Distract them. Give them something else to focus on other than Bailey, or myself."

Her chin rose. "All due respect, we haven't even gotten to the shit show of you."

Oh. She had balls. Big hairy ones.

Kash's eyes narrowed, but he opened them like normal just as quick. He didn't raise his voice or change his demeanor.

"I am not your client. I'm not interested in having my 'story' being spun in any way. You want to take my grandfather on?" He waited.

She gulped. That gave her away.

He kept on. "I didn't think so. Focus your energy on Matthew and trying to distract from Bailey as much as possible. We have one month before she's to go to graduate school. I'd like a plan put in action that'll slowly diminish curiosity about who she is." He stopped, pausing on Matthew, and then he sighed. "Fuck. Give them Matthew."

"What?" My brother's head shot upright. He'd been slouching down in his seat, but also enjoying the back-and-forth around him.

Kash nodded. "Yes. Give them Bonham. The divorce. The affair. The poisoning."

"Fuck you!" Matt's chair was shoved back, and he was advancing on Kash. "Forget that. No way—"

"It's a good idea."

"Do it."

He paused, halfway around the table. His body almost fell over from how abruptly he stopped. He went to Martha, who said the first, then to Peter, who added the second sentiment. Both were careful about their words, low but firm.

Martha was nodding at Kash. "If the focus is to pull attention away from Bailey, then you're right. We need to use what we have."

"*Dad?*" Matt's jaw was on the floor, but it was the pain that had guilt pooling in my stomach. He braced himself on the table. "You can't possibly be saying—"

Peter paused from the computer and turned to his son. "Think about your sister."

Sister.

Jesus.

I didn't know if I liked hearing that or . . . Warmth was next to the guilt, overtaking it. Almost. There was still guilt there, because Matt was shook. He was truly shook.

Peter kept on. "You're not losing anything here. You've had gossip sites report on you for years. Your partying. Having an affair with a married woman is nothing new for you. They'll find you were poisoned, not that you overdosed. You will get judgment, but also perhaps some sympathy at the same time. Or the very least, opinions will not have changed. You have never cared what the public thinks of you, so you will do this. You will help distract from the attention focused on your sister, because you need to remember the reason she came to us in the first place."

Straight to the point. *Damn.* A not-so-subtle reminder of what I was guessing the PR team didn't know about, based on their confusion now.

Understanding brought some color back to Matt's face. "Oh. I see." He glanced to me, embarrassment showing, then that cleared too. Resolve had him raising his head farther, and he nodded again. "Okay. Yes." He said to Martha, "Use me. I can release texts from Amanda and any other sordid detail you'll need."

Martha was looking from Peter to me to Kash and to Matt. Back and forth. Her eyebrows firmly pinched downward. Then she came to a decision, and they smoothed out.

"Okay," she said to Kash. "You are not our client. I was not aware. Good that I am now, and our most important priority is shielding Bailey. We can adjust to these parameters and do this. You'll cooperate?" The last question was to Matt.

He nodded, his lips thinning once again. "I said I would." But he wasn't doing it happily. That was clear.

Martha turned to her team. "Okay. We can go and start moving on this." Her gaze fell to Chrissy, and she faltered as her workers began leaving the room. "Unless there's another matter we haven't addressed?"

"There isn't." Peter spoke up before my mom could. He had gone back to his computer. "Bailey's mother is here for her daughter. That is all."

It was a nice dismissal, but I was sure there was an added sting being sent in my mother's direction. Her eyes clouded over, so I was right, but Kash was standing. His hand on my wrist. He was pulling me with him, shaking his head when I looked up at him. He was warning me against getting between the two.

Matt was trailing behind the PR team, talking to the two girls.

Martha was moving ahead of us, so once we cleared the doors, we still didn't say a word. Kash didn't want my father's PR team to learn anything more, but we did move to the elevator with them all.

I glanced back.

Chrissy was coming down the hallway with Marie, their heads together, talking in quiet tones.

The elevator opened. Kash waited as most of the publicists got on. Matt looked to remain once it was filled, but Martha stepped back and nodded to him. "You stay. Go with them. I'll catch the next one."

The door closed.

Marie and Chrissy joined us, and we were all silent. Waiting for another elevator to ping its arrival.

Once it did, Kash still didn't go.

Marie and Chrissy moved around us, pausing as they stepped inside.

He said to Marie, "Take Bailey's mother to the estate. We'll be coming later."

Martha was clearly hoping to go with us, but when he gave her a pointed look, she got on. Slapping a hand to hold the doors open, she lowered her voice. "I have been aware of who you are while I've worked for Peter Francis. I didn't know all the details, and I'm impressed with how much you were able to keep quiet. But make no mistake. That time is gone, Mr. Colello. You are firmly, and I believe permanently, in the spotlight—your holdings with Phoenix Tech, who your grandfather is . . . and I have a feeling you have more you are attempting to hide. But you are not only a national interest but global as well. Governments are going to be interested in you. Do not put off moving on your public perception. You will be shocked how much it will help if we work *with* the press rather than against them."

Those were her parting words before she stepped back.

The door closed between us and them.

FORTY-EIGHT

I assumed we weren't going with them.

Kash's hand was on the back of my shoulders, guiding me into the elevator when it opened again, and as soon as the door shut he was crowding me against the wall. There was a camera in here, but damn. I was not caring. Watching me, almost close enough to kiss, he hovered over me as he pushed the button for us. I thought he'd close the distance, but he didn't. He was just standing against me, looking into me, and feeling my heartbeat speeding up.

Not one word was spoken.

We were there, right there, with each other. Seeing each other. Feeling each other. Our chests were rising, matching, and as soon as that started, I saw him. He was torn. He was tired. He was twisted inside. And seeing that I was seeing him, his hand raised like it always did. He touched my chin, his thumb grazing over my lips. His eyes darkened and he began to bend down, his lips just a trace away from touching mine.

The door opened, and someone cleared their throat.

He swore under his breath, moving with his hand behind my back, and we pushed past a small group of onlookers. Eyes were wide as they put two and two together. I was assuming Kash wasn't a regular fixture at the building. I was wondering if my father was, because we weren't at the headquarters, just one of his buildings downtown.

He guided me outside, where a car was waiting for us. So were the press. Cameras started going off as we climbed inside. People were asking Kash questions. A few were sent my way, but the publicist was right. Everyone was enamored with Kash.

He leaned forward, telling the driver, "My place." Then he was sitting back, capturing my hand and threading our fingers. He held on to me as if he needed my touch to just be. My heart was in my throat, feeling all of that and letting it roll over me. I was just embracing it, until our driver pulled into the basement parking garage and we were getting back out.

"Kash," I started, as soon as we got to his place, but he wasn't having it.

He caught me up, lifting me in the air, and I was carried to his bedroom.

I felt his urgency.

He stripped me bare, laying me down, and then he worshipped me.

He needed this. I felt it in every inch of my being.

He needed to love me, to make me come—over and over again, if I was basing this off past nights—and then, only then, would he allow himself release. And as he took the rest of his clothes off, every inch of him taut and hard and just a masterpiece for me to appreciate, he came back to me, and I was right.

He took his time, making me cry out and plead and scream. He waited until my voice was hoarse, until I was begging for him to enter me, and only then did he pull on a condom and sheath himself inside of me.

Long. Deep. He pushed in, held, and his eyes holding mine, he began to move.

Thrusting.

Slow.

So fucking controlled.

I was going with him. I was trying to make him lose control, but he was locked in some form of restraint that I couldn't penetrate. I tried. I kissed him. I raked my nails down his back, his chest. As he pulled out, I reached for him, but he only caught my hand and pinned it back beside my head. He pushed back in, still so goddamn fucking slow, stretching me, making me feel every single inch of him, before he pulled back out, then in.

"Kash. Please."

He bent his head down, his forehead resting on my shoulder, and a deep groan escaped him. He pushed harder, deeper, and then something snapped.

He moved faster. More forcefully.

It was building. Rising inside of me, mixing with a deeper emotion, twining together, and as he pushed, grinding to the hilt and his hand coming to my clit, I cried out.

Gripping my hip tight, he turned his head into my neck.

A growl ripped from him and I felt his body jerking, falling down onto me, as we both climaxed, our bodies trembling.

"Fuck," he bit out, catching my body as he slipped out.

He tucked and rolled us both so I was half sprawled over him.

He didn't talk, just nuzzled into my neck, until he lifted me so I was lying completely on top of him. His arms tightened around me, helping me turn so I was facing him. My breasts were on his chest. Hips to hips. I felt him starting to stir, but he didn't do anything else. His eyes were closed, head bent into my shoulder and neck, and he skimmed his lips there.

"Fuck, Bailey." A soft groan from him. His head rested against his headboard, just barely meeting there, and he opened his eyes to see me.

Anguish looked back at me.

My breath paused.

Alarm raced through me, and I raised myself up, a hand pushing off from his chest. "What's wrong?"

"Nothing." He blinked, and when he looked at me again, the anguish was gone. He was focused solely and completely on me. He almost looked drugged, a contentment swimming deep in those cognac eyes.

"Hey." I pressed my hand against the side of his face. "What's wrong? You need to tell me."

He didn't speak for a moment, turning his head. Cupping the back of mine, he raised himself up until his mouth was on mine.

He didn't tell me.

He didn't say anything the rest of the night, instead rolling me back underneath him, and it wasn't long before he was sliding inside once again.

We stayed in the rest of the day, that night, and for the next few days as well. Just him and me.

It felt perfect. But it wasn't.

Kash wasn't letting me in.

FORTY-NINE

I don't want to say we all hid after that, but we did.

We stayed out of the spotlight. Gone were his trips to try to find out what my kidnappers were doing, or what his grandfather was planning. Once it came out who Kash was related to, where he was, and that there was a clock running on him taking over his shares in Phoenix Tech, the buck stopped there. Something was coming. No one knew what it was, but everyone felt it, and because of that, we were tense.

I mean, everyone was pretending we weren't, but we were.

Kash and I stayed at his place until press found out where he lived, and after that, even though we could go in and out with relative privacy because of his basement parking lot, there was a trapped feeling that came with them knowing what building we were in. He'd gotten a few calls from the lobby about people trying to come in under the guise of delivering flowers or gifts. Kash told me he'd never dealt with that anyway, so the fact that he was getting calls said a lot. If he got any delivery before, whatever it was had been signed for by the front desk and placed aside until he retrieved it in his own time.

Management had also called to let him know that his neighbors were starting to complain.

Kash's response was, "Deal with it, or I'll buy the entire building and kick them out." The calls stopped after that, and really, were his neighbors actually going to move out? This would all die down. Eventually.

Right?

Kash didn't want to wait. After a few neighbors had started to try to meet, chat, or "socialize" with him as we crossed the lobby, or when one of the guys approached me when I was using the exercise bike in the gym—

Yes, let's all fall over in shock. I worked out. Once.

I felt fate was telling me to get my ass in running readiness.

It didn't last.

Back to the guy, though, because it wasn't that we were being rude. At first, I liked some of the neighbors trying to reach out and be friendly. I did; Kash didn't. He wasn't like that, anyway. He didn't need to make friends. In that respect, I was the more outgoing one. And it'd been a nice change from the earlier complaints. But this guy had been too much. He was hitting on me the second he saw me, propositioning me so I could feel what a *real* stud felt like.

My relationship with exercising had been quick and brief. Just like how that guy got handled.

A quiet phone call occurred, after I told Kash about the guy, and the next morning I saw him carrying boxes to a moving van.

Kash got the guy evicted.

And that was also the time we went to the Chesapeake and stayed at his villa. I'd talked to my mom on the phone, so I wasn't altogether surprised when we got there and found her, fitting in like she'd never not been there.

Matt was staying in his old bedroom, which was in its own section of the mausoleum.

Seraphina and Cyclone were ecstatic. They now had Marie, Theresa, *and* Chrissy *and* Matt full time there. Kash and I were back, and they were over the moon.

Cyclone wanted to celebrate by having a bowling party, so we had pizza and bowled that night. We used their private bowling lanes on the estate, which was connected to the bar.

Somehow, that translated into a party, and a few of Matt's friends came over.

So that night I got the pleasure of meeting Fleur, Victoria, and the third friend all over again. They were a lot nicer now, knowing who I was in relation to Matt. All except Victoria. She was frigid, but I hadn't expected otherwise. She came in with her nose wrinkled up, seeing Kash next to me, and her attitude only got worse. It might have affected another person, but not me. I was glad she kept her distance. The other guys in Matt's group, not so much. They came over, treating me and Kash like we were long-lost friends.

Chester. Tony. I learned the blond guy was named Guy. It was a family name for him, too. He was officially Guy IV. And of the males, after Matthew, he was the friendliest. Or maybe he was the most easygoing. That was a better word to describe him. He didn't seem affected that I was Matthew's sister, or intimidated by Kash.

He was the first to come over, slap Kash on the back, and ask him for a loan.

That was followed with a wink, but it broke the ice. Everyone in this group already knew who Kash was, but now that it was out, they weren't sure how to treat him. They came in cautious, but when Kash rejected Guy based on his credit, everyone relaxed.

Well, for them they relaxed.

Victoria was still pissy. Chester was still dirty. Tony leered, and Matthew had a restless edge to him, but that was just them.

It wasn't the first night Matt had his friends over, but over the next month, it wasn't a common event. They came over twice more, mostly to commiserate with Matthew after he did a new interview, fulfilling the publicist's plans.

We got an update from Martha, and according to her, it was working . . . regarding me.

Because I had completely left the spotlight and there were no sightings of me, I had fallen off the society pages and gossip sites.

There'd been a few exposé pieces about me. They attempted to interview people from my past, but I looked and was glad hardly anyone from my local town was quoted. That said something. They were keeping quiet.

Martha was quick to inform us that this didn't mean they forgot who I was, just that Matthew's affair and the police charges brought against Drew Bonham were getting more press.

She didn't say anything about Kash. The furtive glances she gave him said enough. And after a search online (which I had also taken a break from), I saw my guess was right.

He was still everywhere, but now the story was being moved to other sites, such as the financial pages, in addition to the normal gossip sites. The articles talked about how his new presence at Phoenix Tech would affect its stock and whether there would be a battle between Peter Francis and Calhoun Bastian, who reportedly had started buying shares in competing tech companies.

Interesting.

And alarming.

Kash saw me reading one of these stories, came over, shut my laptop, and picked me up. He was doing his whole thing of not talking by doing other things with me. It was working. I wasn't putting up much of a fight, but the time would come.

Until then, I let him carry me to bed.

The next morning he asked me not to worry about "that stuff."

Stuff. That's what he called it.

I was gearing up for a battle one time, when he dipped his head down to my shoulder, his hand skimming over my body, and settled on top of me. Feeling the worry and exhaustion from him, I bit my tongue. Literally. He didn't want me worrying because that's *all* he was doing.

I did what I could, which wasn't much.

I enjoyed my time with Kash through August. I enjoyed having my mother there. I wasn't understanding the dynamics between her, Peter, and Quinn, but I wasn't looking to cause a problem. I liked having her there. And I soaked up all the time I could with my siblings.

I continued work on my security system, and I searched Calhoun Bastian.

It was one of those nights when everyone was at the pool. A movie screen had been pulled out and positioned with a projector. They were planning to have a drive-in sort of experience, but lounging on inner tubes in the pool. Pizza, soda—and some healthy options were provided, because Quinn was supposed to be there, too.

I'd been swimming earlier, but excused myself. A whole buzz of hostility and forced politeness was in the air, and the longer Quinn stuck around, the more it grew. I felt bad because she was Seraphina and Cyclone's mother. They wanted her there, but my mother was there because of me, and so a whole layer of guilt coated over me, weighing me down.

I brought my computer out to a lounge chair behind Kash's villa. I was on the chair, my laptop between my legs, and I could still hear their laughter from the pool area.

And because I couldn't help myself, I was doing my usual digging around for any information I could find on Calhoun Bastian. If Kash was going to take him on, which everyone felt was coming, I wanted to give him as much ammunition as possible.

"He knows, you know."

Oh, snap.

I straightened upright in my seat, and I looked around to Kash's patio door, which was open. Peter Francis was standing there, his hands in his pockets, his button-down shirt untucked from his pants, and his hair rumpled. He looked like he'd had a hard day at the office. His tie was gone, and he had the five o'clock shadow working on his jaw.

I could tell. A long-lost daughter just could.

A shiver went down my spine, one of those again, and I knew.

This was the talk. *The* talk.

Or I was assuming, since the first time we'd been alone had nothing to do with personal stuff between father and daughter.

I was ready. I was more than ready. This should have been done long before now.

Then he said, "You're not helping Kash."

He got me with *that*? He wasn't fighting fair.

"What do you mean?"

Head down. Voice hoarse. I could do this. I could handle him. Just been years in the making, right?

He moved to the lounge chair beside me and sat, facing me, resting his arms on his legs, bent over.

I watched him, side-eyeing him, but he didn't lift his head up. He kept it forward, looking at the ground or at his hands, I didn't know. I just knew my father still couldn't bring himself to look me in the eye.

"If you think Kash hasn't been ready for this war since he was six, you don't know who you're sleeping with."

It was another sucker punch.

I closed my eyes. I didn't think I could do this while looking at him.

His voice dropped. "I met Calhoun Bastian when I was around your age, had my head filled with thoughts and plans and ideas like you do. I was going to conquer the world, and damn it, I got fucking close." An edge of regret lined his words. He looked up now, his eyes ringed with the same emotion. So much of it. "I know this has been a long time coming, but for the life of me, I didn't know what to say."

About Kash?

No.

Comprehension flared, and I jerked forward.

Oh.

Oh!

Me. He was talking about me now.

I tried to close it down, but emotions surged up. My throat swelled. A lump was pending, and the waterworks were on deck.

No, no, no. I could not handle that.

Not anymore.

But he didn't know any of that, and he spoke, his tone softening, "Want to know the most humbling moment in someone's life?"

I frowned.

"It's trying to explain to the daughter you always knew about, whose mother made the decision to keep her away and out of the limelight, how I wanted to care for her, love her, support her but I couldn't—and that now, somehow, the reason it had been decided to keep her a secret never mattered, because here she is, her life threatened all the same."

Whoa.

That was a *total* knockout.

He got me. Smack in the feelings.

"Um," I whispered.

Stellar genius, here. Yours truly.

"I have nothing to say in my defense, especially after finally having you here and still not talking to you." He laughed ruefully. "Your mother chewed me back and forth from China for that one. I got a fresh set of road rage this morning. The tire tracks are still smoking." A soft laugh, filled with so much regret still.

"Truth is that I've no idea what to say to you. Still don't. I'm here and I'm trying to figure it out, get my legs under me, but I'm failing. I'm totally failing, and I have no idea how to talk to the daughter who's the most like me of all my kids. Messed up the first time I saw you, too."

Something was opening in me. Something small, but *something*.

A small crack.

He kept on, still not looking at me. "I should've said this to you the first day you were pulled in after the kidnapping attempt.

Hell. I should've just tried harder. Then I heard what happened and . . . shame."

I was focused on my seat. My hands were picking at the chair.

"I was ashamed. The reason your mother decided to keep you away was the exact reason you were coming to me, and I was elated. I'd finally get to see my daughter in person. Not just a report on my desk, or a sound bite. Or knowing that she was applying for my scholarships, that she wanted a job where I worked. My daughter. Mine.

"You won those scholarships on your own, if you ever start doubting yourself. You did. Not me. I had no bearing on the team who picked the winner, but I was glad. I was damn proud of you, because I was still a part of your life, though there's no reason you ever need to give me the time of day. You. I am proud of who you have become, and"—his voice dipped—"I am humbled, because all of that was your mother. Not me. I don't know if you would've turned out the way you have if you'd been under my care."

I knew who he was referencing.

"You don't give him enough credit." I lifted my head now. Matt deserved that from me. "Give him structure. Give him purpose. He'll blow you out of the water."

He held my gaze, his own eyes filling with a sheen of tears.

He said, "We tried."

I bit out, "Do it again." Matt would've owned a company by now, if he'd been pushed how I was. He hadn't been. He was given what he wanted. "Challenge him, but not from disappointment. From pride. From respect."

Peter nodded, ducking his head and rubbing his hand over the back of his hair. He gripped his neck before dropping and lifting his head again. "I'll do that. You're right. I've let things go lax since his mother died." His voice grew thick. "I won't do that anymore."

Then we sat there in silence.

I didn't feel I needed to say anything, to explain myself, to prove myself. Perhaps call me cocky, but I felt my record spoke for itself. And him . . . He'd already shared enough. Maybe it was good enough for the first real talk between us?

"I'm not going anywhere." He needed to know. I spoke up, my chin lifting almost defiantly. "Just so you know. I ain't going nowhere." Grammar be damned. I spoke from the heart. "Matt. Seraphina. Cyclone. They're my family."

Kash.

I was staring back at him, daring him to challenge *me*.

His mouth curved up and he nodded. "I wouldn't let you go anyway." He nodded again before standing. "I have more to say, but we can talk another time. I think we should talk often, actually." He started for the door behind me, but paused and pointed to my computer. "Calhoun has his own team. Every search you've done for him, I promise that he knows it's you. And he's reading enough from it if you don't cover your tracks. He'll know you care for his grandson. He'll know your skill level, and he'll know where you are every time you search."

Why, I oughta . . . I straightened to my fullest height. My pride was hurting. "I've been covering my tracks. I had a whole program running to throw every IP address it can think of to block them."

"It won't be enough." He gave me a sad smile. "You're not the first to try and battle Calhoun like that. I've been warring with the man for twenty years now, ever since I met Kash's parents. And when I say that man isn't like anyone else you've handled, I mean it. You can do what you can against him, but it won't be enough. I know it. Calhoun knows it." He quieted a moment. "Kash knows it. If you want to help take him down, let Kash take the lead. He knows his grandfather the best. He's the only one who has a chance at beating him. Trust me on that. Trust *Kash* on that."

Trust Kash on that.

He said my man's name in a tone like I didn't know my own man.

I gazed down at the laptop screen after he left, an icon blinking, giving me Calhoun Bastian's location, and I sighed, turning it off. All of it.

Maybe he was right. Maybe not.

What I did give him credit for was that he'd been playing this game a lot longer than me, and this was for Kash. I cared too much to be reckless. And with that in mind—and with the whole conversation between my father and me, which was letting me walk with my head a little higher, with an extra bounce in my foot, with a little less weight on my shoulder—I went in search of my man.

I went in search of my family.

FIFTY

"You talked."

It came out as an accusation, from my own mother. She was sneering as she said it. The pool was in an uproar, as Matt's friends had just arrived, and I tuned all of them out.

"What are you talking about?"

"You and your father." She was full-on sneering at me. It wasn't even slight. It was covering her whole face. "You and he talked. I can read it on you." She hiccupped to herself, turning away. "Damn shame."

"Hey!" I snapped. "He's my father. It was about time he came to me, and you know it. I don't get why you're all pissed about it. He said you chewed him out for ignoring me."

She stopped, then huffed. "I did, but . . ." She half turned away, dropping her voice low. "Just don't forget about your mama, okay?"

Oh, God.

I reached for her, but she stepped away and grabbed Cyclone up as he was running by. He laughed, trying to pull away, and the two were in a game of tag within seconds. She was darting, veering around everyone, and somehow Seraphina ended up pushed into the pool. Cyclone pivoted back and pushed my mom in as she was extending a hand to Ser, then jumped in over them.

He was happy.

Seraphina was happy, too.

Glancing over the pool, I saw Quinn smiling fondly at both of them, too. Then her face tightened up when my mom's head popped back up, and her head lifted, finding me across the pool. Her smile faded completely and, her shoulders stiffening, she headed inside the house.

"You're temporary, you know."

Damn.

I turned. Victoria had sidled up next to me, and—bully for her—I just now realized I had pulled back until I was standing in the corner. No one was within hearing distance. She got me. But wait. No. Bully for me. She'd been pissed about me since the beginning. I had a gut feeling it was always about Kash, with everyone saying he was her ex, but maybe it was time I found out.

I sighed. "What's your problem with me?"

She grinned, holding a wineglass in hand. "Just one?"

She'd darkened her hair so it looked like a sunset, a wheat blond mixing in with bright highlights. Long limbs. Long legs. A pastel yellow tunic, sheer enough that her white bikini could be seen, ended just over the tops of her legs. She didn't wear shorts, just her bikini bottoms. Her heels were high, but sparkly and pink. Sunglasses covered her eyes, and she had a slight smattering of lip gloss coating her mouth.

I didn't rise to her bait. "How long did you and Kash date?"

Her eyebrows shot up. I'd caught her off guard. But she recovered quickly, shifting back on her heels and saying smoothly, "We were together for two years." She hesitated before plunging forward. "But I've known him forever."

I was trying to see it. I was.

I was trying to run the math in my head of Kash with her, but I couldn't see it. This was a conversation I should run by Kash, not her. I'd seen too much to know I shouldn't believe whatever she had to say. I wasn't a jealous person, though I could feel intimidated, pushed down.

I'd just feel hurt, not anger.

Which was happening now, slightly, because there was a small voice in the back of my head wondering why he picked me.

I tuned back in to what Victoria was saying.

"Kash and I are meant to be together. Everyone knows it. Why do you think Quinn has me come over for Seraphina?" She was so haughty as she was talking. "I'm family. Already. He'll get tired of you. You're just a novelty to him, a brand-new shiny toy. Trust me; he'll come back to me. He always does." She sounded so assured.

But I still couldn't see it because he had not once looked at her, not ever. If Victoria's name was mentioned, he never even paused.

He would have. There would've been a look, if he had cared, if she was the one he was meant to be with. So I told her my thoughts.

The look on her face. Dark and stormy.

"You don't know anything." She lowered her head, almost hissing under her breath. "They'll all get tired of you, and they'll remember why you weren't brought into the family in the first place. There's a reason you were kept a secret. Once the press stops giving a shit about you—and that'll happen too—you'll be shipped back to where you came from. Everyone will forget you. Matt. Seraphina. Cyclone. They'll all move on, continue with their lives, because you're beneath them. You're a secret. You aren't worthy of this family."

The words stung.

I gritted my teeth. "You don't know anything."

"I know that—"

"Enough!" A growl erupted from behind us, and we both whirled.

I gulped.

Victoria paled.

Peter was standing there. Hands fisted. Steam coming out of his head. Jaw clenched. He was pissed. He swung his gaze to me. "Is that what people have been saying to you? That you aren't worthy of this family?"

"Mr. Francis—"

He didn't cut her off. He didn't *say* anything to make Victoria jump back, but he looked at her. That was it. Just a look. One deep and withering look that said everything. If the girl spoke up again, she was risking her life

and

That.

Was.

Awesome.

Suddenly, all those words she'd said to me weren't so piercing anymore.

But he was still waiting for me to answer, and as he looked back to me, I ducked my head down. It was one thing seeing how he eviscerated Victoria with a look, but it was a different thing to have the father I never knew, who'd been ignoring me, who finally just spoke to me for the first time tonight, look at me as if he was viewing me with a whole new filter.

Things. Annoying things were clogging my throat.

"What's going on?"

Matt and Kash came over. Kash spoke over my head. "What'd you say, Vic?"

Vic.

God. He had a nickname for her.

"Nothing—"

Peter overrode her. "She spewed out a bunch of bullshit, that's what she was saying." He took a beat, saying more softly, "Bailey." He waited. Then, "Look at me. Please."

I did, but I didn't want to. I didn't have the emotions in check, and a tear slid down my face.

I heard Chrissy gasp as she was rounding the pool, too.

Hayes women didn't cry. We endured. We were tough. We kept going.

We did not cry.

Except these eye things kept leaking. They were broken.

"What the hell?" There was my mama bear, growling. "What'd you say to her?" But she wasn't accusing Victoria. Her words were directed at Peter, her finger in the air.

He threw his head up, an incredulous look on his face. "Keep your hate in check, woman. I'm trying to make things right, for once. And I'm done waiting around." He swept the entire pool area in a gaze, his eyes falling and pinning to me. He spoke up. "Labor Day is in a week and a half. We will be having a party that day."

Quinn came forward. "Honey?"

Matt frowned. "Dad?"

His jaw clenched. "It's time I announce my daughter to the world."

He wasn't done.

He turned to my mom. "I am never letting her go, not again. Do not push me on this, and do not make this difficult. I will take you on if I have to."

"She's an adult. No one's got custody of her," Quinn was saying, coming forward in her own high heels and wearing an outfit remarkably similar to Victoria's. "She can make her own decisions—"

"Exactly!" He was skewering his wife and my mother at the same time, with the same look. "She's a part of this family from now on. I will hear nothing against this, do you both understand?"

I was confused. Not about Quinn, but my mom. Chrissy hadn't been trying to talk me into leaving. She had stayed. She was just as locked in with Seraphina, Matt, and Cyclone as I was. But I still saw that guilt. That was there for a reason.

A hand came to my back. Kash. He slid it up to my nape. "Security will have to be tight."

Some of the fight left Peter, and he dipped his head in an abrupt nod. He raked a hand through his hair, rubbing it briskly over his face, but his other hand was still in a fist. "Yes. We'll put together a protocol." He said to me, "I hope you're okay with this, but you *are* my daughter. You have always been my daughter, and it's time everyone realized how your place is here with us and should've always been." He glowered at Victoria once more, but she had faded from my side, starting to turn so she was hidden behind her friends.

He stalked off after that. Quinn went after him.

My mom faltered, watching me, and I shook my head. I didn't want to hear whatever she was going to say. My mom always meant well, but maybe she wasn't always the right person to listen to.

Kash then clipped out, "*What* did she say to you?"

FIFTY-ONE

I was a mess.

The ten days had gone by so fast. So much happened when everyone was getting ready for the party. It was a big to-do. My alerts had been going nuts from people posting about it. Security was going to be insane. They had a helicopter going over the property. I was trying not to focus on all the speculation or how livid Martha had been when Peter told her his plan. He hadn't cared. He said it was happening and she needed to adjust her plan, so she did. She was proficient, if anyone needed one word to describe her.

The Bonham poisoning affair/pending divorce scandal was nipped in the bud and, instead, glowing stories came out about me. They talked about things I had forgotten had happened, like awards I won in elementary school or how I applied for and won so many Phoenix Tech scholarships when it wasn't known I was his daughter. I had earned those on my own, and the competition for them had been stiff.

They talked about my photographic memory, the graduate program I was attending, and how even that was prestigious. The wow factor was in full effect. All these people coming to the party were now coming not only because they were nosey a-holes who wanted to see the ins and outs of Peter Francis's family but also because they were curious about me.

Another person being buzzed about in the papers: Kash's grandfather. The financial papers reported he was in the United States and traveling to our area.

Camille Story wasn't the only blog speculating about whether Calhoun Bastian would make a surprise appearance at the party, even though he wasn't invited, and they were reporting that Kash had brought an order of protection against him. That had been news to me, and since Kash had closed up regarding everything except having sex with me, I hadn't brought it up.

When I say "closed up," that wasn't an exaggeration.

He didn't talk. Literally.

He was silent. He was tense. And he was affecting everyone.

The tension had been building over the last month, but it was on steroids now. Kash was readying for a fight, and it seemed he thought he was the only one going to handle it. I tried to ask about his grandfather, but he'd just pick me up or kiss me or, well, basically he'd carry me to bed, and what girl could say no to that? One touch and I was a melting puddle for him. The tingles zapped me just by a look from him. But I knew he was worried. There were nights when I woke to find him sitting in the living room, in his office, at his kitchen table, alone and in the dark. Sometimes a glass of bourbon was set in front of him. Other times, it was just him and the darkness.

I'd either fold myself onto his lap or he'd stand and pick me up, taking me back to bed. My questions were hushed by his mouth, and I was exhausted every morning, when I would wake later—much later. We were averaging three hours of sleep per night because of that, and because of my own nerves about myself, knowing that Matt's uppity friends would be coming to the party, Seraphina's bully friends, too, and some of Cyclone's. Quinn just seemed to get frostier and frostier toward me, and my mother hadn't been much better. I was ready to explode.

Or have a nervous breakdown.

I was secretly hoping for the latter, because that might mean hospital time and—score!—an expensive-as-hell vacation. That's what those stays were for, right?

Even my humor was slipping. That was lame.

"Are you prepped for the itinerary of the party?"

It was Martha.

I turned, coffee in hand, and wrinkled my nose. She was literally breathing stark professionalism. A headset over her head, a thin mic resting just past her cheek, and a full clipboard in hand, with lists. So many lists. Her phone was in her other hand, and she was dressed to the nines, like always. High heels. A flowing tulle skirt. A sequin top. Her hair wrapped up and twisted all around with flowers and baby's breath intertwined to make her look like she was an earth goddess.

"You are way too awake for me right now." I looked away. It was seven in the morning. If she was like this, when had she gotten up? Maybe she didn't sleep. Or breathe. Maybe she wasn't even human? That was more like it.

She and Kash were both members of the same species.

Lame. *Again.* I was being so lame.

Rubbing a hand over my jaw, I bit back a yawn and went for the coffee again. I'd need this in an IV, at this rate.

She stepped next to me, looking at where I was looking, over the yard, where all the chairs and tables were being set up. Theresa manned the kitchen, but today they had brought in extra catering, given how big the crowd was going to be. Security guys had been walking the premises for the last few days, and as we stood there, looking out, three walked past, doing their sweeps.

"This must be overwhelming."

I glanced sideways at her. She sounded different. More understanding? I didn't trust it.

I sipped my coffee again.

She added, "You were plucked from one world and put in this one, and it wasn't by choice. You were forced here. That has to be . . ." She was studying me now. "I've never really thought to consider from your point of view. Are you handling everything okay?"

My coffee was really interesting—like, super interesting. I could taste the texture of it. The way the mug was warming it. I mean—crap. There's the emotional lump forming again. Why'd she have to go there, look at me like a person?

I sniffed, draining the rest of my coffee, and jerked up a shoulder.

More understanding, more than I was comfortable feeling, had her softening her tone even more. She touched my shoulder, patting there. "Everything will be fine today. Your father wants everyone to take note: you are a Francis now. They will treat you as a Francis after this, and Kash has been working tirelessly with the security. No one is getting in unless they were invited personally. Even the extra catering staff were all checked out. The computer program you wrote helped with all of that, too."

Finally. A topic I could talk about. "Yeah. Well. It's in its early stages. It's just a beta one right now."

"It was helpful. You are a very impressive young woman."

Damn it. The lump. It tripled.

"And you are very loved."

God. No tears. Hayes women didn't cry. I wasn't starting now, and I was ignoring the last time a few tears slipped out. They'd been manipulated out of me. I was going with that lie. I cleared my throat, pushing that boulder back down. "The itinerary?"

"Oh, yes." We were back to business. She pulled her clipboard up. "Food for breakfast will be put out in an hour, for family and close loved ones who have already arrived. It's a buffet-style meal, so go when you'd like, but everything will be taken down by ten. Eleven thirty is when the brunch will be put out and it will be refilled throughout the day. That's when the next wave of guests are due to arrive. Business colleagues. Extended family members. Matthew's friends. Seraphina's. That group. Brunch will be dismantled around two. The drinks will be maintained all day, but we have extra bartending staff coming in around five, and then dinner will be served at six thirty. This will be when everyone will be in attendance. Your father wanted to officially make a statement about you. A slideshow will be played."

A slideshow?

"And then, after that, it'll be dancing, drinks, and hors d'oeuvres for the rest of the night. You are to be seen, mingling and smiling. Your father will take you among the groups after the announcement to personally meet some of the guests." She tucked her clipboard under her arm, focusing on her phone. "You cannot skip any of the events. This one day. One day that you have to be 'on.' Everyone invited is important, either locally, nationally, or globally. We have CEOs of billion-dollar companies, celebrities who make million-dollar donations, top government officials. In some ways, this is the first day of your new life. You will officially be in the public eye now. People are going to expect you to change your last name to Francis. They'll expect you to wear the latest fashion trends. They'll expect greatness from you—"

"Get out."

I'd been tensing the more she talked. Every word, the less air I had in my chest. My lungs were fully depleted. Hearing Kash's growl gave me a reprieve. I bent over, gasping for oxygen.

Martha gave me a distracted frown before focusing on Kash. "What?"

"Get the fuck out of my villa."

She turned to square off against him, lifting her chin. "Kash."

Even her tone sounded condescending.

She was in trou-uh-ble.

"Get out." He growled again. "Now."

She just shook her head. "There will be expectations of her now. No one's informed her. She has to know before she goes out there—"

"She's not going out there alone. She'll be with me. Her father is making the announcement. That's it. She can be there if she wants, she can be gone if she wants. She doesn't have to do a damn thing, and you're going to back the fuck off if you think you're going to start ordering her around."

Now she got it.

Now her eyes widened.

Now she stepped back.

Now she was wary.

Now was too late. Kash was almost in her face. He was re-straining himself, but still closing in.

I whispered, "If I were you, I'd make a run for it."

She gave me an incredulous look, those eyebrows shooting up, but heeded my warning. She was gone within a second.

"You okay?" He drew me to him, folding me into his arms, one hand coming to cup the side of my face.

It felt better, feeling him, and I tipped my head up to smile at him. "I am now."

His eyes darkened. "You are always."

"Always."

We shared a grin before he groaned, stiffened, and dipped his head into the crook of my shoulder and neck. "She's not totally wrong. We have to make appearances tonight."

I smoothed a hand down his back. "If you stick with me, we'll be fine."

And the funny thing was that I believed that. I really did. Everything would be fine. I wouldn't enjoy the night. I never did, with big parties, but I understood why my father was doing this. It was time. And with that reassurance in my head, I trusted that all would be fine as long as Kash was next to me.

I was wrong.

FIFTY-TWO

I broke the "Be with Kash at all times" rule within the first hour.

He got called away for a security briefing, and my stomach growled. And me being the super smart one, I went for brunch. But—score again!—I snuck in. Grabbed a fancy-looking dough-nut, a coffee, an apple for the nutrition gods, and got back to the villa with nothing happening.

I could hear the energy outside, the conversations, laughter.

It got louder and louder as the day went on.

Chrissy texted to check in. I was fine, and that appeased her. She was getting fitted for a dress for the whole day. Matt checked in too. He was at the main house, his friends had just arrived, and he wanted to know if I wanted to come join. I declined, stating I was getting ready in Kash's villa.

To an extent, I was. Sorta.

I'd had all my fittings the week prior, and one of Martha's team members brought over a few different options for me to wear for the day. Actually, they brought more than a *few* options. I had a whole rack. Three different outfits to choose from for breakfast. Three more for brunch, and four different dresses for the evening.

Hair was scheduled in the morning, in Quinn's bedroom, but they should have known I wouldn't go there. I could do my own hair. How bad could it be? Pin it up. Put in a fancy brooch, and voilà. Fashion-magazine ready.

Wrong. So wrong.

I was panicking by around two o'clock. Kash was still doing

his thing, whatever that was, and my hair was flat as a pancake.
I needed help, stat.

My options were limited. My mother, but I didn't want to
endure any griping she might do about the party in general. Matt,
who . . . was probably wasted and balls deep in some girl. Let's be
honest here. So I called Torie.

"What's up, superstar?"

Music sounded from where she was. I frowned. "Are you
working?"

She laughed. "Hardly. But kind of. Your man wanted me at
your shindig in case you needed any help."

She was a gift.

"Know anything about hair?"

She laughed. "I don't, but my roommate's a hair stylist. Want
me to sneak her in?"

I hesitated, but decided. "Yes. Give me her name first, though."

Tamara Harris.

She was roommates with Torie—

"What's your last name?"

Torie chuckled. "Hanson."

Right.

After I did a quick search for her on my own, sending Kash
the details of what was happening, she was flagged through, and
an hour later I was looking back and forth between the two.
Tamara had platinum blond hair that framed her face so it looked
like a heart. She had plump lips, heavy red lipstick, smoky eye
shadow, and thick eyeliner. She was wearing a plaid cropped skirt
and a white button-down shirt, tied at the waist. Black hooker
boots that ended at her calves.

Next to her, with her brown hair slicked down, looking like
it was wet, but that was how it was styled, was Torie. She was
wearing a black leather skirt. The same white button-down shirt,
but it wasn't tied at the waist. It was left out, the ends hanging

over her skirt. And she had cream white heels with diamonds on the straps.

They were fashionably edgy.

They were aliens.

I felt two feet tall in front of them and had only the latte Torie had brought from the house as my shield. I gripped it tight.

Torie's mouth dipped up. "You're freaking, aren't you?"

Tamara nodded with her, eyes never leaving me. "Freaking. Totally freaking."

Oh. Gah. I was.

My lip quivered. "I am not."

They both snorted. "You are a shit liar right now."

Tamara added her two cents, still nodding. "Bad liar when freaking."

"Totally." Torie grunted.

Neither ever looked at the other. They remained fixed on me. *That* was freaky.

I gulped, and Torie saw the motion, her eyes narrowing. "Right. Okay." She was taking charge.

Thank God.

"Show us the goods. Tamara will do your hair, and I'll do your nails."

My nails? I held them up.

As if reading my mind, she laughed. "No way you're heading out there to that group without a proper mani and pedi. Get in the shower. We'll pick your outfit."

I was out of my league. I recognized it now. And after showering, I gave up any control I might have been trying to cling to.

Torie and Tamara could have their own reality or beauty show. They both moved around the other like they'd been working together for years. One-word statements were apparently questions for the other, and somehow the word *Now* meant for Torie to switch up an entire outfit for me. Both looked, nodded, and approved, and they bent over to keep working.

That was just one example.

They were cool, and if I could be friends with them, I might have reached friendship paradise.

I was just getting done when Chrissy popped in. Her eyebrows shot through her forehead, and her mouth fell open. I rarely saw my mother speechless, but I was doing the same, looking at her.

"Mom." I was choked up. "You look amazing."

She wore a gold, glittering dress, her hair curled around her face. More glitter was in her hair, matching her diamond earrings and necklace.

"Where'd you get the jewelry?" I asked.

She was busy taking me in, but her hand went to her necklace. "Oh." A small line formed in her forehead. "This was an old gift. I just haven't worn it in forever."

A gift? "From who?"

She shook her head, coming forward. "You look beautiful, Bailey." She was awed, still looking at me from top to toe.

I was beginning to get uncomfortable—I mean, more than I already had been. I was at a good solid eight, and her compliment, mixed with the surprise, was putting me at a good cemented ten. A bit more and I was going to blow a gasket.

Nervous breakdown. Hospital room. I could only wish.

She began blinking rapidly, her hand wiping at the corner of an eye. "Oh, honey. You look just . . . just so beautiful." Her throat was moving up and down, and she sniffled.

We were moving into the red zone of expressing feelings.

"Thanks, Mom."

Torie and Tamara had been watching our exchange. I introduced them.

Chrissy nodded, giving both a smile. "It's nice to meet you. I'm glad that Bailey had friends to call on for help with this stuff. We don't . . ." She was blushing. Slightly. "We don't do this that often in our other life."

"Mom!" That came out louder than necessary.

"Have you eaten?"

Relief. "No."

She was nodding, smiling. "I'll get you something. Just something small?" She headed for the door. "Maybe something to drink as well?"

I was pretty sure the drink was for her.

I smoothed a hand down my dress. We were nearing five o'clock now, but I hadn't looked at myself in the mirror. I was scared. What if I didn't recognize her? What if this was the new person I was supposed to be from now on? What if—what if I didn't measure up?

A new person came to the doorway, and I had no words.

All my thoughts about myself vanished. They upped and flew out of my head like a bird fluttering away.

I had no thoughts now.

I had no jokes even.

"Kash." I could only murmur, moving toward him. "You look . . ."

A tuxedo that his shoulders filled out, cut in over his slim waist and hips, and I knew what was underneath that tux. My mouth was watering.

Kash was stunning on a daily basis, but him in a tuxedo? He was a goddamn weapon.

His eyes were locked on me, and the air sizzled. No joke. I felt steam in the air.

Might've been from my coffee.

He looked me up and down, and as his eyes darkened, I knew he liked what he was seeing, too. That had my blood on a good simmer, fast heading toward a boil, but I tried to settle down. I wouldn't be able to get through this night if I just wanted to jump him every time he looked at me.

Snap out of it, Hayes!

Why my inner voice sounded like my seventh-grade gym

teacher was something I'd never figure out, but I smiled. "You look *hot*."

Someone snorted, but not me, and not Kash.

His eyes warmed and he took my hand. Bending down to my ear, his hand going to press lightly on my back, he pulled me against him, saying, "I want to strip this off and spend the rest of the night deep inside of you."

Oh, dear Lord.

He chuckled softly and pressed a kiss to my cheek before whispering, "You look beautiful." Then he bent, his mouth sliding and hovering over my mouth.

My breath. Gone. Again. He could do that in one look. Then he was nodding to me and the girls behind me. "I'll be at the door."

My whole insides were trembling.

Torie was shaking her head again. "Is he always like that?"

A weak and shaky laugh was my only response, and her eyes widened at that.

"Wow."

I nodded to that one. "Wow."

"Okay. Let's finish up." Tamara had pulled my hair back into a messy braided bun behind my head. Loose tendrils framed my face and were sprayed for volume, with a few pink roses stuck overtop the bun. My dress was an A-line V-neck with spaghetti straps that pressed over my top. It didn't look tight, just smooth, like it was hugging me. The bottom had a slit up the thigh, with a shimmering silver-blue tint. As I moved, I felt the dress sliding sensually over me. There was no back, so no bra, and I felt the air graze over my back. It felt nice.

I headed out to meet Kash. He opened the door, and I heard him draw in his breath.

His hand came to my back, splaying out protectively, and he bent close. "Are you wearing underwear?"

I only grinned at him. "You'll find out tonight."

His hand pressed on me harder, and his eyes flashed. "If you think I'm waiting for tonight, you're mistaken."

I had to stop, lean against Kash for a second. His hand smoothed down to my hip before sliding up my back, and he caught my nape. He held me still, positioning my head back, and he dropped a kiss to my mouth. He held me there, his lips demanding over mine, but then he groaned. His body tightened, and he forced himself to lift up again.

"You make me want to forget the world." His lips whispered kisses to the corner of my mouth and up my jaw before he found the crook of my shoulder.

I was shaking. He wasn't alone.

I placed a hand to his chest, needing to help hold myself upright. He centered me, and his hand found mine, covering it. He lifted his head up again, a deep raw need in his depths as he raked me over again. "You okay?"

I shook my head. I couldn't talk. I knew what I had to do.

He started forward.

But then I did. I knew exactly what to say.

"Wait." I pulled him back.

He faced me completely, and I spoke low, because I wasn't going to repeat myself.

"You and me, tonight, you're not driving anymore."

His eyebrows pinned together.

"We're talking, and when I say 'talking,' I'm referring to using our vocal cords to make sounds that can string along sentences." I stepped close, my hand on his chest. I felt him stiffen, but I wasn't done. "If you and me are going to be a you and me, we're actually going to be a you and me. That means you talking, me talking, you listening, me listening. Equal. Got it?"

And I didn't wait. This time, I led the way outside.

FIFTY-THREE

There were people everywhere. They were wealthy, privileged, powerful, and I was officially freaking. Forget that they were here for me, though I knew that was just the excuse. When Peter Francis threw a party, people came. That was the sentiment I felt, and I knew it was true as I saw three politicians, a mega pop star that I was fangirling over inside, and—oh boy—a queen of a television network. She was laughing with a group of television anchors and my mom.

My mom?

I stopped walking. Kash stepped next to me, following my gaze.

He chuckled, but it was strained. He hadn't said a word about my "talk" to him. "Why am I not surprised to see Chrissy Hayes fitting in like she owns this house?"

I threw him back a frown. "Speaking of that, have you gotten a feel on the dynamics between her and my dad? And Quinn? They've all been tight-lipped about letting any of that out. It's weird."

He shrugged, tugging me forward now.

A server went by with champagne, strawberries inside, and I snagged two. I wasn't even going to pretend I got the other one for Kash. He wouldn't drink, so call me Two-Hands Fister. It was my party. I could drink if I wanted to.

"I think there's history between the two that neither wants to talk about," he said.

As soon as people started noticing us, conversations quieted. Eyes turned to track us. One would think they were watching me. Nope. I wasn't buying it. All those gazes were on Kash, then dipping to his hand, which was now on my back as, yep, I was holding both of my champagne glasses. Classy.

I could fix that. I quickly drank one of the glasses.

Kash was pulling me over to where Matt was sitting. He was with his usual group of friends, sitting on the lounge chairs by a glass-enclosed fire pit. Matt jerked his head up in a nod, grinning as we drew nearer. He moved to meet us, separating from his group, and one of his hands went into his tuxedo pocket. "You two look fucking smashing." His eyes were twinkling. He looked me over. "Shit, Bailes. You look hot, even for a sister of mine." His lips tugged further upward and he motioned around the entire backyard. The party tables were set up on the bricked patio, behind the mausoleum, but the people had spread so they were standing on the greens that were a part of the estate's private golf course. A few even were on the basketball court, and I saw a couple kids running around shooting hoops at the far end. Cyclone was with them.

Seraphina was standing in a group of other girls. I made a mental note to find out the names of each and every one of them. I remembered the online journal I hacked from Seraphina's account. It hadn't boded well then, and it boded even less now.

Big protective sister was here to stay.

We stayed with Matt and his friends, friends who were very keen and interested and now suddenly all wanting to be friendly with me. Shocker. They were also noticing the hand that Kash kept on my back.

I liked how we were.

I wasn't leaning on him. He wasn't claiming me. He didn't pull me to his side, but he was next to me. There was some space

between us, but his hand was behind me in case I needed him.
It was almost perfect.

Matt sometimes stood on my other side, sometimes maneuvered in front of us so it was the three of us and his back was
keeping everyone else out. Sometimes he just moved aside and
grinned when people came over to "meet" me.

It was his friends first.

Fleur and the third girl in her trio with Victoria were next,
though no V.

I figured Victoria was around somewhere.

Torie and Tamara were at the snack table, then at the edge
of our circle. They were laughing with Chester and Tony. Torie
glanced over at one point, sharing a look with Kash before skimming to me and giving me a smile. She tipped back her champagne glass and turned back to whatever Guy was saying. He had
replaced Chester at some point.

The more time passed, like a clock ticking off every second,
the more tense I grew. I hadn't moved out of our spot, but I knew
it was coming. Then it came.

Conversations quieted as Peter nodded hello to the outer circle first, moving toward where Matt, Kash, and I stood.

He paused, looking uncertain for the first time. His eyebrows dipped together. He raked a look over Matthew, then
Kash, and coming last to me. His lips thinned and he settled his
shoulders back. His head rose a centimeter and he cleared his
throat.

"Are you ready?"

Matt stepped back, glancing to Kash, who moved forward.

Kash asked, "For what?"

Peter looked to him. "I was going to introduce her to people."
He paused, just the slightest of pauses, dropping his voice low.
"You know I have to."

"You don't have to do a thing."

Peter pressed his lips together, the exhaustion coming from him for the first time. I noticed an extra line of bags under his eyes. "I do, actually. It's the only way to make it right, for her. You want something long-term with her, you know this will make things easier. If I don't walk around with my daughter, at a party *for my daughter*, it'll look like I don't want them to address her as *my daughter*." He kept giving Kash a meaningful look each time he said that phrase.

His head lifted again. "Networking isn't something I enjoy, and I know you hate it, but it's a necessity. It might not be for you and where you are going to be in the hierarchy, but Bailey's not that lucky—or unlucky, however you prefer to see it. If I don't walk around with her on my arm, she'll look like an embarrass-ment and"—his eyes flickered to mine—"she's anything but an embarrassment."

Now he turned right to me, focusing on me, only me. "This is overdue. She deserves this respect."

Tears.

My throat was swelling up.

This was not boding well for me.

I needed a joke. Stat.

Matt grinned, seeing my predicament, and leaned in. "Yeah, sis. Don't choke. Suck it down. Be a Quinn."

Peter threw him a disgusted look, his eyes flaring. "Are you kidding—"

Matt gestured to me with his drink. "It worked."

A laugh burst from me, and I was coughing, trying to get the rest of those annoying things out of me. I was damn near hacking. Could not process. Could not think, feel. It was robot time.

I touched Kash's arm, not surprised at how tense he was. "It's just a roundabout, then I'll be back."

His scowl never left his face, but his eyes flashed over my shoulder to Dad. "Don't introduce me."

Introduce Kash? Then I saw what he meant.

Peter—I was adjusting here. Dad/Peter . . . I was going with Peter now—nodded, saying, "Fine."

My dad/Peter, myself, and Kash behind me.

My dad introduced me to people. Some, I tried not to swoon, because—hello—they were huge names. It was the ones in the tech world that had my knees buckling. A couple government officials and the few celebrities, they had my stomach all fluttering, but they didn't pack the punch of the cyber conglomerates.

My dad introduced me, drawing me forward to the circles. I shook hands, kept a nice smile on my face, and every second question I was asked, I responded with one in the same vein.

Everyone was nice, but I wasn't the only reason they had come. As soon as the introduction was done, and sometimes before it even started, their eyes trailed behind my shoulder.

They all wanted to know Kash.

A few tried. The government officials tried to reach out for a handshake, but Peter moved in with a question or a comment and the attention was diverted.

When we were done, I snagged my fifth champagne. I was heading left. Peter grabbed me and veered right, and I heard Matthew snorting somewhere behind me. I tried to throw him a glare, but then Peter was leading me to my absolute nightmare.

I should have been prepared. I *was* prepared.

I knew this was going to happen, hence the five champagnes, but then everyone was being moved farther down the backyard. Peter was leading me to the top of the patio/deck area, so— *gulp*—it was like we were on a stage.

This. Right here. Worst nightmare ever.

I so wasn't prepared.

I was suddenly realizing how much I hated attention—like, dreaded it. Like I made an entire career plan so I wouldn't get attention. Ever. And here I was. I was also remembering the benefits of not being known as Peter Francis's daughter. Yeah, yeah. I couldn't have it both ways, being claimed as his daughter and not getting attention. It was what it was. But I could gripe about it, couldn't I? So I was griping. Actually, I was drinking. I was almost done with my fifth champagne, and as Peter was talking, a microphone was placed in his hand—did we really need that?—and I was trying to catch the eye of a nearby server. Refills, sir. Refills.

". . . are moments in life that we will always remember, and the day I heard I had another daughter was one of them."

I was clueing in, and I saw how Peter stood to the side, a smile on his face, no sparkle in his eyes, and the microphone in front of his mouth. He was grandstanding. He was making a show here. This was supposed to be just an announcement, just to tell them who I was and how happy he was that I was a part of his life. That wasn't what he was doing.

He was lying.

He'd been told from the beginning.

My hand clenched my champagne glass and I fought to keep from weaving on my feet, but he was lying. I hated that. Detested it. It wasn't one of my big rules. I was pretty lenient on the whole being-fake charade. But right now, hearing the father who hadn't acknowledged me in forever now acting like I was this big, grand surprise to him—I was gritting my teeth.

I wanted to tear into him, rip that mic out of his hands, and tell everyone the truth.

He kept on, so damn smooth. "She wrote to my office, and we didn't take her seriously." A *har-har-har* laugh from him. The crowd joined in, thinking he was hilarious.

What was going on here?

He was kind, then kind again, attentive even, and now this? I was not following a thing, not at all. Nothing was making sense to me.

My blood was starting to simmer.

His eyes hardened, seeing my confusion, but he kept his voice so light and happy. How did he do that?

He was saying, turning back to the crowd behind him, "And then we realized that she truly was my daughter, and no one could imagine the whirlwind that happened after that."

Damn, he was good. He almost sounded sincere.

The simmering was moving to the next stage.

His voice was low, husky even. "We had hoped for some privacy while we got to know each other, but it's time now." He turned, facing everyone, his free hand holding up his champagne. "Join with me as I toast, as the entire Francis family now has one more member, my daughter." He turned back, his eyes warming, now being genuine, and he blinked back a tear. His voice broke into the microphone, but it only added to a swoon effect. I saw some of the women wiping away tears of their own.

I shot past the boiling stage. There were flames.

"Welcome, Bailey. I want the world to know about you. I want the world to love you as much as I already do." And then he couldn't say any more. A second tear was sliding down his face, and his Adam's apple was bobbing up and down as he tried to control his emotions.

He just stopped.

He sighed, raised his glass up, everyone else raising their own, and he was beaming at me as he took a drink.

Lies. All the fucking lies. I was sick of them.

A cheer rose up from below us, then Peter was moving toward me. He wrapped me in his arms, hugging me, and he whispered into my ear, out of everyone's sight, "I had to keep with the script our publicist gave me, but I meant every word. I already do love you, and I am so happy that you came to us, even if it was in an unorthodox way." He pressed a hand to the back of my head as I resisted, but shit. I was weak.

I hugged him back.

I felt the emotion rippling through him, and damn if that didn't do something to me. I was melting, so I pulled back. "Thank you." It was all I could get out.

He blinked away a tear, then someone called his name and he stepped away.

How fitting.

FIFTY-FOUR

"You were supposed to never be a problem."

A chill went down my back and I turned. I was standing on the back patio, a bit of food in my stomach, so the full buzz I'd felt earlier was just a nice, small tickle. We were into the night hours, though I'd lost track of time. Everyone was having a good time, myself included. It wasn't something I'd expected, but I wasn't stopping it, either. The publicists' lying speech aside, I'd been moved by how moved Peter had been at the end, and that feeling stuck.

And I let it.

Cyclone was still running loose with his friends. I saw Seraphina giggling with her friends. I still wanted to look into them, but she seemed happy that night. Chrissy was in full flirt mode, an older man and her had been sitting at the same table for the last hour. I'd never seen her laugh so much, so I was enjoying it.

Kash even relaxed.

Matt's group had gone inside for a while but then returned a half hour ago. They took up residence around the same bonfire as earlier. All were sitting, lounging. The fire was going, the flames licking over the crystal rocks inside. Drinks had been flowing. Laughter as well. A few of the girls were around. I recognized Fleur, sitting on Matt's lap, leaning back, with his arm around her hip to anchor her in. She kept sneaking glances at Kash, though. The third friend was on Chester's lap. Torie and Tamara had taken off, saying their good-byes to me before letting me know they were heading to Naveah, and the rest talked about ending the night at the club, if I wanted to join.

To say that I was surprised Quinn was the one approaching me would have been an understatement, but then I clued in to her words and all that died down. Yeah. Not so surprised now.

She was stepping out of the open patio doors, still looking amazing. Her hair was swept up, pinned to the top of her head in a form of hair crown. Loose tendrils fell down, framing her face. Her makeup didn't look smudged at all. With her blond hair, the light blue of her dress, she was giving me an ice queen look, and that chill just doubled when I saw the calculation in her eyes.

She wasn't drunk at all. Oh no. Those eyes were alert, sober, and there were plans, so many plans in them.

I glanced over, reassuring myself that Kash was within shouting distance. She couldn't do anything to me, not here, not with everyone so close—though the sounds of the party were still loud. The DJ had been playing for the last two hours, and trailing my gaze past her and into the house, I saw that the inside was empty for the moment.

"I wasn't supposed to be a problem?" I needed a drink. Right? Maybe not. Maybe I needed to have as much of my faculties as possible for this conversation, because I was feeling it wasn't going to go well.

"No." She stopped next to me, turning to take in the entire backyard behind us. She lifted her head, drawing in a good breath of air, and her eyes closed for a moment. Opening them, her head held high, she turned to face me. Her side rested just so slightly against the railing behind us. Her lips tugged up, that small grin not inviting at all, and she moved even closer, dropping her voice even though no one was near enough to overhear. "Peter and I have had problems since the beginning."

I relaxed, slightly.

She was confiding in me. Opening up. That was a good sign, right?

But my gut was still tightening up, and my instincts were telling me to get away from her. Instead, I reached for the railing and held on, my hands wrapping around it.

A soft laugh from her, and she dipped her head down. "Peter's a cheater. Always has been, even with his first wife. Colleen wasn't even that bad of a wife, but it didn't matter to your father. He was an up-and-coming tech genius. Everyone in Silicon Valley wanted a part of him. Then his mother back in Saint Louis fell ill and, well, you know what happened after that. He and Colleen hadn't ended things, but it was in the works. It was a matter of time."

She stopped, a hard glint coming back to her eyes. Her mouth pursed together, pinching.

A rougher note fused with her tone. "Peter loved his mother. It devastated him when she took her last turn for the worse, and he wanted to spend more time with her. Said he'd just be out there for the time being, that nothing would change. He was going to leave Colleen."

Her words ground together, biting with disdain.

"I'm telling you this so you're aware your mother wasn't special. You weren't special."

I was almost captivated, in a horrifying way.

"No one worked with Peter until I came into his life."

I couldn't make myself pull away, and I only wanted to hear what else she had to say. There was a point. She was getting to it. The charitable Quinn was not beside me tonight. She was an altogether different sort of animal.

Bitterness. She was filled with that emotion. And it spilled out as she kept going, a cruelness peeking out over her face, pulling all of her features into a distorted twist. I'd never seen that on another human being. It was fascinating.

"My father was indebted to Calhoun, but he wasn't the reason I seduced Peter—though *seduce* is a broad term for Peter. I looked at him, lowered my shirt a little, and promised him he could take my ass."

So not needed. So not.

Wait.

"My father was indebted to Calhoun . . ."

Seduce.

Then a different voice, a memory. *"Quinn knows Kash's family . . ."*

Off. This felt off. And wrong.

Where was Kash?

I turned, looking for him, frowning. He was heading our way, but Victoria was there. Of course. Fucking cosmic timing, right? I expected him to pass her by, ignore, but no. That wasn't happening. She touched his arm.

He was bending his head toward her.

A concerned look on his face, but his eyes lifted. He looked at me.

She said something more, tugging on his sleeve, and he looked back at her.

What was she doing? What was *he* doing?

I was stung.

This wasn't normal Kash. He ignored her. He snapped at her. That was what he'd done before now. But then I flashed back to my speech. I had told him how it was going to be. I was declaring my feelings, saying he had to talk to me.

A stab of doubt pierced me. Had I been wrong to do that?

With horror, in slow motion, I saw him give me a hardened look before he turned and followed her.

He followed her.

What the hell?

I started to go after them, but Quinn got in front of me. She blocked me, and her mouth was moving. She was still speaking.

What was she saying?

She kept on. "He was only too eager. It wasn't hard work to ensnare Peter, make him fall in love with me, or at least give him all the promises that he wanted. Infidelity was part of our agreement. I was fine with him being with other women. It was what I could offer that Colleen couldn't. Your father had never curbed his need for women, still hasn't, though his focus has been more singular lately."

What was going on here?

Why was Quinn coming to me, telling me all this? Why now? Or—a lump was forming in my stomach—why here?

Because she felt safe.

No. I dismissed that thought, though it came to me in a whisper, from the back of my mind. That made no sense. None of this was making sense.

"Arcane was sent by someone who knows my grandfather . . ."

"Everything's been fine. Everything's been wonderful. Peter could fuck whoever he wanted, but so could I." She paused now, looking at me again. Her eyes narrowed to slits. "That was, until your last essay to get that Phoenix Tech scholarship for graduate school. You talked about the father you never had, the lie your mother told you."

I wrote that essay so long ago.

Go, get Kash.

That thought nagged at me, speaking up in the back of my mind.

It was a personal piece. We had to include our mentors growing up, along with the prospects of a proposed graduate project. The best of the best didn't have to go to school, not in this career path, but Chrissy pushed school. She wanted a degree by my name, said education was the best way to cement your future. She didn't understand the technology world, but as long as I could continue going to school with those scholarships, I went. I went for her, and I had learned it was my real father who had paved the way.

And that essay.

I should get Kash. It was more insistent now.

I talked about the father Chrissy told me about, the one who had fought for our country and died in an attack. She gave me names and credentials, and she had friends from the VFW who helped along her lie. She talked about my father and I poured all of that into that essay, saying I wanted to help our country but in a different way. I wanted to use the skills I had to continue his work, and I was just now remembering it.

My voice was so small. "Peter read that essay?"

"Quinn knows Kash's family . . ."

"Read it?" She snorted. "He was infuriated by it. It pissed him off that he'd been replaced by a military hero. Your father isn't a perfect man. He has faults, but he does have good qualities, and stepping back, respecting your mother's wishes so you could have a normal and safe life, was hard for him. I had to respect him for it. He was trying, but he has an ego. He has pride, and learning how you were, that you were being guided by a memory of a lie, it set something off in him. He started talking more and more about that time with your mother. He started watching you more. He'd always kept tabs, but it was more. He asked Kash to personally take an interest, and once Kash started, he became captivated. I knew we were headed down a bad path."

Kash?

"Arcane was sent by someone who knows my grandfather . . ."

He'd been watching me that whole time?

I looked over to where he was, but he wasn't there. An alarm sliced through me, but it wasn't enough. Kash wouldn't have stepped away, not completely. He would have worried about me, made sure I was fine.

But he wasn't there. In fact, the entire group wasn't there. They were gone.

I looked around, now seeing we were almost completely alone.

"*Quinn knows Kash's family . . .*"

I was being plagued. Haunted.

What was happening?

"Drew Bonham is right now causing a scene at the front gate."

Drew?

What?

I was confused, but then she kept going. "Victoria has probably pulled Kash into a bedroom. I've no doubt she's trying to seduce him. No one is here to save you. No one is here to rescue you. At this moment, Drew is doing what he was told to do. So while you think you're safe because everyone is around, they're not." She was so cold, but smug at the same time. "They're all running, at this very moment, in the opposite direction. Away from you. And you, my dear, are completely alone."

Drew . . .

His name was familiar . . .

Get Kash now!

Bonham.

Thoughts and pieces of the puzzle were fitting, forming—clicking.

Drew Bonham. The husband. Matthew.

The guy who tried to poison Matt, whose wife was sleeping with Matt—was helping Quinn now?

I was going to be sick.

Cold sweat dripped down my back.

"*Arcane was sent by someone who knows my grandfather . . .*"

"*Quinn knows Kash's family . . .*"

The voices. The memories. Round and round.

"*My father was indebted to Calhoun . . .*"

Round.

Again.

And then, nothing.

Calm.

Silence.

I knew.

I knew who hired the kidnappers.

Her smile was evil, her words soft. "You're a very stupid little girl, aren't you?"

It was too late to get Kash.

FIFTY-FIVE

Quinn's words were cutting, but she was smiling, speaking them almost lovingly, and she reached over, resting her hand on my arm. Then she grabbed me in a tight grip and reached forward, pressing something into my side.

I felt a sharp pain before jerking away. "What—"

She grabbed for me again, jerking me to her and hissing under her breath, "You are a problem. He was supposed to poison *you* that night, not stupid Matthew. He wasn't supposed to have found out his wife was fucking my stepson. I mean, my God, why would he care? He was fucking me, but he wasn't the only one.

"You have no idea how many years of planning you have royally fucked up. You weren't supposed to come into my family and mess everything up. I was set for life. I have no problem that Peter likes to screw around. I enjoy it too. Hell, sometimes we share. But that was all until you came, until your father started remembering your mother, until he started feeling all these insidious feelings, like love, and suddenly he's getting other sorts of ideas, like commitment and monogamy. He wants to be a *role model* for his children growing up."

She laughed, so harsh and ugly sounding. "He wants to be a new man, a better man." She drew in a sharp breath at that word. "He's being foolish, but once you're gone, which I put into action a long time ago, he'll go back to how he was. He'll be heartbroken, and there I will be. Knowing him, knowing all his little guilty desires he enjoys, I'll have him wrapped around my finger once more. You were never supposed to even be a problem.

I wanted you taken care of before your father made the final decision to reach out to you, but stupid fucking Arcane. They messed up."

I almost couldn't keep up.

The outside was beginning to swim around me, moving in circles.

Quinn's voice was looming, her face and body growing up to a giant size.

She had drugged me. That's what the prick had been. And now she was spewing out everything.

She was behind the kidnapping attempt.

Because of my essay, because Peter was starting to think of coming for me.

And he loved my mother. Was that right?

But Kash.

She said things about Kash.

What else about Kash? Other planning for years? Was that all about Peter?

I couldn't run away. I turned, trying to, but I was falling. I was going to face-plant on the patio brick. That was going to hurt.

But then someone caught me, and I was being whisked up into the air.

I looked, feeling a strong chest behind me.

Kash, I thought.

But no.

It was the guard from before. Helms. The one Kash had suspended.

He was speaking over me to Quinn. "Did you have to drug her?"

"Shut up. Arcane is in the back, behind the DJ's van. I got them in and now I'm delivering her to them. I'll expect a steep discount for doing their work."

"What if you dosed her too much? They're hoping Calhoun will want to meet her."

"Don't be stupid. Kash's grandfather has no idea this was in the works. There's no way Calhoun Bastian would sign off on this. Too many strings. Hurry. Drew was supposed to do enough to distract everyone, and Kash is distracted too, but they won't *all* be gone for long. I talked too much. Get her out of here." She snapped one last time: "Now!"

Helms cursed under his breath, and he was going fast, carrying me around the back of the house. Or I thought? I could still make out a little, but the woozy factor was strong. I was going to be sick. I was sweating and shivering and moaning, and the guard was trying to tell me to shut up.

I wasn't listening.

I'd been drugged.

Shit. I'd been drugged! I needed to get out of there.

Kash!

Quinn was psychotic. I had to tell everyone. I had to save them.

She'd do it to someone else.

No. I had to save myself.

I was going to die—that last one helped. Primal fear coursed through me and I started struggling. Or I started trying harder. I was swinging around. My arms. My legs.

I could try and headbutt the guy even.

Helms cursed, tucking me more firmly against his side, trapping me completely so I couldn't fight even a little bit. "Fucking bitch. She should've drugged you, then lied and told you I was carrying you to bed. Why the hell'd she have to spill all that to you?"

I wasn't answering. I couldn't. But I could do something else. My mouth was pressed into his neck and, rearing back, opening my mouth wide, I sank my teeth into him.

He screamed, jerking and dropping me.

As soon as I was clear, I was screaming alongside of him.

The sound that came from him sounded like an animal having its skin pulled off while alive.

"What the fuck?"

A rush of feet came around the back. I could see them on the ground. The same boots, and I was back there, back in my old house.

Boots was coming. Literally.

Then I recognized the voice from before. It was the boss. Arcane.

"Shut her up!" A hand came down hard on my mouth.

I bit that too, and he cursed. "Damn it!"

A piece of tape was slapped on me, hard enough that I felt tears falling down my face from the force. I could smell blood. Just didn't know if it was mine or not, and the stars above were circling again. They were almost a complete line by themselves—they were going that fast.

Arcane bit off a growl. "Are you serious? You scream like that and drop the cunt?"

"She just took an entire chunk of skin out of my shoulder. This bitch." Helms rotated, bringing his foot back and kicking me in the side.

Pain blinded me, tearing the breath out of me.

It also helped push back against the drug.

Rough hands grabbed me, and I was hauled back in the air. I would have bruises everywhere tomorrow . . . if I had a tomorrow.

I got a glimpse of the guy holding my legs. Clemin. Boots hadn't moved, so I was assuming it was Rafe who was grabbing the top of me. They were both running now. I was being jostled in their holds, but they only tightened their grips. A van door was being opened. I heard the squeak and I was thrown inside.

It was completely dark.

They jumped in behind me. I heard rustling sounds. God. That was a tarp.

This was it. This was the end.

The doors were shut behind. Then the van was starting.

"Everyone down. Guards are going to do a quick scan."

That was Boss. Arcane again.

Was Chase here?

All of this—they were going to win.

Quinn was going to win. Kash was going to blame himself. Chrissy would be heartbroken. My dad, Cyclone, Seraphina—they'd be scarred. Matthew. Oh, man. Matthew. He'd blame himself.

This couldn't happen, but I couldn't move.

I couldn't make a sound.

The drug was winning.

A polar bear was racing to me, and I had enough wits about me to know that was a hallucination. Then, suddenly, there was a screech behind us.

The van came to an abrupt stop.

Cursing. Shouting.

Doors were being yanked open.

They were gone.

I heard them running. Was that the pounding I heard?

Then—hands. Gentle hands.

"Oh my God, Bailey."

Kash.

It was *Kash*.

I started crying. I couldn't stop myself even if I wanted. I'd been drugged.

Kash was lifting me up, being so gentle and tender and loving. He was in front of me. He was holding me, and touching my face, cursing, and then murder. Just straight murder.

He left.

More pounding.

People were still running?

I heard Matthew calling his name.

Another voice. I couldn't make out their words anymore. I could only make out who was who.

Peter.

"God. I'm so sorry."

Who was crying.

Chrissy? My mom?

There were others.

Someone was screaming.

Kash was back. He wrapped me up in a blanket, covering me, though I didn't know why, and he was moving away from the crowd.

When had a crowd formed?

But I was safe.

And as Kash was looking down at me, with an emotion I knew he wasn't ready to tell me yet, I knew I could go. Finally.

"Bailey!"

His shout sounded so far away . . .

And then I was gone.

FIFTY-SIX

"*Bailey*." A whisper.

"*Bailey*." Again.

My name kept coming to me, pulling me back from the dark. I was swimming to the surface, and with a last kick, I pushed through. My eyes opened, but I was back in the dark. No. Wait. It was a bedroom.

A soft glow filtered under the bedroom door and, feeling my entire body aching, I sat up, reaching over to turn on something. There had to be a lamp. At least a nightstand to help me get my bearings. I felt something—there it went. I heard a thump as I knocked something over, feeling the splash on my hand.

Crap. Someone must have put out a glass of water for me.

Finally feeling a lamp, I switched it on, and it took me another few seconds to figure out where the hell I was.

I was in a bed. Red sheets. A red armchair in the corner.

Yeah . . .

I had no idea where I was, but I heard voices out in the hallway, so, sitting up, I took inventory of myself. Plaid sleeping pants. A baggy T-shirt. BROOKLEY COMPUTER CLUB, WE BYTE BACK stared back up at me. My mother had changed me, or insisted that whoever did put these clothes on. They were the same pajamas I slept in in high school. Damn. I could still fit in these clothes? *Hell* to the *yeah*!

A different sort of *damn* hit me.

Rushing to the bathroom, I paused in the doorway, grabbing hold of the frame for a second. A wave of dizziness hit me and I was blinking back stars. I'd stood up too soon, so I quickly sat and did my business. Gravity realigned with me. Then I looked in the mirror, after washing up, and I blanched.

I totally and completely did a Golden Girls.

My hair could have laid eggs for eagles. There were scrapes and bruises all over my body. I pulled the front of my shirt and looked down. Shit. The bruises extended all the way down too. And now it was like my brain was catching up to what I was seeing, because I was aching everywhere. My fingernails hurt. My cuticles were angsty. The dead skin on my heels—yes. Even those were in pain.

Every single cell and nerve were in agony. I could hear them in my head. They were all saying, "Bailey, what did you do to us? We want a spa. Bailey. Spa. Bailey. Spa. Spa . . . spa . . ."

I was going nuts. My mind was bruised as well, apparently.

I tried to tame my hair, what I could, and I pressed a washcloth over my face. Raccoon eyes were a real thing. It looked like someone had tried to clean off my makeup, but not all of it was gone. The eyeliner decided to go through a rainstorm.

Catching a whiff of my breath, I wrinkled my nose.

"Bailey?"

I turned, or I started to. The room decided to race me, and it won. I grabbed the bathroom counter, holding on, and Kash was at my side in a flash. He caught me.

He lifted me up and carried me back to bed. After settling me down, making sure I wasn't going to topple out of the bed, he returned to the bathroom.

He came over with my own teeth-cleaning setup. It was a whole thing.

A new glass of water, two towels, and a toothbrush and paste ready for me. I brushed my teeth, spit into the glass I'd spilled. Kash cleaned it up and handed it over. New water. And I wiped my mouth again. My mouth was refreshed, and now all the kissing could commence.

Kash took everything back to the bathroom. He came back, hitting the lights, and I heard his clothes being shed.

I didn't want to process anything.

I knew maybe I should, but I was on strike on the emotional front.

I wanted to sleep. I wanted to sleep in his arms, because he was my man and no one was going to take either of us away. And because I was still having a hard time forming words, I closed my eyes as he pulled me into his arms.

I let the warmth take over. Again.

I was lying in Kash's arms the next day.

I first woke around five in the morning. Brushed my teeth. Bathroom.

Went back to bed.

The next time we woke, it was because someone was knocking on our door.

A guard stuck his head inside, keeping his eyes averted. "Guests have arrived, and they refuse to leave."

Kash sat up. "Her mother?"

"Yes, sir. Matthew. A girl named Torie."

I grinned at that.

He kept on. "Her father." He hesitated now, before saying, "And a police detective."

Kash hauled himself out of bed, crossing to the closet. "Lawyers?"

"They've been here since eight this morning."

A second grin from me. I had a picture of three lawyers sitting on a couch together, hands on their knees, backs sticking upright, dressed in their fancy long coats, with their briefcases at their feet, and then sitting, sitting, more sitting as the hours literally ticked away.

"Okay." Kash pulled on pair of pants and a Henley.

Good God. That Henley.

Mouth not dry anymore.

There's a fair chance I was doing everything I could do *not* to focus on what had happened to me, but the cavalry had literally arrived. They were outside, in the living room of wherever we were, and my vacation away into Sleepland was done.

Time was up.

Kash nodded, saying, "Give us another minute."

The guard nodded, pulling back and shutting the door.

Kash swung those piercing eyes my way, and he stared. His brows pulled together. The seconds ticked away before he sighed. "I have things to say to you, but none of that's happening with the brigade outside. I just need to know, are you ready for all of this? If you're not, shake your head and we'll slip out without anyone knowing."

Oh man. When he said things like that, I was drooling.

But I sighed too, and nodded. "I'm ready." My voice came out hoarse. His eyes darkened, but he just nodded, raked a hand through his hair, and stepped into the bathroom. I had gotten up and gone through a bag my mother must have packed. All sorts of Brookley clothes were in there. I had on an old pair of jeans and a sweatshirt when he came back out.

He stopped, taking me in, before his top lip tugged up.

"What?"

Amusement flashed in those eyes. "Nothing. I just got a glimpse into how you must've looked in school."

I flushed. "I was a nerd in school." Well, kinda.

"I doubt that."

Yeah. His voice dipped low, sending tingles through me, going low as well. I tried to school my features into a scowl. I was sucking at it. My lips kept curving up, and then I just sighed and lay back on the bed.

He came over, leaning over me. His arms rested on both sides of my head. He held himself up, just gazing down at me, and all sorts of promising swept over his face. "Your mother is going to come in and fuss all over you."

He was saying this, asking if I was okay with it.

I nodded.

He added, "Matt is going to curse, look angry, but he's just terrified about what almost happened to you."

Another nod.

I didn't want to think about that, either.

"Your father is going to bark orders, probably fight with your mother, and get irritated with Matthew. It'll be because he has no idea how to talk to you, but he's just as scared as Matt about what almost happened to you."

Again with the reminder. Did he have to go there? But I nodded a third time.

Kash gentled his tone. "Torie is here for you. That's her job. If you need me, tell her. She'll get me. If you need space from your mom, she'll scurry you away for a breather. She's informed me she'll do anything you need except perform sexual favors, unless it's on a specific guard that she's had her eye on. She wanted to make sure I quoted her exactly with that. You okay with all of that?"

Oh boy. I was smiling, just slightly.

He took it as a fourth nod, and his tone hardened next. "The police will need a statement from you. You passed out from the drug Quinn gave you, and they tried to question you at the hospital when you were checked over. You weren't even lucid. The detectives weren't happy when the lawyers pushed back, saying you needed to know what you were saying before saying anything. They've been impatient, and that's saying it nicely. But in the end, they just want to make sure they have a good enough case to make Quinn do time."

Quinn. Time.

It was now sinking in what she'd done to me. I felt a *woosh* inside of me, a wave crashing over my mind, and I was back there.

Rafe. Clemin. Arcane. They were coming for me.

Quinn. How she grabbed me.

I winced now, feeling it all over again.

Kash tensed, then cursed under his breath. He was gone, and I cried out. I didn't want him to go away, but he was saying something in the hallway. Then the door was shut and he was back. The bed dipped under his weight and he pulled me back into his arms. He rolled around me, as if his entire body could cushion the nightmare ripping through my mind. It couldn't. He couldn't. But I was grabbing on to him, too, as if he could.

I was sobbing. Or someone was. It was probably me. I heard myself outside of myself, and I knew it was inevitable.

I was sinking once more.

FIFTY-SEVEN

Everything happened as Kash had warned me.

Chrissy fussed.

Torie was my guard dog, complete with her own drool.

Matthew couldn't sit still. He kept going in circles around the room.

Peter was a mess. He was sniping at Matt, then bickering with Chrissy, then asking Kash questions in a serious voice. He'd stop, stare at me, and his mouth would tremble before he'd bark something at Matt and the cycle would start around again.

The detectives were nice. I'd expected gruff and impatient, but the session with them was just long. The lawyers intervened at times, but not much. Everyone wanted the same thing: to make sure Quinn paid for what she did.

Quinn. Man.

Over the next two weeks, I didn't really let myself think of her.

The day the detectives finally got my statement, once I wasn't a blubbering mess, I stuck to the facts. If they needed more detail, I gave it to them. They were surprised at how much I did remember, until Peter said I had his photographic memory. Their eyes got big, and I swear their ears perked up after that. That just meant more questions, though, and it was a long time later that night when they finally left.

Kash told me the next day that my father had found enough damning evidence—text messages, emails Quinn thought she'd deleted, burner phones, fake accounts, and so much more—to put the picture together. Piecing it together with what she'd said to me, it turned out that Quinn thought Peter had always been in love with my mother, even back then despite what she said to me. She thought her days were numbered if Chrissy or I came back into his life, and she was desperate enough to reach out and then hire the Arcane team.

Peter confessed that he might have exaggerated his fondness for Chrissy when he talked to Quinn about the past. He didn't elaborate on why he did this, or if it was true presently or not, and when I asked Chrissy what she thought, I was given a pat on the arm and told that I needed rest.

That's the answer I had gotten for most things over the last two weeks.

In that time, a therapist came to Kash's new loft, which is where we were the first night I woke after the attack. He had moved out of his last place because the media knew his address, so this one was more secret. Even I didn't know where we were, because I hadn't left his place. Not once.

Everyone agreed that I should take my time, rest, seek counseling for almost being kidnapped and then finding out that they were going to kill me, but the truth is that I was hiding. I was late in starting graduate school. Kash said the school understood and gave me an extension. If I couldn't start before midterms, then I'd have to wait for the second semester. That was their final timeline.

I wasn't doing that. Hell no. Did no one realize how much work I would be behind by that time? Not to mention, who wants to be the student who starts a semester after everyone? No one, that's who. I know how graduate programs work. You start with a group of students and they become your ride-or-die through projects and speeches. I needed that support, so I waited until my last counseling session to inform the counselor it was my last session.

She blinked at me a moment, crossed her arms over her lap. "Excuse me?"

"It's time I rejoin the world, starting here. I'm fine. I don't need any more sessions."

She sputtered. She protested. She fixed her bun.

None of it mattered.

I wasn't the scarred girl everyone was treating me as, and while I had indulged and hid away, I knew it was time. Face the day. Feel the sunshine on your face. Smell the coffee. All of those sentiments. I had to get on with my life. Quinn took two weeks from me. I wasn't letting her take any more, and I really wasn't as traumatized as everyone thought I was.

They were traumatized.

They were the ones who saw me being lifted out of that van, who saw all the guys bloodied on the floor. All that pounding I heard when I was drugged? I thought it'd been people running for us. No. The running had already happened. That pounding sound was actual pounding, from Kash.

He said Victoria kept insisting on an emergency, said a water valve had broken in one of the bedrooms. Yeah. Shit liar. Kash stopped halfway to the room and came back for me.

He saw me being put in the van.

He made one radio call, notifying the guards, and then he was on them.

He was an animal, taking on three of them. A guard got there after, helping, but Kash took out the last one. It'd been a sight to see, as Matt told me during one of his visits.

I had seen Kash's hands since. Took four days for the swelling to go down. Cracked and bruised. I thought they were broken, but he had them looked at. They were fine.

Still. I was traumatized at seeing his hands, but everyone else had been affected by seeing me that night. I was wrapped in a tarp, my breathing already slowing enough that they worried I was dead. It'd been a side effect from the drug Quinn gave me, but it wasn't one she intended. She wanted me killed later, not by her actual hand, but I had a bad reaction to her drug.

I laughed so hard at that. A bad reaction to the drug that she used so that she could eventually have me killed. No shit, a bad reaction.

No one else thought it was funny, but come on. The whole thing was a bad reaction. But now they were worried about what other drugs I might be allergic to. I just thought a good way to avoid them was to not be drugged again. Solved.

No one thought that was funny, either.

But back to my current obstacle: Kash.

There was no more danger. The Arcane team was going away. No bail. Nothing. They were going to a prison that even other prisons didn't hear about. And even Kash's grandfather wasn't a scare anymore. Why he had been in Chicago and in our area, no one knew. The rumors that he was here were proved wrong by footage of him in New York. It was reported that he had flown to Dubai.

And it wasn't the counselor. She left, a disapproving pinch to her mouth, but I didn't care. I shooed her out, thanked her for her services, and shut the door when she started to repeat how she didn't agree with me.

Like I cared.

What I cared about was seeing Cyclone and Seraphina again, in person. We had FaceTimed together. They both started crying when they saw me, but I cracked a joke. That helped. Seraphina was giggling not long later, and Cyclone was asking me questions about a robot ninja. The rabbit was old news. A woman passed behind them, and I had a slight heart attack. I thought it was Quinn.

Kash said it was their aunt. She had flown in from California to help Chrissy and Marie take care of them. My mother had moved back to the estate, once she realized I didn't need her doting on me because I just wanted to jump Kash's bones all the time, which he didn't let me. He waited until my visible bruises had faded, and only then did he gently move inside of me. It was the most frustrating sex I'd had with him. There was no loss of control. It was as if he was scared he'd hurt me, but him being so tender and loving and restrained was what was hurting me.

I wanted him to growl, do his own firm pounding in me, swear. I wanted him rough and passionate. I hadn't seen that side of him since before the party. That's what I needed to move on and get over what happened. I needed him, just him.

So, after kicking the counselor to the curb, I was ready to complete my second task.

Make Kash Lose Control.

I met him at the door when he came home from a meeting.

He stepped inside, and a slight breeze grazed me before he shut the door.

He saw me, then stopped. A grin curved up. "What is this?"

I was standing in the entryway, holding a letter for him.

The air was turning hot again, sizzling. His eyes darkened the farther he got in the letter, until the end, and then he groaned. "Jesus Christ, Bailey."

I knew what words he'd just read, and my throat was feeling raw.

I could only get a whisper out. "I mean it, every word of it."

He was shaking his head even as he stepped toward me. "You have no idea."

I countered with, "I might, actually."

Another head shake, but another step. "No, you don't. You don't know how you looked in that van."

I wet my lips. "So tell me. You have other things to tell me, too."

I didn't even care what he said. I just needed him to talk. And after a moment of silence, I thought he would ignore me. I thought it was like all the other times. He would reach for me, distract me, shut me out. But he didn't.

He started slow at first, but he talked.

He talked about others. About me. About the event. About

the aftermath. About what I should expect. But not about him. He never said a word.

"I can't." He looked away, his hands forming fists.

"Yes! You told me you had things to say to me, but you never did. You have to tell me. You have to let me in, too."

I'd been aching for those words. He had no idea. There was a wall around him. He kept it in place between him and everyone, the world. I needed a peek behind it. I was desperate for it. If he lifted it up, or curled back a corner, I could do the rest. I *would* do the rest. I'd get in there, be my own Cyclone, and tear the rest of that wall down. I just needed an inch.

So I was going to force an inch now.

Stepping to him, closing the distance, my hand came to his chest. "Let me in, Kash."

His chest shook under my touch, his breath sucking in, holding, then coming out in a sudden rush. Then he shoved away, turning, giving me his back.

He spoke, but he wouldn't look at me.

"You want to know how I feel?" he bit out.

Why would he spit those words?

He started, harsh. "I fell in love with you before you even knew me. When your father asked me to watch you. After we found out Arcane was targeting you. It was then, during all of that time that you became mine. You just didn't know."

Those words should've been said beautifully. They weren't.

He kept on, "I thought about walking away. I did." His shoulders bunched under his shirt, stretching the material out. "It's why I left, once you got to my villa. I had you somewhere safe—or I thought you were safe. I knew that what we were about to head into was going to be bad. It would be bad and there would be nothing I could do to shield you from it. Nothing." He spun. His face was rigid. His hands in fists. His jaw was clenching. "You want to know what's been eating me up every fucking night I'm inside of you, every morning when I see you sleeping, every time you send me a text that makes me laugh? Me. *I* am. I am leading you into a storm, and I will be lucky if you come out even half alive."

He stepped toward me, his eyes burning and fierce.

"Because *I* won't be. Because my grandfather is coming and he will kill me. Maybe not my body, but he will do what he did to my mother. And if you stay with me, stay here, then all that dark shit will come on you, too. I will destroy you. You might not know it. I might not even catch it, not at first. It might be slow, but it'll be there. It'll be gradual, until one day you wake up hating me." His nostrils flared. "That's what's going on inside of me, every fucking time I want to tell you that I am completely in love with you."

He spat it out. "Death. Darkness. Hatred. You stay with me, that's what will happen to you."

He stopped, looking down at me. His eyes were black, clouded over.

I reached up without thinking.

I cupped the side of his face.

"The world is already fascinated with you." Those were my words. More came out. "And whatever comes our way, I will handle it. I'm here. I'm with you. And, my God, Kash. If you try to leave me, I won't have it. You got that?"

I could speak just as harshly.

He didn't say anything. Neither did I.

We were glaring at each other.

The room was shrinking in on us, and then the doorbell rang.

Kash cursed, his eyes closing. His head tipped back, but it rang again. And again.

Stalking over, he pressed the button, then went stock-still.

Blood drained from his face.

Every hair on my body stood straight up.

I was standing at the end of the hall, and I stepped toward him, out of instinct. "Kash?"

He didn't answer. He didn't look at me.

Whoever it was, they'd gotten past the front desk. They were on our floor, just on the other side of our door.

Cursing, he wrenched open the door and faced off against whoever was on the other side.

"Get. Gone!"

Their response was quieter, calmer. "Hello, Kash." A man. An older man.

Ice ran down my spine. I was moving faster, hurrying to be at his side, because this time Kash needed me. Then Kash was moving. He blocked me, holding me back. He slammed the door shut, engaging all of the locks. He flicked off the security camera feed so I couldn't see, then hit the buzzer. "Call the police. Now."

He held me back until we heard the elevator open, close, and travel down.

I stepped away from him, getting a glimpse of what a cornered feral animal might look like. Unease traced through me. They were whispering at me, in the back of my mind, riding down my spine.

I asked, "Who was that?"

He didn't look me in the eye, but his hand tightened over mine.

"My grandfather."

BONUS

Bailey's Letter to Kash

I told you before that I wanted more nights with you.

I demand more nights with you. I demand longer nights with you.

I see the outside you. I demand to know the inside you.

I want the words, the actions, the secrets. I want the you and me that no one else will ever know.

I want to hold your hand. I want to feel your hugs.

I want to get cards from you. I want dinners and roses and chardonnay. I want champagne, but I want the other good stuff. I want the sunset hand-holding. I want the sunrise coffee together. I want the laughter in the day, flirty texts, dirty sexts.

I want it all, and I want them with you.

I want to know your haunts. I want to tremble from them, alongside you.

I want the full picture of how you became you, from your first memory to your last memory, and when a new day starts and when that memory refreshes, I want those too.

I am greedy because I want all of you. Not some of you. Not a third of you. Not the good part of you, or the bad part of you. I want the lover, the friend, the part that will walk with me wherever I go, the part that will ride next to me, the part that will fight with me, for me, beside me.

I know you think I need more time. I don't.

I know you think I was scarred. I wasn't.

I know you think I need to heal still. Fuck no.

I'm good to go, so besides all the other gushy stuff in this letter, I want you to come over here.

I want you to take me, make me yours, because I already am. I'm yours, Kash. If you haven't figured it out by now, I love you. So *fucking* give me you, okay?

ACKNOWLEDGMENTS

To my agent, holy crapola, Kimberly! Thank you!

To Monique! To everyone who worked on this book and helped get it where it is. To Macmillan.

To the ladies in Tijan's Crew. To the group in Tijan's Audiomen. Just, whoa, to everyone.

Every author dreams of going to a bookstore, walking in, and finding their book on the shelves. This has happened sporadically for me; I've mostly been an indie author until this publisher decided to take a chance on me.

I'm really truly hoping everyone loved Bailey and Kash as much as I loved writing them! I'm grateful and happy to have been able to bring this entire world and cast from *The Insiders* to life, and I hope you guys continue on with the next book in their series.

Bring on some graduate school!

ABOUT THE AUTHOR

TIJAN is a *New York Times* bestselling author who writes suspenseful and unpredictable novels. Her characters are strong, intense, and gut-wrenchingly real with a little bit of sass on the side. Tijan began writing later in life and, once she started, she was hooked. She's written multi-bestsellers including the Carter Reed series, the Fallen Crest series, and *Ryan's Bed*, among others. She is currently writing to her heart's content in northern Minnesota with an English cocker spaniel she adores.